A DETECTIVE'S LIFE
SHERLOCK HOLMES

MORE ANTHOLOGIES FROM TITAN BOOKS

Associates of Sherlock Holmes
Edited by George Mann

Further Associates of Sherlock Holmes
Edited by George Mann

Encounters of Sherlock Holmes
Edited by George Mann

Further Encounters of Sherlock Holmes
Edited by George Mann

Sherlock Holmes: The Sign of Seven
Edited by Martin Rosenstock

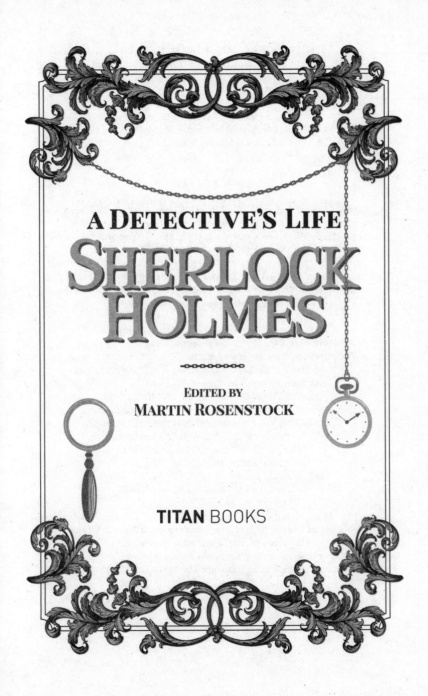

A DETECTIVE'S LIFE

SHERLOCK HOLMES

EDITED BY
MARTIN ROSENSTOCK

TITAN BOOKS

SHERLOCK HOLMES: A DETECTIVE'S LIFE
Print edition ISBN: 9781789098747
E-book edition ISBN: 9781789098860

Published by Titan Books
A division of Titan Publishing Group Ltd
144 Southwark St, London SE1 0UP
www.titanbooks.com

First edition: September 2022
10 9 8 7 6 5 4 3 2 1

A CIP catalogue record for this title is available from the British Library.

Printed and bound by CPI Group (UK) Ltd, Croydon CR0 4YY

CONTENTS

INTRODUCTION

In 1906, G.K. Chesterton, who knew a thing or two about detective stories, observed that Sherlock Holmes was the only truly familiar figure in modern fiction, someone each and every reader would recognise. Holmes had been solving cases for twenty-five years by that time; two years before, Arthur Conan Doyle had completed his third set of stories featuring his detective. Since Doyle's and Chesterton's days, James Bond has made his appearance, as has a whole pantheon of American superheroes, their presence in turn enlarged by film and television into towering proportions. These figures all might challenge Holmes's exclusive claim to universal recognisability. Everyone today also knows 007 and Batman.

Chesterton's main point, however, remains as valid in 2022 as it was back then: Sherlock Holmes is an omnipresent global icon. The stories of his adventures are to the detective story what *The Magic Flute* is to classical music: the inescapable, quintessential embodiment of the genre. In some sense, everyone writing such narratives today looks towards Holmes and Conan Doyle, just as all classical musicians have Mozart on their minds. This book tells the story of the great detective's career, from the early days in Baker Street to his retirement on the South Downs, and even a little beyond. That is quite some arc to traverse, but luckily twelve dedicated and talented writers each volunteered to take us on a section of the journey.

I count myself lucky to have had the privilege of working with every one of these writers. I have learnt much from them in the course of editing this volume, and I hope to have done their work justice. My thanks to all of them, and also to the team at Titan Books for their unending patience and support. At the risk of sounding a little Victorian, allow me please to wish you, dear reader, as much enjoyment as you peruse this collection as I took pleasure in assembling it.

And thus again, Holmes.

MARTIN ROSENSTOCK, Kuwait, 5 April 2022

PROLOGUE

By and large, putting pen to paper has come easy to me over the years. Yet today, as I apply the final touches to this manuscript, my hand feels leaden. I drag the stylus over the page, and every few minutes my eyes wander through the wood-panelled lounge of my club, quiet as usual on this spring afternoon. I am no longer the man I once was. Father Time has been kind to me, but as of late he has been collecting some of his dues. However, even if the present task had fallen to me a decade earlier, it would have been none the easier. In fact, I am thankful the Fates saw fit to spare me until the race was almost run.

What task? Allow me, cherished reader, to take you back to a November morning some months ago. It had rained during the night and the ground squelched beneath our feet. A few patches of blue shone with anomalous pallor in an iron sky. The wind blew mild from the southwest and rustled the remaining leaves of the poplars, as we all gathered to pay our respects to a man who had in some form or another made our sojourn on this earth more agreeable. A man who lived a full life and lived it well, who possessed an immense capacity for friendship, a generosity of spirit second to none, and the gift of telling a tale.

The line of mourners was long that morning at the grave of Dr. John Watson. As my turn came to stand in front of the open wound in the earth and to look down upon the coffin with the chrysanthemums piling up on the mahogany, it seemed to me that I heard the man's voice as clearly as if he were standing next to me. A calm deep voice, the voice of a doctor who had given solace to many a patient: "Chin up, Arthur. We played our parts well, you and I. Did what we came here to do. Cheerio, old fellow." "Cheerio, my friend," I thought. "We'll meet on the other side, before too long, I assume…"

I dropped a flower into the grave, closed my eyes to regain some composure, and then stepped over to express my condolences to Mrs. Watson. We had not seen each other in some time, and I thought she looked frail in her black dress and black gloves. A veil covered most of her face, but I could see that her features were shaking. Her hand lay in mine like a small bird.

"Thank you –" her voice faltered "– thank you, Sir Arthur." And then she added: "Why don't you come by in two or three weeks? There is something I should like to show you."

"Certainly, madam. It would be my pleasure." I nodded and moved along, so as to make room for the person next in line.

As I walked back to my automobile, I felt a tap at the elbow – "Mr. Doyle."

Upon turning, I beheld a hazy figure of an odd step-like shape. I wiped my face with the back of my hand and the figure disassembled itself into two: the lanky frame of Mr. Holmes and to his side in a wheelchair, which Mr. Holmes had apparently been pushing, the massive figure of his brother, Sir Mycroft. They were both all in black with black toppers. Sir Mycroft closed his eyes briefly like a large cat, as he is wont to do by way of greeting.

Mr. Holmes cleared his throat. His pale, haggard features appeared unreal in some manner, as if they were an overexposed photograph – I cannot quite explain what I mean. Of course, I have much respect for the man. Who would not? His mind is certainly first rate. Yet even though we have generally interacted in cordial enough a fashion, truth be told, I had never much cared for Mr. Holmes. He always struck me as someone who had replaced a vital dimension of humanity with something other, as if he were both less and more than one of us mere mortals.

Perhaps, I suddenly thought, however, I had been unkind in my judgment. A few reddened veins traversed the whites of Mr. Holmes's eyes, and he held his lips pressed tightly together as if he were trying to prevent them from trembling. He extended a hand, and I took it, mutely. We must have stood there in silence for a few seconds, before Mr. Holmes finally did speak.

"Thank you, Sir Arthur. I know you have been a great help to John over the years."

I coughed, somewhat at a loss for words. "It was the honour of my life."

He let go of my hand. We both raised our hats. I nodded to Sir Mycroft, and then I turned and left. I am glad Mr. Holmes and I parted on good terms. This was, I am sure, our last encounter. No doubt he will outlive us all. I wish him well.

*

Two weeks later, I drew up at the modest, yet well-appointed Belgravia apartment building where the Watsons had made their home some time ago. On the third floor, a maid showed me into a parlour furnished in solid Edwardian style and served me tea. While I was sipping it and watching some pigeons huddled in the barren chestnut tree outside the window, Mrs. Watson entered. We shook hands and then took our seats. John's widow appeared thoroughly composed now, and occasionally even a wistful smile played upon her delicate features. We talked of better days long gone by, as people commonly do in circumstances such as these.

"You know, Sir Arthur," she finally said, "John trusted you a lot. 'Sir Arthur,' he would say, 'Sir Arthur does not give his word lightly, but he always keeps it.'"

"I am gladdened to hear that," I said. "John himself was the most reliable of men. A rock."

Mrs. Watson nodded silently and then leaned forward to top up my tea, before reaching for the crystal bell on the table. When the maid opened the door, Mrs. Watson said, "Lizzy, please bring us the box we talked about the other day."

"Yes, ma'am."

Two minutes later, Lizzy placed a box full of papers between Mrs. Watson and myself on the table, curtseyed and withdrew. I immediately recognised John's neat handwriting on the topmost page. Mrs. Watson placed her right palm on the stack.

"I don't know if John told you, Sir Arthur, but the past few months he was working on what he liked to refer to as 'The Terminal Twelve'."

"Oh. He never mentioned this."

Her blue eyes looked steadily at me. "I believe he worried he would not be able to finish everything. In fact, I am not quite sure he did. His idea was to tell a tale from each period of his friendship with Mr. Holmes, going back to their days in that place they shared in Bloomsbury. Some might also be old stories he never published. I believe he was in touch with Sir Mycroft at some point. John was in much pain the past few weeks, but he kept working. Perhaps the manuscript is almost complete. I do not know. I have not had the strength to read it…" She lifted her hand. "You would be doing me a great favour if you had a look at the matter. Perhaps there is a book there, perhaps there isn't. I leave the decision up to you, Sir Arthur."

I admit I felt a weight descend upon my shoulders. I have assembled many a volume, and it is no easy task. Yet what could I do in the face of such a request by John's widow, but nod and assure her that I would see the task through if seen through it could be. It was both the least and the last I could do for my oldest, dearest friend.

*

And thus I have been sitting in the lounge of my club for the past three months, organising John's final set of tales of his adventures with Mr. Sherlock Holmes. To very few of us it is given to complete all the tasks we have begun in life, but John had done most of the work. Some polish here and there, a few rewrites, that was all that was required on my part. It has been my privilege over the years to serve as John's agent, and now to have done him this last honour of serving as his literary executor.

What lies in the future for those of us who are still here? More importantly, for those who will still be here when we old ones are gone. Much darkness, I am sometimes afraid. It will no longer be my fight. Many of you who read these words, however, will need to face what is coming – I fear for you. Yet now, for a few brief hours, let us forget both the present and the future. Please, extend me the honour of returning with me to the beginning, to those days in Baker Street a lifetime ago. From there, we will wend our way through the decades with John, and some other worthy men, as our guides. We will conclude quite close to the here and now, and at that point, I am afraid, both John and I will have to bid you adieu.

These are the last tales. There will be no more.

ACD, London, 5 April 1930

THE ADVENTURE OF THE SPIRITUALIST DETECTIVE

STUART DOUGLAS

Were it not for the necessary prohibitions placed upon me by matters of state, and the need to maintain a certain circumspection when discussing the security of the nation and its most illustrious people, I could compile a long list of cases which my friend Sherlock Holmes inexplicably dismissed as being of no interest to him. Kings and queens, presidents and prime ministers, each of them have sent emissaries to Baker Street and been swiftly rebuffed.

Holmes will tell you himself that he is not a man to court publicity, nor one for whom fame is of any great concern. But place before him a case which contains some element incapable of rational explanation and, no matter how prosaic it may otherwise seem, he will be reaching for his hat and coat before even you have finished recounting your tale.

This fascination for the unusual and the incomprehensible was the only explanation I could initially contrive for Holmes's involvement in what seemed to be the most trifling of cases in the summer of 1881, soon after we began to share rooms in Baker Street.

*

"The fact of the matter is, Mr. Holmes, I won't allow that Liberal rag in the house, and the servants know that. It's more than their jobs are worth to be seen reading the likes of that claptrap, far less leave a copy on display for all to see. I would have sacked the lot of them if the newspaper hadn't been so old!"

The speaker was a stout woman of early middle age, clad in brown hiking boots and a gentleman's green tweed suit. Her hair was cut short and worn parted to one side, and she affected both a monocle and an ivory cigarette holder, through which she smoked continuously.

The name she had given to Mrs. Hudson was Leslie Spooner, with no indication of her marital status, and when Holmes attempted to ascertain how best to address her in the absence of such information, she curtly informed him that the unadorned *Spooner* would suffice.

To me, she seemed the strangest of creatures, and her reason for appearing at our door was equally ludicrous. I felt sure that Holmes would dismiss her out of hand, as he had every other potential client that week.

I hoped, however, that he would not. He had been poor company lately, rising late and spending the day slumped in his chair, silently smoking an abominably strong tobacco, and vanishing every evening on business which he would not discuss with me, but which kept him absent until the early hours of the morning. Perhaps a new case, even one so mundane as this, would put him in better fettle. I had noticed on the sole previous occasion I had been involved in a case with him that his mood improved immeasurably when his mind was active.

I was pleased (if surprised) therefore, when, as Leslie Spooner finished speaking, he leaned forward with every sign of fascination. He steepled his fingers in a gesture I was beginning to recognise as denoting keen interest, and began to interrogate her.

"The newspaper was twenty years old, you said? And its appearance is merely the most recent in a series of similar unexplained oddities at your home?" he asked.

"It is. First there was the odour of kippers – a fish I cannot abide in any form – on the staircase, then a half-consumed bottle of beer left right outside my room, and yesterday, very clear and large footprints in the dirt to the rear of the house, leading from the back door to an old potting shed."

"And there is nobody in your household, no male servant who might have made the footprints?"

"I employ only female servants, Mr. Holmes. It is a strict rule I have, and well known to everyone."

"Might one of them perhaps have a follower?" I interjected, now at something of a loss as to exactly what Holmes was even being asked to investigate. The elderly newspaper was strange, admittedly, but kippers, beer and large footprints indicated the presence of a man; there hardly seemed much deduction required to discover which of the female staff had illicitly entertained an admirer.

"Certainly not!" The lady could scarcely have been more outraged had I suggested that the killer of the recently murdered American President Garfield had breakfasted in her kitchen. "I do not allow any of my staff to entertain gentlemen callers, nor do I allow them admittance to the house. No living man has set foot in my home since the day I moved in." She looked me up and down in a manner which I felt sure was intended to be insulting, and then turned back to Holmes. "You will be the first, Mr. Holmes. I should have preferred to engage a female investigator, in fact, but there are, it seems, none such to be had, and you have come highly recommended."

Holmes smiled thinly and nodded. "I am delighted that you have seen fit to honour us with your case," he said. "There are certainly several elements of it which will bear closer examination." He settled back in his chair and lit a cigarette. "You are wondering, of course, whether this is the work of a restless spirit, or perhaps even a poltergeist, as the Germans call it?"

I had known Holmes only briefly at this point, but had already heard him make some entirely unexpected remarks. Even so, this statement attained to a level of apparent eccentricity fit to match that of our guest. If my new colleague felt it necessary to consider the possibility of ghosts and ghouls in every case, I wondered if his sanity was all that it should be.

Before I could give voice to this thought, or one with similar meaning but less likelihood of offence, our prospective client emitted a short, barking laugh and pointed at Holmes with her cigarette holder.

"Bravo, Mr. Holmes!" she said, and clapped her hands together loudly. "Exactly so! It is good to know that the reports I have had of you were no exaggeration." She swept her hand through the air in front of her. "But you must explain, how did you know that I suspected a supernatural incursion?"

I was at a loss as to how to react to this exchange, but Holmes merely bowed his head slightly in acknowledgement, and gestured towards the lady with a languid wave.

"It was not a difficult deduction to make," he said, blowing smoke in a perfect circle towards the ceiling. He held out a telegram which had arrived earlier that morning. "When you contacted me regarding these unexplained appearances at your home, you called them 'manifestations'. Not an unknown word, I grant you, but uncommon, and with almost the weight of a technical term among the spiritualist fraternity when referencing the returned dead. Furthermore, you were at pains to stress that no *living* man had ever entered your home. That is not, I would wager, a modifier most people would feel the need to employ. Then, of course, there is the tiny pin in your lapel which, unless my eyesight has deceived me, reads SAGB. The Spiritualist Association of Great Britain is the foremost such society in this country. Given your membership, it is no great leap of logic to deduce that you would be inclined to supernatural explanations."

Holmes stopped and fixed Leslie Spooner with an unblinking stare. "And, of course, I have a keen interest in all matters spiritualist. Who does not, who has read of the lives of Philippe de Lyon or the Fox sisters?"

Our client took a few moments to reply, fiddling with the top of her holder as she affixed another cigarette before looking back at Holmes.

"It is gratifying to hear that, Mr. Holmes. Not everyone is as enlightened as you, nor as convinced by the evidence, clear though it is to all but the wilfully obstinate. As I said, I should have preferred a woman for choice, but in the absence of such an option, it seems that those in the Association who suggested Sherlock Holmes were not mistaken." She smiled. "If you come away from my home with no possible explanation save the spiritual, what a boon it will be to our movement to have your public support in addition to your private beliefs." She placed the end of her holder in her mouth, and I leaned across to light her cigarette. "And I have no doubt that that is exactly what will happen."

Holmes nodded once, slowly. "Very well," he said. "Expect Dr. Watson and myself tomorrow morning, at around eleven. I should be grateful if you would collect up the various objects which have manifested themselves, so that I might examine them myself, while looking over your home in general." He stood and opened the door, inviting the lady to leave. "I trust that, even though we are gentlemen, we will be welcome?"

Leslie Spooner passed through the door in a trail of cigarette smoke. "Of course," she said. "I am not so foolish as to ask you to investigate, then refuse you access to the scene. Besides, the spirit intruder is clearly of the male persuasion – perhaps you will not be the first man to enter my home, after all, and at least *you* will be invited."

*

The address we had been given belonged to a large house at the end of a long, otherwise empty lane, with thick woods all around. Holmes instructed our cab driver to deposit us on the street in front of the house and to wait until we were ready to depart, leaving us to approach the front door on foot.

The atmosphere had been rather strained on the long journey across town, with Holmes sunk in his seat, lost in thought, and unresponsive to my attempts at conversation. I feared that he had taken offence at my suggestion the previous evening, after Leslie Spooner had left, that spiritualism was more akin to a native cult from the Far East than a religion suitable for an Englishman. He had said nothing at the time, simply glared at me with red-rimmed eyes, but he had gone out for the night soon afterwards and we had barely exchanged a word since his return just before breakfast.

Now, rather than immediately knock, he stepped back, peering up at the front of the house with obvious interest.

It was an impressive sight. The door before which we stood was large and black, with three windows on either side of it and, on the upper floor, a matching set of six more, with another, larger and more ornate, directly above the doorframe. All but the two windows directly adjacent to the front door were shuttered, but the two rooms into which we could see were large, bright and airy. To our right, a copse of apple trees took up a significant portion of the garden, extending to the edge of the property and round the side of the house, while to our left, a path meandered through a series of magnificent flower beds, before vanishing round the corner and presumably leading to the back garden.

Holmes slowly walked along the right-hand path, while I admired the flowers. He was lost from sight for a moment among the trees, but soon returned, bearing an apple in his hand, which he tossed to me.

"An apple a day, Watson," he said, with an unexpected grin. "I hope you will forgive my mood recently. I have been… preoccupied, I fear, and not the best companion."

I returned his smile and assured him that there was nothing to forgive, but I did secretly wonder if life with Holmes was destined always to be like this: periods when I might as well live alone, for all the interaction I had with my new friend, followed by bursts of energy and good humour, when a more stimulating associate could not be imagined. Very unlikely, I reassured myself. The past week was sure to be an extraordinary one, I decided – how could Holmes make his living as a consulting detective if he refused to be consulted?

"Are you coming, my dear fellow, or do you intend to stand there all morning?" Holmes's voice broke into my thoughts and reminded me that we had been engaged to carry out an investigation. (In truth, Holmes alone had been so engaged, but he had insisted I accompany him, one of the few things he had said to me the previous evening. Again, I wondered if this was to be the normal way of things, and if I should need to explain to him soon that I could not be at his constant beck and call, and must attend to a medical practice in due course.)

I joined him at the door just as it opened in response to his loud knock. A striking young woman, in her early twenties, with blonde hair piled high on her head and piercing blue eyes, stood before us. She wore a black dress that might or might not have been a maid's uniform, but eyed us suspiciously, then very deliberately crossed her arms, as if waiting for us to introduce ourselves. The experience was slightly unnerving, but no stranger than I expected at the home of Leslie Spooner.

Holmes, however, was unperturbed. "Good morning," he said, removing his gloves and hat as he spoke. "My name is Sherlock Holmes, and this is my friend, Dr. Watson. We are expected." He dropped the gloves into the hat and attempted to enter, but she stood firm in his path.

"Are you now?" she said impertinently. There was the slightest hint of an accent, which made me think of a holiday I had once taken in Tuscany. "I do not think so." To my astonishment, she reached for the door, obviously intending to slam it in our faces, but Holmes was too quick for her and planted a foot in the way.

"Perhaps you should go and consult your mistress," he suggested calmly. "I am aware that this house does not routinely welcome gentlemen callers, but on this occasion…" His voice trailed off, but he held her eye until she grunted churlishly and let go of the door.

"Wait here, then," she said, and disappeared through a doorway on the left. A moment later, I could hear voices raised in apparent argument, and then the girl reappeared. Red-faced and plainly furious, she pulled open the door and indicated that we should enter.

Holmes handed her his hat and gestured to the left. "Your mistress is through here, I presume?" he asked. Without waiting for an answer, he strode past her. I followed, wondering just what sort of household we had come to.

Ridiculously, I experienced some mild disappointment on discovering that the interior of the house was entirely commonplace. I am not sure what I had expected, but the comfortably furnished, warm and welcoming sitting room with a pleasant view in which we found ourselves was not it.

Leslie Spooner rose from her armchair as we entered and gestured towards two other low leather chairs. "Take a seat, gentlemen," she said with a frown. "And please do accept my apologies for Millie's dreadful manners. She is unused to anyone of your sex appearing at the door, but none the less, she should have known better than to be so rude to my guests."

"Is she one of the household staff?" Holmes asked, his eyes flicking about the room as he spoke. Already, I knew that his mind would have catalogued its contents and filed away a dozen areas which required further examination. "She is wearing a dark dress and an apron, but I fancy she is not a maid."

"No," our hostess said slowly. "Millie is not exactly a maid."

"A companion, then?" Holmes pressed. "She obviously lives here."

"She fills many roles, Mr. Holmes. Sometimes she serves as my secretary, and sometimes she helps the housemaid with the housework, or the cook in the kitchen. As you have seen, on occasion, she answers the door to visitors."

It was not a complete answer, I was sure, but Holmes appeared satisfied, for now at least. "Is that the entirety of your domestic staff? A cook, a housemaid and the young lady we have just met?"

"Exactly. There's only me rattling about in here, and I've never felt the need for a large staff. The cook – Mrs. Hanby

– looks after the kitchen, Emily is the housemaid, and Millie is… well, she's Millie. Or Miss Detford, if you wish to be formal." She smiled, and I had the oddest sensation that there was some joke I was missing. If there was, Holmes showed no interest in it.

"I shall need to speak to all three of them in due course," he said. "But for the moment, perhaps you could have someone lead me to the back door of the house, and allow me the freedom to go where I please?"

"Naturally, Mr. Holmes, but do you not wish to see the objects which the spirit left for me first?"

A frown creased Holmes's forehead and I thought he would say yes, but after a moment he shook his head. "While it is tempting to examine immediately items which may have passed to this realm from another, certain evidence is of a more earthly and, I fear, transitory nature," he said. "You mentioned footprints in the dirt?"

Our hostess waved her holder in agreement. "I admire your resolve, Mr. Holmes, and you are quite right, of course," she said. She reached for a small golden bell at her elbow and gave a firm ring. While we waited for this summons to be answered, she lit a fresh cigarette, and Holmes crossed to the back window, which looked out over the garden.

"That is the potting shed of which you spoke earlier?" he asked, gesturing through the glass, though he seemed strangely uninterested in the answer. Though his actions were hidden from the rest of the room by his back, I was positioned in such a way that I could see that he was testing the lock of the window as he spoke.

"It is – and this is Emily." Another young woman had entered the room, darker haired and heavier than Millie, and far more obviously suited to a maid's position.

She blushed and gave an awkward bob of greeting as her name was mentioned, then stared down at the floor as her mistress told her to show us to the back door, adding that we were to be given free rein to go where we wished in the house.

"Yes'm," the girl said, and led us out of the room. As we exited, I looked across the hall through an open doorway directly opposite, and saw the mysterious Millie seated in the window, smoking a cigarette and leafing through the pages of a magazine with no obvious interest. She glanced up as I watched her, and the look she gave me was one of unexpected malice.

I had no time to remark upon this, however, for the little maid hurried us along the hallway to the kitchen, where a heavy-set, middle-aged woman, obviously Mrs. Hanby, looked across as we passed, but demonstrated no curiosity in us, and quickly turned her attention back to the pot she was stirring.

"Did you see the girl Millie?" I asked Holmes as soon as we were alone in the back garden. "I think she may have taken a dislike to us."

He made no reply. Instead, he knelt at the fringe of a stretch of grass and pulled a tape measure from his pocket. I joined him on my haunches and peered down at the indentation which had caught his eye. It was a heel mark, very distinct in the soft earth at the edge of the lawn, with the faint impression of the front sole just about visible in the grass itself.

"A size eight boot, rather than shoe, of inferior manufacture and excessive wear. The owner is a heavy man, upwards of twenty stone in weight, and with a tendency to allow his foot to roll inwards when walking." He leaned forward slightly, using one hand to balance himself, and examined the grass just in front of us. He tutted in what might have been disappointment, but sounded more like irritation.

"Approximately six foot three."

"A tall man," I offered.

"Too tall," Holmes agreed cryptically with another frown. He jumped to his feet, but rather than proceed to the potting shed, as I assumed he would, he turned back to the house.

"Don't you want to take a look inside the shed?" I asked, in some surprise, but he shook his head. There was a strange look on his face, one I had not seen before. He looked over at the shed, which was larger than I would have expected from its name, and resembled more a small summerhouse than a place to store gardening tools. It was the perfect location for an illicit romantic assignation.

"No," he said, finally, turning his attention back to the rear of the house. "I do not think that will be necessary."

Suddenly, utterly without warning, he gave a strangled cry and raised his hands to his face. I started forward in alarm, but he pushed me away. His face was contorted in a way I recognised from my time in the Army – fear, even terror, gripped him. "Do you not feel it, Watson?" he groaned, stumbling backwards until he struck the wall of the house. "There is an unquiet spirit nearby, and I fear it wishes us ill! My God! Do you not feel it!"

He rolled himself along the wall until he reached the door, which he wrenched open with sufficient violence that it slammed against the brickwork, then fled inside. As I hurried in behind him, I heard him shout that the house was cursed, and that he must be free of it. I caught a glimpse of his back as he stumbled through the kitchen, along the hallway and out the front door, without even stopping to wish our client good day.

I did so on behalf of us both, explaining to the lady that we would be back the next day. If she was at all perturbed by Holmes's bizarre behaviour, she gave no sign of it, and indeed seemed to welcome his sudden, noisy departure.

"He felt something, did he? It often happens that way. He may have thought he believed before now, but today, in this house, he felt the direct touch of the other world. He's not the first to run in fright from that. Cursed, he says, but he should say blessed. It's not everywhere that the spirits feel welcome enough to pass back over, but they do here. And they've touched Mr. Holmes."

It would have been rude to contradict a lady in her own home, but I was certain that the spirits had done no such thing. I was worried about Holmes, though. He had until now seemed a man of science like myself, and I could not fathom what had produced in him such terror, or why he had left so precipitously. Still, I did not know him particularly well, and perhaps this was another manifestation of his eccentric nature.

I had no wish to cause offence by casting aspersions on the lady's obviously deeply held beliefs, so I simply repeated that we would return the following day, made my excuses, and departed.

A further surprise awaited me outside, however. I was naturally keen to speak to Holmes, but there was no sign of him. I walked a hundred yards or so along the road, but he was nowhere to be found. Eventually, after five fruitless minutes, I gave up the search, pulled myself into the waiting hansom, and told the driver to take me back to Baker Street.

It had been a peculiar and, I could not help thinking, wasteful manner in which to pass the day.

There was no sign of Holmes at Baker Street, nor did he return all that day, which I spent in catching up on recent medical journals and considering whether I had been wise to take lodgings with so erratic an individual. I could make no sense of his behaviour that morning. Discounting the ridiculous notion that some type of ghostly spirit with a sense of humour had decided to play a series of tricks on the household, it remained plain that either Emily the maid, or Millie the... whatever she was had a young man paying her court, a fact she did not wish her employer to discover, lest she lose her position. If pressed, I should have favoured Emily, who seemed a timid creature, for the guilty party, rather than Millie, who I could imagine was scared of nothing and would always do exactly as she wished. The cook, I decided with a smile, remembering her sturdy frame, could probably be ruled out entirely.

A five-minute interview with the two young women would soon expose the truth, I was sure, but instead Holmes had allowed his unexpected spiritualist beliefs to complicate matters unnecessarily – and waste a reasonable portion of my day for no obvious reason, when I should really have been thinking about restarting my medical career.

The longer I sat, the more annoyed by this aspect I became until, as the sun set and Holmes remained absent, I decided that I would need to speak to him the next day, and make it clear that I could play no part in this odd profession of his in future. With this thought firm in my mind, I retired to bed, determined to tell Holmes that he would need to conclude the current investigation on his own.

*

"Do you have your service revolver to hand?"

Someone was shaking me and, for a moment, I was confused and had no idea where I was. "Damn you, Carruthers," I snapped, disoriented and thinking myself back in Afghanistan. "Will you stop heaving at me like that? Of course I have my revolver."

"Excellent. Bring it with you when you've dressed. A cab is outside and we need to be on our way."

Holmes's voice in my ear was enough to bring me back to my senses. I opened my eyes and blearily registered that I was in my room in Baker Street, that the curtains were open, and that he was standing over me, impatiently gesturing that I should rise. Perhaps it was the look on my face, but as I glared up at him, he murmured, "I shall wait for you outside," and left me alone to dress.

Of course, I had no choice but to accompany him, and though I fully intended to discuss the previous day's events with him on the journey, as soon as I began to speak, he held a finger to his lips and began to lay out the case for the Spooner house being haunted. As he muttered about lines of energy and the illusory nature of time, I knew there was nothing useful I could say to pierce his seemingly growing delusion, and that it might even prove dangerous to do so. Instead,

I let him talk and passed the time watching the nature of the city change, as we travelled out towards the suburbs and the buildings thinned out, and patches of greenery began to appear. It was, in truth, a pleasant enough way to spend an hour and eventually Holmes, receiving neither encouragement nor ridicule from me, fell silent and closed his eyes in sleep.

The moment that we arrived at the Spooner house, however, he roused himself and leapt to the pavement with almost manic energy. He had reached the front door before I had even stepped down from the carriage, and I hurried to catch up with him, now genuinely worried for his sanity as he knocked loudly and demanded entry.

The maid, Emily, answered and thankfully proved more courteous than Millie had been the day before. Holmes bustled past her and made his way straight to our hostess's sitting room.

"Good morning," he said, his head shifting this way and that as he spoke, almost as though he feared an attack from some unseen foe. I noticed his fists were clenched so tightly as to whiten his knuckles and his voice was unnaturally loud. I stepped forward and laid my hand gently on his arm, but he started away with a strangled curse and frowned at me.

"Careful, Watson!" he cautioned. "There is… something… here, in this house. I felt its touch on my shoulder as soon as I crossed the threshold. Can you not feel it?"

Unsure what to say for the best, I indicated some chairs and suggested we take a seat. Holmes stared at me for a moment longer, then nodded and, to my relief, sat down. His foot twitched and his fingers drummed on his leg in a surfeit of nervous energy, but he at least stopped the disturbing movements of his head.

Leslie Spooner was as delighted by Holmes's behaviour as I was concerned. From the instant he had entered the room, she had watched his every movement with eager interest. She had even stubbed out her cigarette and taken a notebook from a table at her side, and begun to jot down what I could see were notes about my friend's strange actions. Now, as Holmes nervously arranged himself in the chair, she laid the notebook aside, and rang the same bell as yesterday.

"I confess I am gratified that you have had such a strong reaction, Mr. Holmes, but I assure you there is no need to fear," she said. "Even if the spirit is a malevolent one – and such manifestations are rare, as I'm sure you're aware – we have in this house one of Europe's greatest mediums, one with experience of every possible type of spiritual event. She will guide and protect us."

Before she had finished speaking, I realised who she meant. Sure enough, when Emily the maid answered her mistress's summons, it was Millie that she was ordered to bring to the sitting room.

"Not just Millie," Holmes interjected, before the girl could leave. "The cook, too. I must speak to everyone in the house."

This request appeared to amuse our hostess, but she nodded and instructed Emily to follow Holmes's instructions. A few minutes later, the door opened once again, and all three women entered. Neither the cook nor Millie made any attempt to hide their displeasure at being summoned, and I wondered again at the unconventional nature of the household.

"I'm sorry to trouble you, ladies, but Mr. Holmes wished to speak to you all." Though she addressed herself to everyone, Leslie Spooner's eyes never left Millie. "Especially you, I think," she went on. "I believe we may have need of your talents in particular, Millie, my dear."

"We certainly do," Holmes replied before the girl could speak. The agitation in his voice was plain, and his hand trembled as he indicated Millie. "Your mistress is entirely correct that your assistance is vital if tragedy is to be averted." He grimaced as though in pain, and continued to speak only with obvious effort. "We must immediately conduct a séance, and everyone in the house must be present. To do otherwise would be to invite disaster!"

A séance! My faith in Holmes's rationality had been waning, but even so, this was unexpected. I knew of such things, of course. Mystical gatherings, in which the participants sat together around a table in darkness, each holding the hand of the person next to them, while a medium – someone with a supposed special talent for speaking to spirits – attempted to make contact with the dead. It was the most arrant nonsense, in my opinion, designed to gull the foolish and the unwary, and I would have thought it most unlikely to gain the approval of Sherlock Holmes.

But he was insistent. "I see that you do not all agree," he said, rising to his feet, "yet it is surely the only safe course we can take. I was invited to investigate apparently inexplicable manifestations, and I admit – for all that I am sympathetic to the spiritualist cause – I expected to arrive and find a simple, wholly corporeal source." He smiled thinly, and indicated me with one hand. I could see beads of sweat on his forehead. "My colleague, Dr. Watson, is convinced that there is nothing more sinister at work here than a maid with an undisclosed suitor, and my initial thought was along similar lines, I must say."

As he spoke, I noticed Emily the maid flush and lower her head. The thing was so obvious that I almost accused the girl there and then. Only concern that it might prove dangerous to interrupt my friend while he was clearly in the midst of some episode of mania caused me to hold my tongue. Holmes himself obviously noticed nothing, for he carried on speaking, without pause.

"But from the second I arrived here, I knew there were forces at play beyond the corporeal. In the house, I felt a chill hand on my breast, and I followed this sensation to the garden and then back inside, at every moment consumed by anxiety and, yes, even fear. Now, I do not claim to have any special talents in the realm of those who have passed over, but I have the blood of the Romany in my veins, and perhaps I am more susceptible to the spirits than most." He shrugged. "In any case, I am convinced that the recent manifestations which have plagued this house, the sinister appearances of these seemingly random objects, the scents which so outraged the sensibilities of our gracious hostess, even the spectral footprints in the grass, each of these is the work of the same unquiet spirit, and the only way in which we can hope to be rid of it is to find out why it has remained tied to this earth, and what we can do to assist it to move on and pass across the veil."

Holmes had worked himself into a fever pitch as he delivered this ludicrous speech, and as he reached its end, he gave out a great sigh and fell, senseless, back into his chair. Our hostess was at once most solicitous and ordered Emily to fetch a glass of water, while she took it upon herself to loosen Holmes's tie for him.

"Don't distress yourself, Mr. Holmes," she said, waving a fan about his face. "I blame myself for not warning you that a first exposure to the other world can be a terrifying experience. But you need fear no longer, for as I told you, we have one of the most gifted mediums working today under this very roof." She frowned. "I admit to reservations – a séance is not a matter to be entered into lightly – but if you're certain that that's what is needed, then I'm sure Millie will be delighted to lead us!"

I was not so sure this was the case, for Millie frowned and shook her head as her mistress finished speaking. But Emily had returned with the water, which she handed to Holmes, and the next minute or so was taken up with the maid being given a short list of necessary items to procure from about the house. Séances, it seemed, required little equipment.

"…and set it all up in Millie's room," our hostess concluded. The girl scuttled away, and I checked Holmes's pulse, suddenly recalling my responsibilities as a medical man. It was strong and steady, and in truth he seemed entirely recovered from whatever faintness had overcome him. He pulled his arm away from me and jumped to his feet.

"Is that the room we saw you in yesterday?" he asked the medium as he crossed to the door and threw it open. "That one just across the hall?"

Millie nodded stiffly, apparently still unhappy at the idea of carrying out the séance. Why that should be, I had no idea. Perhaps she – understandably – feared being exposed as a fraud. In any case, she grudgingly followed Holmes out of the room, our hostess, the cook and I following behind.

*

Emily was putting the finishing touches to the room as we entered, closing the heavy curtains and lighting the gas lamps as low as possible, so that our shadows were cast against the wall in what I felt was intended to be a suitably theatrical manner. The table at which I had seen Millie sitting the previous day had been covered in a black velvet cloth, and a jug of water and glasses for each of us placed in its centre. Everyone took a seat, Emily last of all and with obvious reluctance, with Millie farthest from the door at the head of the table, directly opposite Holmes. I sat beside the little maid, and waited for the séance to begin.

"Please, can everyone reach out and take the hand of the person to their right and left?" Millie asked. "I will seek to contact the spirit world, and discover if there is any unquiet spirit who wishes to speak to us." She glowered across at Holmes. "Though I can't sense anything at all, so we might end up wasting our time."

Feeling something of a fool, I rested one hand on top of Holmes's and carefully took Emily's in my other, then sat back and waited for the tomfoolery to begin. I had watched a broadly similar ceremony in a marketplace in Afghanistan, and it had been a loud and colourful affair, with the local fakir jerking about in spasms of alleged possession, while his assistants banged drums and threw green and red dye in the air. I very much doubted we would see anything quite so extravagant in an English home, but I was prepared for a certain degree of theatricality.

I was to be sorely disappointed. In the dim light, Millie asked, in an uninterested tone, whether there was anyone there? We sat in silence for several dreary minutes, punctuated only when she repeated the question in an increasingly flat voice. Needless to say, nobody answered. Finally, after what seemed an age, she announced that no spirit was present and that we should give up the attempt. I admit, I had a good deal of sympathy with the suggestion.

"No!" Holmes's voice was loud and firm. "How can you not sense the presence in this room, Miss Detford? I feel it like a cold breath on my neck, as real as you or I." He turned to our hostess. "Spooner," he implored, and I winced involuntarily at what seemed like unforgivable discourtesy, "I beg of you, do not stop now! I am certain there is a spirit in this room, at this very moment. Imagine if we were to make definite contact. Think of the publicity it would bring to the Association!"

The lady frowned and glanced across at her medium, then turned back to Holmes. "Yes, Mr. Holmes! I can feel it too!" she cried. "You're quite right, of course you are. We must go on! Millie, my dear, try again – there is a spirit nearby, I know it!"

And so we endured another half hour, while Millie called, with less and less conviction, on a spirit to show itself, and Holmes urged everyone to continue the effort, even in the face of constant failure. By the time that the cook stood up and announced that she had a roast to put on, regardless of how other people might like to waste their day, I had decided that I would start looking for new lodgings the next day. I was by no means certain I would find accommodations as comfortable and reasonably priced as those at 221B Baker Street, but equally I could not bear to remain living at close quarters with a man who held such self-evidently ridiculous beliefs.

In fact, I had decided that I would depart the séance alongside the cook, no matter whether Holmes was determined to continue or not, but the need to do so was rendered moot when he himself rose to his feet and carefully straightened his waistcoat.

"I think that will do," he announced gravely. "Clearly, I was mistaken." He bowed slightly in the direction of our hostess and then walked across to the window. "If you would be so good as to close and lock the door to this room, Watson," he continued, "I should be most grateful. You might also wish to draw your revolver."

I stared at him in dumbfounded confusion, for his manner had changed completely. Where only minutes previously he had been possessed of a maniacal fervour, and shrilly vocal regarding the spectral presence he claimed infested the room, he was now as calm as I had ever seen him, and appeared to have lost all interest in the spirit world.

"The key is in the lock," he prompted. "If you could just turn it, my dear chap, that would be splendid."

Later in our acquaintance, I would have obeyed Holmes's request without a second thought, but I was still unclear as to what was happening, and so I remained where I was. I wondered if our hostess would protest, but she seemed as lost for words as I was myself. Miss Detford too was staring at Holmes, but she said nothing. Then, to my surprise, Emily the maid pushed herself to her feet and did as Holmes had asked.

"The door's locked, Mr. 'Olmes," she said. Like Holmes, the girl had undergone a sudden change in personality. Gone was the timid, easily embarrassed servant of only an hour previously, and in her place stood a confident young woman who met Holmes's eye with unmistakable self-assurance. "You can go ahead now," she added, mysteriously.

Holmes, however, obviously knew what she meant. He gathered a curtain in each hand and, with a dramatic flourish, threw them open, allowing bright sunlight to flood the room. The sudden change from dark to light pained my eyes and forced me to shade them with my hand, but even with my sight thus impeded, I saw a mass of uniformed men rush from the street outside towards the front door of the house. Moments later, I heard the door crash open and the sound of many feet thundering through the hallway and up the stairs. The unmistakable crack of a shot being fired was swiftly followed by shouts of warning and, finally, a loud smash as something, or someone, took a heavy fall.

A similar sound much nearer to me caused me to glance to my right, just in time to see the maid, Emily, kick a pistol from the hand of Millie Detford. Holmes, in whose direction the pistol had been pointing, gave the smallest nod of thanks, and calmly suggested to the other two ladies in the room that they might perhaps be safer hiding under the table. Both did so, with alacrity.

"What on earth is going on, Holmes?" I asked, belatedly pulling my revolver from my pocket. Plainly, all was not as it had seemed.

As though in response, there was a hard knock on the door, repeated three times, and a voice called from the other side. "Mr. Holmes, are you in there?"

Holmes quickly unlocked the door, and a familiar figure entered. I had met Inspector Lestrade when he was investigating a mysterious and bloody murder in Brixton, and knew he and Holmes had kept in touch since then. He was a dark-eyed and sallow-skinned man, but efficient enough, if prone to taking the credit for cases solved by Holmes. "All done and dusted, and as neat as you could wish for, Mr. Holmes," he said as he strolled into the room. "Marcelli is upstairs in handcuffs, nursing a sore head, and there's enough papers and plans and maps and what have you to keep Scotland Yard busy for a month of Sundays."

Holmes smiled grimly. "And you can add Miss Maria Marcelli to your collection, Inspector," he said, indicating our erstwhile medium, who was seated in her chair, rubbing her arm and glaring at Emily, who stood watchfully over her.

"Well, that is good news, Mr. Holmes," Lestrade grinned. "I admit I'd forgotten all about her in the excitement." He would have said more, I think, but just then he noticed the two women hiding under the table, and gave a startled exclamation more suited to a gentlemen's smoking room. Recovering himself, he held out a hand and helped our hostess to her feet.

"You must be Mrs. Spooner," he said, as the lady brushed herself down. She did not object to the title, I noticed, but from the wide-eyed manner in which she looked from Lestrade to Holmes and across to the women who had, until half an hour previously, made up two-thirds of her household staff, I doubted she even really heard him. Neither did she protest when Lestrade summoned a constable to lead both cook and mistress away.

"We best be going too, Mr. Holmes," he announced. He pulled a set of handcuffs from his pocket and slipped them onto Miss Detford's – or rather, Miss Marcelli's – wrists. "We wouldn't want to be losing you, now would we?" He grinned. "Not when Mr. Holmes and his friends have gone to such pains to catch you for us."

He nodded in Holmes's direction. "Thank you again, Mr. Holmes. I know I expressed my doubts that this plan of yours would work, but I'm man enough to admit when I'm wrong. Very neat this has been, very neat indeed." He chuckled and, still chuckling, led his prisoner from the room. Moments later, we heard the front door shut. I looked out of the window and saw Miss Marcelli and a fair-haired man of narrow build, presumably Mr. Marcelli, being marched towards a police carriage.

It had been a hectic and confusing few minutes, and as the carriage disappeared down the long path leading away from the house, I suddenly felt as though I were a puppet whose strings had been cut. With a heavy sigh, I dropped into the nearest chair and demanded an explanation of Holmes.

He took his time to answer, lighting a cigarette and offering the case to me. I waved it away, and he pushed it along the table to Emily, who had taken the seat recently vacated by Miss Marcelli.

"Thanks, Mr. 'Olmes," she said, in a rough Cockney-accented voice. "I've bin gasping all day, and that cook says that ladies don't smoke." She shook her head and inhaled deeply, blowing the smoke in a thick cloud towards the ceiling. "Well, I ain't no lady, am I?"

Holmes grinned and gestured towards her with his own cigarette. "Dr. John Watson, please meet Violet Cushing. Violet," he went on, "is one of that select group of irregular troops whom you will recall I employed during the Jefferson Hope case. I placed her here as a domestic servant some weeks ago and asked her to carry out one or two small tasks for me."

"He asked me to plant evidence, is what he did." The girl seemed to think this improper, for she frowned at the memory. "Din't seem right to be putting stuff into a house, if you get my drift?"

"Violet was, at one time, one of London's foremost pickpockets, and also an occasional cat burglar," Holmes explained. "She has seen the error of her ways, but old habits die hard, I fear."

"Too right they do," Violet agreed. "Very 'ard indeed. But still, you done me a good turn, Mr. 'Olmes, and I din't forget that. So I did what you said, even if it seemed a bit loony."

"What did you do, exactly?" I asked.

"Well, I cooked some kippers while her Ladyship was out at her club, and I left 'alf a bottle of stout outside her bedroom door, which was a waste of good stout, if you ask me. Plus I made them footprints out the back."

"Where you failed to carry out my exact instructions," Holmes chided, though with a hint of a smile to remove any sting from his words. "You applied too much pressure and left too large a gap between the prints, creating a veritable giant of a man!"

Violet was unabashed. "Yeah, well, it was pitch black out there, wasn't it?" She grinned. "I stuck that ol' newspaper on her favourite chair, though, din't I?" She shook her head and gave Holmes a mocking smile. "See what I mean – a bit loony."

"You arranged for the... what did she call them... manifestations, Holmes?" I asked, now thoroughly lost.

"Of course, and I also arranged for the Chairman of the Spiritualist Association of Great Britain to recommend me to Mrs. Spooner when she asked him who would be best placed to investigate what could either be a haunting or a disobediently amorous servant."

"But why?"

"As with most things, it is simple enough, really, once explained. You saw the fellow being led away by the doughty Inspector Lestrade? That is Luigi Marcelli, an Italian anarchist wanted on the continent for the murder of, at last count, two judges, one police chief, and at least three high-ranking politicians. He is known in anarchist circles as the bomb-maker supreme, and he has been in England for the last two months, planning some new atrocity on these shores. Unfortunately, as soon as he arrived, he disappeared and had not been seen until today. However, I have –" he paused and smoked in silence for a moment, as though deciding what to say next. "– I have... an acquaintance who works at a high level inside Her Majesty's Government, and he approached me and asked me to do what I could to lay hands on Marcelli. I was not able to find him, though I spent several nights combing the docks and opium dens of London in search of him, but one of my informants did find his sister, Maria, working in this house as a medium, of all things. It did not take long to discover that the householder was a well-known spiritualist, nor to deduce that Maria had positioned herself here in order to help her brother in some way."

"So you arranged for Miss Cushing to take up a post here, to spy on Miss Marcelli?"

"Exactly so. As you saw, she is an excellent actress, and she can be quite pleasant when she chooses to be."

"I assume that she discovered that the brother was hiding here, but what I don't understand is why any subterfuge was required in order for Lestrade to take him into custody. Why not just knock on the door and arrest the man?"

The look on Holmes's face was one of wry amusement. "Ah yes. I am afraid that I owe you an apology for my recent behaviour, Watson." He walked over to the window and gestured towards the street. "You see how things are laid out beyond the garden gate. The only access is by way of that lengthy lane in front of us, and there is no cover along it for a good hundred yards. It would be impossible to approach the house undetected, particularly with Maria seated in the window watching the road all day. And the land to the rear is dense woodland, in which a man, given warning, might lose himself within moments. In short, this house might as well be a castle, so well placed is it for defence. Doubtless, that is the reason the Marcellis chose it.

"Luigi Marcelli is a dangerous man, Watson, with no compunction about killing. Had Lestrade attempted openly to bring his men up the lane, I have no doubt Marcelli would have killed the occupants of the house, and then he and his sister would have fled through the woods."

Holmes grimaced at the thought, as well he might, for the idea that innocent women were not safe even in their own homes was repulsive to any Englishman.

"I knew that I had to get into the house myself, but how to do so, when one of the eccentricities of its most eccentric of owners was that no man might cross its threshold? I admit that the answer, when it came to me, was sufficiently outlandish that I had some difficulty convincing Lestrade it would work. But how better to come to the attention of a spiritualist than by creating a spirit? I had Violet scatter random objects about the house, objects which could not possibly have been accidentally placed, and then allowed Mrs. Spooner's imagination and willingness to believe complete the task.

"And you know the rest. By feigning belief in the presence of a spirit, I obliged Maria to conduct a séance, thus preventing her from watching the street and warning her brother. In that way, Lestrade was able to bring his forces to bear… and now he has both Marcellis safely in custody."

"But where was Luigi hiding? Could he not keep watch himself?"

"He was secreted in the attic, which thankfully has no windows. As soon as Violet arrived, she began to keep an eye on Maria's movements and quickly realised that she was taking food to her brother every evening. He could go nowhere else, of course – the very prohibition against a man setting foot inside the house, which worked to their benefit everywhere else, worked against them in this sole respect."

I have no doubt that Holmes caught the look of relief which crossed my face as he finished his explanation. The news that his histrionics had been a ruse was most welcome indeed, saving me the trouble of finding new lodgings on my meagre daily allowance of eleven shillings and sixpence. In the future, I would have to remember, however, that my new friend was a superlative actor.

"Shall we go?" he asked, with a smile. "Though I fear we should have hitched a ride with Lestrade. I doubt that there are many hansoms plying their trade nearby, and it may be quite a walk until we find a cab."

THE ADVENTURE
OF THE MISQUOTED
MACBETH

———— ❊ ————

DERRICK BELANGER

The Bible instructs us to love our brothers, but I confess I felt little of the sentiment in question as I stared at the letter from San Francisco. I had a strong sense of what kind of news the missive contained.

"This one's travelled a long way, Doctor," Mrs. Hudson said, holding out the letter.

I had just come home from a long day of work; fortunately, Holmes's day was even longer than mine and my detective friend had not yet returned from his investigations. I knew his current case concerned the murder of a mudlark. It was the type of case he took when the client, in this case a desperate street Arab who was the victim's kin, had nowhere else to turn. Holmes did not profit from these cases, but they kept his mind occupied and proved to me there was a heart inside his cold exterior.

"Em, do me a favour, Mrs. Hudson, and please don't mention this letter to Mr. Holmes. It, em, involves a surprise I'm planning for him," I blubbered, uncomfortable at telling my landlady a falsehood.

The creases around Mrs. Hudson's eyes flattened as she opened them wide. "A surprise? For Mr. Holmes?" she said, astonished. Then she let out a soft chuckle. "You don't need to worry. Your secret's safe with me." I was unsure that she believed me, but I was certain she would not breathe a word to Holmes.

I quickly ascended the steps to 221B and tore open the letter, reading with dread. As my worst fears were confirmed, nay, exceeded, I felt my face reddening and anger rising within me. My brother was penniless and very ill, residing in a hospital. He asked me to journey to see him one last time, for he feared his drinking had finally got the better of him. The signature was in a shaky hand.

I tore the letter into pieces and threw them in the wastepaper basket. Then I reached for paper, ink and pen and wrote a frenzied response telling my brother how much I despised him, how he had squandered his life as a drunkard and run through our father's inheritance without ever doing an honest day's work. When I reached the final lines and saw the loathing and ill will inked upon the page, I had second thoughts. I crumpled my letter into a ball and tossed it away, realising that I needed a clearer head before deciding on a course of action.

*

It was but a few days later, on a chilly spring afternoon in the year of 1884, when a case was brought to Sherlock Holmes that serendipitously led me to a conclusion on the matter of my kin. I had returned to 221B Baker Street in a foul mood, lamenting to Holmes over the crowded London streets and the unseasonable cold. The frost really was not out of the ordinary, but since receiving my brother's letter I had found a long list of things about which to complain. Holmes must have noted the change in my mood, but he did not comment, nor did he say anything when I built a fire in the hearth. We could have easily worn wool and drunk tea to stay warm and not wasted the coal.

I was sitting in my armchair across from Holmes, grumbling about the new French Minister of Foreign Affairs, when the bell rang downstairs, and soon after Mrs. Hudson came to our door. She handed Holmes a card. My friend read it and gave a nod.

"Send the gentleman up."

"A new client?" I asked.

"That depends on whether I take his case." Holmes had been smoking his clay pipe and looking towards the flames, puzzling over some problem. A new case might prove beneficial since he had brought the mudlark investigation to a swift conclusion. The less he had to do, the more likely he was to become bored, and that was when he chose less savoury ways to occupy his time.

There was a knock and Holmes called out, "Enter!"

I turned, and started at the sight of the man who might become Holmes's next client. It was as though the giant Antaeus himself were stepping into our sitting room, a massive figure who had to stoop so as not to scrape his head against the doorway. His chest was Herculean, his arms were thick as tree trunks, and his looks brutish. An unevenly trimmed black beard hid some of his pockmarked face, and a lion's mane of hair fell over his forehead. His nose was stubby, his eyes dark and beady.

"Which one of you is Sherlock Holmes?" he asked in a baritone, guttural voice.

The appearance of this creature had me at a loss for words, but Holmes gave a few coughs and whisked away smoke from his face. "Excuse me," he said, calmly extinguishing his pipe. "I wanted to get in the last few puffs of this excellent Turkish blend. I am Mr. Sherlock Holmes, and this is my friend and associate, Dr. Watson. Please join us."

Holmes motioned for the goliath to sit in the cane-back wicker chair between himself and me. The giant sauntered over and lowered himself, the chair giving a long, pitiful creak.

"Watson, this is Mr. Phineas Armstrong. At least that is what his card indicates. I believe the name is an alias, isn't that right, Mr. Armstrong?"

The brute glowered at Holmes. "What are you getting at?" he snarled, leaning forward in threatening fashion.

My friend studied his fingernails. "I do believe it is time to file these down," he mused. "Have no fear of our guest, Watson. While he is a sizeable man and appears quite menacing, Mr. Armstrong is as gentle as a newborn babe."

I am not sure who had a more startled look upon his face, Armstrong or I. Holmes, unruffled, elaborated on his statement:

"Look to his hands, Watson. Note how they are smooth

and free of calluses." Holmes made a fist to show off his own rough hands. "Unlike mine, the hands of a fighter.

"You will also observe the high quality of his suit. It is new, well pressed, and with rather expensive silver cufflinks. An unusual fashion choice for a man who wears his hair as though it were brushed by a whirlwind and speaks as though he made his home in Limehouse.

"Lastly, the name Armstrong furthers his act. A brutish outer appearance coupled with the name Arm-strong suggests a man you would not want to cross." He turned to our visitor. "Now, Mr. Armstrong, I should appreciate it if you dropped your charade and told us your real name, and more importantly, why you are here."

I had been watching Armstrong's expression turn from one of shock to one of absolute pleasure, like that of a child beholding a magic trick.

"Well done, Mr. Holmes, well done," he said now in the Queen's English. "You're everything Lestrade said you'd be."

Holmes arched his brows. "Lestrade sent you?"

"In a manner of speaking. He's mentioned you. Said your detective skills could almost keep up with his own –" Armstrong stared blankly "– and your fees were reasonable, too."

"Did he, now?" Holmes responded, his lips closing in a thin line.

"Oh, don't you worry, Mr. Holmes. You'll be well compensated for your work."

"I do not yet know what that work is," Holmes answered. "Nor do you know if I shall accept your case."

Mr. Armstrong raised his hands as if telling a robber not

to shoot. "I understand. I probably shouldn't have mentioned that bit about Lestrade…" He shook his head. "Let me tell you the nature of the case and then you can make up your mind."

Holmes nodded his approval.

Armstrong leaned forward and began his tale, moving his hands expressively as he spoke. "I should begin by telling you that Hale, Chauncey Hale, is my birth name, though I did legally change it to Armstrong, and debt collection is my game. I didn't set out to be a debt collector, no, sir. Chemistry was my field of study, and I started out at King's, thinking that would be how I made my way in life. Fate took a bad turn, and a case of the pox left my face as cratered as the moon. Always looking for a way to flip my luck from bad to good, I saw how intimidated people were when they encountered me with my new face, and I thought there had to be some money in it for me.

"So, a few years back, I turned to debt collection, and not just any debt collection, but the collection of large sums. You see, I can charge twenty per cent of the debt for my services. Fear makes the men pay up. Banks are much happier to get their money and pay a hefty fee than to send a client to debtors' prison where the person may never work off what is owed. Better to pay me and have eighty per cent immediately."

"Your work must be quite lucrative," I said, thinking of all the people I knew who had gambled away their fortunes. Even I myself had been in debt several times from making bad bets at the races.

"It is, Doctor. I have a gentleman's salary. There's no end to those who owe money, regardless of whether the markets are up or down. And if I keep bringing in payments, I should be in business for the rest of my life. And that brings me to why I'm here."

Holmes leaned forward. His gaze became more focused, and I could see that he would concentrate on the colossus's every word.

"Continue."

"Yesterday, I had three payments to collect. All were for large sums of money from gentlemen who had fallen on hard times. The first two were easy enough to... let's say coax into finding the necessary resources. Alas, I'm sure that they ended up even deeper in debt by borrowing to cover what they owed." He shrugged. "Better than hanging from a noose tied with their own hands."

"Really, sir!" I was disgusted at how nonchalantly this brute discussed the misery of his fellow man.

"It is but the truth, Doctor," Armstrong answered casually. "I take no pleasure in this. No one ought to be blamed for a task society considers necessary."

I was about to reply with some choice words, but Holmes held up both his index fingers.

"Mr. Armstrong," he said in a tone of boredom. "Pray, keep the asides to a minimum."

Armstrong grumbled that he was only trying to defend himself. "It was late in the afternoon," he then continued, "when I came to my third and final collection of the day. Since the first two had taken longer than anticipated, I was torn about how to approach this one. You see, I keep a red setter at home. I pay the neighbour lad to take her out each day after he gets home from school; however, he had some oral examination yesterday, so I had to get home and give Lady a run of the park before she made a mess of the house.

"My last scheduled visit of the day was to the home of one Jacob Snerley, a former bank manager who owed five hundred pounds. The man had worked for Horace and Sons, but when the bank discovered how much debt he was in, he was sacked. They thought it looked poor for a company that was entrusted with people's fortunes to have a manager who was so bad at managing his own."

"Understandable," Holmes agreed. "And who owns Mr. Snerley's loans?"

"A lender by the name of Bentley mostly, but there are a few brokers as well."

"Thank you," Holmes said, and I could tell he was storing this information in his mind. "Carry on."

"I decided that I would go over to Snerley's house in Upper Grosvenor Street, threaten that I'd return to see him that evening and he'd better have the money or I'd haul him off to prison myself. That would give him plenty of time to gather the necessary funds and myself plenty of time to care for my dog."

"Weren't you concerned that he might flee in the interim?" I asked.

"That was a concern of mine, Doctor," the giant said with a grin. I could tell he was a man who enjoyed the sound of his own voice. He was having a grand time telling his tale. "However, when I got to the house I knew, or at least I thought I knew, that he wasn't going anywhere. The property was worth vastly more than what he owed, a two-storey house with a manicured lawn. If the man fled, then the loan agency could foreclose on his house. Before I rapped on the door, I already knew that I'd suggest Snerley take a small mortgage, easy to arrange for someone who's worked in the City—"

"One moment," Holmes interrupted the potential client. "Just because a man can lay hold of some money doesn't mean that he will act upon your request. There must have been more to your certainty that he would not run off without paying his debts."

"You are an observant fellow, Mr. Holmes. Yes, I noticed through the window when I approached the house that the furniture had beige cloths draped over it. I figured Snerley was having the house painted. Someone who improves his property isn't going to up and leave. The man appeared to have resources; he just wasn't directing them properly."

Holmes thought for a moment, nodded, and then said, "*Appeared...*" as though he were questioning the debt collector's word choice. "Very good, Mr. Armstrong. Pray continue your story."

"I was surprised, gentlemen, that when I knocked on the front door, it was answered by Snerley himself, and he was as tall and almost as ugly as I am, and also scarred. Before I had a chance to introduce myself, he handed me a thin envelope and said, 'I've been expecting you. Here.'

"I thanked him, but he sneered at me. 'Don't dawdle. Be off with you, now,' he said. I did not like his tone of voice, but this was a stroke of good fortune, so I simply tipped my hat and turned on my heels.

"I caught a hansom to my house in Marylebone, took Lady

for a long stroll, and then spent the remainder of the evening catching up with the news. It was not until this morning when I was preparing to hand in the debts I had collected that I opened Snerley's envelope." Armstrong ground his teeth while taking an envelope from his inner pocket. "Here, Mr. Holmes, have a look. No cheque inside. Only a piece of paper with some gibberish on it."

Holmes opened the envelope and took out a sheet of paper, which he proceeded to unfold. I noted that his eyes widened for a fleeting moment. He scoffed and then handed the paper to me.

I was surprised to see scrawled there in pencil a number of the opening lines of Shakespeare's *Macbeth*:

FIRST WITCH: When shall we three meet again?
When the moon neither waxes nor wanes?

SECOND WITCH: When the hurlyburly's done,
When the battle's lost and won.

THIRD WITCH: That will be the arrival of the sun.

FIRST WITCH: Where the place?

SECOND WITCH: Upon the Saint.

THIRD WITCH: There to meet with Macbeth.

"Tell me," said Holmes in a rather uninterested voice. "What did you do next?"

"Well, after I cursed and complained to my poor dog, I took a cab over to Snerley's residence. When I arrived, I saw this little fellow slipping a letter through the letterbox. I asked if he happened to know whether Mr. Snerley was home. He told me that he wasn't. We struck up a conversation, and it turns out the man was Snerley's landlord! So, not only did Snerley not own the house, but the place was furnished, so he didn't even own the furniture. I had nothing to use as collateral and the thief had slipped away. If only I'd opened that envelope when it was handed to me!"

He used some rather uncouth words to describe himself before continuing. "So, that's about it, Mr. Holmes. I have to find Snerley and collect the debt from him, if possible. I can probably get a few days of grace from my employers, but after that, they'll drop me, and I'll lose my payment. Twenty per cent it is, Mr. Holmes, but more than that, I'll lose my reputation for always collecting my debts. In fact, if you can get Snerley and the money to me in forty-eight hours, I'll give you half... no... sixty per cent of my fee as payment. What do you say, old man?"

Holmes's face still displayed an expression of ennui. He glanced over the paper that bore the *Macbeth* quote one more time, then reached out and let the paper glide into the fire. Armstrong's jaw dropped, just as my own did, on watching Holmes destroy what appeared to be a piece of evidence.

"What'd you do that for?"

"Because, Mr. Armstrong," Holmes said as he grabbed the poker and stirred the fire, "the message provided no value to your case, but it does provide a touch of warmth to the room." He returned the poker to its rack and leaned back in his seat. "Now, Mr. Armstrong, your fee is quite generous, and I do believe I can bring your case to a conclusion within the time you have in mind."

At Holmes's words, the Hercules let out a sigh of relief. "Thank you, Mr. Holmes. Lestrade was right to recommend you."

"Just a moment," my friend cautioned. "I do have a few questions before I give you my final agreement."

"Of course."

"First, you mentioned that Snerley was ugly and scarred."

"That's right. A truly repulsive fellow."

"How so?"

"Well, he has a twisted face, as if his eyes and ears don't quite line up. They are misaligned, with his left side higher than his right."

"And the scar?"

"Ghastly, Mr. Holmes. It stretches from here –" Armstrong tapped his left temple then moved his finger down his face, from just under his eye to the corner of his lips "– to here."

Holmes nodded. "Well, he should be easy enough to find." He then asked, "What additional information did you learn from Mr. Snerley's landlord?"

"Not much. He said Snerley was a fine tenant who always paid on time. In fact, he is paid up until the end of the week. I'll be honest, Mr. Holmes. I find it odd that Snerley pays his rent and fixes up the interior of his home, but doesn't make any payments towards his debt."

"A good point, Mr. Armstrong. One that I hope to clarify for you."

*

Once Armstrong had departed, Holmes practically threw my coat to me from the wardrobe. "Get ready, Watson. We must hurry to Snerley's house."

I buttoned up my outer garment. "Why the urgency?"

Holmes swung open the door, cape in hand, urging me to head downstairs. "I must inspect the house, though I fear it has already been cleared."

We exited into Baker Street, damp and rather glum this afternoon. Fortunately, we did not need to wait for long. A four-wheeler approached, and soon we were off to Snerley's residence.

"I take it there is more to the case than an escaped debtor," I remarked dryly.

"There is indeed, Watson. How much more I hope to elucidate when we arrive in Upper Grosvenor Street."

Holmes settled into a monk-like trance as he focused on the fragments of the case. I also reflected on what I knew, wondering if there was any significance to the letter Holmes had thrown into the fire. I decided against it, for why would my friend destroy a piece of evidence? Still, his methods sometimes appeared to make as much sense as the ramblings of a Bedlam resident.

Despite my best efforts to focus on the problem at hand or even to clear my mind and just listen to the clopping of the hooves upon the cobblestones, my thoughts returned to my brother and his situation. A bitterness grew in my heart. I remembered our good times together growing up, playing rugby in the field near our house, jumping off rope swings into the pond near our school. What a waste for a lad with so much promise to end up a hospitalised drunkard in a faraway land.

*

The Snerley residence, handsome and well kept, was nestled between a Georgian cottage and a row of terraced houses. Upon our arrival, Holmes awoke from his trance and practically sprang out of the carriage, not even pausing to request that our driver wait while we inspected the house.

My friend rushed up the garden path to the entrance. He tried the door, found it locked, and removed a pick from his trouser pocket.

"Stand behind me," he commanded, so that I blocked anyone from seeing us breaking in.

While Holmes worked, I turned my head and looked through the front bay window, where I could see a fine but worn green couch. Something about it puzzled me, but I could not place my finger on why that particular piece of furniture should draw my attention. The lock clicked open, and Holmes entered the house. I followed, shutting the door behind me.

The front parlour was sparsely furnished. There was the green couch I had spied through the window, with a matching set of cushioned chairs. A small mahogany card table stood in the centre of the seating arrangement. The table was quite worn and looked as if it might serve more frequently as a footrest than as a device for playing bridge.

Holmes stared at the floor. "Bah!" he let out, clenching his right hand. He stepped over to the dining room behind the parlour and let out another "Bah!"

"It is as I feared, Watson. Just look at the floor."

"Could do with a touch of the mop."

"Exactly." Holmes bent down and swiped his index finger

across the wooden boards, then showed me the dust upon its tip. "It will be like that throughout the house. In every room, except in the front parlour."

"Why would Snerley only clean the parlour?"

"Because that is where he and his unsavoury guests met." Holmes returned to the parlour, crouched down by the furniture, and began moving the chairs around and peering underneath. "This ensures that they can't be identified. I should almost say that the precautions they took suffice to identify them, but without conclusive evidence I—aha!"

Holmes had moved the couch back, and now in one corner picked up what appeared to be a long strand of white hair. He held it up to the window, a look of triumph taking shape upon his face. "Ah, Watson, as I suspected. I will verify with my microscope at home, but I am certain this strand of hair is from our adversary." Holmes gave one of his odd silent laughs. He was certainly in high spirits.

"I don't recall Armstrong saying that Snerley had white hair."

"He didn't. In fact, my friend, Armstrong never met Mr. Snerley."

"Really, Holmes, you are making little sense."

"Come, Watson. Our cab is waiting and I have what I need. We shall return to Baker Street, and there I can explain everything to you."

*

We rode back to Baker Street in silence. I wanted Holmes to give me a hint at least as to what he had discovered, but I knew better than to press my friend. Back in our rooms, Holmes went straight to his desk and placed the hair he had found under his microscope. He looked through the lens for just a second, then turned to me, a wry smile upon his face.

"As I suspected."

"What is so suspicious about a strand of white hair?"

"It is the type of white hair. It is a strand not from an elderly man but from one who lacks pigment."

"Albinism?" I asked, surprised that Armstrong had left out this important detail. "You believe that Snerley is an albino."

"Not Snerley, no. But one of his two associates is. The other is the man whom Armstrong met."

Holmes saw my befuddlement. He invited me to join him in our seats by the hearth so as to explain himself, though not before calling down to Mrs. Hudson to request warm brandy. Once our landlady had served us our drinks, my friend leaned back and revealed all to me.

"As you surmised, Watson, when Mr. Armstrong first brought me the case, I didn't think it was worth my time. It was only when he showed me that note he had received that my interest was piqued. When he described Mr. Snerley, I knew we were dealing with true villainy."

"But you destroyed the note," I countered. "Why would you destroy a piece of evidence?"

Holmes took a swig of his brandy before answering. "For two reasons. First, I had gleaned all the information I needed from the note. Second, I wanted Mr. Armstrong to see me destroy it in case our antagonists were to go after him. If he told them he had spoken to a detective who destroyed the note because it was worthless, there was a better chance they would do him no serious harm."

"I see," I said curtly, wishing that Holmes had told me the logic behind his actions earlier. "So, the note was never intended for Armstrong?"

"No, I am certain that our client was mistaken for a courier."

"Armstrong? If he showed up at my door, I'm not sure I'd hand a letter over to such a character."

Holmes gave me a look of disparagement. "Remember, the man who greeted Armstrong told him not to dawdle. The letter needed to be delivered promptly. I am sure that the true messenger showed up after Armstrong had left. That's when the coverings were removed from the furniture, and the parlour was cleaned."

At Holmes's words, I recalled Armstrong telling us that the furniture was covered in cloths as though the room were being prepared to be painted. At this point my mind started working. I understood why I had thought there was something odd about the green couch I had spied through the window. There was no covering. I remembered Holmes's remarks on the parlour having been cleaned.

"That is where the villains met. They covered the furniture and later, when they cleaned everything thoroughly – though not thoroughly enough – they removed the coverings. They did not want any evidence, such as a strand of hair from an albino, to be discovered. If they had not abandoned the house in such a hurry, I am sure that they would have left no trail for me to follow."

"And you couldn't share any of this information with me?"

"Do not be offended, Watson. Until we inspected Snerley's house, all was mere speculation. I had to see the evidence, and then determine how seriously to take the plan laid out in the note."

"Plan? It was just a quote from *Macbeth*."

"Ah, that is where you are mistaken, my dear Watson. While the words are taken in part from *Macbeth*, they are misquoted. The original quotation reads: 'First witch: When shall we three meet again, in thunder, lightning, or in rain? Second witch: When the hurley-burley's done, when the battle's lost and won, that will be ere the set of sun. Third witch: Where's the place? Second witch: Upon the heath. Third witch: There we go to meet Macbeth.' If you recall, Watson, the note Armstrong received quoted several of those lines incorrectly. The first witch said that the three witches would meet again *when the moon neither waxes nor wanes*, not in thunder, lightning, or in rain."

"I do seem to remember that, Holmes, but I'll have to take your word for it since you destroyed the note."

My friend nodded. He knew that I lacked the faculty of etching something into my mind by way of a mere glance.

"The note also said that the time they will meet is on the arrival of the sun instead of at the setting of the sun," Holmes explained. "And the last change was that they would meet Macbeth not upon the heath, but upon the Saint."

"Most interesting, Holmes, but what does it all mean?"

"It means, my friend, that our three ne'er-do-wells are planning to meet at Saint Katharine Docks at dawn on Thursday."

"Thursday? In two days? But…" I blubbered. "How could you read all that from the note?"

Holmes fixed me with a steely-eyed gaze. "The pieces are all there, my friend. I simply had to look for what had been altered from the original. First, the time of the meeting: when the moon neither waxes nor wanes. That would mean a new or full moon. There is a full moon tomorrow evening. This is followed by the line that the time is at the arrival of the sun, so that would mean dawn, the dawn after the full moon, ergo, Thursday morning. The quote concludes by saying the three will meet upon the Saint to find Macbeth. While there are many churches and cathedrals in London named after saints, the wording that they shall meet *upon the saint* would indicate a location such as a field or a dock. The most likely answer, then, is that the three men will meet at Saint Katharine Docks."

"Remarkable, Holmes!" I said, once again astonished at my friend's skills.

"Merely logic, Watson."

"But who are the three men of whom you speak? There's Snerley, but what of the other two?"

"Have you read in *The Times* of a notorious thief known as MacAlister?"

"Yes…" I whistled. "The less respectable papers call him the Albino Butcher. Works alongside a nasty brute named Fibbs, a man with a ghastly face and…" I paused. "Holmes, that means…"

"Yes, Watson, it means that Snerley is working with two of London's most notorious criminals. I now must learn why."

"Isn't it obvious? The man is in debt. He's reached for the bottom to dig himself out of the hole he's created for himself."

Holmes tapped the fingers of his right hand on the arm of his chair while his left hand held his chin. "Perhaps, Watson, but a man, a professional man, doesn't usually delve down so quickly. You could be right; however, I wonder if there is more to it in this case. Tomorrow, I shall make enquiries as to the character of Mr. Snerley. I believe I can answer many of my questions, and those that I can't shall be answered by Snerley after we apprehend him."

"You are certain that you can catch him."

"I am. We now know the time and location. The question still remains as to why they are meeting at Saint Katharine's. It is either to perform a robbery of some sort or to flee the city. A robbery appears more likely. All will be revealed in just over a day's time."

*

I had a light schedule the following day, and while I supplied routine medications to my patients, my mind kept turning to Holmes and the case of Mr. Snerley. I could not help but wonder how a banker could drift into a life of crime. Then I thought of my own problem with gambling and how I, at times, had to watch myself to make sure I did not lose all of my savings. I also thought of my ill brother and for the first time felt a pang of sympathy for the man. He had fallen on hard times and was in hospital. He could have become a thief, or worse.

Before going home for the day, I made sure to clear my diary. I knew that I might be up all night and not find rest until early or even late in the morning. I would be in no condition to treat patients.

When I returned to Baker Street, I opened the door and found a well-groomed, bespectacled, elderly man sitting by the fire.

"Ah," he said in a high-pitched, scratchy voice, "you must be Dr. Watson. Mr. Holmes told me about you, said you were a fine fellow."

"That's very kind of you to mention. Is Mr. Holmes here?"

The lined face of the elderly man softened, and I noted the steel-grey eyes of my friend. "Why, Watson, he is right here. I have just arrived, haven't had a chance to change out of my disguise."

I complimented Holmes on his extraordinary outfit and asked what the occasion was.

"Why, to gather information on Snerley, of course. A stern yet well-dressed older gentleman can take on many roles. Today, I used this disguise to impersonate a bank inspector, an officer of the law, and a visiting professor of medicine."

My friend invited me to sit with him. He lit a pipe and I cut myself a Cuban cigar. As smoke began to drift to the ceiling, Holmes began his tale.

"I first went to Threadneedle Street to visit the bank which formerly employed Snerley, an institution by the name of Horace and Sons. At first, the owners were tight-lipped about any information on a former employee. Some stern gazes and veiled threats helped loosen their tongues and they then answered all my questions. Mr. Snerley was a model employee and well regarded. The man is relatively young, in his thirties, and had built up a reputation for kindness and competence. But, as Mr. Armstrong said, when a debt collector came to the bank enquiring about Mr. Snerley, the owners felt compelled to show him the door.

"They did not know the reason for Snerley's debt. They asked him, but he refused to answer, merely agreeing with some sadness to leave their employ.

"I also enquired about any special new assets set to arrive at the bank. Michael Horace, the elder brother, was surprised I asked, because they had been advised that a rare jewel would be delivered to the bank late this evening."

"Don't you mean tomorrow at dawn?" I asked.

"Actually, I must humbly admit that I was wrong on that count. The jewel that is being delivered is a large rare yellow diamond of an intense and vivid hue. It is called the Australian Sun – the sun referred to in the misquoted *Macbeth* – and is set to arrive on a special freighter this evening at ten o'clock."

"Snerley and his associates plan to steal it at the docks, eh?"

"Yes, but I've already notified Gregson, and he assures me the force will be out in full to protect the diamond and arrest the trio. We shall join them at the dock shortly after dinner."

After leaving the bank, Holmes continued, he had gone to Snerley's residence in the guise of a police inspector. He claimed that he was investigating the disappearance of Mr. Snerley. From the banker's former neighbours, Holmes learned that Snerley was the type of person who helped carry in baskets for elderly people returning from the market.

One neighbour who had been close to Snerley revealed that the man had a sister who, like my brother, was the black sheep of the family. She was a drunk who squandered money and had ended up in debtors' prison. When his sister became ill, Snerley borrowed heavily to pay off his sister's debt. She died soon after being released. That was all the man knew.

"You said that you took on the guise of a bank inspector and an officer of the law, but you also mentioned you were a professor of medicine."

"Ah, very good, Watson." My friend nodded. "I ended my day at the hospital where Snerley's sister had been treated. I claimed I was doing research on the effects of excessive alcohol on the female body. It is there that I verified that the death of Miss Snerley was indeed from liver failure.

"Now, Watson, do you have your trusted Webley?"

"Give me a minute, and it will be at my side," I responded, patting my hip.

"Excellent. You might need it at the dock later on."

*

The fog for which our fair city is so noted was absent that evening, and the dock was well lit by the light of the full moon. As Holmes and I watched, together with Inspector Gregson and his men, the steamer carrying the Australian Sun docked. None of us saw any signs of the criminal trio we were hoping to apprehend.

The guards from the bank arrived with an armoured carriage to transport the rare jewel to the vault of Horace and Sons. Gregson spoke with the head of the guards and Holmes walked around the carriage, ensuring that it was secure. I began to wonder if the villains might be scared off by the presence of so many officers.

"Looks like you were wrong about this one, Mr. Holmes,"

Gregson told my friend in a flat voice. Unlike Lestrade, Gregson did not take every opportunity to gloat. He had in fact hoped to apprehend two of London's most dangerous criminals that night.

"Perhaps," Holmes responded, deep in thought. After a brief pause, I could see a gleam come into his eyes. "Inspector, I have an idea that will ensure that the diamond arrives safely at its destination."

"Go on."

"Let us have the bank carriage leave the dock, but instead of carrying the true diamond, it will carry a decoy along with us and an additional two of your men."

"And what of the actual diamond?"

"We shall leave it here, under guard by your best men. Surely nothing will happen to the gem with so many officers around."

Gregson agreed. Per Holmes's orders, the inspector called on one of his men to fetch a small box from the ship containing a much less valuable jewel than the Australian Sun. In the cargo were a number of gems worth only a few hundred pounds. While the jewel was being retrieved, Gregson beckoned over two of his best constables, Lockley and Stark, and Holmes related the plan to them.

A few minutes later, a sergeant handed the replacement jewel to Lockley, and the two constables entered the armoured carriage. Holmes and I followed, and soon we were travelling along the streets of London.

If the villains were watching, as Holmes surmised, then they would now believe that we were escorting the Australian

Sun to the vault of Horace and Sons. We were in the back for half an hour. The mood was tense as the officers and I clutched at our guns, waiting for the fiends to strike. Holmes remained calm, biding his time.

Constable Stark grumbled that he wished he had a touch of snuff, and Lockley used his sleeve over and over to wipe the sweat from his brow. Like mine, their minds must have wandered to the possibility of Holmes's plan going wrong. What if the villains overtook the carriage and forced us into a gang hideaway where their sheer numbers could overwhelm us? I shuddered at the thought of fighting a wave of ruffians, armed with sharp blades, furious at finding they had been tricked. But then the carriage stopped and we heard noises outside; no sound of violence, only regular chatter. A man in a thick Scottish accent said:

"We just need to make sure nothing's gone amiss."

A key turned in the lock and Holmes nodded towards us to be at the ready.

"Here you are, officer," said the guard as the back of the carriage swung open and moonlight streamed in.

"Now!" Holmes shouted, and we jumped out, surrounding two police officers and one of the guards. The guard, of course, was innocent. The two police officers, on the other hand, were none other than MacAlister, the Albino Butcher, and his grotesque henchman Fibbs, both in disguise.

"What is this?!" shouted Fibbs as the darbies closed around his wrists.

MacAlister made no attempt to conceal his true self. He threw a satchel at one of the officers, trying to break through their ranks. He might have succeeded, had I not been standing directly in his path, the barrel of my Webley aimed straight at his face.

The albino growled, but gave up the fight. "It was that fool Snerley who tipped you off, wasn't it?" MacAlister spat at Holmes. "I should have killed the traitor when I had the chance!"

Holmes did not respond. The two villains kept yelling threats as they were locked away in the back of the armoured vehicle.

We would have driven off right then and there, had not a loud moan come from an abandoned building next to the scene. A search of the premises revealed the two constables whom MacAlister and Fibbs had stripped of their uniforms, as well as Mr. Snerley himself. All three were bound and gagged. When freed, the constables explained that Snerley had stopped Fibbs from killing them. The banker had threatened to shout for help if the officers were harmed. He thus compelled the villains merely to tie up their victims. Then, however, MacAlister hit Snerley over the head from behind, knocking him unconscious. Fibbs tied him up as well and said that he planned to kill all three of them once they had obtained the diamond.

"I never wanted any of this," Snerley lamented to Holmes. "I only wanted to save my sister."

Snerley was the opposite of his henchmen, a rather handsome fellow with striking blue eyes, a soft face, square jaw and broad shoulders. I could tell that he was the kind of man whose character was solid, but who had taken a wrong turn. He explained that after losing his job, he had been unable to lay hold of the funds to pay off his debts. Desperate, he began looking towards the underworld. MacAlister had got wind of the banker's plight and approached him with an offer. If he helped in stealing the Australian Sun, he would receive one third of the money from the sale.

"I had knowledge of when the jewel was arriving, which I provided to MacAlister and Fibbs. I knew how dangerous those two were, but I told myself that they were sincere when they assured me that no one needed to get hurt."

The plan was to stop the armoured carriage as constables in disguise and claim that a police informant had relayed a rumour that the diamond might be stolen. MacAlister had a fake diamond in his satchel. His intention was to swap it for the real one. It would most likely have been days or even longer before the forgery was detected.

"I've ruined my life, I have," Snerley choked, trying his best to contain his tears. "But I'd do it all over again, to provide my sister with the opportunity to die in the comfort of her home. I had to give her that. After all, she was my sister."

*

The plight of Mr. Snerley moved not only me but also Sherlock Holmes. My friend used the power of the press to have Snerley's story told as though he were working as a police informant, a man who had risked his life and career to stop two of London's most notorious villains. The constables who were captured with Snerley spoke of his valour and how he had saved their lives. Within a few weeks, the banker became a hero of London. He served as a witness against MacAlister and Fibbs, and for his help the charges against him were dropped.

"After all, Watson," Holmes explained to me. "The man's motives were pure even if his means were illicit. In the end, little harm was done. He saved the lives of two constables and ensured that MacAlister and Fibbs will spend their lives behind bars."

I concurred with my friend. Due to all the coverage in the papers, Horace and Sons rehired Mr. Snerley. A hero brings in exceptional business, and they paid all his debts to free his mind of this burden.

Holmes, for his part, earned his payment from Mr. Armstrong and then had his time occupied by a case involving a high-level Member of Parliament.

As for me, the tale of Mr. Snerley led me to realise the importance of family. After much contemplation, I informed Holmes that I would be away on a lengthy sojourn to San Francisco. Holmes never enquired as to the reason for my leave. Perhaps he knew and was kind enough to remain silent.

I was fortunate to arrive in time and to spend the few weeks my brother had left in his company. It was during those precious weeks that I learned much about myself and what it behoves one to hold dear to one's heart. It was also the time during which I met the first true love of my life, though that is a tale for another day.

THE TRAGIC AFFAIR AT THE MILLENNIUM MANOR

DAVID MARCUM

The drapes were suddenly pulled back, letting in the weak morning light. I groaned and shut my eyes tighter, but it was too late, and I was not surprised to hear Sherlock Holmes say, "Five minutes, Watson! Downstairs. The lady seems insistent on sharing her story."

With my eyes shut, I heard him walking from the window to my bedroom door and closing it behind him without another word. His statement held no meaning, and I had no idea as to the identity of the lady in question.

We were in Keswick at the urgent request of one of Holmes's old school chums, Sir Kelvin Demery, in regard to a missing painting with deep historical significance to the area. Locating the item itself had been easy enough, but doing so had revealed a wider and more subtle conspiracy, seemingly against the knight, his younger wife, and their infant son. A final reckoning had occurred late the previous night during an aborted sacrifice of the child at the Castlerigg Stone Circle, revealing that the threat against the family came from within – specifically Demery's ne'er-do-well younger cousin.

Circumstances were such that afterwards we could not remain at the Demery estate in Watendlath, some five miles to the south of the Druidic ring of stones. It being far too late to return to London, we had instead settled into a nearby inn of rather dubious quality and a surly landlord (irate for being awakened at such a late hour) for the remainder of the night, until we could make our way to the Keswick railway station, and so on back to the capital.

Wondering if this morning hubbub was related in some way to the Demery affair, I made my ablutions and then descended the narrow staircase to the small inn's common dining room where Holmes was sitting in the shadows near the fireplace, his back to the wall, and facing a young woman. I could not see her face yet, but her dark clothing seemed to be of good quality, and heavy enough to protect her from the sharp autumn chill that permeated the room.

I glanced to the bar where our host stood, holding a mug of coffee. He nodded, seeming not quite so irascible this morning as when we had knocked him awake after midnight – just a few hours earlier, I sadly noted, stifling a yawn. He raised the mug with a questioning look, and I nodded gratefully before moving to join my friend and the unknown lady.

She heard my footsteps and stood, turning to reveal that she was just in her early twenties. Her complexion was dark, as was her hair, and even in the dim light of the room I could see that she was a rare beauty indeed. As I had thought, her clothing was moderately expensive – not gaudy, but well-made and serviceable. She presented confidence and poise, and yet her fingers were twisted anxiously around a crumpled handkerchief.

Holmes stood. "Miss Thirkell, this is Dr. Watson, my associate."

We greeted one another and seated ourselves, and at that moment, the landlord placed the much-appreciated hot coffee before me. Holmes and Miss Thirkell already had their own mugs. Holmes had made a good start on his, while the young lady's was untouched.

"Mr. Holmes," she said, "I learned that you were here from our cook, Mrs. Weaver – she's friends with the cook at the Demery house – and I knew that I had to ask for your help before you departed – or I think that I shall go mad!"

Her voice rose in tone, and I leaned forward to urge that she calm herself and take a sip from her cup. She nodded and did so, visibly relaxing while Holmes spoke.

"Before the Doctor joined us, you stated that you are being watched – 'terrorised' was the word you used. Has this been the case since your return to England, or did it begin in India?"

She looked up sharply, surprised at his simple deduction. However, even I could see that her naturally dark features were even more so because of long-time exposure to hot and dry weather and that her simple jewellery was clearly from northern India, where I myself had been not so many years before. I noted these facts for her, and she nodded.

"I only returned a short while ago, after leaving India in late summer, summoned home following the death of my uncle Raymond. It is an uncomfortable situation – he had named me as his sole heiress, in spite of the fact that he had two sons, one of whom is especially deserving. I... I'm not sure that I wish to claim this inheritance, but my presence was necessary to disentangle certain legal questions. Now... now I wish that I had never returned!"

"And someone is watching?"

"I'm – I fear that my fiancé, Philip – he is the younger of the two sons – is watching me."

Holmes raised an eyebrow. "That statement is rather unusual, and vague – not indicative of your level of distress. You fear your fiancé? Pray explain."

She nodded. "I'm telling it out of order. You see, I've only been back in England for less than a week, and I expected Philip to meet me when my ship docked. Instead, I learned that he'd angrily departed from our family home more than a month ago, following an argument with his elder brother, Sterling, and there has been no sign of him since.

"Soon after I arrived here, I felt the need to move out of the large house where I'd been staying, not far from here, and into a small cottage on the property. Since then, I've had the impression that I'm being watched. At first, I didn't know who it could be, although I suspected that it was Sterling, as he'd hinted since my return that he also harbours a romantic interest in me." She lowered her voice. "He was the reason I left the main house for the cottage."

Holmes raised a hand. "Your story indicates that you

were initially staying at your fiancé's family home with the two brothers, but you also called it 'our family home', and these brothers are your uncle's sons. Are we to make the connection, then, that these two brothers are your first cousins, and it is their father who left the fortune to you, rather than to either of his two sons?"

She nodded. "Yes, I'm sorry that I wasn't more clear about that."

"And you do not trust your elder cousin, Sterling – it is due to him that you moved to the cottage – but it is your missing fiancé, Philip, that you fear."

She nodded. "The cottage where I've been staying, on the grounds of the estate, is surrounded by a number of large trees. Sometimes, when approaching my window, I've seen movement among the nearby trunks by the drive leading to the road as someone seems to slip into hiding. Last night around dusk I went out to see if there were any signs of who it could be.

"I was no more than fifty feet from the cottage, but I felt as if something were wrong – a vague sense of alarm. And I felt a chill that had nothing to do with the cold. Then, alongside one of the trunks, I found this."

She reached into her bag and pulled out a bracelet. It was silver, with large links and a wide flat plate. She handed the bracelet to me first, as I was closer, and I saw that it was engraved with the initials *PT ST*. I read them aloud before handing it across to Holmes.

"Philip Thirkell, no doubt," Holmes clarified as he examined. "And the letters 'ST'?"

"My first name is Sheila. It was a gift from me to Philip before I left England. It expressed my feelings for him before we openly acknowledged them, and made our plans for marriage."

"And it was simply lying on the ground?"

She nodded. "Near the trunk of one of the larger trees, quite obvious. As I picked it up, my hand was shaking – had Philip dropped it inadvertently while watching me from this hiding place? Was he still nearby? Had it been him watching me all along, instead of his brother Sterling, as I'd first thought – and feared? If it is he, why has he not made any effort to communicate?"

As she spoke, Holmes continued to turn the bracelet this way and that, holding it to the light, examining the links with great attention, and even holding it to his nose. He raised an eyebrow slightly – one who did not know him probably would not have even noticed – and then handed the accessory back to Miss Thirkell.

"I called out, but there was no answer," she continued, replacing the bracelet in her bag. "Just the sound of the birds in the trees. I hurried back inside and locked the door. Later last night, when Mrs. Weaver came down to check on me as she has often done since I moved from the main house, I broke down and told her what I'd found, and how it had unnerved me. She sympathised, but could offer no explanation. She was certain that Philip had departed in anger more than a month ago, following an argument with Sterling – she'd seen him herself walking away from the house towards the station, carrying his bag. She said that if he was back, he would have notified me as soon as possible. She thought that perhaps Sterling had been watching me, although she couldn't explain the presence of Philip's bracelet, and she stated that this situation needed to be resolved – that it's unfair to me to be left in such a position of ignorance. That's when she remembered hearing from her friend that you were here, and that you might be able to offer some advice, based on your experience.

"After she left, I pondered her words, and later, as I read my Bible and said a prayer, I realised that she was right – I'd be best served by asking for your help."

She looked to Holmes with a hopeful countenance – an expression I had seen on many a face in the years that I had known him and been a witness to his investigations. By that point in our friendship, I knew that Holmes was able to accomplish what ordinary men could not.

Holmes took a sip of coffee, leaned back, and said, "I am intrigued, Miss Thirkell, but I think that a clearer picture of the situation would help before we move forward. Please go further back. How did you end up in India to begin with?"

She composed herself for a moment. "My family has lived around here – Watendlath – for a long time. Centuries in fact, and Thirkell Hall has been our ancestral home for several hundred years. Through the generations, the family fortunes waxed and waned, though over the past two generations mostly the former. My grandfather, Eustace Thirkell, went to sea in his youth and came back with a fortune. He then made a number of improvements to the original house while cannily keeping track of his investments, increasing his wealth many times over. He never revealed the source of his fortune, but I gathered that it wasn't earned honourably, which may have had something to do with his behaviour in later life, as he tried to atone for past sins in his own way. He turned his attentions towards religion in a most unique and fervent manner and even stepped away from the running of his businesses.

"He had only two children: Uncle Raymond and my father, Desmond, the younger brother. Upon reaching adulthood, Raymond followed his father into business, further increasing and consolidating the family wealth, while my father joined the Church – although not pursuing the same strict path that his father, Eustace, would later settle himself upon.

"My father married a young woman from his congregation and I was born in 1866 – twenty-one years ago next month. My mother died when I was small, and as I grew, Father and I moved around from parish to parish. We would, however, regularly return here to see my uncle Raymond and his two sons – my cousins Sterling and Philip. Grandfather and Grandmother had both died by then, passing away before I had any memories of them.

"As I explained, Sterling is the elder of Uncle Raymond's two children – around thirty now. Unfortunately, their mother died in childbirth when Philip was born. Philip is nearly my age and, being motherless like me and much younger than his brother, we were always particularly close, although we only saw one another every year or so when father and I would journey back here to visit Thirkell Hall House. However, Philip and I have always corresponded, even when Father decided that we were going out to India.

"As he grew older, Father's faith sustained him less and less, but rather than give in and abandon it, he only delved deeper into its pursuit. When he heard of the opportunity to carry out missionary work overseas, five years ago, it seemed to awaken a new spirit within him, and I was willing to go along. And it was the saving of him. Once there, he had the energy of a man twenty years his junior, and he was instrumental in setting up a hospital that served a number of poor villages. Then, early this year, he was suddenly struck down with a fever, and died within a week."

She paused, not to swallow any grief, which had apparently subsided long ago, but instead to have a sip of coffee.

"I remained there," she continued, "in India, to carry on with Father's work. I wouldn't have stayed my whole life, but it was a plan for the meantime, and I knew that what I did was important. Throughout, I maintained my correspondence with Philip, and over time – perhaps due to the safety provided us by distance and carefully crafted letters – we came to have an understanding that when I decided to return home, he and I would wed.

"In the late summer, I received a wire from England – most unusual, as the correspondence that typically arrived was by letter – explaining that Uncle Raymond had passed away unexpectedly from an apoplectic seizure, and that I must return home as soon as it could be arranged, since he had named me as his heiress. Other wires arrived, and my responses followed. I was surprised at Uncle Raymond's decision, but perhaps I shouldn't have been, as Uncle Raymond had become more unpredictable with age. He had also become more cantankerous, as Philip had intimated in his letters, particularly when expressing his disappointment in his two sons, leading to a widening estrangement – more on his part than theirs. In one of the wires from the lawyers, I learned that, after an argument with Sterling in which he felt that Philip didn't take his side to a sufficient degree, Uncle Raymond had the family lawyer remake his will in my favour – something, I surmise, he would have changed back soon if death hadn't taken him so quickly afterwards. Neither the property nor the fortune is entailed to the elder son, and so legally I find myself the sole possessor of more than I'd ever imagined – and of a burden of which I never wanted any part.

"I settled my affairs in India and turned over the running of the hospital to several locals who I hope will continue its success. After a long and tedious journey to the coast, and an equally monotonous return home by sea, I set foot on the dock in Portsmouth a little over a week ago in a cold autumn rain. It was a great shock, having been away for five years, to find such a different climate and way of life. I had sent a wire when I departed, telling of my scheduled arrival, and another when we briefly docked in Bilbao, so I was expecting to be met by someone – particularly Philip. However, there was no sign of him – or anyone – when the ship made port, and rather than leave for Watendlath on my own and miss him, I sent a message. The return wire from Sterling shocked me. That was when I first learned that a month earlier – around the time of my departure from India – he and Philip had fallen into a bitter quarrel, after which Philip was seen leaving the house the next morning and hadn't been heard from since.

"In haste, I returned to Thirkell Hall House on my own, finding it much diminished since I'd last seen it. Philip had given some indication that his father had become rather stingy as he aged, and I could see that in the past few years he'd barely done anything towards the upkeep. Sterling greeted me when I arrived, and even though I wished to discuss where Philip might be, he instead began an immediate and ongoing litany on both the unfairness of the new will and on what needed to be done towards the improvement of the estate, now that his father was out of the way.

"As those early days passed, I also noticed an uncomfortable fact: Sterling seemed to be paying attention to me in a rather bold way – more than he ought – as if he had conceived a romantic interest in my direction that was never before demonstrated. He began to press his attentions on me immediately during my very first evening back, after he'd had a bit too much to drink and when dinner had concluded, and I had to ask pointedly if he was aware of the understanding between his brother and me. He admitted that he was, but he stressed that clearly Philip had changed his mind, fleeing from the house before my arrival would force him to honour his promise.

"He then shared the details of their argument, which had begun with a discussion of the inheritance, and had progressed to the point where Philip revealed that he had regretted our arrangement almost from the beginning, and that the added weight of my inheritance made the match most unsuitable, as he wished to continue his preparation for the ministry, and such wealth on my part would be intolerable. Sterling had argued to him that I was on my way home, and that he would change his mind when we were together once more, but that had only made Philip more adamant and upset, and he had angrily vowed to find a new life before he would ever allow himself to be trapped in one with me.

"'After he left,' Sterling explained, 'I sent wires to his old school and his friends, but he hasn't returned to his classes, and no one has heard from him. I also informed the constable, who put some questions about at Keswick station to see if his direction could be determined, but nothing was learned. It seems that he simply didn't have the backbone or the stomach to wed you after all, my dear.' And then he stood, with something of a leering smile on his red face, as if he intended to join me where I occupied the sofa – perhaps to provide me with something that he conceived of as comfort. Since I found that idea quite distasteful, I arose and quickly excused myself.

"What he told me made no sense. Philip and I have always had the same sensibilities, and I'm quite in agreement with his view that the inheritance is an added weight that neither of us needs. Surely if he and I could talk, we could find a way forward. I simply cannot comprehend that he changed his mind about our engagement. His expressions of love and affection, which grew over time, were always most sincere and proper, as he is a quiet and thoughtful man. The idea that he could argue with his brother, and reach the level of anger described to me, suggests he might have been under some other strain of which we know nothing.

"Over the next day or so, I found Sterling watching me more and more, or looking for further excuses to attempt conversations *tête-à-tête*, ostensibly about the estate, but his underlying intentions were obvious. Finally, I had the idea of moving to the cottage beside the Millennium Manor, and to Sterling's surprise, I relocated there the next afternoon."

"The 'Millennium Manor'?" I asked.

She paused here and took another sip of the now cold coffee. "It is an old stone building on the property, built by Grandfather Eustace in his later years, related to his religious beliefs. There is a tidy little cottage – the Woods Cottage, as it's called – to one side, which is where I moved to escape Sterling's attentions. It's always been well maintained, in contrast to the Manor, although rarely used.

"It's much more suited to my needs than the large house, and I can take care of myself there – a fact that has confused the servants no end, as they don't quite know what to do with the fact that after I had the place stocked with provisions and my possessions moved over, I've proven quite self-sufficient. I let the lawyers know where to find me, and of more importance, I indicated to Sterling that he should keep to himself as well – without quite stating explicitly that his attentions are offensive.

"I've been there ever since, reading and enjoying my solitude, and worrying about Philip, and considering what the lawyers have told me during their almost daily visits. The wealth of the estate is much greater than I'd imagined, as Grandfather Eustace had originally left things in the hands of good managers, and Uncle Raymond and then Sterling proved quite capable in their own right. At times, I believe that I could happily walk away from it all, although I'd decided – while considering the situation during my long journey home – that I would remain involved after Philip and I were married, at least initially, until I understood the entire situation. And yet, with Philip's disappearance, I'm now completely at odds and ends as to what to do.

"As the days have passed, I've become more and more anxious, and except for the lawyers, my only visitor has been Mrs. Weaver, who comes down from the big house to check on me. I had always gravitated to her company when I was small during our visits – perhaps she has been like the mother I never had – and I still find her a comfort now. She can offer no explanation as to where Philip might have gone, or why. The staff were aware that he was angry that night – they could hear his voice through the closed doors during his argument with Sterling, and it seemed most unlike him. The engagement between Philip and myself wasn't common knowledge, but Philip had told Mrs. Weaver after swearing her to secrecy, and she believes that he was happy in the anticipation of us marrying. Now she's as worried as I am.

"Two days ago, I visited the constable, and he had nothing to tell me, having had no success in tracing Philip following Sterling's original request. And so I wait, with the feeling that there is something wrong. It has only grown worse in the last few days – and with the sensation that I'm being watched, and finding Philip's bracelet..." She leaned forward. "Can you help me, Mr. Holmes?"

I expected that he might ask more questions, but instead Holmes stood, surprising both the young lady and myself. "Do you have a carriage waiting outside?"

"I do. When I decided to come here, I walked up to the main house to tell Mrs. Weaver, and she roused the driver."

"There are aspects of this that make me uneasy," Holmes responded. "Watson, join me upstairs to retrieve our coats and hats."

*

A few moments later, I stepped into the upstairs hall, having donned my coat. Holmes met me in his Inverness and with his fore-and-aft cap in hand.

"I heard the same story as you," I said, "but nothing seemed terribly urgent."

"Ah," he replied, "but you didn't thoroughly examine the bracelet."

"I saw nothing unusual."

"Likely not. But you didn't take the opportunity to smell it."

With that, he led me back downstairs, where we joined Miss Thirkell outside and settled into the carriage for the drive, which she assured us was only a few miles.

There was a frost on the ground, and as the sun rose, its light muted by the overcast sky, I could see that we were passing along a narrow roadway, with hills sloping up steeply on either side. Everywhere I could see were rocks, broken and scattered aeons ago, untouched by man throughout that entire time. It was a bleak landscape, and I could only imagine how one might feel on returning to it after a sojourn of five years in the hot and colourful climes of India.

"I am intrigued," said Holmes, breaking the silence. "You mentioned a stone structure near the cottage where you are staying – the Millennium Manor, I believe you called it. What is the story behind such a place?"

"The tale is as strange as the name implies," replied Miss

Thirkell. "I've told you of how my uncle Raymond and my father became estranged from their own father, Eustace. This was due to his ever-increasing interest in religion – not in the way that my own father was interested, in terms of ministering, or Philip's interest in being a pastor. Rather, it was an apocalyptic belief in the end of the world, as described in the Book of Revelation. This had been developing within him for many years before I was born, and was very much the cause of the separation between him and his sons, who did not share his convictions.

"As his mind increasingly turned towards the end of the world, Grandfather Eustace began to believe that he was one of the Chosen, the 144,000 righteous souls described in the seventh chapter of Revelation – although he was not a member of the Tribes of Israel, as specified therein."

"'Do not harm the land or the sea or the trees until we put a seal on the foreheads of the servants of our God'," quoted Holmes. "'Then I heard the number of those who were sealed: 144,000 from all the tribes of Israel'."

The young lady nodded. "That's right. Assuming himself to be one of the Elect, Grandfather planned to live on earth with Jesus for one thousand years after the Lord's return, which he had calculated to be imminent. He and his wife, Enid, without any aid from servants or other labourers, began to construct a home in which to live out the millennium following Jesus's return.

"Over the course of eight years, both of them, then in their sixties, laboured together to create an Apocalypse-proof, thousand-year-strong fortress. I'm told that Grandfather often explained it by stating, 'I believe in preparing to live instead of preparing to die.'

"They rejected any building material that would rot or rust or burn, such as wood or metal, instead gathering the stones which lie in abundance here in Watendlath. They burrowed into a wooded hillside not too far from the main house and built, all of rock, a two-storey monstrosity with fourteen rooms. It's estimated that the two of them together hauled and placed hundreds of tons of stone, and then mortared it all together with over two hundred tons of cement. One can only imagine the curiosity they generated among the locals. Working alone, they built wooden forms for the walls and ceilings, and then stacked rocks over these forms using Roman arch-and-key methods. Theoretically, we were told once by a visiting medieval expert, the structure alone was self-supporting, but by pouring the cement over the top of it as they'd done, its solidity was increased by two or three hundred per cent, and it could in fact stand for one thousand years.

"Sadly, Enid died soon after the building was completed, and Eustace lamented that 'her faith just wasn't strong enough'. He, however, remained firmly committed to his belief that he would live on earth with Jesus for the next thousand years – and by his own interpretation, he was certain that such would begin any day. He died, however, just a few years after his wife. They're both buried near the manor in unmarked graves, as he wished. I must confess it adds to my agitation when I think that I might have inadvertently strolled across their final resting places.

"After their deaths, the stone house – which came to be

called 'Millennium Manor' – was abandoned. After all, it is nearly indestructible, unless someone intentionally attacks it with carefully placed explosives, or with picks and hammers. But while the place was being constructed, Eustace and Enid hired someone to build an attractive little wooden cottage beside the stone house, where they could live closer to their tasks, and because the ostentatious vastness of Thirkell Hall House had become distasteful to them. Since their deaths, the only visitors to the Manor, as far as I know, have been the servants, who sometimes look around while caring for the cottage, and Philip and I, when we played there as children."

As she finished speaking, we turned off the road, and after a hundred yards or so we stopped before a pair of most dissimilar buildings, set near a grove of trees. We stepped down beside the closer of the two, a charming wooden cottage, well maintained and constructed to resemble a sort of fairy-tale dwelling. It showed strong, exposed timbers, mullioned windows with complex metalwork, and a sturdy-looking thatched roof that might last a century. But as interesting as I found the cottage, my attention was inevitably drawn to what loomed behind it – the Millennium Manor.

As described, it was completely made of stone. Two storeys tall, it was rough looking, and the stonework showed no obvious skill or eye towards beauty. No stone was regularly shaped, and each was stacked in place solely with the thought as to where it would fit with its irregular neighbour. There was what seemed to be a main doorway centred in the ground floor, as well as several other doors and openings for a number of windows, all abandoned to the elements now and lacking any kind of jamb or frame. The upper floor had several curved arches, as if in the shape of a three-humped camel. The builders, the old man and woman of deep religious convictions, had indeed made use of ancient Roman methods. I could not imagine what force would be required to take this building apart.

It was a brooding place, and one could almost imagine the ghosts of the builders watching from within. I shivered, and my reaction was merely related to the coldness of the morning. The grim atmosphere was made complete by a number of ravens, some perched on top of the building, others sitting on the ground. Their raucous speech was the only sound except for the sigh of wind in the denuded branches of the nearby trees.

The house seemed to hold a dark and immediate fascination, and I made a move to step that way, wishing to see the place more closely, but Holmes held up a hand. "In a moment, Watson," he said. "Miss Thirkell, can you point me towards the tree where you found the bracelet?"

She nodded and indicated a tall tree at the perimeter of the nearby grove. Though clearly a type of oak, the tree looked somewhat unusual to my layman's eyes, and it oddly retained its dead and darkened leaves, even this late in the season.

"Thank you. If you will wait inside with Dr. Watson, I shall make a quick examination."

With that, he turned away, heading not directly to the tree, but rather into the old stone house, passing through the ground-floor doorway and into darkness. I went inside the cottage with Miss Thirkell, who offered to make tea, but I declined, as Holmes might need us to join him at any moment. Instead, we sat in the cold, the fire in the stove having long gone out, and discussed common memories of India. At times, I could see Holmes moving back and forth across the narrow field of vision provided by the window. He went to the oak and the other trees around it, looking here and there at the ground, sometimes getting down upon hands and knees. He spent some time peering up into the tree, and then walked over to the carriage driver, with whom he had a short conversation. I saw the fellow nod, climb down, and walk towards the cottage. However, he did not come to the front door, but instead went around one side, returning a moment later with a ladder that must have been kept there for when it was needed during routine maintenance. Meanwhile, Holmes approached the cottage and then knocked on the door. I opened it, and he gestured for me to join him outside.

"Watson," he directed softly as I pulled the door shut behind me, "I need you to take Miss Thirkell to the main house and leave her in the care of the cook. Then, find out from her which servants can be trusted, and have them ensure that Sterling Thirkell makes no effort to depart. Have the cook summon the constable to join us here. Then return with Coggins, the driver, as soon as you can."

"What is this, Holmes?"

"Deviltry." He turned away, back towards the tree. "Oh," he said over his shoulder. "When you return, bring a long rope."

I made my way back into the cottage, summoned Miss Thirkell, and explained that we needed to go on to the main house. Thus, we were soon back on the road, travelling at a brisk pace north. She questioned me, but I could offer no explanations, and refrained from describing Holmes's instructions.

She then turned to the driver, asking, "Coggins, what did Mr. Holmes do?"

The driver, however, simply shook his head – which rather surprised me, as he was accustomed to take orders from her. He had seemingly received instructions as well.

We drove to the rear of the main house. As we stepped down to enter via what turned out to be the kitchen door, I beckoned to Coggins and asked him to find a long rope. He nodded and I followed the young lady inside, where I requested that she let me speak with Mrs. Weaver. I could tell that by then Miss Thirkell was becoming quite impatient at being kept in the dark. When the cook arrived, she being a woman of trustworthy mien in her late sixties, I quietly and to one side explained who I was and what Holmes had asked. She seemed to understand that something grim was in the offing and led Miss Thirkell deeper into the house. I returned outside to find Coggins, along with three other steady-looking fellows. The driver showed me a long rope he had found. Then, together we returned to the cottage.

*

I shall never forget that grim and terrible task. Holmes explained what he had found during his search of the grounds, and we were soon spread around the large oak where Miss Thirkell had discovered the bracelet. Holmes placed the ladder against the trunk and called me over to point out a pair of deep marks in the soil.

"Note, Watson, that those were already present. Someone

has placed a ladder here before. The leaves on the tree protected the marks from the weather."

With that, he climbed the ladder to a point within easy reach of the lowest limb. From there he stepped into the tree, working himself higher, climbing steadily. I looked up to see his goal, now somewhat visible in the morning light. I could scarce believe my eyes.

While we stood there, the constable arrived, and Coggins whispered to him while pointing up into the tree.

Holmes had carried the rope with him, and by then he had secured it to the object hanging high above us before cutting the other rope that fastened the object to a strong branch. He thereupon proceeded to lower the body of Philip Thirkell slowly to the ground.

Coggins identified what was left of him and turned away. The poor fellow was greatly decomposed, and the ravens had been at him.

"He's clearly been here a while," Holmes explained, "likely since just after the argument between the two brothers, and just before his supposed 'departure' for parts unknown. Does the older brother, Sterling, have a limp?"

"He does," confirmed the constable.

"His footprints are all over the place," responded Holmes. "In the dust on the floors of the stone house, and in the soil under these trees. This is *Quercus palustris* – the pin, or swamp oak, native to North America, but transplanted to England in the early years of this century. They hold their leaves through the winter, shedding them only gradually instead of all at once. After Philip Thirkell died – and we do not yet know the reason – his brother Sterling chose to hide the body, rather than make his brother's death known. Sterling brought the body here, thinking this to be the most out-of-the-way place for quick disposal. He couldn't dig a grave – the ground is too rocky, and he might have been seen, or the excavation noticed. Here, he could hang the body where it would remain undiscovered for quite a while. The leaves would conceal it, even after the season changed, giving him time to think of a better place. He likely believed that no one would come here – not realising that harassing his cousin would drive her to move to the cottage almost immediately."

"But how did you know where to look?" I asked.

"I mentioned to you that the bracelet she found below this tree had an odour. I know it well – that of a rotting corpse. If you had smelled the bracelet, you would have recognised it yourself. When the body was hung, the weather was warm – it has only just now turned cold – and decomposition proceeded rapidly. Over the last month, the wasting of the hand and wrist progressed to the point where the bracelet slipped off and fell – probably in the last day or so. Thus, I already suspected that the body was hidden in the tree. When we arrived here, and I saw the limping footprints, I was certain. The footprints were quite obvious, both from when Sterling Thirkell hung the body, using this same ladder which is kept beside the cottage, and from when he lurked around here during the past week, both in the stone house and underneath the trees, spying on his comely cousin."

Our return to the house was a terrible affair. Miss Thirkell broke into uncontrollable sobs upon hearing of her fiancé's death, and before we could stop her she ran to the wagon which held his body, throwing back the tarpaulin and seeing the terrible wreckage of her longtime companion and love.

Sterling Thirkell was still asleep upstairs, hung over from his drinking the night before. He was a lanky man, old before his time and clearly dissipated. When he understood that the truth was known, he collapsed, repeating over and over again that it had been an accident. He and his brother had argued over Miss Thirkell's return. Sterling had wanted to bully her into relinquishing the inheritance, or if not that, then he had insisted that he be the one to marry her, as he was the elder brother, and the one with the strongest claim to becoming the owner of their late father's estate. Words led to blows, Philip had fallen, and his head had split on a fireplace andiron. In a panic, Sterling had wrapped up the body, hidden it first behind a sofa, and then transported it to the trees by the Millennium Manor in the dead of night. After hanging his brother's body out of sight, he had returned to the main house. Early the next morning, he walked away in Philip's hat and coat, carrying his brother's bag, making painfully sure to move without his customary limp and to be seen by Mrs. Weaver and the others in the kitchen. He had spread the story of their argument and Philip's angry departure. No one had believed that the man they had seen leave could be the older brother, as he never rose that early.

Sterling Thirkell was arrested, but the magistrate believed his story of an accidental death, and in spite of his heinous actions the case never even came to trial. Even in our modern times, justice is an elusive good in our country, particularly in rural districts, whenever the wealthy and well-connected are concerned. Against all advice, his cousin relinquished her inheritance and returned to India.

*

I happened to be in Watendlath again several years later, this time without Holmes and on my own business, and I decided to stay at the same inn. Finding the host much more genial when not bothered after midnight, I spent some time talking with him. It was he who told me that Sterling Thirkell still lived in the big house and that his business was still vastly successful, no thanks to its proprietor. The man was slowly drinking himself to death.

I did not mention to my new friend that I had stopped by the Millennium Manor the previous evening, intending to explore it further, having missed the chance some years earlier. The cottage beside it was empty and dark, and the wind was up, sighing through the trees, one of which was the swamp oak in whose crown of foliage Holmes had found the unfortunate Philip Thirkell's body. As I approached the building, the ravens' cries became louder, and some landed nearby as if they meant to defend it. The place may have been built to await the Saviour, but there was something sinister about it, and after many long minutes considering whether to press forward and enter that darkness, I turned away.

I learned one additional fact of interest from the innkeeper: Miss Thirkell had insisted that her fiancé, though dead, had still found a way to warn her of the dangers posed by his elder brother by dropping his bracelet where she would find it below the tree. Throughout her remaining time in the village of Watendlath, he told me, she had grasped this bracelet as though it were a talisman, twisting it around her white fingers and never once letting go of it.

I only knew her for a couple of hours and have no idea where she ended up in the world, but I shall never forget that look of wrenching despair when she realised that her love was gone. I feel as if there was some sort of lesson in her anguished features, but all these years later I have yet to find words adequate to express what I should have learned at the Millennium Manor.

AN ENCOUNTER
WITH DARKNESS

AMY THOMAS

One evening in the spring of 1890, I requested my brother Sherlock's presence at the Diogenes Club, so as to entertain a friend alongside me. I did not mention the friend's name, but I knew Sherlock trusted my reasons – "I suppose you know what you are doing, Mycroft," he had said. As expected, my brother turned up punctually, as did our guest, the well-dressed man of heroic exploits, victor in many a skirmish in the farther-flung corners of the Empire, Colonel Sebastian Moran.

As I had counted upon, my brother did not betray surprise or dismay. He simply accepted the introduction and sat down to drinks. Moran and I spoke of nothing consequential, exactly as he and I had agreed upon. After half an hour of chitchat, the Colonel took his leave of both of us, turning to march off, all military stiffness in his bearing. The moment was a tricky one; behind Moran's back, I indicated to my brother to leave as well, which he readily did – before returning a quarter of an hour later.

"Whatever do you mean by this?" Sherlock's eyes flashed with rare passion. Back in our school days there had been many a row between us, but our adult lives were marked by few such incidents.

"Mean by it? My dear brother, you have joined me at my club and helped me to entertain a friend. Whatever meaning need there be beyond that?"

"You do not entertain, and you do not have friends."

I could not help smiling. "Clearly, you know the man."

"The height of London villainy!"

"Highest but one."

"Oh, stop it, Mycroft! Why were you entertaining Colonel Moran, and why did you require my company to do so?"

"Quite simply, his master, the renowned Professor Moriarty, wished to test my loyalty to him, and you were the assurance. I was to invite you, without warning, in order for Moran to ascertain whether my lips are as tightly shut as I claim them to be. Simply, I was to prove that you know nothing of my involvement with Moriarty's outfit, which I considered would be aided by you actually knowing, well, nothing."

"What if I had betrayed my surprise? You could have provided a hint, at least." My brother continued to glare at me across the Stranger's Room table.

"They no doubt intercepted the note I sent you to make sure there was no hint. Besides, you need not be modest about your acting abilities. I was sure you would instantly comprehend the assignment and carry it out with aplomb."

My brother leaned across the table, eyes still on fire. "They're clever, brother, cleverer than any of the ones before them. You do not consider that others may possess faculties equal to your own, or mine. Your determination to infiltrate them yourself, while courageous, is imprudent. What is to stop Moriarty from assuming that my ignorance was an act?"

"I'm glad you at least retain some faith in our collective mental energies," I said, before continuing: "You are giving Moriarty and his men too much credit. You convinced Moran you do not know of him beyond his public reputation, and he will tell Moriarty so. Additionally, my trustworthiness will soon be proven in an even greater way."

"Are you absolutely sure they trust you? That this isn't some elaborate game to dangle you like a worm on the end of a hook?" My brother clenched his fists atop the tabletop, and he spoke too quickly, even by his standards.

I gave him a long look, forcing a silence because I knew he would thus regain his composure. "You of all people know the burden I bear and the secrets I carry. I put you in a difficult position just now, but please have some faith in my decisions. I thought you would be pleased to find that, for once, I am doing my own field work, if you will."

"I do not doubt your abilities," he finally acquiesced, calming visibly. "But what is to be done now?"

"Now," I said, "is the time to tighten the noose. This test passed, I have promised Moran some classified documents, to be delivered to him personally."

"You wish to use this transaction to apprehend the lot?"

"No, I wish to lure them into an artificial calm through one successful transaction. To do so, I need to give them something that will be deemed valuable, while discommoding no one, creating no inconvenience for the government, and without harming the country. What I give them cannot be inconsequential, for they know my position – or, at least, enough of what it is to have heightened expectations."

"And you do not want to attempt to capture them the first time, as you expect them to suspect a trap and prepare accordingly?"

"That is one factor, my dear brother. Beyond that, my hope is that the first transaction will lead to a second and eventually a third one, and that the whole gang, including the man himself, will eventually be encouraged to step boldly forward towards their own demise."

"I gather from the level of trust you have already attained that you have placed yourself in a position of considerable risk for some time now. You might have told me – allowed me to shoulder some of the burden."

"It is to your credit," I said, meeting his gaze, "that you don't object to being placed at risk by association."

"There is no one else who can go after them except you and I. I was never in a position to infiltrate their gang. Moriarty knows too much of me; no one knows anything of you, not personally, anyway."

"And therefore you must help me, because we must finish it and end their villainy once and for all."

My brother smiled. "It's been quite some time since I have seen you righteously passionate about something."

"There has never been anything of this kind before."

"True indeed. Of course, I shall help, with pleasure."

"Excellent. Then come around to my rooms tonight, and we shall discuss the matter further. I understand Dr. Watson to be much preoccupied with his domestic life, but in any case, I'm afraid I must ask that he not be present."

My brother breathed out sharply. "Yes, he is rarely at my disposal now, and I do not expect to see him for another week hence."

I am not inhuman; I felt for my brother, who was comforted and aided by the good Doctor's presence, but under the current circumstances, I was relieved by Watson's absence. It simplified matters.

"Very well," I said. "This evening, we shall plan, and I shall explain further why Moriarty chose you, my brother, as his test of my loyalty."

I did not answer Sherlock's question about why I had decided to undertake the task without him for as long as possible. I could have lied and said that it was because of my position or my knowledge of certain affairs, or for some other reason born of circumstance. The real reason, of course, was that I feared for his safety.

*

I had not received my brother at my rooms in Pall Mall for some time, before I welcomed him that evening to discuss the plans I was to hand over to Moran. Sherlock cared little for his outward surroundings, whereas I preferred a curated life of beauty and elegant comfort. I suppose many would have been surprised to see how sumptuously decorated and well-appointed my rooms were, but that would have betrayed how little they knew me. I am not a man who denies himself the amenities of life.

My brother arrived after dinner, and I provided a decanter of Spanish wine and a few of my favourite delicacies, which I knew he was unlikely to touch. For my sibling, problems of the intellect were delicacies enough; his palate was purely cerebral.

"Thank you for coming," I said, as my man, Carlton, helped Sherlock out of his coat.

He nodded. "Have you the plans?"

I handed him the packet, amused but unsurprised by his abandonment of social graces in favour of the objective.

"They're real," said my brother, incredulous, staring at the plans for a new, high-powered weapon.

"I told you they must be real."

He looked at me for a long moment. "If you give them this document, what is to stop them from having the weapon manufactured or from selling the plans to someone who will? The French, say, might be interested. From what I read, they are having some trouble with their little war in West Africa…"

"These plans only show half of the process. They are real, but incomplete. The next set will complete the instructions – but they will be incorrect."

He nodded thoughtfully. "Now, explain how this has come about."

"Sit down."

My brother took his place in the brown chair he always occupied in my rooms.

"Three years ago," I said, leaning back in my office chair,

"I was informed that one of our men, who worked as a stockbroker's clerk, had reported in after a long silence. We had placed him in his position because we suspected his employers of involvement with our nation's enemies. Our man was extremely capable and had worked his way into being considered indispensable. Nothing appeared out of order for over a year, until the day when the owner of the firm had a meeting with a certain Mr. Smith. Our man was present because he had become knowledgeable as regards some South American investments. There was the usual financial talk, but as our man sat by, mostly quiet, something else emerged. Smith, it appeared, was a subordinate for the leader of a criminal organisation. Our man did not get a name, but after the meeting he made it clear to his employer, who was by then quite trusting, that he would be pleased to partake in whatever this business might be.

"To omit tedious details, though they prove what an efficient operative our man was, he had himself integrated into the scheme in question and finally began working hand in glove with Moran himself. It was my office that had already deduced, as you did, the connection between Moriarty and Moran, so we understood immediately what the ramifications were.

"Most unconventionally, I instructed our man to give up the truth of his connection to the British government – with the promise of delivering me up to Moran as one who wished to join their operation. I had little doubt that Moriarty was aware of me; he could hardly be credited with his level of ingenuity in this city if he were not.

"Moran proved quite susceptible to flattery. He would have accepted me quickly, believing that since my man had not turned them in, I must be trustworthy and my avarice must be as great as his own. In that, he is not wrong; he simply fails to understand that some men may be as avaricious for power within the bounds of the law as he is for power and money outside of them.

"Moriarty, I have no doubt, is the one who devised the following tests of my loyalty, though he has not come himself to witness any of them. He trusts Moran enough to oversee that aspect of things. I've had no trouble playing their little games until these final two, which were the duping of my own brother and the delivery of a truly classified document."

"What is to stop him from thinking you are sitting here now, telling me all this?"

"Moriarty will know the plans are real," I answered triumphantly. "Once I hand them over, with you by my side feigning to believe the business to be above board, he will be convinced that I am entirely compromised. As he believes in your integrity, I am now trustworthy by way of being, in his eyes, unable to be honest with you, even if I wished to. The next exchange will reinforce this impression further still. He will believe that I have lied to you in order to escape admitting the damning truth of my criminal involvement, for if Sherlock Holmes knew his brother was passing secret plans to a gang of criminals, no doubt he would try to put a stop to it. Quite simply, Moriarty knows that you are well aware of him and of his villainy, but he believes you, and most of the world, to be as yet unaware of Moran's.

"Moriarty's belief in your integrity, which is, of course, quite warranted, leads him to think that I am now in an impossible position. On the other hand, if I had been playing a long game all this time, I would no doubt have alerted you and aborted the operation before handing over a set of genuine and highly classified plans."

"You think Moran himself is entirely without suspicion of all that I actually know?"

"Yes, but it hardly matters; his every opinion is filtered through Moriarty's suspicions, which are enough for both of them. Moriarty persists in believing that no one, including you and I, is smarter than himself. That will prove his downfall, I should think, though he shows greater caution and meticulousness of thought than his subordinate."

"Moran is more than a crack shot," my brother observed. "He has a keen mind, of a more practical bent than his master's. I understand Moriarty's trust in him."

"Moriarty sees the web, Moran only one or two filaments, but those in perfect detail. Fine prospects for the sort of work I do, if they both hadn't chosen to use their talents in such disappointing ways."

"Not from their point of view. In your world, they would be subordinates, cogs in the machinery of the Empire. In their world, Moriarty is king, and Moran has but one master."

I shrugged. This might have been an engaging topic, but whatever darkness in Moran's heart had impelled him to throw in his lot with the master criminal at that precise moment held but little interest for me. For my brother, though, understanding the criminal mind was a near obsession, irrespective of whether such understanding was immediately useful or not.

Moran, I was quite sure, thought me an outright simpleton compared to himself and his master. I fancied his hubris far exceeded that of Moriarty, and this made him vulnerable. The Professor, however, was far too clever to think I had attained my present position while being a simpleton. Besides, he had seen my brother's intelligence at first hand, as he had foiled many of the Professor's schemes. All I could do was aid the Colonel in becoming as persuasive as possible in his arguments.

*

"I'm going out," I said, late in the evening three days after my brother's visit.

Carlton was too well-bred to express surprise with more than a subtle lifting of the eyebrows. I did not blame him. At times, I would go for weeks without venturing out anywhere except to my office. I particularly disliked evening amusements, with their crowds and uncomfortable rooms.

"My brother and I attend Colonel Moran at his club tonight."

Carlton nodded, almost imperceptibly, and I knew he understood. He was not only my valet; he was my most trusted associate. His position in my home was a secret assignment of sorts. It enabled me to apprise him of whatever was needed and to enlist his services easily, without prying eyes. His mind was prodigious, and he was constantly amused at the pretext of being a gentleman's gentleman, though he performed the role with conscientious attention to detail.

"I wish you success," he said, helping me into my coat and then opening the front door for me.

I have been called unsociable, and I was reminded as to why when half an hour later my brother and I approached the sanctum of Moran's club. It was refined enough, on the outside, but as we entered I heard raucous laughter and loud voices.

"Loathsome," I murmured.

"Unpleasant, perhaps," my brother answered, "but it is where humanity is found and elucidated, not in your temple of the tight-lipped."

I recalled that Sherlock had been known to conduct reconnaissance in opium dens, and I did not argue. His business was what it was.

"Gentlemen!" The place had many servants, young and sleek, of course. One approached us with a false smile.

"We're here to see Colonel Moran," I said.

The man nodded. "Right this way; you're expected."

He showed us to a quieter room with a fireplace and comfortable chairs. Even I could not find fault with the place, especially with my brother and myself as its only occupants. Moran made us wait a fair amount of time, obviously with intent. As irritating as this was on principle, Sherlock and I both knew without the need for words that if the Colonel thought he had bested us, bent us to his will, so much the better.

Finally, Moran entered, puffed up with his usual arrogance, his moustache seeming to bristle with self-importance. "You have the plans?" he asked after the curtest of greetings. The Colonel had with him a small fellow, older and bespectacled. "I have brought Mr. Burns here to assess them." He looked pointedly at me. "We wouldn't want to pass on anything incorrect, would we?"

"Of course not," I said smoothly, "though I take umbrage at the implication, Colonel. I should have supposed by now that you and your associates have reason enough to trust my information."

Moran did not answer. He merely took the packet from my hands and gave it to Burns, who grabbed it with bony fingers and began to read eagerly, rather like a glutton going after a slab of choice beef.

"Just as you have your insurance," I said, "I have my brother here to make sure I do not constantly need to glance over my shoulder."

Moran gave me a look of distaste, but he could hardly argue at my methods, with his own expert in the midst of inspecting the merchandise.

Burns handed the packet back within a few minutes. "Genuine."

Moran performed his own cursory investigation, more for show than because he knew what he was looking for. My brother remained silently watchful, letting the Colonel believe whatever he chose about what I had told him.

After a while, Moran tapped approvingly on the sheaf of papers and handed me the promised compensation. It was a ridiculously large amount, but I had known that I could not ask for less and remain credible. "The first instalment. Our shared leader will allow me to give you the rest upon the next delivery." He did not say Moriarty's name, and my brother sat by acting none the wiser.

"Thank you."

This was a game of patience, and it would not do to be

rattled by Moran's patronising manner.

"You have been surprisingly helpful, Mr. Holmes," said the self-satisfied man. This was a good sign, a sign he believed me to be susceptible to blandishments.

For the first time in many years – decades, in fact – an impulse to throttle a man arose in me. If he or any other of Moriarty's creatures ever laid a hand on my brother, I would tear them limb from limb. The idea that Sherlock might be caught in the crosshairs of this vile game was nearly enough to cause me to break from the character I had set myself to play.

Thankfully, I have not held government secrets for this many years without learning to wear an aura of detachment like a suit of armour. "I assure you," I said, "that we are both mutually pleased by our arrangement."

He shook my hand, and I resisted the temptation to break his arm.

"Our leader values your insights greatly, Mr. Holmes."

"He's welcome to attend and hear them himself," I said coolly. "It is not my habit to work for a man whom I have never met." This was a bald-faced lie, but I hoped it might make an impression on Moran, who I thought would understand such a sentiment.

"I will convey your thoughts, though he's not a man to be threatened or cajoled."

"Nor am I," I answered, "and you may tell him so."

I was taking a firmer stance. Being overly amenable might awaken suspicion. On the other hand, if I pushed too hard, I might well find myself out of the association.

Moran turned to my brother. "It's been a pleasure making your acquaintance."

"Likewise," came the answer, assured and impassive, with a blank nod, as though my brother understood nothing of what had just occurred. Including him, once again, had served as assurance that I was to be trusted.

*

"Burns is a fraud," said Sherlock, as we walked out of the club and into the mild evening air.

"Really?" I asked, genuinely surprised.

"Don't worry. You missed no signs. He's devilishly clever, is Oliver."

"You know him?"

"I do. He would be incapable of identifying a forgery if it came with a label attached." My brother shook his head. "Burns had better hope he is not discovered. Deceiving Moriarty can be unhealthy."

Sherlock and I had examined a few cases together, but doing so was generally a pleasant undertaking. I found his company stimulating, as if my mind could expand, no longer pressed into service by the bureaucratic chicanery of Whitehall.

"You are a better man than you let on," said my brother now.

"As are you. Dr. Watson has had a beneficial influence."

He smiled. "I fear I may soon have nothing left to offer him but danger and absence," he said, alluding to our darkest conversations about Moriarty and the lengths to which we might be pushed.

"Watson is not the sort of man to be undone by any course of events."

"You're right. But I shall miss him, if it comes to that."

I did not remark on the humanity of this utterance, though I felt it. The brother I knew in the past would not have admitted to so much sentiment. He had changed – not in the cataclysmic manner of a hero in a cheap romance, but in the natural, incremental way by which human beings change in the presence of another person, like a stone being sculpted until a form is revealed.

I could not help thinking how empty the city might feel without the spare figure of my brother within her borders. We did not see each other or communicate often unless a case demanded it, but nevertheless we had an understanding of shared presence. I felt more grief than expected at the thought of enduring London without that understanding to punctuate my days. That this absence might be permanent, I did not allow myself to contemplate. This was not the first time my employment had placed my brother in harm's way, but the situation did not feel any better for being familiar.

"You are worried, Mycroft. And angry. You have the exact look you had on that day in our boyhood when you gave Harold Wilcox a broken nose."

"Yes. I'm most concerned about the state of England."

My brother half-smiled and laid a hand on my arm. "Rest assured. England is a well-armed old lady."

I put my hand over his for a moment. My brother's departure might prove inevitable if even the smallest detail of our plans failed. Not for cowardice did I rule out doing myself what needed to be done. My position did not allow me the freedom he had. I did not like this situation, any more than I had liked finding him knocked from his feet when he had been a little boy by that oaf Wilcox. I intended to do to Moran and the others what I had done to Wilcox, only this time they would suffer more than a broken nose.

*

Two nights later, to Carlton's astonishment, I entertained again, my brother and also Dr. Watson this time, who had agreed to take an evening away from his charming wife. The Doctor had, for lack of a more accurate term, a soothing presence. I had ceased to question his involvement in my brother's affairs soon after meeting him. He was not without his own abilities, but, most relevant to my concerns, he seemed to facilitate my brother's. Sherlock was calmer around him, less likely to resort to his seven per cent solution or any of the other unhealthy habits he had cultivated to relieve boredom and mental strain.

"Good evening," I said, as the Doctor was shown in, and received a friendly greeting in return. Watson looked happy, and that was all for the best. If things went as my brother and I had begun to fear they might, the Doctor would need his reserves of good cheer.

I handed him a brandy, which he took with equanimity. "Thank you for the invitation. I have dined in few places without Mrs. Watson since my marriage, and while I consider her presence to be a reward, a fellow likes to have a night out once in a while. In fact, this place feels a bit like our old lodgings in Baker Street."

My brother arrived a few minutes later, and we sat down to some marvellous steak frites crafted by my personal chef.

The man cost a great deal to employ and was worth every penny. In time, however, business was at hand. I had invited Watson on purpose, to allay any suspicion by Moriarty's subordinates who were always watching my address. They would not assume it possible that I might engage in sensitive business with the Doctor present.

I am well aware that some people believe all heroes of war are, by nature, impressive people. Had a person only made the acquaintance of one Dr. John Watson, he might be forgiven this misconception; however, this belief ignores the existence of a vast group of others who, instead of performing what one might consider necessary evils in the service of the greater good, actually enjoy the evils as the object and do not give a fig about the greater good. Sebastian Moran was one of these. He delighted in his skills and in their use, wherever he might employ them. The Bible commands us not to judge, and generally I abide by this dictate. I am myself, after all, far beyond reproach. However, when a man's pleasures encroach on the safety of England, they do become my business, and I do judge.

My brother had been aware of Moriarty long before I became aware of Moran. That the Professor had chosen one so different from himself as his subordinate was unsurprising. Moriarty was clever enough to understand the advantages of having a more visible proxy with strengths different from his own, just as my brother found his own work more effective when combined with Dr. Watson's presence as a sounding board.

"You have the second package?" Sherlock asked, pipe in hand.

"I do. And I should like both you and Dr. Watson to ascertain whether its contents appear genuine."

Both men looked at the second half of the plans for the weapon.

"I am no expert," said Watson, "but they appear genuine enough to me."

My brother nodded in agreement.

"Thank you," I rejoined, taking back the packet. The good Doctor did not pry into the business any further.

"Your man," said my brother, puffing away, "he is more than a valet, isn't he?"

"What leads you to that conclusion?"

"He has the calluses of a frequent writer, but I know your habit of always conducting your own correspondence. Merely taking care of his own would not lead to such a feature, unless he had an unusually high volume of writing. He also dropped a folded paper from his pocket, which, when I picked it up, appeared to be a page of an official dispatch. You would hardly grant a simple valet access to it."

"Quite right," I said. "Let us drink to Carlton's health, my right-hand man."

I had every intention of telling Carlton about this exchange later on, knowing that he would find it humorous. He took his meals with me when we were alone, but never when people were about, so as not to undermine the appearance of the conventional servant. I drank to Carlton, but in my mind I drank to my brother's future health.

*

Four days hence was the appointed date of the second transaction, which was to take place in my office late in the evening. I had suggested this location, and the apparent brazenness appealed to Moran. The guards at the gate of Pall Mall were informed to let anyone pass who wished to see me.

My brother appeared an hour ahead of time, and I saw no reason to conceal what I knew.

"Burns is dead," I said. "Your misgivings were correct. He was discovered by his landlady this morning. The cause appears to be a stroke, but you may surmise otherwise."

"He double-crossed the wrong man. He ought to have known better." I could tell by the brittleness of Sherlock's voice that the news affected him.

"It's not as if his judgment of the plans was incorrect," I said.

"No. Moriarty must have caught wind of the man's deception some other way; Burns is not unknown in criminal circles. He was a fool not to recognise the danger."

We lapsed into silence until voices could be heard outside. As soon as the men entered, I saw an almost imperceptible change in my brother's expression. It alarmed me, so I studied the three narrowly: Moran, a thin young man the Colonel introduced as Bryant, and the third man, elderly with a few wisps of grey on his head, to whom Moran gestured, saying, "Butler."

I did not perceive a problem, but I trusted Sherlock's keen eyes. "Please, gentlemen, sit," I said, pouring drinks, while my brother stood silently by. I knew that I must end the operation, and likely my whole involvement in the affair. Someone else might wonder why a slight shake of my brother's head would suffice to effect such a course of action, but in that case they must not know Sherlock Holmes or the bond between us.

"I am afraid, Colonel Moran, that I shall be unable to supply the package," I said firmly. "After our last exchange, my superiors have been watching me like hawks. I did not cancel today's meeting for fear that they would suspect something, since they are no doubt monitoring my appointments."

"Superiors?" Moran's eyes flashed anger. "I thought you had none."

"Everyone has superiors, as your leader well knows. Please convey to him my strongest regrets that I shall be unable to assist him beyond the first exchange."

Moran rose abruptly. "You had best hope you don't hear from him," he said, losing some of his gentlemanly veneer, and then nodded to his two associates.

"He will not take me on, directly or indirectly," I said, "and if he does, he will not like the results."

As the three men passed from the room, I realised the implications of what I had just done. By removing myself I had failed in my attempt to keep Sherlock out of the whole affair – not that he had ever wanted to be out of it.

The door slammed shut behind the three men.

"Why did I do that?" I asked my silent brother, once the visitors were well out of earshot.

"Do you not know?"

"Do enlighten me, please, and help me to feel that my implicit trust in you was justified, for at present I feel that I've practically given up the British Empire."

"Did you see the shoes of the elderly man, Butler?" My brother's voice was even, but I could not fail to notice a faint air of self-satisfaction.

"Boots. Nothing out of the common way."

"Perhaps not for one of your means, but certainly out of

character for a man who otherwise gave the appearance of abject degradation. They are the boots of someone with an income."

"Perhaps a gift for his services."

"Perhaps," said Sherlock, "but once I noticed them, I began to notice other incongruent details."

"Out with it," I said, unable to hide my annoyance.

"It was exceedingly faint, but on the side of his face there were flakes of colour. Peeling make-up. From there, I noticed his stature, which he was attempting to alter by stooping, and I detected other signs of falsity in his appearance. He is thinner, taller and paler than he wished to seem."

"Moriarty," I intoned, my ire instantly rising. "I might have known he would contrive a way to appear!"

"It is precisely what I would have done under these circumstances," Sherlock nodded. The idea of facing an opponent of an intellect equal to my brother's and my own did not delight me. "With Moriarty present, I judged that going forward with the exchange was inadvisable, given that we no longer had full control or knowledge of the situation. Our current course is no longer tenable. Whether or not he genuinely believes that I am ignorant of your reasons for producing these documents, our position is now compromised."

I remained stock still for a moment, facing my sibling, who stood impassively near the corner behind my desk.

"Now, you don't blame me for signalling to end the operation, do you?"

"Of course not, but you know what this means. Now that I have failed to deliver, I am no longer useful to them or to you in this matter. I had hoped to dismantle this gang of villains without endangering you as directly as I now fear will be necessary."

My brother stepped forward and placed his long, thin hand on my shoulder. "Moriarty was never going to be a Guy Fawkes, going down with one swipe at the nation. His net is wide. He prefers to work patiently in many small rooms. Every once in a while, a gunshot or a scream. He was always more likely to be my prey than yours."

I did not find this comforting, though I knew it to be true. "Moran wants more. He holds anger towards the country he once served. Moriarty cares little for such things."

My brother shrugged. "But without Moriarty the Colonel is a cipher. You made a valiant effort. Yet this was never truly your fight to win."

"You still believe it can be won?" I asked, not feeling my most hopeful in that moment.

"I don't know," he answered thoughtfully, "but I must try."

Neither my brother nor I could tell exactly what Moriarty's aim had been in coming to the meeting, but his appearance indicated with clear finality that I could no longer manoeuvre as before.

"I'm sorry," I said, words I had not uttered to my brother, or anyone, in many years.

"Whatever for? Everything was well conceived. He simply chose to act unexpectedly. Perhaps it was wishful thinking on our part that he would leave Moran to handle such important business alone."

"I'm sorry I couldn't keep you out of it."

"Moriarty was always determined to have me into it,"

he replied, almost cheerfully. "I suppose I am glad to know where things stand."

I did not feel as sanguine, but I filled a glass with my strongest stuff and handed it to him, filling another for myself.

"Do you want to toast Queen and country?" he asked with amusement.

"No," I answered. "I just need a stiff drink."

Half an hour later, my brother walked out into the night. He looked nothing like the small boy I had once protected from Harold Wilcox, and yet in some way he did. For all our strategising, it had taken but one unexpected move by Moriarty to bring our plans to naught. He had forced our hand. Perhaps he knew or suspected more than Moran had let on. Should I have predicted that Moriarty would step onto the stage so late in the drama?

*

"So it has come to this," Sherlock said softly, as soon as he arrived in the Stranger's Room at the Diogenes Club one week later.

"So it has."

"You will do as I ask," he said, his voice taking on a commanding tone.

"I will," I answered, feeling the thing pass out of my control and into his.

"All is not lost, not by any means."

"And yet –" I said, not wanting to finish the thought.

"And yet," he echoed. "It is my turn. You must not keep all the excitement for yourself."

"Yes. But I dislike it, and I reserve the right to continue."

My brother smiled. "Please do. I should like to know that

whatever happens to me, you are back here scowling at the miscreants. I find the thought to be motivating."

"It'll be all right," I said stupidly, patting his back. Quickly, he pulled away, turned, and left the Stranger's Room.

I hated James Moriarty in that moment, more than I have ever hated any other human being. That night, I paced for hours before I went to the kitchen. Carlton was long abed, so I brewed my own tea. It tasted bitter because I made it too strong. How apt that seemed.

THE WILD MAN OF OLMOLUNGRING

CAVAN SCOTT

FROM THE JOURNAL OF SIR ERNEST HENNING, JANUARY 1893

Of all the strange, strange things I expected to encounter in my search for Olmolungring, the events of the last few days have been the most curious of all my travels. Even now, as I sit in the safety of a lodge in Kathmandu, I pause before committing what occurred to paper, not sure what to believe or to think of the singular individual I first met on the slopes of Mount Kailash.

We had come to Holy Mountain in search of the fabled Mi-rgod, the Wild Man of the old Bon religion and guardian of the sacred city. I had first discovered mention of the legendary man-beast during a visit to the Murknight Archive at Cinderwick, stumbling upon a woodcut depicting the mythical creature, both worshipped and feared by the ancient

Lepcha of Tibet. The image of the beast, with its long, loping arms, vicious claws and burning eyes, stirred my imagination and I became a man possessed, seeking out any reference to the creature. Few shared my enthusiasm, and when I announced my intention to travel to the region and discover if there was any truth in the legend, only two men agreed to accompany me: Percival Reddick, so keen to make a name for himself as a young adventurer, and William Livermere, son of my old friend, the Bishop of Rushwell.

William in particular had been excited to set sail. His good humour hadn't wavered, even in the early days of our journey when the Fates seemed against us. First, we struggled to find a native guide, most locals refusing point blank to lead our small party, insisting that the slopes of Kailash were cursed, a proclamation that didn't seem so outlandish when, on day two of our hike up the mountain path, I slipped, injuring my leg. Nothing was broken, thank God, although I was forced to rely on a stick as we continued on our way. Was it foolish of me to press on as if nothing had happened? Maybe. Yet we had come too far and sacrificed too much to turn back at the first sign of hardship.

I must admit that by day three I was beginning to doubt my decision. A blizzard had whipped up, seemingly out of nowhere, taking us by surprise and putting the fear of God into our Tibetan guides, a father-and-son team who had agreed to accompany us despite serious misgivings.

"It's no good," Tenzin, the father, told us. "We shall have to make camp here."

"Are you sure we can't keep going?" Reddick asked with

typical impatience, forever attempting to hurry us on. "The storm could still pass."

"Or we could stumble off the side of the mountain," Tenzin told him plainly. "We camp here."

Reddick sighed, even as Livermere began to unpack the gear from the sled. "What do you think, Sir Ernest? Can we afford the time?"

But I wasn't listening and instead peered into the whirling snow.

"What is it?" Reddick asked, stepping closer.

"I'm not sure," said I, wiping rime from my goggles. "I thought I saw something on the path ahead."

"I don't see how...?" Reddick said, before breaking off. "No. No, you're right. Is that... is that a figure?"

Indeed it was. A shape was looming out of the snow, tall and shaggy, waving arms that looked too long in the blizzard. Instinctively, I raised my own hand, waving back.

"No," Tenzin snapped, going so far as to grab my arm and pull it down, nearly sending me spinning from my feet. "It could be the Mi-rgod."

"Then it's what we've come for!" Reddick exclaimed. "The evidence we have been seeking since day one!"

"The evidence that might get you killed," Tenzin told him.

That's when we heard the cry, calling over the gale; not the roar of an ancient beast, but the call of a strident, decidedly human voice.

"Hello? Hello, is someone there?"

"Yes," I called back, ignoring the glare from our guide. "This way. Over here. Can you see us?"

The response to my question was a whoop of laughter, tinged, I thought, with just the merest hint of hysteria.

"Oh, thank the Lord. For a moment I thought you were a mirage, my half-frozen brain playing tricks on me."

All of a sudden he was upon us, his lumbering silhouette revealed to be a mass of furs, a thick hood concealing his features. He kicked up snow as he surged forward, stumbling and falling as he reached our party to land face down at our feet.

"There's no need to prostrate yourself," I joked, leaning heavily on my stick to offer him a hand, which he took gladly. "You're safe now."

"Yes," he said as Reddick and Livermere moved to assist. "Safe. I must admit, I thought I was... how do you say... done for."

There was a Scandinavian lilt to his voice, although the beard we could see on the thin face within the furs was as black as night. The stranger's eyes were hidden behind a curious pair of goggles fashioned with leather, with thin vertical slits where the glass should have been.

"What the devil are you doing out here on your own?" I asked as my companions helped the man back to his booted feet.

"A good question, my friend," he said, gasping for breath. "A good question indeed, and one I might ask if the shoe were on the other foot, as I believe the saying goes. I was part of an expedition, much like you, I see."

"Then where are your people?" Reddick asked. "Your guides?"

"Lost," the stranger said, trembling slightly. "All of them. I became separated from the party in the storm and have been wandering ever since. I fear… I fear they have gone over the edge, or fallen into a crevasse. It has been a while since I heard the dogs. I'm afraid I have lost all sense of time. The snow, you see… the winds."

"Are you hurt?" I enquired, and the fellow shook his head.

"No. I don't think so. Hungry, yes. Disorientated, definitely, but not hurt."

"You must stay with us," I told him, clapping a mittened hand on his shoulder, bony through the thick furs. "We are about to make camp. Maybe we'll put out some traps for food. We're only just above the tree line. We might have some luck."

"That sounds good," he said, shaking gently beneath my palm. "You are most kind."

"Nonsense," I told him. "It's the very least we can do…" I trailed off, realising that I didn't know his name.

"Sigerson," he offered, realising my predicament. "Erik Sigerson. And you are?"

"This is Sir Ernest Henning," Reddick answered for me, irritation creeping into his voice. "But maybe we can save the introductions for *after* we have pitched the tents?"

"Of course," our new friend said, his voice as cheerful as Reddick's was terse. "And I shall help."

"There is no need," I said, concerned that the fellow would collapse any minute. "You must rest."

But Sigerson wouldn't hear of it. "It is the least I can do," he insisted, pulling himself up straight, although there was no mistaking how he wavered in the force of the mountain wind. Little did I know how strong he actually was beneath all those furs, or the true reason he was wandering alone in the snow.

*

It was only later, once we were safely under canvas, that Sigerson finally pulled down his hood and we beheld a sharp-nosed face that looked as tired as I felt. However, there was nothing weary about the grey eyes that were revealed as he took off his curious goggles. While his bushy, ice-covered brows bordered on the comical, those piercing eyes were always on the move, darting here, there and everywhere as he seemingly committed the interior of our small tent to memory. For a moment, I felt a pang of unease. The man's demeanour was pleasant enough, but I couldn't help but feel we were being weighed up, examined as microbes are studied beneath a laboratory microscope. Reddick, in particular, had taken an instant dislike to the fellow and, while I thought he was being paranoid, I admit there was something odd about the way our new acquaintance watched Reddick struggle to remove his boots.

"Do you require assistance?" the Scandinavian enquired, only darkening Reddick's mood.

"I can manage, thank you," he replied in clipped tones, even though it was obvious that nothing could be further from the truth.

"This is your first expedition," Sigerson commented as Reddick's failure to extract his left foot continued. It wasn't a question, but a statement of fact.

"Of course not," Reddick replied. "Whatever gave you that impression?"

"Your boots," Sigerson answered. "They are new. Well, compared to Sir Ernest's, anyway," he added, acknowledging my own footwear. "The same goes for your suit. Jaeger, if I'm not mistaken, the finest camel hair."

"Of course," Reddick huffed, finally releasing his foot to massage his toes through the thick socks. "Although what difference it makes is beyond me."

"Sir Ernest's suit has obviously served him well for a number of expeditions, its cut a style favoured ten, maybe twelve years ago. And then there is the issue of the pin…"

"Pin?" Reddick repeated, becoming more annoyed by the second. "I am not wearing a pin."

"Exactly. And yet, Sir Ernest is wearing his proudly." Sigerson pointed a thin finger at the left lapel of my suit. "A silver compass fashioned with the initials I.A.C."

"The Intrepid Adventurers Club," I said, without thinking.

"Indeed," Sigerson agreed. "An illustrious society housed on Biggs Lane in London."

"You've been there?" I asked.

"Once or twice," he replied. "As a guest, of course. Not a member. Perhaps we have a friend in common, Sir Ernest? Tell me, do you know Lord Frederick Goodrich?"

"I should hope I do," I said, not wanting to admit that my association with the gentleman, known throughout the Empire for his exploits in lands far and wide, was passing at best.

"Then maybe we should all meet up the next time I am in London," he said, turning back to Reddick. "You too, of course, as by then you will be eligible for membership, having completed at least one expedition. That is the requirement, yes?"

Reddick grumbled that it was, turning his attention to his other boot. "What about you?" he muttered, shooting a look at Sigerson's furs. "I assume that all this is rather new for you as well."

"What makes you say that?" the Scandinavian asked, drawing a snort from my companion.

"I thought that would be obvious. You are correct. My suit is new, as are my boots, but as for your…" He paused, looking Sigerson up and down. "For your get-up…"

A frown creased Sigerson's brow. "My… get-up? I'm sorry, I do not know this expression."

"He means your clothes," I explained, gesturing at the loose hides that hung from the fellow's lanky frame. "The furs and whatnot."

"Hardly the outfit of a gentleman," Reddick added.

"Percival," I exclaimed, appalled at his rudeness, although Sigerson merely chuckled, looking down at his clothes as if seeing them for the first time. "You are probably right, Mr. Reddick. I imagine I look a fright to both of you, although maybe not to your guides."

It was true. Sigerson's furs were similar to those worn by Tenzin and his boy, a fact that Reddick found necessary to underline with his usual tact.

"Exactly my point. They're useful chaps, but hardly what you call civilised. I doubt Frederick Goodrich would be seen dead wearing something so…"

"Primitive?" Sigerson asked.

"Quite so," Reddick smirked, thinking he had won the argument.

Sigerson, on the other hand, showed no sign of being insulted. "Yes, they are primitive, compared to your own tweeds, but they have their advantages."

Reddick scoffed, still unable to remove his remaining boot. "I somehow doubt that. Can't beat camel hair."

"Indeed. The wool of a camel is a godsend when it comes to underwear, especially out here on the mountain, but as an outer covering, well, as I'm sure you've discovered, it provides little if any protection against the wind. And then there is the perspiration…"

"I hardly think we need to discuss such things," I interjected, all too aware that Reddick's mood was worsening by the second.

"Quite right," Sigerson agreed, apologising with a bow of the head. "I have no desire to offend your sensibilities, only to suggest that maybe looser furs like these allow for more movement while also keeping you warm, a benefit proved by generations of Sami. As do these," he added, kicking out his fur-covered boots, as soft as Reddick's boots were hard. "Reindeer skin, lined with sennegrass for insulation. Quite wonderful. Moreover, they barely ever freeze, unlike…"

He let his voice trail off, his point made as Reddick's boot remained stubbornly on his foot. "Are you sure you don't require any help?"

That was it. Reddick's temper boiled over. I should think that Tenzin and his boy could have heard his rebuke from their tent, as could have Livermere, even, wherever he was, out setting traps in the snow.

"So asks the man who managed to lose his entire party on the side of the mountain!" Reddick all but exploded. "A man we found floundering lost and alone in his oh so miraculous furs!"

"Percival, please…" I interrupted, but Reddick wouldn't be silenced.

"I'm sorry, Sir Ernest, but I'm not going to sit here and be insulted by such a man as this. For all we know, he's here to sabotage our expedition."

"I meant no disrespect…" Sigerson began, only to be cut off by another question from Reddick.

"What *were* you searching for, hmm? Why are you on Kailash?"

"For the same reason as you," the Scandinavian said simply. "To locate the lost city of Olmolungring."

"A-ha!" Reddick cried out in triumph. "He admits it. He is from a rival party."

"That much is obvious," said I, aware that there was little other reason to be in the region, especially as Tibet was, for all intents and purposes, closed to visitors and had been for more than a century. We had been forced to smuggle ourselves across the border, which had been a trial in itself, but whatever hardships we had endured to get here, I had no desire to argue with this stranger. Yet of course, it was not I whom Sigerson seemed determined to insult.

Thankfully our guest appeared to realise that he'd crossed a line and raised his hands in an attempt to pacify the situation. "I have offended you, and for that I wholeheartedly apologise, especially after you have all shown me such kindness. I have no need, or desire, to sabotage your expedition. I only guessed why you are here thanks to the maps that I see peeping from that pack over there by the entrance, the work of Bon monks if I am not very much mistaken. Ninth century?"

"Tenth," I confirmed, impressed by his knowledge.

Sigerson smiled, somewhat sadly I thought. "Excellent. My people, on the other hand, were relying on oral traditions and folklore, which is no doubt why our venture ended in such… calamity. I ask that you forgive my gibes about your suit…"

"And my boots," Reddick grumbled, one foot in and one foot out.

"And your boots, yes," Sigerson acknowledged graciously. "If I am honest with you, I am a little ashamed to have been found 'floundering around', as you quite rightly put it, miraculous furs or not. Have you heard of the term 'transference'?"

Reddick begrudgingly shook his head.

"It is used in the study of psychology to describe the habit of projecting one's own feelings of guilt or inadequacy onto another. It's a crime I am guilty of today, as I have been many times in the past. In days gone by, I was… accompanied by a dear, dear friend who would quite happily point out the error of my ways, but recently… well, suffice it to say that he is no longer at my side, and I am much the worse for it."

A wave of melancholy had come over the man, a sadness that stole both the edge from his voice and the wind from Reddick's sails.

"I'm sorry to hear it," Percival said, his tone kinder than it had been all evening. "Was he a member of your party?"

That, at least, made Sigerson chuckle. "Good heavens, no. The very thought of such foolishness would have had him running for the warmth of hearth and home. But I miss him. I miss him more than I thought possible."

The tension broken, the argument abated and we sat for a moment listening to the wind howling outside, the frame of the tent creaking in the storm. Finally, it was Sigerson who broke the silence, laughing self-consciously and asking what was keeping young Livermere. Reddick agreed, absentmindedly checking his watch, despite the fact that the works had frozen solid days ago.

"You're right," he said, wiping the iced face against his waistcoat. "William should be back by now. What do you think, Sir Ernest? Should we have a look around outside?"

There was no need, as seconds later Tenzin's boy burst into the tent, babbling excitedly in his native tongue about a body and blood and terrible wounds.

*

It was William all right, laid out beneath the clump of evergreens we had passed shortly before making camp. The lad had gone back to set a trap, thinking that he might catch a hare or some such to supplement our dwindling rations. Now, the snow beneath Livermere's body shone red and there was no longer a need to worry about having too many mouths to feed.

"What happened to him?" asked Reddick, his face as white as the crystals whirling in the light of Tenzin's lantern.

"He found what you came for," Tenzin spat at my companion, a mixture of fear and anger in his voice. "Or rather, it found him."

"What do you mean?" I asked, but before the guide could answer, Sigerson pushed past me to crouch down beside Livermere.

"I say," Reddick began, "what are you doing?"

"Examining the body," came the reply, the Scandinavian's accent clipped and severe. He reached over, running his gloved hand down Livermere's jacket.

"The *body*," Reddick parroted, scandalised. "That, sir, is our friend."

"Was your friend, I'm afraid," Sigerson replied. "He's quite dead."

His hands halted at the tears on Livermere's chest, the thick tweed of his jacket sliced to pieces. Sigerson didn't even flinch. Instead he pulled the mittens from his long fingers and started to undo the buttons.

"Sir Ernest!" Reddick protested. "We can't allow him to do this!"

"We need to know how Livermere died," I told him, my eyes fixed on Sigerson as he pulled aside the boy's shirt to reveal the identical slashes in Livermere's undergarments, the cuts long and deep.

"What could do that?" Reddick asked, sheer terror eclipsing his outrage as he saw the wounds that had sliced Livermere open from belly to chest. "A bear?"

"I think not," Sigerson replied, assessing the poor boy's neck, presumably for more signs of violence. "Bears have five claws on each foot—"

"Exactly!" Reddick interrupted.

"And yet here," the Scandinavian continued, "we can clearly see three slashes across the young fellow's chest. There are more here, across the neck."

Sigerson turned Livermere's head so we could see the marks,

livid in the gleam of the lantern. For all his bluster, Reddick jerked his head away, a hand going to his mouth, and for a moment I thought he was going to be quite unwell. It was all I could do to look at the boy myself. It wasn't the blood, or the injuries, but the frost-covered eyes. So wide. So sightless. For him to meet his end this close to our camp. How could we ever forgive ourselves?

Our guide, it appeared, agreed with Sigerson's theory. "Not a bear," Tenzin growled as the Norwegian did the decent thing and closed Livermere's sightless eyes. "Never a bear. That is the work of the Mi-rgod."

I'm ashamed to say that, for the briefest of moments, the mention of this name had me forget the tragedy that had befallen us. My heart skipped a beat, and I whirled upon the local, asking him if he was sure.

He looked at me with something resembling disgust… or maybe even pity.

"You came here to hunt the Wild Man, and now the Wild Man hunts you. I warned you. We all warned you and yet still you came."

"And you with us," Reddick reminded him. "For the right price."

Tenzin's jaw clenched as he considered this. "That was wrong of me," he finally admitted, the lantern unwavering in his hand. "I should have walked away, refused to guide you, maybe persuaded you to return to your own land, but my greed led me here –" he looked around, his expression like flint "– into the Mi-rgod's realm."

Sigerson rose, turning towards the guide. "Those words you used… the Wild Man… the Mi-rgod… do you mean the Yeti?"

Tenzin snorted, and for a moment I thought he was going to spit on the ground, such was the look of revulsion on his weathered features. "That is not a word we use. It is… disrespectful, just as our presence here on the Holy Mountain is disrespectful."

"But this is evidence," I stammered, my brain working double time just to keep up with what had happened. "This is evidence that the Wild Man exists."

"Wild Men," Tenzin corrected. "They never travel alone."

"Can you hear yourselves?!" Reddick exclaimed, finally recovering his voice. "Livermere is dead and you're talking of evidence, for God's sake."

"This is why we came here," I reminded him, even though my heart burned with shame. "I am sorry for Livermere's death, of course I am…"

"Sorry?"

"But the boy knew the risks." I shot a look at our guide. "We all did. We came up this mountain to prove that the Mirgod was real…"

"And you won't be content until we're all lying on our backs with our guts steaming in the snow."

"Percival!" I snapped, taken back by the starkness of his words.

"Oh, I'm sorry. Did that offend you?" The young man was looking at me in disbelief. "Maybe you'd like to discuss that with poor William. Oh, you can't, can you, because he's been butchered not one hundred yards from our camp."

"We should leave," Tenzin suggested, looking back the way we had come. "Tomorrow, when the sun rises. We should go from this place and never return."

"What of Livermere?" I asked, glancing at the body.

"We take him with us," Reddick said, as if this were the most obvious thing in the world. "For a proper burial."

"Oh, be sensible," I told him, shaking my head. "How do you imagine we will get his body across the border, let alone all the way back to England?"

"You cannot take him from the mountain," Tenzin said. "He belongs here now. To the Mi-rgod. They will come for him. They will come for us all unless we retreat. We have stumbled too close to Olmolungring. They will not allow us to take another step."

"Poppycock," said a voice we hadn't heard for a while. It was Sigerson, who had been listening without comment as the argument raged on. "There is no such thing as a Yeti."

"Then how do you explain those injuries, hmm?" Reddick said, sweeping an arm around to take in Livermere's body. "You said yourself that it was no bear."

"It was no bear that I know of, but I could be wrong. We will not know unless we investigate further."

"Investigate for what?"

"The storm has already covered any tracks that the beast may have left behind, but we should check the surrounding area at first light."

"For what?"

"For further evidence. For scraps of fur on the trees or claw marks against the rocks."

"Do not test the Mi-rgod," Tenzin warned the Scandinavian. Warned us all. "We have already outstayed our welcome." As he spoke, the old man swung his lantern around to peer into the gloom that pressed in from all sides. "The Wild Men could be out there right now, waiting for us, watching us. And they will claim us as their own unless we leave their mountain."

"Oh, we're leaving all right," Reddick told him, "but not without giving William a decent English burial."

"Percival," I interjected, raising a hand to calm him. "I've already told you—"

"That it will be impossible to get the lad home, and you might be right," Reddick admitted, "but I'll be damned if I'm going to leave him out here for those creatures to come back and pick over his bones. If we can't bury him at home, then we're burying him here, on the mountainside. We owe him that at least."

*

It turned out, of course, that burying Livermere was nigh on impossible, the ground beneath the trees frozen solid. Instead, we had to make do with a cairn of scavenged rocks, covering his poor slashed body one back-breaking stone at a time. Exhausted and drained, we returned to camp, Reddick falling asleep before I even had chance to open the rations. As I lay there, I could hear Tenzin and his boy already packing up their gear. As sleep finally took me, I wondered if we would wake in the morning to find our guides gone, having fled the mountain to avoid an encounter with a demon from their culture's long past.

And yet, Tenzin and his boy were still with us when we peered out of the tent at first light. I had hardly slept a wink, and my stomach gurgled, partly from gnawing hunger and partly because of the decision I had already made, a decision neither Reddick nor the Tibetans would welcome.

"We're not going back," I announced to the company. "We came here to prove the existence of the Mi-rgod and we won't turn back now. *Especially* now. Livermere's sacrifice will not be in vain."

Tenzin complained, Reddick immediately joining in, but Sigerson merely stood in his reindeer furs, stoically watching and waiting before delivering his verdict.

"I think you have chosen well, Sir Ernest. We have all come too far to give up now."

"*We?*" Reddick spluttered. "Must I remind you that you are *not* part of this expedition."

"He is now," I said, leaning on my cane. "With Livermere gone, we need every man we can muster." I turned towards our guides. "And that includes you and your son, Tenzin. Will you stay?"

The local didn't answer, but neither did he leave. We packed up camp and spent most of the morning doing as Sigerson had suggested, searching for evidence of the Wild Man that had so savagely attacked Livermere the previous night. The storm had abated and the air was crisp, but the newly fallen snow had covered any tracks or clues we may have missed in the dark. And so we pressed on, heading further up the mountain path, Sigerson turning his expert eye to the maps, comparing the cryptic cartography with the evidence his own party had gathered.

Evidence, it appears, that was worth more than he had first suggested.

Not three hours into our ascent, Tenzin's boy issued a shout and pointed high up the slope. Something was glinting on the side of the mountain. Could that be…? Yes, yes, it was. There was a building carved into the rock, windows shining like angels while a pair of enormous statues flanked an imposing wooden door carved with ancient runes.

For a second, Tenzin froze, staring at the grotesque effigies, a single name on his trembling lips.

"Mi-rgod."

I had recognised them myself, from the woodcut back in Cinderwick. Broad as they were tall, the Wild Men of the mountain bore proud but fierce faces, their jaws crammed with monstrous teeth and their brows heavy. Long matted hair flowed over wide shoulders, and even fashioned in stone the creatures looked as though they were ready to pounce on anyone unfortunate… or foolish… enough to stumble into their path, each mighty paw tipped with three sickle-like claws.

"Is that it?" Reddick breathed next to me, transfixed by the vision. "Is that…"

"Olmolungring," Sigerson said quietly, completing the sentence for him. "The divine city of the ancient Bon."

"We go no further," Tenzin intoned, his breath fogging in the chill air. "You go if you need to, but we stay here."

I tried to argue, but the guide was resolute. He couldn't stop us, but would not endanger his boy. I acquiesced and so, our pulses quickened, Reddick, Sigerson and I continued towards the ancient city, navigating a path that was barely wide enough for a mountain goat. We inched towards the great doors, clinging to the rock face. More than once I stumbled, having been forced to strap my cane across my back, and would have toppled into cold, thin air if it hadn't been for Sigerson's strong grip. Finally, we reached the ancient doors, and found them unlocked. One shove was all it took to gain entrance, snow tumbling from creaking hinges as we pushed our way inside. Barely able to speak, we ignited torches and moved deeper into the building, unsure what we might find within its walls.

It's fair to say that legend had been kind to Olmolungring. It was no city, but rather a temple. Once the walls would have been daubed with frescoes, but the colours had sadly faded, leaving only ghosts in their wake, echoes of former splendour. Gone also were the treasures that had been said to line the corridors, Olmolungring's once great libraries empty. My heart ached as we walked from one echoing chamber to the next. Is this what Livermere had given his life for? Is this what the Mi-rgod, if they even existed, guarded with such ferocity? Suddenly, our expedition seemed foolish. All the legends and the myths, the planning and expense… had it all been for this, a collection of empty rooms in an icy wilderness?

It was clear from Reddick's face that he shared my disappointment. Sigerson, on the other hand, bounded ahead, hurrying from one chamber to the next. Every now and then, he would crouch down to inspect the floor before springing back to his feet to run his hand across the time-worn walls. I found myself becoming increasingly annoyed by both his manner and the smile that was plastered across his gaunt face. What possible reason was there to be gleeful?

The expedition thus far had been a complete and utter disaster. There was nothing here. Nothing at all.

And yet, as if to prove me wrong, Sigerson plucked something from a crack in an arched doorway, turning on his heel to present his findings as if he had discovered the treasures of Olympus itself.

"What do you think of this?"

I shrugged, unsure what to say. Reddick at least leaned in closer, scrutinising whatever Sigerson held grasped between his thumb and index finger.

"It's a thread."

"Indeed it is, my good fellow. A thread snagged as someone passed this way, brushing up against the rock."

"Hardly something of note," I said, dejected and weary.

"It is *everything* of note," the Scandinavian insisted. "How long do you estimate it has been since anyone walked these corridors?"

"Olmolungring has been lost for centuries," Reddick told him. "Millennia perhaps."

Sigerson's grin expanded with his words. "And so explain to me how wool woven in Germany attached itself to that wall. Wool dyed by modern industrial means."

Reddick frowned. "How could you possibly know that?"

"The pigment and the weave. They are quite distinctive. It is impossible that the sheep which once carried that fleece originated on this mountain or any of her neighbours. I once read a monograph on the subject. Quite fascinating. Written by an English gentleman by the name of Sherlock Holmes? Have you heard of him?"

Of course we had, but Sigerson didn't wait for our answer, turning around to take in the mosaic-clad floor. "And then there are the corridors. The main thoroughfares through the building. Have you noticed the floors, gentlemen?"

"A simple enough design," I said. "Although I would have expected more colour."

"No, no, no, not the mosaic," Sigerson interrupted, waving away my expert opinion as if it were an irrelevancy. "The dust, Sir Ernest. The dust."

"Dust?" Reddick repeated, completely baffled.

"The dust," the madman repeated. "The rooms we entered… the chambers… they were all covered in a thick layer of dust."

"As is to be expected," said I.

"And yet," Sigerson continued, "these corridors have been swept clean. You can even see the odd bristle. They have been cleaned regularly and thoroughly in recent days, maybe even this very morning." His eyes gleamed in the torchlight. "I was right, gentlemen. He *is* here, I am sure of it."

"Who?" I asked, confused. "Who is here? What are you talking about?"

Again he didn't answer, but instead snatched the torch from Reddick's hand and plunged through the doorway, moving so fast that we could barely keep up, especially with my dratted stick clattering against the mosaic beneath our feet. Sigerson was like a bloodhound that had caught a scent. He wouldn't pause for a second, not even as he found a curved stairwell that led to who knew where. He bounded up the steps without hesitating, taking them two, sometimes three at a time. We followed, and eventually heard him stop at the summit, an exclamation of triumph echoing back down towards us.

"What is it?" I called, my heart quickening. "What have you found?"

"Not what," he replied, "but *whom*."

My mouth dropped open as we reached the top of the stairwell. There was no need for the torches now. Flickering oil lamps lit the chamber. Deep rugs lay on the floor, and fine wood cabinets stood arrayed along the walls, behind them tapestries, each a riot of colour and design, displaying scenes of huntsmen charging through what could only be the English countryside.

And yet, vibrant though they were, the tapestries weren't the most startling item in the room. That was the bed that stood opposite us.

A bed with a solitary occupant.

Sigerson held out the torch and Reddick took it without comment or complaint, too dumbstruck even to speak. How could this be? Who was this man lying on a feather-down pillow as if he were reclining in a stately home rather than a crumbling ruin halfway up a snow-blasted mountain?

Sigerson strode closer, silently observing the fellow beneath the covers. Whoever he was, the poor chap was in a bad way. A bandage was wrapped around a prominent domed head, the man's sunken features ravaged by badly healed scars. His nose had obviously been broken, what should have been his right eye little more than a mass of scar tissue. One side of his mouth was permanently pulled down by a hastily stitched gash, and he was missing an ear on the same side as the butchered optic. Even though I had no idea of his identity, I couldn't shake the feeling that he had once been a giant of a man, as strong and imposing as the building in which we stood. Now, however, he looked shrunken, even beneath the blankets, his breath as he slept shallow and wheezing.

At least, we assumed he was asleep. The patient's eye flicked open the moment Sigerson drew near, the obscene tip of a withered tongue moistening those ruined lips. And when he spoke, the voice that issued from the wreck of a man was little more than a croak.

"Who... who are you?"

"I might ask you the same question..." Sigerson responded, but his voice had changed, the accent we had become accustomed to gone as he added one final knowing word, "Professor."

"Professor?" Reddick asked, starting an avalanche of questions now that the spell was broken. "Do you know him? Who is this man? Who are you? What is going on here?"

Sigerson, if that was even his name, didn't respond, but stared at the man in the bed as the man gazed back.

"This is why you came here, isn't it?" I asked, wanting to grab our companion and shake him by the shoulders. "You were looking for this fellow?"

"I was," he nodded, having the decency not to lie.

"Was there ever another expedition?"

At that, he shook his head, incredible though the admission seemed.

"You came here alone?"

"I have been tracking this... gentleman for two years straight, following leads and hearsay, chasing all across Europe and far beyond." His attention turned back to the patient, his tone level but bristling with... what? Pride? Anticipation?

"I knew you had survived, Professor. Knew that the waters of Reichenbach had not claimed you for their own. Your own people gave up on you, your lieutenants stating, even when pressed that they had heard nothing from you for months. Others would have given up the chase, but not I, not until I knew for sure. Your organisation was being dismantled piece by piece, your allies vanishing like smoke, and yet there was one story I could hardly ignore, about a school for assassins high in the mountains, once funded by the late, lamented Napoleon of Crime. Killers trained there were said to have murdered the Duke of Vensoria in 1878, and the owner of the Golden Fleet Shipping Line just three years later. The school was closed now, of course, its students scattered, but the rumours persisted that the building itself, housed in a once holy city, still existed. A bolt hole. A place to lick one's wounds. Your tracks were covered well, on that I congratulate you, but it soon became clear to which location you had crawled to recover. And now, finally, I can bring you to justice. The game is at an end."

"The game?" The accused's voice, whoever he was, was so faint we could barely hear it, as fragile as leaves trodden underfoot. "There is no game."

"No longer. Now that I have found you and your 'wild man'."

In one fluid motion, Sigerson pulled his hand out of his furs, producing a revolver, cocked and ready to fire.

Instinctively, Reddick and I moved, not wanting to see this stranger we had taken into our midst murder a defenceless soul, whatever crimes he may have committed in the past. Reddick got there first, grabbing Sigerson's outstretched arm and trying to yank it to the side, anything to pull the handgun from its target. Sigerson grunted, yet didn't seem perturbed by the intervention. Instead, he swivelled at the waist, the gun sweeping around to fire multiple rounds harmlessly into the tapestry of the hunting party. Now I was on him, clamping my stick across his chest to wrestle the man back.

"No, Sir Ernest," he protested, as I grabbed his furs and pulled with all my might. He stumbled, his arm dropping long enough for Reddick to deliver a punch to the fellow's bearded chin. Sigerson went down on the bed, the gun slipping from his grasp, and he shouting at us that we didn't understand. I twisted his arm behind his back, yelling at him not to struggle.

Again, he repeated over and over: "You don't understand! I didn't come here to kill him. The gun was not for Moriarty."

The name meant nothing to me. I only cared that we had saved the man who lay wheezing in the bed. Reddick was already moving to examine the old fellow when there was a blur of sudden movement from the tapestry Sigerson had decorated with his bullets. The fabric was pushed aside, revealing not more wall as expected, but a hidden doorway. A figure somersaulted from the ingress, bouncing up to slash an arm across Reddick's side. Reddick cried out in surprise and pain, his knees folding beneath him as he collapsed to the floor, an arm clutched tight across his midriff.

His attacker, a wiry Tibetan in long flowing silks, snapped round to face us, his hands raised to reveal long knives attached to both wrists by metal bands, the blades curved over his bunched fists like claws. The shock of the assault had loosened my grip and Sigerson pushed me away easily, telling me to run, a task all but impossible with my bad leg, and thus I stumbled and fell, landing in a heap on the floor.

Freed of my clutches, Sigerson was looking around for the revolver, but it was nowhere to be seen. Nor did he have time to search, for the assailant lunged forward, his knives arcing through the air. I cried out, expecting those dreadful blades to sink into Sigerson's shoulder, but instead the Scandinavian jumped back, the knives finding only billowing furs. For a moment I thought Sigerson was about to stumble on my stick, which had slid across the floor. Instead, he seemed to know where the instrument lay, ducking as the assailant spun around to deliver a flying kick with his bare feet. The Tibetan's leg sailed over Sigerson's head as he dropped to the floor, snatching up the stick and bringing it around to take the attacker's feet from beneath him. The Tibetan jumped like a jackrabbit, leaping over the flashing stick, and it cracked harmlessly into one of the bed's thick legs. Sigerson's arm snapped back, bringing the cane around to block the next attack. The makeshift weapon did no good, the claws slicing through the wood as though it were paper. The Tibetan swivelled, bringing his other fist to bear and punching Sigerson in the side. A gasp escaped Sigerson's lips as those dreadful blades were buried deep into his furs and he slumped forward onto the bed. There was nothing I could do as the attacker raised his claws high, ready to deliver the final, fatal blow. Sigerson was finished, of that there was no doubt.

And yet, just as hope evaporated, a shot rang out like thunder before the knives met flesh. The Tibetan was knocked from his feet, crashing to the floor where he lay silent, unmoving, blood soaking into the thick rug. For a moment, all was still, the sudden violent end of the fight taking us all by surprise. Sigerson pushed himself up, one hand pressed against his side, while I struggled from the floor, wondering how I would now cope without my stick. Reddick lay worryingly still, but I couldn't go to him, not while the figure in the bed pointed the gun in my direction. The barrel shook in the old man's hand, but he had shot once. Surely he could again.

"You missed, Professor," Sigerson said, his voice breathless from the fight. "Your wild man of the mountain is dead, while I still live. A mistake, to be sure."

"No mistake," the old man croaked, finally dropping his arm to throw the revolver out of his own reach to the foot of the bed, a look of disgust on his ravaged features.

"A trick," Sigerson concluded.

"A *decision*," the patient responded. "I couldn't let him kill you, not before... I could ask... one final question..."

"And that is?" Sigerson asked, still pressing his hand to his side.

"Am I a monster?"

For once, words seemed to fail Sigerson. I limped over to Reddick, pleased to see that, while obviously wounded, my young friend was alive, the slash marks not as deep as I had feared. Sigerson, meanwhile, remained where he was, his mouth bobbing open and shut until he uttered words I imagine were somewhat alien to him.

"I… I do not understand."

The old man gasped for breath before replying. "I have no memory of being brought here. No memory of the accident that left me this way. But most importantly, I have no memory of the man I used to be, the 'Professor' of whom you spoke. There has been no one else here… all this time… no one but the man who attacked you…"

"The man you killed," Sigerson reminded him.

"Yes," the patient whispered. "As he tended to my injuries, he told me stories… stories of the man I used to be… They have haunted my soul, Mr…"

He paused again as he realised that he didn't know Sigerson's name. Neither did I, it appeared, as the man we had met on the mountainside responded with a different title, one he had already mentioned that very day.

"My name is Holmes," he said, searching the Professor's face for a glimpse of recognition. "Sherlock Holmes."

"Sherlock Holmes," the old man repeated, as if hearing the name for the first time. "And we know each other?"

"We do."

"Then you must answer my question."

"Are you a monster?"

Sigerson… Holmes… was silent for a long moment, his eyes studying the man's gaunt face. When he finally spoke, he drew himself up to his full height, his voice and demeanour changing as if he were standing in an auditorium addressing an audience instead of conversing with an obviously dying man.

"I realised I was on the right track when we found the body of poor Livermere last evening. Our guide, the redoubtable Tenzin, believed that he had been attacked by the Yeti or, in his own words, the Mi-rgod, the so-called protector of Olmolungring. While it's true that Livermere was killed by a being protecting this place, it was no creature of myth. Nor did he die from the claw marks across his chest. Those were delivered post-mortem, after Livermere had either stumbled, or been knocked onto his back. An examination of the back of his head revealed a fracture to his skull, which I believe killed him instantly. The claws, as found around the wrists of your most singular nurse, were raked across Livermere's chest after he had died. This was clear not only from the little bleeding from the wounds, but also from the fact that the slashes in his suit corresponded perfectly to the cuts in his body. Victims have a tendency to struggle, especially while in the grip of a savage beast. Whether your assassin killed Livermere or simply found him dead, the claw marks were left as a warning, in the hopes that we would retreat down the mountain.

"However, those claws, and many like them, have slit the throats of a great many people on the orders of one man, the man who funded this facility, the man I saw topple over the edge of the Reichenbach Falls. Was he a monster? Undoubtedly. Is he lying here in front of me? Did he just save my life?" The man I had known as Sigerson paused, deep in thought for a moment before continuing. "No. That man is dead, leaving…"

"Leaving a broken shell in his place," the patient said for him.

"Maybe. Maybe not."

"You think it a lie? An act?"

"It is possible, although not likely."

"Then what will you do?"

Holmes considered this for a moment, glancing down at the hand that he had finally pulled from his side, his palm less bloody than I had expected.

"For once in my life, I am not sure," he said, still examining the offending appendage. "What would you do, if you were in my position?"

The old man didn't miss a beat, clearing his throat before speaking. "I would go through the hidden door you noticed as you entered the room."

Holmes smiled at that as if addressing an old friend, thus acknowledging that he had seen the tapestry shifting in the breeze.

The patient didn't comment, his voice weaker than ever as he continued. "I would go through the door and find the medicine and bandages that until today have been used to tend my injuries. I would then see to the wounds of your friend on the floor, as well as those in your own side, before leaving…"

"With my quarry clapped in irons?" Holmes asked.

"You said your quarry is dead and gone."

"I said I was unsure."

"Either way, there is little he could do. Alone, a monster trapped in his own corpse… You came to deliver… your professor… to justice. I believe it…"

The sentence remained uncompleted. The person who had begun it was gone, the broken body in the bed finally at rest.

Justice had been served.

The man who had introduced himself as Sigerson barely spoke as we made our way back down the mountain. He had helped dress Reddick's wounds, before seeing to his own superficial injuries. His only request was that we should never speak of what we had seen in Olmolungring. We had come looking for a monster, as had he, and yet had found a man waiting to die.

As for his request, well, it will be easy enough to keep. Who would believe me anyway? I can barely believe all this myself.

*

Note from John H. Watson:

The extract from Ernest Henning's journal was sent to me on the event of the explorer's death. It was attached to a hand-drawn map allegedly showing the location of Olmolungring on the slopes of Mount Kailash. I once asked Holmes whether the account was true. He only smiled and walked away, although I did notice his hand going to his side as if to rub an old wound as he exited the room.

THE ADVENTURE OF THE WITANHURST GHOST

PETER SWANSON

In all the years that Sherlock Holmes has been my friend I have rarely seen him fall under the spell of female beauty, the notable exception being Irene Adler. And yet, despite this, I am aware that Holmes, while being an extraordinary man with extraordinary gifts, is still just a man. Not only that, but he is of such an observant nature that he could hardly fail to recognise a beautiful countenance. He may not be moved by beauty, but I do know that he comprehends it, and that he is well aware of how the female member of our species can cause even the most unflappable, the most logical, of men to lose his mind temporarily.

I was thinking about this subject even before the arrival of the telegram from Maude Carradine, an old acquaintance of

Holmes's and mine, and a woman of such perfect beauty that I admit to thinking of her with some regularity in the years since we had met. The telegram arrived in the midst of one of those mornings in which I could feel Holmes's gaze stalking the room like a tiger in a cage at London Zoo. November was upon us and he was in one of his dark moods, his violin sitting restless on his knee. I understood his feelings well. Not only had the days been growing shorter and colder, but London seemed drained of all colours. For a fortnight our already grey city had been smothered by such a low and pestilential sky that on some days the top floors of regular four-storey townhouses were obscured by clouds.

"A telegram, Watson," Holmes said, upon hearing Mrs. Hudson's step approaching the door. "Let's hope it is of some interest."

"How can you be sure she's bringing a telegram?" I asked, looking up from my book.

"She walks about twenty per cent more briskly when she has a telegram to deliver."

Indeed, he was right. Mrs. Hudson delivered a message that Holmes quickly read before passing it over to me.

MR. HOLMES, I AM IN A DIFFICULT SITUATION AND BEG OF YOU TO HELP. MAY I COME TO YOU TO DISCUSS THE GHOST THAT IS BEDEVILLING ME.

MISS MAUDE CARRADINE, WITANHURST HOUSE, HAMPSTEAD HEATH.

"An interesting missive, indeed, Watson."

"Miss Carradine," I said with some enthusiasm. "I remember her well. I am surprised her name remains the same. I thought she might be married by now."

"Did you now? But certainly not to the man she was on her way to meet when we made her acquaintance?"

It had been a rather full train on that sunny Monday morning in early June when Maude Carradine joined Holmes and me in our first-class carriage. We were travelling to Moreton-in-Marsh at the request of a retired colonel named Nigel Atwill. Atwill laboured under the belief that his collection of hunting paintings had been replaced by forgeries, and while neither Holmes nor I believed that Atwill, who was in his ninth decade, was fully compos mentis, the weather was good and we were both happy to take the short train ride to the Cotswolds. I was made even happier when the young redheaded woman settled down across from us in our compartment. She was attired in a green dress of a shimmering material that matched her equally brilliant eyes. Her skin was an alabaster white, her cheeks rosy, and her hair the palest, softest red I had ever seen. Upon taking her seat, she removed a book from her handbag and immediately began to read.

As the train departed, I noted how fast she was speeding through the pages, never taking her eyes off the text. I surmised that she was a young woman of bookish disposition, head always in the clouds, not remotely aware of what was happening around her. But as we passed through Didcot she did raise her eyes to glance through the window towards the bustling station platform. Before she resumed reading, I observed her flipping to the last page of her book, then riffling through the pages as though assessing just how much was left in the story. In order to perform this manoeuvre she lifted the book from her lap enough that I could recognise its cover artistry.

"Ah, *Winnetou*. By Karl May," I said aloud, pleased to see that she was enjoying the German fabulist's thrilling novel of the American West.

The young woman looked at me, surprised, I believe, that she was not alone in the carriage, and said, with what sounded like hope in her voice, "Have you read this book?"

"Indeed, I have."

"Then can you tell me, sir, please, what happens in it?"

"I could," I responded. "But that would deprive you of the pleasure of reading it for yourself."

"I would gladly deprive myself of that pleasure if you could only provide me with the basic narrative and maybe some of your favourite scenes. I would be forever in your debt."

I was surprised by her insistence and did not reply immediately. That was when Holmes, whose eyes had been closed for most of our journey, suddenly spoke:

"While I have not read the book in question myself, I do believe, Watson, that you should divulge the details of the story. That will alleviate the young lady's anxiety about finishing the novel by the end of this train journey."

I began to protest that she would have more time than this journey to finish the novel when the young woman raised herself in her seat and declared that Holmes was correct; she did very much hope to reach the end of the story by the time she arrived at Shipton-under-Wychwood, only a few stops away.

"But why do you need to finish the book by then?" I asked her.

It was Holmes who responded. "She is going to visit a young man to whom she hopes to become engaged. It has been some time since she has seen him, and at their last meeting he gave to her a book, *Winnetou*, asking that she read it. Because she has been particularly busy with her job as an actress in the theatre she has not had time, and now that she is meeting him again, she is attempting to prove her affection for the German gentleman by finishing, or at least appearing to have finished, his favourite novel."

I watched her appraise him. Some astonishment was evident in her eyes, but mostly there was amusement. At last, she said, "I only take exception to your saying that I hope to become engaged to him. I have not decided any such thing."

"But in all other details I was correct?"

"Yes, you were correct. Is it some kind of magic trick?"

"It is no more than simple observation. If it were a magic trick then I would already know your name, and I do not. My name is Sherlock Holmes and my companion is Dr. John Watson."

"My name is Maude Carradine, and I have heard of you, Mr. Holmes. I have heard of both of you."

"And I am familiar with you, as well, Miss Carradine," I said. "I believe you are currently appearing in a new play by Oscar Wilde."

She turned her eyes to me. "Now that is something you would know by simply reading the newspaper. But how did Mr. Holmes ascertain that I was an actress and that this book had been given to me by a German gentleman?"

Holmes reached into his jacket pocket for his pipe, and while tamping it, explained. "It was easy enough to see that you are an actress. For one, when you first entered this carriage you removed a handkerchief to wipe your brow, and on that handkerchief is a smudge of make-up, the colour of which is only ever used in the theatre. I also noticed that your posture is extremely elegant, as though you have been trained both in dance and the theatrical arts, and that while you read you often move your lips silently, a habit you have no doubt formed from reading plays and practising dialogue. It is also a Monday, not typically a day to go on a trip to the countryside, unless Monday – a day when no respectable theatre is open – is your day off.

"As to your visit to see a gentleman, you are wearing a brand-new frock, the colour of which has been selected to accentuate your eyes. But more important than that is the book that you are at such pains to finish. Karl May's novels, and again I'll admit I have not read them, appeal to young men of a certain type, often young German men. It is certainly not a book that appeals to actresses on the West End stage. Therefore, the book was given to you by a man you are travelling to see. May I suggest to you that he will be so pleased to see you that he may not even notice that you have yet to read his favourite story?"

Miss Maude Carradine smiled widely at this, a smile that I imagined had caused audience members in the very back rows of theatres to fall in love with her. "That may be the case," she said, "but why take the risk? Dr. Watson, time is running out. Please recount to me the plot of this book so that I can stop worrying about it, and the three of us can continue this delightful conversation."

This encounter had occurred three years earlier, but I suspect that Holmes had as good a memory of it as I did. Our conversation with Maude Carradine was certainly more interesting than the case of Nigel Atwill's forged paintings; it turned out that Atwill had noticed a change in these only because his housemaid had been neglecting to dust them.

"Let us reply at once," Sherlock Holmes said, the telegram from Maude Carradine back in his slender fingers. And indeed we did, settling in to wait for the appearance of our former acquaintance, now bedevilled, as she put it, by a ghost.

*

When Miss Carradine arrived at 221B Baker Street shortly before dusk, her appearance alarmed me. She was still striking – a few years could hardly fade such beauty – but dark circles lay underneath her eyes, and her nails appeared bitten to the quick. She settled into her seat, managing a rather unconvincing smile, and telling us she was pleased to see us again, despite all appearances to the contrary.

"Tell me," I said, "whatever happened to your German suitor?"

"Oh, I had forgotten all about him. As it turned out he had invited me to his friend's house in the country in order to tell me that on his recent trip back to Germany his parents had forbidden him to marry a woman who made her living on the stage."

"Oh dear!" I exclaimed.

"He wasn't the man for me, though, and I did make sure to accidentally leave my copy of *Winnetou* at his friend's house. I am always happy to shed an object for which I no longer have any use."

"I am glad you are shed of both the book and the man. I believe it is his loss," I said. "And I am pleased to see you, but sorry for the reason. Tell us about the circumstances."

Her shoulders fell, and I noticed a slight quiver of her chin. For a moment I thought she was going to succumb to tears, but she lifted her head and began to tell her story. "I am currently living in a small house in Hampstead that my uncle left to me two years ago. He had no children of his own, and I was his favourite niece. I have been happy there, at Witanhurst, despite its distance from the West End, until, that is, one month ago. That was the morning I awoke to find a note on my bedside table. That was the first shock, of course."

"You live alone?" Sherlock asked.

"I do live alone. While I employ a housemaid, she only comes during the daytime."

"And she has her own key, I presume?"

"She did, Mr. Holmes, until recently. I've had all the locks changed, but I am afraid that there is still a presence in my house."

"Did this presence… leave the note?"

"He did. It came from a man named Ralph Mercer. He was an actor. We shared the stage for two weeks in a rather second-rate performance of *Lear*. I was Goneril and he played Oswald. During the course of this production, he became enamoured of me. Indeed, he proposed to me on closing night, despite the fact that I had given him no encouragement. I knew of his feelings, of course, since he had written me several heartfelt letters during the run of the play. Because of this I immediately recognised his handwriting on the note I received one month ago. It was unmistakable."

"What did the note say?" I asked.

Maude Carradine reached into her embroidered purse and produced a half-sheet of paper. I rose and took it from her. It was cream stationery, of quite good quality. "M.," I read out loud. "Nothing will come of nothing. R."

Passing the note on to Holmes, I said, "That is a quotation from *King Lear*, I believe."

"It is. Lear says it to his daughter. It's a threat in the play and I believe it is a threat, as well, in this note."

"Most certainly," I said. "And I suppose you would like us to find out how Mr. Mercer was able to enter your house and leave this for you. I suspect you have already been to the police?"

Before Maude had a chance to respond, Sherlock spoke:

"Watson, I'm afraid you are wrong. Miss Carradine might have been to the police, but it was not to report an intruder. It was to report a ghost. Am I correct?"

At the word ghost, our lovely visitor could no longer hold back the tears. I quickly produced a handkerchief, and she soon regained control of herself. When she was able to speak, she said:

"Mr. Holmes, it *is* a ghost that I have in my home. I cannot believe I am saying those words, but it is what I believe. Ralph Mercer has been dead for well over a year."

"How did you know this, Holmes?" I said, amazed.

"I would like to dazzle you, Watson, with a level of observation you do not possess, but in this case I simply remember the unfortunate demise of Ralph Mercer. He took his own life in a rather morbid fashion, if I recall, utilising the trapdoor of the Gaiety Theatre in order to hang himself."

"He did," our guest confirmed. "It was a few weeks after I had last seen him. I was called to testify at the inquest because he had expressed to several of his acquaintances that he no longer desired to live, in part, or in whole, I suppose, because I had not reciprocated his feelings."

"My dear, I hope you have not suffered any torment because of this," I spoke. "His death, much like his life, was not in your hands."

"I will admit that his death shook me, but I have come to the realisation that I was not at fault, had done nothing to deceive him, nothing to lead him to an understanding that I shared his feelings."

"I am sure of it," Holmes said. "And what did you feel when you received this note?"

Her nostrils narrowed slightly as she took in a deep breath. "I was terrified, naturally, but I believed the note to be a forgery. Still, that did not explain how the note had arrived in my bedroom while I slept."

"Did you go to the police immediately?"

"I did, and they suggested that someone was playing a particularly cruel prank."

The note was now back in my possession, having been passed to me by Holmes. I spoke:

"Surely you don't believe that Ralph Mercer, even if he has

returned to our plane of existence, would be able to leave you a note? To hold a pen and place words on paper?"

"I didn't believe it, but the note has only been the beginning. A week later I entered my kitchen in the morning to find that there was a spill of flour across the table. And in this flour a finger had drawn a perfectly recognisable hangman's noose."

"Was this before or after you had the locks changed?"

"Immediately before. But since I have had the locks changed there have been several more incidents. Small objects have been moved about the house. The playbill for *King Lear* suddenly appeared on the drawing-room floor, and there have been more nooses, sometimes appearing on my mirror in the bathroom or else on dusty surfaces. It's absolutely impossible, but it is happening. I have searched the entire house and there is no one in there, and yet something, some spirit, is in my house.

"And it is not just these incidents. I feel a presence, all the time. I feel I can hear him moving about in the night. You will tell me that I am simply hearing the creaks and sighs of an old house, but it is more than that."

"I assure you I shall not tell you that what you are hearing is merely an old house," Holmes said.

"So you believe me?"

"I believe everything you are telling me, Miss Carradine, but I am not quite ready to believe in a ghost."

"I don't either, but what other explanation could there be?"

"I assure you there is one, and I assure you I shall find it."

With that, Sherlock Holmes stood, with a purpose that I had not observed in weeks. "I want to visit your house as soon as possible. Do you think you will survive one more night under its roof?"

"I believe so," she said. "I don't feel in physical peril, but I do sometimes worry that I am being driven mad."

"I suggest you put off insanity for a few hours more. We will arrive at Witanhurst at ten tomorrow morning. Before you go I have just a few questions."

"Of course."

"When exactly did you have the new locks put in?"

"It was three weeks ago yesterday."

"And there was no cessation of the haunting after that?"

"There wasn't. On the morning after having the locks changed, I noticed that some books had been rearranged in the library."

"I see. And one more question. Who played Cordelia in the production of *Lear* you were in?"

"Cordelia? She was a Russian actress, Ludmila Fedotik. I believe she came over to England when she was quite young. With a troupe of circus performers. Why do you ask?"

"All will be explained, hopefully, tomorrow morning."

We said our farewells to Maude Carradine and Mrs. Hudson showed her to the front door. I naturally questioned Holmes about his line of thinking, but he responded to me in the same manner in which he had responded to Miss Carradine, promising an explanation the following day.

*

Thus it was with much anticipation on my part that we arrived by carriage at Witanhurst House, a red-brick and white-trim residence near Parliament Hill, set not too far off the road behind an imposing hedge. As we approached the front door I noticed a gentleman upon the stone steps, apparently awaiting entrance as well. For a brief moment I feared that something terrible had happened to Miss Carradine in the night, that this man was here to tell us about it, but then the door opened, and the lovely lady appeared in its frame, attired in a simple velvet frock, the colour of which reminded me of the green dress she had been wearing when I had first laid eyes upon her. The sound of the door opening caused the unknown man to turn and greet our hostess, and she returned his look with one of dismay and annoyance.

"Oh, Charles. I told you not to come. There is no reason for you to be here."

"I will not interfere," he said. "But I will also not permit two unknown men access to every aspect of your house without keeping an eye on things. For that I will not apologise."

Miss Carradine turned now to Holmes and me. "Allow me to introduce Mr. Charles Lowry. He is part owner of the Florentine and knows all about the recent incidents in my home."

Holmes and I introduced ourselves, and I studied the countenance of the young man before me, no doubt another admirer of Maude Carradine. He was broad-shouldered and attired in a fashionable suit, fair-haired but with dark brown eyes under a rather dark brow. His moustache, too, was darker than his hair. He met my gaze with undisguised hostility.

I turned to Holmes, expecting him to be observing this unexpected attendant, but found instead that my friend was studying the array of locks on the front door. "I observe, Miss

Carradine, that when you had your locks changed you in fact had multiple new locks installed."

"I did. I don't know exactly why I thought three locks were better than one but it made me feel safer at the time, a feeling, alas, that was only temporary."

"How long does it take you to unlock all of these?"

"Too long," Charles Lowry interjected. "She stands here on her front doorstep for at least a minute, trying to locate the correct key for each lock."

"Charles, you said you were going to keep your opinions to yourself."

"I'm sorry, Maude," he said, and rubbed his large hands together.

"Shall we all go inside?" Miss Carradine proposed, and we followed her into a dim front hallway with high ceilings, and rather dour paintings on the wall. My initial impression was that the house most likely took after its previous inhabitant, Maude's uncle, but as she led us into the drawing room I saw the influence of the young lady. Everywhere there was colour, from the deep red of the velvet curtains to a Persian carpet with the most intricate pattern of blues and oranges. Any available wall space was filled with framed theatrical posters, plus a rather sentimental oil painting of a young child cradling a kitten. At the centre of the room stood an enormous red velvet sofa. I asked Miss Carradine if it came from the theatre.

"It does, actually," she said. "It was used in my first professional role, playing Alice in a theatrical version of the Lewis Carroll novel."

"It is quite unusual," Holmes said. "Larger, I think, than most loveseats."

"Yes, it was part of a visual effect. I was playing a girl, but since I was fully grown at the time, they wanted me to appear of a smaller size."

"And what of this throne?" Sherlock asked, having cast his eyes to a carved wooden chair in a far corner of the room.

"Yes, that is another piece from a production. A Shakespeare play, but not *Lear*. It was used in a rather dreadful production of *Henry V*. I was Catherine, and I sat on that miserable chair every night for a month."

"And they allowed you to take it home with you at the end of the run?" I enquired.

"Well, I'm afraid our production might have ended the Victoria Palace for good. It was a theatre in Leeds, and after it closed they asked the actors if we wanted any memorabilia. I only took the chair so that I might burn it on Guy Fawkes Night, but now that it sits in the drawing room, I've grown quite fond of looking at it."

Charles Lowry, who had been tugging rather indelicately on his mutton-chop whiskers, spoke suddenly. "Why are we wasting time talking about theatre props, when there is clearly an intruder who comes and goes of his own free will throughout this house?"

"Charles, don't be rude," Miss Carradine said.

"He is being practical," Holmes interjected. "I sense that, as we are, he is concerned with your well-being. To that end I shall take a look around the premises. But before I begin, Miss Carradine, might I ask you: did you receive any visitations last night?"

"I believe I did. This morning I noticed that a photograph of my father, taken just before he died, was turned so as to face the wall in the library. I cannot guarantee that it happened over the course of last night, but I only noticed it this morning."

"Then let us go and look at this photograph first. After that, I should like a tour of the house."

We moved about the house like a regiment of soldiers, Miss Carradine pointing out the areas where strange occurrences had transpired. The house, except for the drawing room and its mistress's bedroom, still seemed inhabited by its previous owner, the deceased uncle who seemed to have revered dark wallpaper and maritime paintings. I will confess that the atmosphere of the place had produced in me an uneasy feeling, as though the sinister happenings might actually be rooted in the spectral world. I particularly felt this when Miss Carradine showed us the windowpane on which she had found the letter R – the first initial of the unfortunate suicide, Ralph Mercer – scratched as though with a sharp nail. A cold shiver passed through me. Holmes merely looked at the R with some interest, then surprised us all by asking Miss Carradine if he could observe her larder.

"Are you hungry, Mr. Holmes?"

"Not at this moment. But if you wouldn't mind…"

We moved as a group to the kitchen where Holmes took an inordinate amount of time looking upon the shelves of dry goods. "You have quite a stock of food," he said.

"I do, at this present time. When I am on the stage, I eat

most of my meals in restaurants, but currently I am between acting jobs."

"And who stocks the larder? Is it you?"

"My housemaid, Edith, does the shopping for me."

"Thank you for this tour," Holmes said. "I have one more request. I should like to observe the outside of your house from all sides."

"Yes, I will show you," she said, but Holmes held up a hand.

"Point the way, Miss Carradine. Is there a rear door I could have access to? And I would ask that the rest of you wait for me in the drawing room. I shall return there shortly."

Maude Carradine made tea while Charles Lowry and I sat by the dying fire. Since the gentleman seemed preoccupied with his own gloomy thoughts, I endeavoured to cheer him up by asking about upcoming productions at the Florentine. Indeed, my strategy worked, as he began to describe in detail a new drama that was being rehearsed. While he spoke, I thought of Holmes, outside in the gloom of the day, no doubt compiling the facts of the case so as to solve the riddle of this remarkable intruder. For, despite my earlier apprehension that Maude Carradine was experiencing a genuine haunting, I had returned to my senses, and now believed that there was nothing unnatural on display. A human hand was responsible for these strange alterations to the interior of the house, and nothing more.

Our tea concluded, Holmes had not yet returned from his outside jaunt. Mr. Lowry was still talking of the theatre and its upcoming production, but he had now turned his gaze to Maude, sitting across from us on a chair with Oriental upholstery, an expression of apprehension on her face. He looked at her the way a gourmand looks at a laden banquet table. I understood him to be in love, and while it was evident that Maude Carradine might not feel entirely the same way, she was obviously amenable to his company. At last, just as our hostess suggested another cup of tea, and possibly a slice of seed cake, we all heard Sherlock Holmes coming back into the house through the rear door of the kitchen. He entered the room, his coat damp with the mist we could see through the windows, and his eyes lit with intensity. It was a look I recognised, a hunter with his prey easily within reach.

"I am sorry for the delay," Holmes said, standing on the edge of a worn Persian rug. "After observing the outside of this house, I wandered down the road, and was shown to the nearest telegraph office by an enterprising youth. At this very moment, detectives are on their way to arrest your ghost, Miss Carradine. All we need to do is wait."

"Do you mean to tell me that there is an intruder in the house at this very moment?" Miss Carradine had stood up, still holding an empty teacup.

"I mean to tell you that the culprit is in this very room," Holmes said. "I shall say no more for now."

Since all eyes were on my friend, I took the opportunity to cast a glance in the direction of Charles Lowry. His body was rigid with tension and his face unreadable. Surely, I now realised, he must be the culprit. It made perfect sense. He partly owned the Florentine, and it was there that he had developed an affection for the actress in his employ. He had devised a way to make it seem as though Maude Carradine was subject to a haunting, thus allowing himself to be employed as her protector. He had probably arranged for the changing of the locks, making sure to procure for himself copies of all the new keys. All he would need to do was to enter the house quietly in the dead of night and produce evidence of a spectral presence. By this means he was no doubt hoping to scare the young lady into accepting his love. I thought again of beauty, and how it often motivates the extremities of human behaviour.

There was soon a knock on the front door, and Holmes went himself to allow two policemen onto the premises, one as portly as a landlord, the other resembling an ill-fed youth. The portly landlord looked as though he had just woken up from a long slumber, and the ill-fed youth seemed faintly annoyed, as well.

"All right, Guv'nor," he said, "which one of these is the intruder?"

I fully expected Holmes to point to Charles Lowry and declare him to be the architect of Maude Carradine's woes. I had already steeled myself for an unpleasant reaction from such a strong-looking man. Instead, however, Holmes indicated the velvet loveseat, and informed the two detectives that there was where the intruder would be found.

We were all dazed for a moment by his pronouncement. Since I was the one closest to the sofa, I dropped to one knee and peered underneath. I saw nothing but bare floorboards illuminated by the tall windows on the far side of the room. Standing up, I declared, "There is no one there, Holmes."

"I assure you there is," he said. "I believe we will find the intruder if we all take one end of the—"

Holmes stopped speaking because, suddenly, rearing up behind the sofa was the figure of what I mistakenly thought at first to be a young boy. Dressed in trousers and a shirt that both looked as though manufactured from some sort of muslin, head swathed in a tight knit cap, this whirligig flew towards the far end of the sitting room, then let out a piercing high-pitched scream that identified her as a female. I admit that I was stunned by her sudden appearance and felt frozen in place, and from the look of both Maude and Charles Lowry I was not alone. It was only Holmes, unperturbed, who took two nimble steps towards the intruder. She flew at him with surprising speed, and he turned his body at just the right moment so that she missed him with a claw-like hand, tripping over his outstretched leg and hurtling into the waiting arms of the two detectives, who managed to subdue her. What followed was a string of unrecognisable words, their origin seeming to my ear to be Russian, and most likely of a vulgar nature.

"That is Ludmila Fedotik," Maude Carradine said, her voice so calm that I imagined her to be in some kind of shock.

"I thought as much," Holmes said. "She has been living with you in this house for some time, I imagine. And she is not a ghost, as we all can see. But a woman driven to mad jealousy by the death of Ralph Mercer."

The actress's knit cap had come off in her struggle and dark lustrous hair fanned out around her shoulders. She had black eyes, a narrow nose and sharp chin, but I could see that there was some beauty there as well, disguised most likely by temporary insanity.

"How?" Miss Carradine said.

"To begin," Holmes said, "she is a woman just small enough to fit into the inner workings of that theatrical prop you call a loveseat, Miss Carradine."

Our attention turned to the sofa, and Charles Lowry now walked around it and remarked upon a carefully disguised slit in the fabric. This allowed Ludmila Fedotik to access the interior of the furniture and thus to hide undetected in our presence.

At this moment, Miss Fedotik yelled, in English and with no Russian accent that I could detect, "Now you know how Ralph felt, driven to despair by your callousness! He was too good for you!"

Before being taken from the room by the two bewildered police detectives she spat towards the group of us, her black eyes wild and darting like those of a trapped hare. Miss Carradine, walking as though she were held up by nothing more than the stiffness of her frock, went to the back of the sofa to observe the slit through which her antagonist had been coming and going. She opened her mouth as if to speak, but fainted instead, Charles Lowry stepping in and catching her with some ease.

*

The following day, as grey as its predecessors, Holmes and I, back in 221B Baker Street, were reminiscing already about the conclusion of such a remarkable case.

"I suspect she broke into Miss Carradine's house to enact revenge on the woman she believed responsible for Ralph

Mercer's death. It was there that she discovered the oversized sofa, with just enough space inside for her to hide. In fact, the sofa had been used exactly for such purposes during its time on the stage, its hollowness allowing actors to hide and then magically to appear. She, like most Russian actresses, was trained in the circus arts, able to control her body and her appetites in a way that gave her the discipline to attempt this most sinister crime."

"But what exactly was the crime?" I said. "Did she hope to drive Maude Carradine out of her mind?"

"Presumably, yes. Maybe she hoped that by constantly reminding her prey of the man who had taken his own life rather than live without her, Maude Carradine would make the same choice. Why else would Fedotik draw a hangman's noose on several surfaces in the house except to remind her victim of the death she believed she had caused?"

"And she must never have left the house after first breaking into it, not after the locks were changed."

"There you are wrong, Watson. She was easily able to climb out of any one of the rear-facing windows, leaving them unlocked for her return. I found her very small footprints in the damp soil at the back of Witanhurst House. She would not have done this often, I believe, and probably only when Miss Carradine was away at work. When there was food in the house my guess is that Ludmila Fedotik was able to sustain herself on scraps from the generously stocked larder while she crept around at night, leaving evidence of a ghost.

"And while Miss Carradine was away, Miss Fedotik would have had free range. Even more so because of all the locks that had been installed. She would have heard Miss Carradine's approach and have had ample time to return to her hiding place within the sofa."

"But what of the note left on the bedside table?"

"It was a note originally written by Ralph Mercer to Ludmila Fedotik. Ludmila, of course, is often shortened to Mila, and that is why he addressed her simply as M. She must have realised that the note could be used to convince Miss Carradine that she was subject to a haunting."

"And because the line from *Lear* in the note – 'nothing comes from nothing' – is spoken to Cordelia you asked Miss Carradine the identity of the actress who played Cordelia?"

"Well, Watson, I am no expert on the practicalities of stage craft, but I recalled that when casting *King Lear* it is important always to have the smallest available female play the role of Cordelia. I learned this from an article I read a number of years ago in the *Daily Telegraph*. An actress playing Cordelia was seriously injured when she was dropped by a rather frail octogenarian actor playing Lear, tasked with carrying Cordelia's lifeless body across the stage. The scribe who penned the article made the point that the only serious consideration in casting the part of Cordelia should be her size and weight, and it was a theatrical detail that fortunately stuck with me.

"You see, Watson, very early on in this case I realised that the ghost haunting Witanhurst House must in fact be an intruder that lived inside the house. It was the only logical explanation. And such an intruder would ideally be of a small size. That is the chain of thinking that led me to wonder who played Cordelia in that ill-fated production of *King Lear*."

*

It was over three months later that I attended the premiere of a new play at the Florentine, a rather delightful comedy called *Black-Eyed Susan*, in which Maude Carradine, now engaged to Charles Lowry, played the titular role. I had thought I could entice Holmes to attend the play with me, now that we were so familiar with the theatrical arts due to the adventure of what I was calling the Witanhurst Ghost. But Holmes, who was never particularly interested in the theatre, turned down my invitation, and I attended alone, enjoying the night despite his notable absence.

THE LAST BAKER STREET ADVENTURE

DAVID STUART DAVIES

With the arrival of the twentieth century, and all the changes that it brought to society in general and to London life in particular, my friend Mr. Sherlock Holmes grew progressively disenchanted with his lot. It was as though the death of the Queen in 1901 signalled the end of an era, a time when he functioned easily and successfully in the great city. This world, which had been familiar and comfortable to him in the latter half of the nineteenth century, was slowly disappearing. "I am beginning to feel like a fossil in my own city," he observed when in one of his low moods. Added to this, clients, and particularly those with intriguing and challenging problems, were less numerous. London was now awash with private enquiry agents and, despite his illustrious reputation, Holmes was not always the first court of appeal for those troubled souls seeking help. A further shadow increased the darkness in his life when I moved out of Baker Street.

As I have observed elsewhere, Holmes was a man of habits, narrow and concentrated habits, and I had become one of them. I was a whetstone to his mind and as such I stimulated his thought processes. My erroneous conclusions often served to make his own flame-like intuitions burst forth the more vividly and swiftly. Thus I was aware that I constituted a reassuring presence in those comfortable rooms at 221B Baker Street and that my absence would dismay him greatly, despite my assurances that I would remain in close contact at all times.

However, for some time I had been itching to return to general practice, to pursue some beneficial activity during those increasing lulls between Holmes's investigations. When a practice, which included modest living quarters, came up for sale in Queen Anne Street, I bought it, and moved there in late 1902. This move coincided with the increasingly close relationship I had with the lady who was to become the second Mrs. Watson.

It was not very long afterwards that Holmes declared his intention to retire. He professed that he had grown dissatisfied with the gloom of London and had begun to yearn for the soothing life of nature away from the smoke and noise of the metropolis. At first, I was not fully convinced by this statement, believing that one of his black moods, prompted by his lack of cases, had produced this revolutionary decision. How well I remembered his old claim, "Give me problems, give me work, give me the most abstruse cryptogram, or the most intricate analysis and I am in my own proper atmosphere." And, to me, his proper atmosphere was London. When we first met, I saw a man who loved to dwell in the very centre of five million people, with his filaments stretching out and running through them, responsive to every little rumour or suspicion of unsolved crime. But, of course, that had been well over twenty years ago, and now there was an unmistakable note of sincerity in his claim about moving to the country that unnerved me a little. I prayed that some challenging investigation would come along and shake him out of this malaise.

Less than a month after this outburst, he sent me a telegram: "Dine with me this evening. I have good news." I was most surprised at receiving such a missive. It was so uncharacteristic of Holmes, a man to whom simple social occasions were anathema. As I travelled in the hansom en route to Baker Street, I wondered what the good news was that my friend had to impart. I sensed that it would not be good for me.

Mrs. Hudson had prepared a simple supper and we dined in easy companionship, discussing old cases in the main. I did not press Holmes to explain the reason behind this reunion. I knew him well enough to be aware that he would do so in his own good time. It was after the meal as we sat in our old chairs, cigars and brandy at hand, that Holmes revealed his dramatic decision.

"I have purchased a cottage in Sussex, on the Downs. It has a splendid view of the Channel. It is there I will rest my weary bones and eke out the rest of my days."

Despite all the hints that had come before, I was struck dumb. Was it really true that this unique, vibrant individual who had turned the detection of crime into an art form was going to desert his profession and rusticate in the country?

Holmes smiled beatifically. "I intend to keep bees. I find these creatures fascinating. I shall be most content in my rural idyll. I do hope that your medical and domestic duties will allow you to come down and visit me occasionally."

"You are really going ahead with this… this venture?"

"Indeed I am, old fellow. I leave Baker Street in a fortnight."

"A fortnight!"

Holmes chuckled. "You are getting into the habit of repeating my utterances."

"So soon," I said quietly, shaking my head. "I'm sorry. It is rather difficult to take all this in."

"Nothing lasts forever, my dear Watson. There are seasons in a man's life as there are in nature and one must accept the change. Spring will turn to summer and autumn to winter. I stand at the brink of the sere and yellow stage of my existence and I know it is time to move on."

I cannot deny that a wave of sadness crashed down upon me at the realisation that Holmes was deadly serious about the move, and about relinquishing his detective career for a quiet life in the country.

"Well," I said, my throat tightening with emotion, "if you have made up your mind and it is what you really desire, I wish you well." I raised my glass to my friend and he reciprocated the gesture. I looked around the room, our old quarters, with the chemical bench, the crowded mantelpiece where Holmes's correspondence was transfixed with his old jack knife, and the shelf with his files. It somehow shimmered before me, provoking so many memories.

"I shall miss this place," I said.

"Oh, believe me, Watson, so shall I, but in essence this room and the stories it recalls will still live here." He tapped the side of his forehead.

"Cheap rooms at a cheap price, eh?" I said wistfully.

Holmes chuckled. "Well, I am still resident here for another couple of weeks, so please feel free to drop in at any time."

"Of course, and I shall be here on your final day to give you the grand send-off."

Sometime later, as I prepared to leave, Holmes took my arm. "Let me accompany you to the door," he said quietly. As we descended the seventeen steps to the hall, there was a sudden loud banging at the front door.

"Rather late for a visitor," I observed casually.

"Certainly too late for one of Mrs. Hudson's cronies," said Holmes gloomily. "That knocking can only mean one thing, I'm afraid: a client. I have no wish to entertain such a creature now. That was part of my old life."

"Nonsense, Holmes," I replied hotly. "As long as you are resident at this address, this is your life."

With a sullen gesture, my friend opened the door. There on the threshold stood a tall lady, whose wild eyes and strained features clearly illustrated her distress.

"Thank heavens," she cried, almost falling into the hallway. "I desperately need your help." Her eyes flashed between the two of us, uncertain which was the man she was seeking.

"I am Sherlock Holmes," he said in answer to her unspoken dilemma. "Come, let us retire to my sitting room, where you can regain your composure and tell me the nature of your problem."

"Thank you, thank you," the lady said with relief.

*

Revived by a tot of brandy, our late-night visitor was ready to explain the reason for her dramatic *cri de coeur*. She was a handsome woman whom I judged to be somewhere in her mid-thirties. Her clothes and manner spoke of wealth and station. She also carried with her an aroma of expensive perfume.

"My husband has been arrested for murder. A murder he did not commit." It was a dramatic statement expressed with deep emotion and she let it hang in the air for a time. Glancing at my friend, I recognised that flicker of the eyes I had observed many times before, clearly indicating that his interest had been aroused.

"Please explain. Give me all the details."

The lady nodded and closed her eyes briefly, as though trying to clear her mind in readiness for her recital.

"I am Leonora Bradley. My husband is Anthony Bradley, the artist. Earlier this evening the police came to our home and arrested him for murder."

"The murder of whom?" asked Holmes, steepling his fingers.

"His brother, William."

"What were the circumstances?"

"William lives nearby and late this afternoon his manservant, who had been out for the day, discovered his dead body in the sitting room. He had been shot – murdered."

"What prompted the police to suspect your husband?"

"They found Anthony's monogrammed handkerchief at the scene of the crime with blood on it. In searching our home, the police discovered a pistol in my husband's dressing room with one bullet having been fired. I have to say that it was well known that there was great animosity between the brothers."

"What was the cause of this animosity?"

Mrs. Bradley paused before replying. "It was connected with the family inheritance. When their father died some three years ago, he left his entire estate to his eldest son, William, his favourite, with the instruction that he should provide Anthony with an annual allowance. My father-in-law, a strict man of business, did not approve of my husband's profession as an artist. He maintained that it was no way for a man to earn a living. William, on the other hand, took over the reins of the family business – a small but profitable building firm. Unfortunately, old man Bradley did not stipulate the sum for this allowance and as a result William provided us with only a pittance. He took great pleasure in seeing his brother struggle financially, while his own wealth increased steadily. There were many rows concerning this matter, but my poor husband always emerged the loser, both emotionally and financially. We have consulted a number of lawyers to see if this matter could be rectified, but have been assured that William's actions, while morally questionable, are legally watertight."

"With the death of your husband's brother, I assume the estate will revert to him," I observed.

"Yes," the lady agreed, with a gentle nod. "Certainly, the police believe this was the motive that drove my husband to murder."

"Well, it is not a very practical way of achieving this state of affairs – ending the man's life in such a melodramatic and obvious fashion," said Holmes softly, almost as if speaking to himself. "Tell me, Mrs. Bradley, have you any notion who might have killed your brother-in-law?"

"I have no idea. But I do know my husband is innocent. He couldn't harm a fly."

"There is no one else who could benefit from William's death?"

"Not that I know of."

"He had no family? A wife?"

Mrs. Bradley shook her head.

"No competitor in the building trade who would benefit from the firm's failure?"

"Well, I know of a rival builder who is often in competition with William's company for contracts, but it seems unlikely that he would go to the extreme of…"

"Quite. Nevertheless, all avenues must be considered. Who is he?"

"Sam Mellor. His business is located in Highgate."

Holmes scribbled details down on his cuff. "Who is the inspector in charge of this investigation?"

"A man called Sullivan. A brutish sort of fellow whose manners were brusque and bordering on the rude."

Holmes pursed his lips. "One of the new breed, Watson. Ambitious, ruthless, but often lacking finesse."

"I know my husband is innocent. My gentle Anthony is incapable of such an act! I appeal to you for assistance. I am convinced that you can prove he did not commit this crime. I have no other hope, Mr. Holmes. Will you help me?"

Holmes cast a glance in my direction before responding. I was aware instinctively of what he was thinking. I knew he could not refuse the challenge. His *raison d'être* was to respond to such dramatic requests. It was not merely out of sympathy for the client's dilemma – indeed, I suspected this was the least of his concerns – but because his detective juices had been aroused. Here was a puzzle that he could not resist, and he knew it was likely to be his last case in Baker Street.

*

After the lady had gone, Holmes requested that I make a long arm and reach down for his gazetteer, a file containing details of crimes, criminals, notable events and biographical details of figures of interest.

"You are obviously looking up the artist Anthony Bradley," I said.

"Excellent deduction, old fellow," Holmes acknowledged with a smile.

He pored over the volume for a few minutes before snapping it shut.

"Anything?"

Holmes shrugged. "He has exhibited a few times at the Royal Academy, but it would seem that his paintings – mainly rural scenes – lack the power and finesse of a really skilled artist. One critic referred to his work as 'mundane'. It would be safe to say that he is not a particularly successful painter."

"Oh dear."

"Indeed. One can understand how he needed this meagre allowance of his. He was married five years ago after meeting

Miss Leonora Coulson when they were both members of an amateur theatrical society."

"Not the history of a cold-hearted killer."

"On the contrary, Watson, he may well be an ideal candidate for the role. A poor, resentful, sensitive artist with a flair for the dramatic could easily be driven to murder," observed Holmes as he reached out languidly for his violin.

*

Early the following morning Holmes visited Scotland Yard to see Inspector Sullivan. I accompanied my friend. I had no intention of missing out on Holmes's final case. I had, in fact, closed my surgery for a few days in order that I should be able to follow him in his investigations. The ease with which he accepted my suggestion reassured me that he was happy to have my company.

Inspector Sullivan was very much as Mrs. Bradley had described him. He was bullish, curt rather than brisk, and showed neither respect nor courtesy to my friend. The fact that the illustrious Sherlock Holmes was interested in his case obviously made no difference to him.

"You shouldn't waste your time, Holmes. We have the culprit in the cells. No doubt about it. Case closed," he crowed.

Holmes smiled urbanely. "I am sure you are correct, Inspector, but for my own peace of mind there are certain 'i's that I should like to see dotted and a few 't's I should like to see crossed. I certainly have no intention of interfering with your investigation. All I ask are a few small favours."

Sullivan seemed intrigued. "What are they?"

"Is it possible to see the murder weapon?"

"Yes. I have it here in my desk drawer."

Within seconds he had produced the pistol, which Holmes studied thoroughly, at one point holding it close to his face. He smiled, nodded, and handed it back to the inspector.

"Is that all?" said Sullivan.

"I should very much like to have a word or two with the accused man."

Sullivan smirked. "A bit pointless, but it's no skin off my nose. I'll get one of the constables to take you down to the cells."

*

"We used to complain about Lestrade and Gregson being short-sighted and self-opinionated in the old days, Watson, but they were never as crass as that fellow," Holmes whispered to me as we made our way to the prison cells in the bowels of Scotland Yard.

Anthony Bradley was a cringing, sad creature. He lay huddled on the straw matting, his longish hair a tangle of brown curls, and he barely moved when we entered his cell.

"Come on, rouse yourself, mate!" barked the constable. "There's two gents here to speak with you."

Slowly Bradley unfurled himself and sat up, blinking hard at us in the gloom, his eyes struggling to focus.

"Your wife has asked me to try and help you. My name is Sherlock Holmes."

"Oh, my God!" he cried. "Thank you. Thank you. Believe me... I didn't do it. I did not..." He clasped his long fingers to his face and began sobbing.

"If we are to progress," Holmes snapped sharply, "you must pull yourself together and let me know the facts of the matter clearly and concisely."

My friend's stern words had a sobering effect. Bradley wiped away his tears with his shirt sleeve and made a determined effort to control his emotions. Despite this, I could not help feeling that he was, in essence, a weak, rather pathetic individual. Certainly not a man with the hardened soul of a brutal murderer.

"I went to see my brother yesterday afternoon," he said haltingly. "My visit was prompted by my wife. Our funds were terribly low again and she urged me to make another attempt to persuade William to increase my allowance. Of course, as I suspected, he was in no mood to comply with my pleas. I literally begged him, but all he did was sneer at me. I left empty-handed and dejected. But believe me, at no time did I threaten him, and I did not shoot him."

"Did you have a pistol with you at the time?"

Bradley shook his head. "Of course not. Why would I?"

"Why do you own a pistol?"

"It was a youthful purchase when I was a boy. I used to shoot tin cans off the garden wall for amusement." He gave a shrug. "I haven't used it for years – in fact I had forgotten I still possessed it. That is the truth, Mr. Holmes."

"And yet one bullet had been fired from it. How do you explain that?"

"I cannot."

"And the handkerchief found by the body? Did you perhaps drop it during your visit?"

Another shake of the head. "No. I still have the one I carried yesterday." He slipped his hand into his trouser pocket and produced a handkerchief, spreading it out on his knee so that we could observe his initials embroidered in the corner.

"So, if you are innocent, who did shoot your brother in cold blood?"

"I wish I knew. I've been racking my brains to come up with an answer to that."

"What about the builder Mellor? We gather he was a rival of your brother."

"Sam Mellor? No, I cannot see him going to such violent lengths to get the upper hand in the building trade. He is a fairly decent man as far as I know. I have only met him once."

Holmes pursed his lips. "Your wife told us that William had no other family or... a sweetheart."

"No more."

"No more? Explain."

"William was for a time engaged to a young lady, but he broke it off. But this was a while ago – some twelve months or so."

"What was the reason for this?"

"I do not know for certain, but my wife was of the opinion that my brother thought his betrothed's motivations were exclusively monetary, rather than driven by affection."

"What is the name of this lady?"

"Daisy Sommerville. She resides with her mother at 31 Priam Gardens, Chelsea."

As we left the cell, Holmes turned to the pitiful figure of Anthony Bradley, cowering in the gloom. "There are many dark corners to this case that need illuminating, but I have a strong belief that you did not shoot your brother. And I have hopes to bring the truth to light before long."

The artist responded with a brave smile, words failing him.

"A sad creature," I observed, as we made our way out of Scotland Yard.

"Indeed. I cannot see him having the courage or raising sufficient anger to pull the trigger."

"But strong emotions can often, on the spur of the moment, lead to desperate acts."

"Indeed, Watson. But the murder of William Bradley was not a spur-of-the-moment affair. The killer had planned to carry out the murder, bringing a pistol along especially for the purpose."

"So, our only other possible suspects are this builder fellow, Sam Mellor, and the former fiancée, Daisy."

Holmes pursed his lips and gave me a swift glance. "So it would seem. We shall need to see them both, but beforehand I would like to inspect the scene of the crime."

*

It was with no difficulty that we persuaded the constable on duty at William Bradley's house to show us the sitting room where the murder had occurred. Indeed, the red-faced fellow felt privileged to be of some assistance to 'the great Sherlock Holmes'. My friend roamed the sitting room, magnifying glass in hand. He paid particular attention to the area where the body had lain, indicated by a dark patch of dried blood. I stood by the door while Holmes carried out his investigations. He examined the ashtray, then scooped up some small item near the doorway and slipped it into his pocket.

"It is interesting," my friend said, returning to my side,

"that we were told this was a bachelor household and yet I have detected the imprints of a lady's shoes on the carpet. A fact that opens new possibilities."

"The only lady in the case is Daisy Sommerville, William Bradley's former fiancée."

"So you say, Watson. Perhaps it would be enlightening to have words with her."

As we travelled by cab to Priam Gardens, I asked Holmes if he had gleaned any other points of interest from his examination of William Bradley's sitting room. My friend placed his gloved forefinger to his lips before replying, "A trinket of sorts which may turn the tables on this case, but I'd rather say no more until I have collected further data."

Daisy Sommerville was a very petite young woman with delicate china-doll features but in possession of a self-confident demeanour. She was in no way discomfited to have two men sitting opposite her in the living room of her private quarters in the family home, intent on making enquiries regarding her former fiancé and his death. It was her mother who had answered the door and she was at first reluctant to allow us entry, but Holmes quickly put her mind at ease and persuaded her that if we could have some private words with her daughter, it would help to prevent a more formal visit by the police.

Miss Sommerville sat demurely before us, a questioning look on those neat features.

"You may have read in the morning paper of the death of William Bradley."

She nodded. "Yes. It is terrible. We were no longer in communication, but it saddened me to learn of the tragedy."

"You had not seen Mr. Bradley – visited him recently?"

"Oh, no. When he broke off our engagement, he made it clear that he wanted nothing more to do with me."

"That seems very harsh. What was the reason for the rift in your relationship?"

The lady gave a sardonic smile. "I suppose that issue is of importance now. It was simply that I made the mistake of enquiring of him the date of our wedding. In fact, I pressed him on the matter. That did not please him. We had been engaged for some time, you understand. He was quite happy to parade me around as his betrothed, a young lady on his arm, which gave him a certain acceptance in polite society, but, as I was to learn to my dismay, he did not harbour any plans for taking the matter further. As he explained in our final interview, he had no intention of, to use his phrase, 'saddling himself with a wife with all the personal restrictions and financial commitments such an arrangement would incur'." She smiled. "I remember the words exactly."

"The man was a bounder," I found myself commenting instinctively.

Miss Sommerville glanced in my direction and her sardonic smile broadened. "That is one of the politest terms to be applied to Mr. William Bradley."

"He must have made you very angry," suggested Holmes.

"Very! And humiliated. However, I now see that I had a fortunate escape."

"His treatment of you must have prompted thoughts of revenge."

"Of course it did. I…" She paused, her eyes flashing, and then suddenly she seemed amused at my friend's implication. "Ah, I see what you are hinting at there, Mr. Holmes. Spurned fiancée resorts to murder in vengeful rage. I am sorry to disappoint you. I certainly would not place myself in the role of murderer. I am more sensible. My life was damaged but I had no intention of ruining it completely by becoming a killer. William Bradley washed his hands of me, and I have now washed my hands of William Bradley. And anyway, why would I wait twelve months before carrying out the deed?"

"Some say that revenge is a dish best served cold," Holmes observed casually.

"A cliché without real substance. I'll throw one back at you. Strike while the iron is hot. Well, sir, I can assure you that the iron is stone cold."

Holmes smiled in appreciation of the woman's wit. "When was the last time you saw William Bradley?"

This question prompted a hesitation. Miss Sommerville's eyelids fluttered nervously. It was as though Holmes had touched a nerve.

"Before you reply, may I suggest that it was yesterday?"

She started with surprise, but saw that denial was a hopeless strategy. "How on earth do you know?"

"Your shoes. Those wedged heels leave a strong, distinctive indentation on a thick carpet. I observed many such indentations in William Bradley's sitting room."

"Well… yes, I admit that I visited him yesterday."

"The day of the murder."

"Yes."

"And yet you have just told me that you had not seen him for a long time, that you had washed your hands of the man."

"And so I have. The meeting was at his request – his insistence."

"Please elucidate."

"He had been badgering me for some time, sending me notes, threatening missives. He wanted me to return the engagement ring. I had been determined to keep it. It was the only beautiful thing that emerged from my unfortunate alliance with this man. He protested that once the engagement was over, the property should revert to him. In the end I grew tired of being bombarded with these letters, which became more threatening. Eventually, common sense overrode any sentimentality. I reasoned that if I did give in to his demands and returned the ring, the letters would stop and my connection with Mr. William Bradley would be severed once and for all. So I agreed to go to his house and hand it over."

"It must have been strange to see your old fiancé after a year?"

"I had no feelings about it. It was a very brief and businesslike meeting. We were both civilised and stoic."

"He offered you no kind words, no feelings of gratitude that you had returned the ring?"

Miss Sommerville smiled. "He was not that kind of man, Mr. Holmes. And I would not have welcomed such gestures. There were no strong emotions aroused in either of us, and I assure you I did not pull a revolver from my reticule and shoot him."

"Have you any thoughts as to who carried out the deed?"

"I can think of no one."

"You know his brother Anthony has been accused of the murder and has been arrested."

A strange look came over Miss Sommerville's face at the mention of Anthony Bradley. "The idea is laughable," she observed with a sneer. "Anthony doesn't have the backbone to carry out such a desperate act. He can't even stand up to his own wife!"

"Really?" observed Holmes.

It was a prompt on which Miss Sommerville picked up. "He is dominated by his wife, or so it appeared to me. She was very subtle about it in public, but it was clear to me that Anthony was her marionette and she was pulling the strings."

*

"A formidable young woman," I observed after we left the house in Chelsea.

"A formidable actress, more like," returned Holmes. "She is not the bold, self-assured creature she would have us believe."

"Oh, why do you say that?"

"Anyone whose fingernails are bitten down to the quick is certainly of a somewhat nervous disposition. I also observed, partly hidden behind a vase of flowers on the sideboard, a bottle of Crampton's Nerve Tonic. A medication, no doubt, that helped her present herself as a confident young woman. She certainly rose to the occasion in our interview, but it was a controlled performance. The constant wringing of her hands in her lap bore witness to her nervous tension."

"I did not observe... she completely fooled me. However, if she is able to repress her insecurities for a short time with the assistance of drugs and self-restraint, is it not possible for her to gain enough courage to commit murder?"

Holmes gave me a gentle pat on the back. "Well done, Watson. That is our dilemma."

"Did you believe her remarks concerning Anthony Bradley and his wife?"

"That, I think, is at the nub of this affair. However, as we have seen before, outsiders do not always interpret facts accurately. It could well be that Anthony Bradley excels in presenting himself as a somewhat put-upon figure."

I was not sure what Holmes meant by this cryptic statement, but I did not press him on the matter for I knew he would explain things in his own good time. "So," I said, "what now?"

"A visit to a certain builder named Sam Mellor."

*

Mellor was a bluff, ruddy-faced fellow with wild thinning ginger hair. As we entered his office, he was studying a sheet of paper spread across the length of his desk. It was obviously an architect's plan for some very large structure. He looked up as we approached, an expression of irritation clouding his features.

"What is it, gentlemen?" he snapped. "I am a very busy man. My secretary tells me you are here to make enquiries about William Bradley. What's he been up to now? Going behind my back with a cheaper estimate, no doubt. He does that, y'know. Says he can do the job cheaper than me and then when papers are signed he finds some 'unforeseen' snag which virtually doubles the bill. Villain." Mellor paused, mopped his brow and cooled his temper. "So, gentlemen," he said at length, "what do you want to know?"

"We shall not take up much of your valuable time,"

Holmes assured him suavely. "Could you inform us of the last occasion you saw Mr. Bradley?"

Mellor screwed up his face in a pantomime of distaste. "Can't say. I know that I have no wish to see him again."

"It's unlikely you will," observed Holmes. "He was murdered yesterday."

Mellor's eyes widened with shock, an emotion that seemed genuine to me.

"Murdered. Who by?" he croaked.

"That has yet to be determined."

"I see. Well, why the devil have you come to me?" He paused dramatically as a thought struck him. "Great heavens, you're not thinking I had anything to do with it, are you?"

"That also has yet to be determined, Mr. Mellor, but at least you could tell us the truth."

"The truth?"

"You already knew that Bradley was dead. You were fully aware that he was murdered. Today's newspaper in the wastepaper basket by your desk would have told you that. And the other truth is that you visited William Bradley yesterday."

Mellor froze, his features stiffening, and there was a look of fear in his eyes.

"Don't deny it," said Holmes. It was clear from the man's demeanour that my friend's claim was accurate and protestations to the contrary would be futile.

Mellor's shoulders sank and he shook his head in dismay. "How do you know?" he asked, his voice rasping with apprehension.

Holmes picked up the ashtray from the desk and pointed at two dark cigarette stubs resting there.

"Russian cigarettes. A rare, imported brand. You smoked one in William Bradley's sitting room when you visited him yesterday, leaving a stub behind in his ashtray."

"So what if I did? It doesn't mean I killed the man."

"I am not suggesting you did, but I am curious to know why you lied to me," said Holmes smoothly.

"It's obvious, isn't it? I didn't want to become a suspect in this affair. It is well known we were enemies – that there was bad blood between us. My presence in his house on the day he was killed would make me an easy target."

"Why did you visit him?" I asked.

Mellor's features darkened. "He'd been up to his old tricks again. We had the go-ahead for a small factory in Hendon and the contract had already been drawn up. Then Bradley went to the firm and offered them a cheaper deal. The unscrupulous villain. I went to threaten him to back off."

"Threaten him with what?" said Holmes.

Mellor paused. "I knew we hadn't a legal leg to stand on – so, I'm ashamed to say, I threatened him with violence. I told him that if he went ahead, he had better watch his back. Believe me, it was an empty gesture. I had no intention of carrying out the threat. I just hoped that it might frighten him."

"What did he say?"

"He laughed in my face. Yes, I confess it crossed my mind that I could have killed him there and then if I'd had a weapon with me, but… I just left. I determined then to play him at his own game and go to the firm and offer to lower my price below his. Now it seems I don't have to do that. Believe me, I did not kill that charlatan, but I am glad that he is dead."

*

"Do you believe him?" I asked Holmes as we made our way back to Baker Street in a hansom.

My friend narrowed his eyes. "Well, he lied to us about seeing Bradley yesterday… There is rather a lot of dissembling in this case. A fog of lies is veiling the truth. This is certainly a three-pipe problem. Silence and an ounce of the strongest shag tobacco should help me juggle the various facts, untruths and misdirections, so as to compose a clearer picture."

And so it was that once we had reached Baker Street, Holmes flung off his overcoat, wrapped himself up in his mouse-coloured dressing gown and puffed heartily on his old briar, filling the room with his own brand of domestic fog. I knew better than to interfere with him. Sitting some distance from the belching fumes, I contented myself with reading a biography of General Gordon, which I had selected from Holmes's bookshelf.

With the warmth of the room, my familiar chair and the rigours of the day, a tiredness soon overcame me. The printed pages began to blur and I sensed myself nodding, when I was suddenly brought back to full consciousness by a cry from Holmes. He had risen quickly from his chair, his features bright with excitement.

"I think I have it!" he cried. "Just a few more brush strokes and the picture is complete."

"What…" I began, but he cut me short.

"Not yet, Watson. Be patient. To round things off, I need to have further words with Mrs. Bradley. Come. The game's afoot!"

*

On arriving at the Bradley residence, a fairly smart town house in Islington, we were shown into the sitting room by a plump little maid with rosy cheeks and an attractive Irish accent. Leonora Bradley, who was resting on a chaise longue apparently reading a book, seemed quite surprised to see us. She jumped to her feet at our entrance, her eyes wide with expectation.

"You have news?" she said.

Holmes nodded in the affirmative, but his features remained stern. "Indeed I do, but I am afraid it is not news which will please or comfort you."

"What on earth do you mean?" she cried.

"My investigations have led me to identify the murderer of your brother-in-law."

On hearing this statement, Leonora Bradley's eyelids flickered erratically and her body stiffened. "Thank heavens," she said, her voice emerging as a hoarse, uneasy whisper. "Who... who is the culprit?"

Holmes paused, a faint smile on his lips. "It is you, my dear Mrs. Bradley. It is you."

The lady gave a sharp laugh. "Don't be ridiculous. Is this some kind of joke...?"

"I speak in deadly earnest," replied Holmes coolly.

"This is madness. And you call yourself a detective!"

"Indeed, I do call myself a detective, for the moment at least. During this investigation it has become clear to me in meeting your husband and from other information I have gleaned that you were right in your affirmation when you stated that he 'couldn't harm a fly'. You should not have pressed this point so forcefully, especially when you wanted me to find him guilty of the crime."

"Nonsense! That is an outrageous assertion. I came to you for help."

"You came to me hoping that I would prove that your husband was a murderer. How could I not when you provided the clues that clearly indicated his guilt? There was the bloodstained monogrammed handkerchief discovered so conveniently near the dead man. However, your husband was still in possession of his own handkerchief when we visited him in his cell. There was also the murder weapon placed in your home so that the police would have little difficulty in finding it. No murderer would be so careless. It was clear to me that you handled the gun yourself. When I examined it at Scotland Yard, I could still smell traces of that perfume of yours. White Jasmine, I believe. A complex spiced fragrance with a predominant note of ambergris. It was very much as though you had left your signature on the weapon."

Leonora Bradley stared open-mouthed at Holmes, having momentarily lost the power of speech.

"And then there was this," said Holmes as he deftly pulled an envelope from his inside jacket pocket and extracted a small pearl. "I found it at the scene of the crime. It matches the seed pearls which adorned the outfit you wore when you visited me in Baker Street yesterday. A fatal clue left close to the body of William Bradley."

"If all this were true, why would I come to you to solve the murder?"

"Ah well, that was indeed your biggest mistake. You no doubt thought that you had laid the guilt so clearly at your husband's door that even I would have to agree with the police that he was the murderer. What greater evidence to the world that he was the guilty man than to have it confirmed by the great Sherlock Holmes? Your husband's execution would leave you to reap the rich rewards of his inheritance, allowing you to indulge yourself in many ways, such as buying extravagant perfumes and even more stylish and expensive clothes. You had long ago lost patience with your husband, his failing prospects as an artist, his inability to stand up to his brother. You were desperate for the wealth that was denied you by William Bradley's miserly treatment. He was your stumbling block."

"Yes, yes, he was," she snapped viciously, her features now harsh and strained. "He was a cold-hearted, tight-fisted worm. I am glad he's dead. And I'm glad that I was the instrument of his demise."

"It is a high price to pay."

"Not if I had got away with it," she said soberly, dabbing her eyes, which had freshly dewed with tears.

"You hoped to kill two birds with one stone. Eliminating William was only one part of the plan. Implicating your husband in the murder would also rid you of a tiresome burden. You would be wealthy and free."

Leonora Bradley sat down slowly on the chaise longue, her hands resting gently in her lap. "He was a great disappointment to me. A spineless creature." She now spoke softly, drained of all emotion.

"The truth is that if you had not come to me for help, you might have succeeded in your cruel machinations. I suspect it was arrogance on your part."

She nodded slowly and gazed at my friend with empty eyes. "You are right, Mr. Holmes. I was trying to use you to establish firmly that Anthony had committed the murder. With your declaration, who would question his guilt?"

"In doing so, you rather over-egged the pudding and, indeed, underestimated me. A failing that has trapped many a malefactor."

*

Later that evening, Leonora Bradley was housed in the cells at Scotland Yard, while her distraught husband was released.

"One heading for the pit of despair, the other en route to the gallows. A very unhappy case," observed my friend as we emerged into the cool air of the evening.

"But a successful one," I added.

Holmes suggested we take a late supper at Simpson's. "It may well be the last time we dine together for a long while."

As we lingered over the fish pie and a fine bottle of Montrachet, I raised the topic of the Bradley case. Holmes took a sip of wine and then, holding the glass before him, he stared at the light shimmering on the pale liquid, a faraway expression in his eyes. He was silent for a moment, lost in thought, then returned to me.

"To be frank, Watson, I suspected Leonora Bradley from the first," he said, replacing the glass on the table. "Her fine clothes and rich perfume told me that here was a lady who craved the good life, one which she was financially ill-fitted to enjoy. She was living beyond her means. It was obvious that William Bradley's unfair treatment of his brother, her husband, regarding the allowance rankled her greatly. To her mind, the only solution was to eliminate the fellow and then all the money would land in her lap."

I nodded. "I see that now. It takes a very cruel woman to implicate her husband in the way she did."

"Indeed. In essence she was planning two murders."

I shuddered at the thought.

"Of course," Holmes continued, "we were presented with two possible suspects and I would have been failing in my duty if I did not at least consider them. Daisy Sommerville had a motive, but if she had desired to kill William Bradley she would not have waited a year to do it. Besides, she was of too nervous a disposition to carry out such an act."

"What of Mellor?"

"He is a bluff businessman and it was clear to me on meeting him that he held a commonsensical attitude to life. Killing one rival would not really ease his way in the competitive commercial world. He appeared a possible culprit, I suppose, but to my mind he did not remove Leonora Bradley from her position as my prime suspect."

"And you were right."

Holmes sighed. "Yes, but it gives me little pleasure. It only reminds me of the miasma of evil and violence that envelops the life of a consulting detective. It makes me even more desirous to leave this dark city. I shall be happy to shuffle off this metropolitan coil and breathe the less tainted air of the countryside."

I raised my glass. "Well, I trust you will find contentment there. In the meantime, I toast your success in your last Baker Street adventure."

Holmes smiled. We clinked glasses and drank.

*

A week later, with a heavy heart, I arrived at Baker Street. It was the day of my friend's departure. A new life awaited him on the Sussex Downs. A red-eyed Mrs. Hudson let me in. We did not exchange words. We both knew what we were thinking and feeling.

Our old Baker Street lodgings were almost unrecog-nisable. Apart from a few sticks of furniture belonging to Mrs. Hudson, the sitting room was bare: the books, the chemical bench, the numerous files, the old coat rack, the pictures and portraits, the desk crammed with papers were all gone. It was a ghost of a room, containing only memories.

Holmes was standing at the window, gazing at the street below. He was dressed in his country tweeds and an ulster, with an ear-flapped travelling cap on his head – his favourite deerstalker. He turned towards me at my entrance and gave me a warm smile.

"I knew you'd come today."

"How could I not?" I said, my voice emerging from a dry throat.

"I am waiting for the cab to whisk me away."

I nodded, and looked around the room, my eyes landing on the 'VR' picked out in bullet pockmarks on the wall. "We've had some magical times together," I said, "most of which began in these rooms."

"Magical times, indeed," said Holmes, moving towards me. Taking hold of my right arm, he gave it a firm squeeze. "And I am so very glad you were there by my side to share them."

Moments later I was standing on the steps of 221B, my arm around a tearful Mrs. Hudson as Holmes stepped into the waiting cab. In an instant he was off, out of our lives.

A hundred yards down the street, I saw his arm extend from the cab window, clutching his deerstalker. He gave a cheery wave with it before he disappeared from view.

THE ADVENTURE OF
THE THIRD CAB

JAMES LOVEGROVE

It was in September of 1908 that I received from my friend
Sherlock Holmes a rather unusual letter, on notepaper headed
with the address of his retirement residence near Eastbourne.
The missive read as follows:

> *My dear Watson,*
>
> *I should be very grateful if you could take it upon yourself
> to visit me on the coast this Friday. It has been far too long
> since last you and I were together and it would be a great
> pleasure to see your cheery face again, assuming, of course,
> that Mrs. Watson can spare you for a weekend. I should not
> want to deprive that admirable lady of her husband's company
> against her wishes.*
>
> *Provided you are free to come down – and I trust that
> that will be the case – I have a few stipulations.*

First, you are to catch the 2.45pm train from Victoria, which arrives at Eastbourne at 5.12pm. No other train will do.

Second, when it comes to transporting your belongings, in lieu of your trusty old Gladstone bag you are to use a travel suitcase in mushroom-grey leather with two straps. If you do not own such an item already, kindly purchase one matching the description.

Third, be sure to bring with you a watercolour set and easel, which you are to obtain from Adams and Sons on Holborn. You are not to buy these items from any other purveyor of artists' materials.

Fourth, you are to avail yourself of a pair of round spectacles with mauve-tinted lenses, although, since you may find wearing them uncongenial, you need not don them until you reach Eastbourne.

Fifth, once you alight from the train you must furnish yourself with a buttonhole from the flower seller on the station concourse.

Last but not least, when you catch a cab outside the station you should get into the third cab in the rank. This step is crucial. You must not take the first or the second cab, only the third. You will not need to speak to the cabman, and indeed it is better if you do not. He will know what is expected of him.

I appreciate that the above list of requirements entails some financial outlay on your part. I shall of course reimburse you in full for any expenses you incur.

I appreciate, too, that what I am asking of you must seem onerous and irksome, not to say downright queer. I

*would merely crave your indulgence in the matter. All will
be revealed in due course.*

> *Yours in eager anticipation,*
> *Sherlock Holmes*

I showed the letter to my wife, who shook her head and
clucked her tongue, not so much in despair as in tolerant pity.
Such had long been her habit whenever she was confronted with
behaviour that strayed from the norm or – which was often the
same thing – whenever I had dealings with Sherlock Holmes.

"I am surprised Mr. Holmes has not specified what sort
of flower you should choose as your buttonhole, down to the
colour," she said. "Perhaps you should wire him to check."

She was speaking in jest, but in point of fact I had toyed
with the notion of sending Holmes a telegram demanding
that he explain his reasons and threatening not to comply
unless he did. Yet I knew this would be futile. I could predict
his response, which would be a brief, stern rebuke along the
lines of "Do as I tell you, Watson. Have I ever let you down?"

"And round spectacles with mauve-tinted lenses?" my
wife continued. "Those are hardly the height of fashion. It all
seems like some bizarre practical joke."

"I must admit, it is rather perplexing," I said, "even by
Holmes's standards. I am used to him being enigmatic, but
never has he given me so exacting a set of conditions to abide
by as these, and certainly not for a social call."

"Now that I think about it, John, did he not enjoin you to
take a third cab once before?"

"Did he?"

"I believe so. It was during the episode you have dubbed 'The Final Problem'."

"By Jove, you're right, my dear! So he did. Holmes and I were in hot pursuit of Professor Moriarty, and he instructed me to send for a hansom and drive to the Lowther Arcade."

"But your man was to take 'neither the first nor the second which may present itself'."

After we married, my wife had diligently and dutifully undertaken to read all my chronicles of Holmes's investigations to date. Now, somehow, she was better versed in them than the fellow who actually wrote them, to the point where she could not only remember their contents with accuracy but, as evidenced here, quote from them verbatim. I ascribed it to the fact that she was over a decade my junior and therefore blessed with a concomitantly sharper brain. I myself, on the other hand, having by this time reached my mid-fifties, was starting to feel the onset of old age, whose effects included a slight but noticeable diminution of the mental faculties. This may also account for the occasional errors and inconsistencies which, despite my best efforts, had begun slipping into my published output.

"Perhaps we are on the trail of another criminal mastermind as fiendish as Moriarty," I averred.

"Perhaps." My wife's tone was sceptical. "But if so, why does Mr. Holmes not simply say as much?"

"It could be that he feared the letter being intercepted by some hostile agency and his intentions becoming known. I take it that I am permitted to go?"

"You do not need my consent to visit your old friend, John, you know that."

"It does not hurt to seek it, though, does it?"

"Certainly not," replied that inestimable, pretty creature, patting my cheek fondly. "That you are so considerate of my feelings is one of the many reasons why I love you quite as madly as I do, and why my friends are inordinately envious of my choice of mate."

I flushed with tender, husbandly pride. She was no Mary, this second wife of mine, but she came close, and in her comparative youthfulness she made me feel not quite as advanced in years as I was, and likewise with her natural gaiety and gregariousness she saved me from becoming as hidebound and reclusive as I, in common with many a widower, might have.

"Besides," she added, "if the letter is more than a mere invitation to visit and Mr. Holmes really is hunting after some ne'er-do-well, can he manage without his loyal second by his side?"

"That," I replied with a wry nod, "is very true."

*

That Friday, I duly boarded the 2.45 at Victoria, bearing both a mushroom-grey suitcase with two leather straps and an Adams and Sons watercolour set and easel. The London, Brighton and South Coast Railways locomotive, with its handsome umber paintwork, puffed away from the platform, lugging its retinue of olive-green rolling stock behind it. Soon the clutter of the smoke-shrouded, brick-girt capital had given way to clear skies and the serene undulations of the North Downs. After a change of trains at Tunbridge Wells, onward I travelled through the High Weald, and the landscape outside the carriage window grew yet more expansive and rural, the scenery made further pleasing to the eye by the tinges of russet and gold that early autumn was bringing to the trees' foliage. Halts at Groombridge, Mayfield, Hellingly and various other evocatively named small country towns came and went, until at long last Eastbourne loomed.

By that stage, I will allow, a modicum of apprehension had set in. Since Holmes's retirement, he and I rarely embarked on adventures as we had in the old days. He deemed his withdrawal from London life and the relinquishing of his career as a consulting detective to be more or less permanent, a state of self-imposed exile from which little could tempt him to stray. I, as a result, had fallen out of practice when it came to the risks and rigours of crime-solving. If this business with the third cab was connected with the stalking of a Moriarty-esque foe, as seemed at least possible, then the game was once more afoot.

However, whereas before I might have faced the prospect of a potentially hazardous escapade with equanimity, and even with a certain glee, now all I felt was unease. I was conscious that, like the dulled blade of a disused knife, I had lost my keen edge.

With some effort I steeled myself. Whatever awaited me in Eastbourne, I was up to the task. I would surely not be found wanting. So my head insisted, even as my heart continued to cavil.

At the last moment, just as the train was pulling into the station, I remembered about the mauve-tinted spectacles. I fetched them out from a pocket and settled them upon the bridge of my nose. All at once the world was cast in shades of lilac, violet and lavender, which I found oddly agreeable.

Having shown my ticket at the barrier, I made straight for the flower seller's stall, where I was greeted with surprising warmth.

"Hello, sir," said the flower seller. "Nice to see you again. What will it be today?"

I presumed the fellow recognised me from my previous forays to Eastbourne, even though these were infrequent and I had never stopped at his stall before. He evidently had an excellent memory for faces, even those that merely passed him by on the concourse. That or he treated all his customers with the same cheery familiarity.

I selected a fine, creamy white gardenia.

"An excellent choice, sir," said the flower seller as I paid him. "It's the end of the season for the late-blooming varieties. Gardenias will be thin on the ground soon. Make hay while the sun shines, eh?"

With the flower installed in the lapel of my overcoat, I strode outside to the cab rank.

Four broughams stood in a row, and I made straight for the third, in accordance with Holmes's directions. This went against the grain somewhat, since by tradition one commands the cab at the head of the queue. It will have been waiting the longest and a 'first come, first served' system is in operation. I feared the two cabmen in front of the third would object, but neither, in the event, said a word. I climbed into the brougham, refraining from speaking, just as Holmes had charged me to. The driver fixed me with a smile, then turned and whipped his horse into motion.

Since Holmes's letter had declared that the cabman would "know what is expected of him", it felt safe to assume that my friend had primed him beforehand with my ultimate destination. This was in all likelihood Holmes's farm, that tidy smallholding five miles outside the town, perched a short way from the chalk cliffs overlooking the Channel. With sweeping sea views from its south-facing windows and the ever-present drone of Holmes's bees humming industriously in their hives, it was an enchanting place, and I looked forward to seeing it again.

I knew well the route thither and was startled, therefore, when I realised that the brougham was leaving Eastbourne in entirely the wrong direction. We were not taking the steep road westward up to Beachy Head and thence towards the rocky bay known as Birling Gap, near which Holmes's farm was situated. Rather, we were northbound, going inland.

I opened my mouth to voice a complaint, then closed it again. If Holmes had advised me not to talk to the driver, it must be for a good reason. I was none the less unsettled, and wondered afresh what this whole rigmarole was about. The suitcase, the watercolour set and easel, the spectacles, the buttonhole, not to mention this third cab that was now transporting me to parts unknown – what did it all signify? There was a real mystery here, and no mistake.

I felt my brow furrowing ever more deeply as the brougham put the town behind it and entered the depths of the countryside. We trotted along mazy, wayward lanes, between high hedgerows whose intermittent gaps revealed glimpses of grazing cows or sheep, and arable fields newly ploughed after the harvest. Now and then we would pass through a village or tiny hamlet, as the bulk of the South Downs grew smaller and smaller at our backs. All the while, I racked my brains, trying to fathom out what was happening.

I attempted to apply Holmes's own methods to the situation. I told myself to analyse the data item by item, as he did. I was not down here in Sussex for purely social reasons; that much was now inarguable. Holmes's invitation bore a hidden ulterior motive, one which involved me adopting a form of disguise. He wished me to be less recognisable as myself, hence the unwonted spectacles and the change of luggage, and hence the buttonhole, too, no doubt.

I considered the watercolour set, with the purveyor's name embossed on the lid, and its companion easel. This was, above all else, the most distinctive of the conditions Holmes had imposed on my visit. Clearly, I was meant to be a watercolourist. Just as clearly, I was here seeking some wondrous specimen of Sussex landscape as my subject matter, which the cabman had been entrusted with finding for me.

The presence of the tinted spectacles suggested that my eyes were sensitive to light or else perhaps weakened through overuse, or both. That would reinforce the impression that I was an artist who had strained his eyesight repeatedly in pursuit of his craft until it had become defective.

But why? What purpose did this imposture serve?

I could only conclude that Holmes was involving me in an investigation, albeit with a brief that gave me little in the way of guidance or understanding. I was the terrier, whose job was to flush the fox from its lair, whereupon Holmes, the foxhound, might pounce.

What sort of fox, though, were we after?

Here, my thoughts took a dark turn. War was looming in Europe. Anyone with half a brain could see that. The continent was riven, with Germany growing ever more belligerent and its allies in the Triple Alliance – Italy and Austria-Hungary – making no secret of their territorial and colonial ambitions. Relations between those three countries and Britain were souring by the day, and Britain had lately strengthened its own tripartite coalition with France and Russia as a counterweight to the mounting threat. Lines were being drawn, and it seemed inevitable that sooner or later some precipitating incident would plunge us into all-out conflict.

As a consequence, Holmes had lately begun to direct his attention against enemies of the realm, agents of overseas powers who were spying on Britain and working to destabilise it from within through sabotage and sedition.

This dawning line of thought cast everything in a new light. Was I, then, meant to be a spy, one currently masquerading as a weekend watercolourist? Was the real spy being detained elsewhere and I journeying in his stead to some assignation? If so, what was I to do when I arrived wherever I was bound? Holmes's letter afforded no clue. I reckoned I must improvise as best I could, reacting to circumstances as the genuine spy would. It would be a challenge. I was no great extemporiser.

Then there was my interaction with the flower seller. Perhaps he was in on the conspiracy. He had seemed to recognise me, after all.

Thus the way was paved for all manner of further conjectures. The choice of a gardenia had been a random impulse on my part, but perhaps it held an inherent significance I was not privy to, a meaning known only to the flower seller. Likewise his response, those casual-seeming remarks about late-blooming varieties and making hay while the sun shines. Could this have been a code? Some message I should pass on, or else a cryptic warning I should heed?

In that case, there was every chance the cabman, too, was involved in the plot. How else would he know where to take me, without having to be told? I could only infer that he had made sure to be third in line in the rank, so that I, his supposed confederate, following some prearranged plan, would know to use his brougham and no other.

Warily I eyed the man's back, the bowed head, the hunched shoulders beneath his cape. Did he have the air of a traitor about him? I rather fancied he did. And what if he had sensed that I was not who I purported to be? What if I had inadvertently betrayed myself somehow? What if he was driving into the middle of nowhere, to find some desolate spot where he could do away with me?

I told myself that should the cabman intend me harm, should some assault be in the offing, he would not find me an easy mark. I might be middle-aged but I remained in decent physical shape and still knew a thing or two about fisticuffs. I was, however, wishing fervently that I had not left my service revolver at home. If only I had perceived the seriousness of this undertaking when I was still in London, rather than now, belatedly.

Of a sudden, the brougham drew to a halt. We were some

distance along an empty lane, with thick woods on either side. Just the place, I thought, for an ambush and an assassination, with not a soul around, nor any dwelling in sight.

I tensed as the cabman turned towards me.

"Here you are then, sir," said he.

I looked around. Was I to alight? It appeared I was.

I clambered out, and the cabman extended a hand to me, palm upward. When I did not move, he raised an eyebrow. It was obvious, from his manner, that he wished to be paid.

I fumbled some coppers from my pocket and passed them to him. He studied them and evinced disappointment.

"Ah, yes," I said, as though in a fit of absentmindedness I had neglected some foreordained nicety. If the cabman and I were on clandestine business together, then naturally his recompense ought to reflect that.

I handed him a half-sovereign, which satisfied him. He lashed the horse, and away the brougham rattled, the cabman not even volunteering me a backward glance.

What now, I wondered as I stood on the verge of the lane with my luggage at my feet. There was nothing here, just the expanse of woodland whose leaves shivered in a whispering wind. I noted a footpath nearby, which ran off perpendicular to the lane, winding narrowly between the trees until it vanished from view. There was no sign of human habitation, not so much as a barn or shack. It was as lonely a location as any I had been in.

Thinking I must be there for some rendezvous, I waited. After perhaps twenty minutes I ventured further up the lane, on the off chance that there was a house nearby, perhaps round the next corner. There was not. Returning to the original spot, I followed the footpath into the woods for a hundred yards or so, but it seemed to lead nowhere, so I doubled back. At the side of the lane once again, I called out a plaintive "hello" several times. The countryside swallowed up my voice, and there came no reply.

By now, the sun had begun to dip and the sky was hazy and dull, as though the day was becoming tired of itself. Nightfall was due in less than an hour. I could remain where I was, growing ever more restless and perplexed, or I could give it up and set off in search of civilisation. After another ten minutes, I made up my mind. Whatever I was there for, whatever errand or objective I was supposed to be discharging, either I had completed it or it had been summarily cancelled. Time to cut my losses. The brougham had passed through a village a mile back. I had seen a pub there, and at that particular moment the idea of a warm hearth, a pint of ale and a bite to eat was a very attractive one. Furthermore, I was sure I might rustle up some local with a dog-cart who was willing, for a shilling or two, to take me to Holmes's farm.

*

In both instances, I was not disappointed, and by eight o'clock that evening I was at Sherlock Holmes's front door, feeling bewildered and more than a touch aggrieved. Light shone in every downstairs window, and Holmes himself answered my knock promptly. He laughed with delight to see me and enveloped my hand in both of his as he shook it.

"Watson, Watson, Watson," he declared. "You have made it at last! Come on in, old fellow. How was the journey down?"

"Protracted and confusing," I replied.

"Yes, yes, I imagine it was. You have eaten, I take it. A hearty pie, judging by the flakes of pastry adhering to your moustache. Steak and kidney? The colour and consistency of the tiny blob of gravy on your sleeve suggests as much. But still, you would probably not be averse to a spot of bread and cheese. I have a superior Stilton in the larder, and a glass of Tokay to wash it down with would not go amiss either, I'll wager."

Ensconced by the fireplace, we ate and drank, and little by little my disgruntlement began to abate. It was always comforting to be in Holmes's presence again, whatever the circumstances. The years seemed to fall away, and it was as if we were once more snug in our rooms at Baker Street, the gas jets hissing, the curtains drawn against a thick yellow London particular that curled and coiled outside the windows, with Holmes busy at his chemistry bench while I perused the newspapers or the latest edition of *The Lancet*, and always the feeling that at any moment the doorbell might ring, signalling the arrival of a client, a plea for Holmes's aid, a fresh mystery in need of unravelling. How long ago and far off those days now seemed, and how bright and exciting that world. The extent to which I missed our old life often, as now, caught me by surprise. It could never be returned to, and the only way I could recapture it was through the narratives that I was continuing to publish, drawing on the fund of notes I had accumulated about Holmes's former cases.

"You are doubtless bursting with questions," said my friend at length, "and now that you have calmed down a little – the Tokay has done its work and the choleric flush has faded from your cheeks – I will do my best to satisfy them."

"I would be grateful if you did. This has been a most vexatious afternoon, Holmes, I must say. I have run the gamut of emotions, from curiosity to trepidation to anxiety to irritation, with a pinch of exasperation thrown in for good measure."

"It was never my aim to incommode you, Watson, at least not unduly. I simply required your participation in a... well, one might call it an experiment."

"An experiment?" I echoed, with some asperity. "As if I were some – some mouse you are testing a poison on?"

"It is not nearly as manipulative as all that."

"It feels a lot like it."

"You have not been in any peril, let me assure you on that front," Holmes said, offering me a cigarette, which I accepted with a grudging nod. "Rather, you have been fulfilling a role – a role, I may add, for which you were eminently suited, more so than any man I know."

"That of ignorant catspaw, you mean?"

"Come, come. Let me lay it all out before you."

"Pray do."

"And in return, you will relate everything that you have discovered today."

"It is not much, but very well."

Holmes settled back in his chair. "You remember Lord Cantlemere, I am sure."

"Yes, of course. From the affair of Count Negretto Sylvius and the Mazarin Stone. As I recall, he was no great aficionado of yours."

"Not to begin with, although by the end of the matter he had rather changed his tune. At any rate, his lordship has a niece, a Mrs. Helena Risbridger, married to Jasper Risbridger, a lawyer of some repute, senior partner with the firm of Fowler, Henderson and Risbridger, of Chancery Lane. On his niece's behalf, Cantlemere contacted me by mail, begging my assistance. It is hard to refuse when so eminent a gentleman desires one's services, harder still when he tenders a large fee. The case, if nothing else, was local to me and had a couple of singular elements that intrigued.

"It transpires," Holmes continued, "that Mr. Risbridger is in the habit of travelling down to Eastbourne every Friday from the family home in Stockwell. He spends the weekend here, returning on Sunday evening. He has been doing this every week, almost without fail, for over three years now. He has developed a taste for watercolour painting, you see, and according to him, the light and the landscape on this particular patch of the coast are second to none. Whatever the season, whatever the weather, there is always something of interest to catch his painterly eye.

"Mrs. Risbridger was quite happy for him to indulge in the practice. Theirs, reading between the lines of Lord Cantlemere's letter, is a marriage whose initial flame of ardour has long since dwindled. They live together contentedly, but relations between them are more cordial than passionate. Not like you, Watson, old chap, who remain as besotted with the new Mrs. Watson as on the day you met."

I felt myself blush.

"I cannot ever see you becoming less than enamoured with

your bride," Holmes said. "But such is not the lot of every married couple, and indeed the majority appear to settle into a kind of distanced companionability as the years go by, with the Risbridgers being a case in point. They are childless, and perhaps offspring might have been their saving grace, affording the glue that would have bound them together more closely. Regardless, if Mr. Risbridger wishes to spend his weekends elsewhere, Mrs. Risbridger is prepared to offer no objection. The temporary separations do not trouble her.

"Lately, however, the woman has begun to harbour doubts about her husband's regular countryside jaunts. At first, he would always return with at least a finished watercolour or two to show for his time away. In recent months, though, he has rarely brought home a new painting, and those that he has done strike her as perfunctory, lacking the care and attention to detail of previous efforts, as though he has been dashing them off simply to maintain the illusion of painterly efforts. With what, then, is he occupying himself during these sojourns away from town if it is not the pursuit of his artistic muse?

"Now, it wasn't difficult for me to observe Risbridger's movements in and around Eastbourne station. I knew from Lord Cantlemere that he habitually catches the 2.45 from Victoria every Friday. I waited on the concourse at Eastbourne to spy on him, adopting a different disguise on each occasion so as not to arouse his attention. Three Friday afternoons in a row, I watched him purchase a buttonhole for himself immediately upon arrival and then make for the cab rank, where he invariably boarded the third cab along, toting his grey suitcase and his Adams and Sons watercolour set and easel."

"So I was he!" I cried. "You had me doing everything today that Risbridger himself does."

Holmes nodded. "And there's more, for as soon as I saw the fellow for the first time, one thing leapt out at me, namely his close physical resemblance to a certain Dr. John Watson. It was marked; I would go so far as to call it striking. He is your age and has your build, your complexion, your hair colour, similar whiskers. Even your gaits are not unalike. With the addition of the tinted spectacles that Risbridger likes to wear, you and he could practically be twins. It was such an uncanny coincidence that I could not help but feel I should act upon it somehow, exploit it to my advantage. His unvarying routine was something you might easily reproduce, with the appropriate direction; and through no amount of stage make-up or play-acting could I render myself more effectively his double than you could, by dint of just being yourself."

"But to what end?"

"Why, Watson, to find out where that third cab took him."

"Could you not have followed him in another cab?"

"Easy enough to do undetected in London, where the streets are crowded and the traffic thick. Not so easy on the lonely, unfrequented roads of Sussex."

"Then mightn't you simply have made enquiries among the cabmen? One of them might have supplied the answer."

"Well now, there we have a problem. Although Risbridger always takes the third cab, the driver is not the same one each time. I have observed with my own eyes the arrangement of the cabs in the rank prior to his arrival. It is wholly random. Whosoever happens to be driving the third vehicle in line, his is the one that Risbridger selects. This implies that every single cabby in Eastbourne knows where Risbridger goes each Friday afternoon. Every one of them is wise to the game, and it is merely the luck of the draw which of them happens to be in third position when the man emerges from the station."

"That ought to simplify things, though, oughtn't it?" I said. "You have plenty of cabmen from whom you might winkle an answer."

"You are right, it should be so," said Holmes, "and believe me, I tried. Your local Eastbourne jarvey, however, is a taciturn, imperturbable breed. There exists within their fraternity a code of silence over certain dealings, or at any rate over this particular one. I found that no amount of cajoling, bribery or finagling would get any of them to reveal where they take the gentleman in mauve-tinted glasses. Nothing I could say or do was of any avail to me in that regard. The reason for their reticence is unknown to me, although I strongly suspect that Risbridger pays them handsomely for their services and this in turn guarantees discretion."

"You are not wrong there. My cabman was content with a fee of nothing less than a whole half-sovereign."

Holmes clapped his hands together and chuckled. "There we have it. What else is there that you can tell me about your journey?"

I described, as best I could, the route we had taken out of Eastbourne and spoke with some bemusement about the driver depositing me in a remote, unpopulated region of countryside, where no one came to meet me and there was not a building in sight.

"Do you think you could find the place again?"

"I believe so. I remember the name of the village I made my way back to – Farthingham – and I'm certain I can retrace my steps from there."

"Capital! Then that is where we shall go first thing tomorrow, to achieve a resolution to the case."

"I presume you know what is going on here, Holmes. You have some inkling as to the reason behind Risbridger's odd, furtive activities."

"I do. The evidence is fairly plain. You have all the facts yourself, and it cannot be too difficult to draw a conclusion from them."

"And yet I remain in the dark. It did occur to me, as I was in the thick of it, that this was all to do with spying and agents of foreign powers," I ventured.

"Oh ho!" my friend declared with a smile. "That, Watson, is your overactive imagination at work. Your writer's brain is always searching for the most melodramatic construction to put on events. No, in this instance, alas, we are looking at something altogether more prosaic."

"Namely?"

Holmes tapped the side of his nose. "Tomorrow, old fellow. Wait until tomorrow."

*

So it was that, the following morning, we hired a trap to take us to Farthingham. We left it at the village, Holmes instructing the driver to wait for us, and set off along the lane on foot. Presently we found ourselves in the wooded expanse I remembered from the previous day, and in no time I located the exact spot where I had wasted the best part of three-quarters of an hour in bootless waiting. I was able to identify the locale thanks to the footpath that led off from the lane into the woods.

Holmes studied our surroundings for a while. Then he began striding back and forth, nose to the air, like a dog questing for a scent. I did not realise that this was precisely what he was doing – scenting – until he said, "Smell that, Watson?"

"I smell nothing except the usual aromas of nature."

"It is quite distinct."

"Perhaps my nasal acuity has been blunted by years of London fumes and fog."

"Whereas mine has perhaps grown sharper thanks to the fresh rural atmosphere of Sussex," said Holmes. "There is a definite tang of woodsmoke in the air, which suggests the high probability that there is a dwelling of some sort nearby. And the odour appears to be emanating from yonder." He pointed along the footpath and wordlessly set off down it apace.

I followed, and soon we were deep in woodland, the lane lost from view. A short distance further on, we arrived at a clearing in the middle of which stood a tiny, tumbledown cottage. A skein of smoke drifted up from its crooked chimney, and outside the front door, beside a modest kitchen garden, a small girl was playing with a ragdoll. The lass could not have been more than two years old, and she was quite the picture of innocence, chatting to the doll in a string of happy childish babble.

She glanced up as Holmes and I emerged from the woods, and when her eye fell upon me, she broke into a broad, gap-toothed grin.

"Dada!" she cried. She leapt to her feet and ran towards me, arms outstretched as though to give a hug. She stopped just short, her face lapsing into a frown. "You are not Dada."

"No, my dear," I said gently. "I am not."

The child looked crestfallen and a touch petulant. "Where's my flower? Dada always gives me a flower. He takes it from here." She pointed at my lapel. "'A flower for my Daisy,' he says."

Now a woman stepped out from the cottage, a pretty young apple-cheeked thing in a plain cotton smock. Clearly, she had been alerted by the little girl's cry. She took one look at us, then beckoned to the girl.

"Daisy," she said. "Come to my side. Now."

Obediently the girl trotted over to her. The woman put an arm around her shoulders and drew her into her skirts.

"Who are you gentlemen?" she asked, with a wary note. Her gaze strayed from me to Holmes and back again. She scrutinised my face, her eyes narrowing. "What do you want?"

"Madam," said Holmes, doffing his hat, "I regret the intrusion. My name is Sherlock Holmes. This is Dr. Watson. And you are...?"

"Who I am is no business of yours." Her voice carried a faint but appealing rural burr.

"I'm very much afraid that it is. Unless I am greatly mistaken, you are an... acquaintance of Mr. Jasper Risbridger."

At the mention of the name, the woman paled.

"Furthermore," Holmes said, "again, unless I am greatly mistaken, little Daisy there is his daughter."

Now the colour drained almost completely from her face.

"How do you...? How can you possibly...?"

"Rest assured, my good lady, we do not mean you ill."
Holmes had adopted his smoothest, most suave demeanour.
"We are here to clear up a few matters, that is all. Would you
care to invite us in?"

The woman's expression hardened. "I am happier staying
out here, if that's all right with you. Daisy? Go indoors, my
poppet. Take your dolly with you. I shan't be long."

When it was just the three of us, she said, "Is it bad news?
Has something happened to Jasper? He didn't come yesterday
as usual, but that does not always mean disaster."

"To the best of my knowledge Mr. Risbridger is well,"
replied Holmes. "He was detained in London overnight by
a social occasion. His wife's uncle put on a dinner party
yesterday evening, at somewhat short notice, and Risbridger
was obliged to attend."

"His wife's…?"

"You know, of course, that he is married."

Hesitantly the woman nodded.

"It is that same personage – his wife's uncle, Lord
Cantlemere – who has engaged me to look into Risbridger's
behaviour," Holmes went on. "In order to help facilitate that,
at my suggestion he invited his niece and her husband to the
aforementioned dinner party, knowing the invitation could
not reasonably be declined. This left the way clear for my
friend here to masquerade as Risbridger yesterday, so that his
true goal in visiting Eastbourne could be ascertained."

"I see. Very tricksy of you, sir. Your friend does indeed
look like Jasper, so much so that when I first laid eyes on him,
I thought for one second that it was he."

"So did your daughter. Plainly, then, Risbridger does not come down every weekend expressly to paint watercolours. Maybe once he did, but no longer. Rather, it is to spend time with you and Daisy."

The woman offered a rueful smile. "It was how we met, he and I. The watercolours. I chanced upon him one day, in a field not far from here. He was at his easel, sketching with a pencil in preparation to adding paints. We fell to talking. I lead a solitary life, in this cottage in which I was born and raised and which is my sole possession, left to me by my late parents. Company is always welcome, and Jasper seemed a friendly sort, and clever, and charming. Before we parted he asked if I would show him some other scenic spots where he could paint, and we arranged to meet the following weekend. One thing led to another, and… well…"

"Now you are the mother of his child, and where, in the past, watercolouring was his single aim in visiting the area, these days he has a paternal obligation."

"He is kind, sir," said the woman. "He loves Daisy, and he is generous to me. As I understand it, he and Mrs. Risbridger have grown cool towards each other. He is happy when he comes here. It is a relief, he says, to be out of the city and in a simpler world, if only for a short while." She spread out her hands. "Am I ashamed of the arrangement? I should say yes, but I am not, for it has brought me Daisy. She is the light of my life. She is my heart, and I daresay she is Jasper's too. He has no children with his wife. He dotes on Daisy and is as good a father to her as any man could be. It is not an ideal situation, far from it, but it is what it is and I have learned to accept it. I must ask, though, what you intend to do, now that you have uncovered the truth."

Sherlock Holmes deliberated a while. "That is hard to say. On the one hand, no real harm is being done here. On the other, a man has broken his marriage vows and is deceiving his wife."

"Were she to find out, it would ruin everything, I am sure."

"Or," I interjected, "she may be forgiving and understanding. There is always that possibility." I spoke more in hope than expectation.

"Please, sir," said the young woman to Holmes. "I am not one to beg, but there is the happiness of several people at stake, not least Daisy. Would you be able to forget you ever found me? Could you see your way to telling his lordship that your investigation came to naught, so that everything can continue as it was?"

"You are asking a hard thing," Holmes said. "You would have me lie."

"I know." She bit her lip. "Well, if you cannot, I shall not hold it against you. Maybe it would be best for all concerned if the truth were to come out. Jasper cannot go on living a double life forever."

"I shall think long and hard on the matter, madam. You have my word on that."

"Thank you, sir," said the woman. "I suppose it is as much as I can hope for."

*

Holmes was in a ruminative mood as we returned to Farthing-ham. I could not get much out of him, and even when we were back at his farm, he remained withdrawn. After he had scribbled a letter to Lord Cantlemere and posted it, he became somewhat more outgoing, and the rest of my visit passed pleasantly enough, although at no point would he vouchsafe the nature of what he had written to his lordship.

I learned the outcome of the whole affair a few days later, via another letter from Holmes.

My dear Watson,

Doubtless you are keen to know what has become of Jasper Risbridger, his mistress and their daughter.

In the end, I decided that honesty was the best policy. I could not cover up something that was bound to come to light sooner or later anyway. No man can hoodwink his wife indefinitely, and Mrs. Risbridger must already have had a good idea of what he was up to behind her back. Women, with their particular sensibilities, are never shrewder than when it comes to matters of the heart.

In the event, upon learning the news that Risbridger has a child by another woman, she has proved more sanguine than one might have foreseen. Lord Cantlemere tells me she is affronted but at the same time resigned. The partial estrangement that existed between her and her husband is now more or less total, and while there is acrimony in the marital home, it is not as bitter as it might otherwise have been, and that most difficult and painful of enterprises, a divorce, does not seem on the cards. She accepts that Risbridger must visit his daughter, so now at least he will no longer have to use his watercolours as an increasingly flimsy pretext for journeying to Eastbourne every weekend.

One might say that his mistress – her name, by the way, is *Alice Ellison* – was correct in suggesting it would be best for all concerned if the truth came out. A boil, unless lanced, may end up contaminating the whole body. You, as a medic, understand that more than most.

One last minor detail to clear up. You like things neat and tidy, do you not? Especially when it comes to a case like this, the sort you are apt to transform into one of those gaudy little narratives of yours. Why, you doubtless wish to know, did Risbridger always choose the third cab in the rank? What difference did it make to the whole enterprise which cab he took? The answer may amuse you, as it did me.

You will be flattered to learn that the fellow is an admirer of your work, and also, by extension, of mine. Having read 'The Final Problem', he was struck by my injunction about engaging neither the first nor the second cab, as a defence against potential enemy interference. He decided to apply the principle to his own situation, in case his wife ever got wise to his duplicity and decided to have him followed or otherwise track his movements somehow. Once he started doing this, within a few weeks all the Eastbourne cabbies had become familiar with his pattern of behaviour and it was common knowledge among them where he went each time. They began treating it as a standing joke, indeed a game, and whichever of them happened to have the third cab in the rank on Friday afternoon at a quarter past five was deemed lucky, for he was the one who was going to be paid over the odds for his services (although he would also be expected to buy a round of drinks for his colleagues in the *pub that evening, so as to share out the bounty).*

Lord Cantlemere explained all this to me, after he confronted Risbridger about his behaviour in the presence of Mrs. Risbridger, and Risbridger came clean.

Finally, an apology. From the outset I had a strong suspicion that Risbridger was an adulterer. What man garlands himself with a fresh buttonhole as soon as he arrives at his destination if not to look his jauntiest and most presentable? And why would that be the case unless there were some feminine influence in play? The flower must originally have been meant to impress Miss Ellison, although in time it developed into a regular gift for young Daisy instead.

I feel moved to apologise to you because I prevailed upon you to impersonate Jasper Risbridger, even when I already knew that infidelity might well be the true motive behind his actions. Although there is some irony in the notoriously uxorious John Watson standing in for a man who has shown himself to be the opposite, I trust you will not feel stained by the association. You and he could not be less analogous.

With fondest regards,
Sherlock Holmes

As I read the letter, I was amazed by the level of compassion Mrs. Risbridger had shown towards her errant husband, albeit perhaps not wholly surprised. I then, having perused the final paragraph, looked at my wife across the breakfast table, studying her as she leafed through her own morning correspondence. Eventually she became aware of my attention and enquired what the matter was.

"Nothing, dear," I said. "Nothing at all. Just thanking my stars for my good fortune."

She aimed a quizzical but approving look at me, and returned to her business, as I did to mine, and not for the first time, nor for the last, I marvelled at the capacity of women to bewitch men with their beauty and charms, and at the same time weather all manner of masculine fancies, foibles and failings. Truly, in every sense, they are the fairer sex.

THE ZEN GARDEN MURDER

ANDREW LANE

"It really is too bad of you," my friend Sherlock Holmes said suddenly. He was hunched in his armchair across from me in the living room of his Sussex cottage with his knees drawn up to his chin and a pensive expression on his face, staring into the fireplace.

"What is?" I asked, without looking up from the jottings I was making in my notebook.

"Still characterising me as a misanthrope when really I am the most clubbable of men."

I laid down my pen and stared at him in astonishment. "How on earth did you know that I was thinking that very thing?"

He shook his head irritably, like a man trying to shoo away a fly. "A simple matter of observation and deduction."

"It may be simple to you, but everyone else finds it amazing. Pray, explain."

"Again? I have lost count of the number of times I have led you through my thought process, and yet despite all of those occasions not only do you continue to be impressed but you also show no improvement in your own deductive abilities. You really are a dull pupil, Watson." His words were harsh, but I could tell from the quirk of his lips and the way he quickly flashed a glance at me and away again that he was not being entirely serious.

"One more time and I might get it."

"I doubt it, but very well." He sighed, a trifle theatrically I thought. "Yesterday we successfully concluded the latest of our many investigations. Today therefore, as is your habit, you will be making your initial notes for what will inevitably be called 'The Curious Case of the Surgeon's Third Ear' or some such, even though neither the surgeon nor his extraneous auricular appendage had anything but the most cursory link to either the puzzle or its eventual solution. The case began, you will recall, on the day after your arrival here, as we dined with Dr. Mordhurst and his wife in Arundel. I noted just now that your hand brushed absently at your shirt front as you undoubtedly remembered spilling your mulligatawny soup down your dickey while Dr. Mordhurst was explaining the details of the blackmailer who had contacted him. Your gaze then drifted to the mantelpiece, to the invitation from the Earl of Chichester for us to join him at his Hunt Ball next week. Despite these two notable social occasions in my calendar, you pursed your lips and shook your head slightly. Your gaze moved to me, then to the table where my latest chemical experiment is bubbling away, and then to the front door. You nodded, as if you had come to a decision, and scribbled a few words in your notebook. I deduced, therefore, that you had decided to adjust the facts of the case so that it starts here, presumably with the two of us receiving a visitor while I am conducting my research, rather than in a crowded restaurant. This is, I am afraid, how you generally begin these stories of yours. You have become predictable."

"Whether you like it or not," I said, "these *stories* are remarkably popular. Readers have formed a view of you—"

"An erroneous view," Holmes interjected.

"Which, should I contradict it or pull against it, would discomfit them. They expect you to be aloof and isolated, and they expect our cases together to start in your sitting room and with the arrival of either a letter or a visitor. These things are expected, even anticipated."

"Expectations must not be disappointed, I see. And don't you think your readers might be expecting to learn at some point the true number and identities of your various wives?"

"That," I replied, feeling slightly stung, "might be a step too far. After all, these stories are about *you*, not me."

"These stories are about a fictionalised version of me that I find risible and brother Mycroft finds highly amusing. Which reminds me –" he waved a hand at a letter, affixed to a shelf of his bookcase with a wavy Malay kris, a souvenir of an earlier case, "– I have received an interesting communication from said sibling. You may wish to read it."

I sprang out of my chair, spilling my notebook and fountain

pen to the ground in my eagerness, and pulled the dagger from the wood. Mycroft Holmes never wrote socially but always for a specific purpose, and those purposes usually led to interesting, if not actively dangerous, sets of events. I pulled the letter from the envelope and quickly scanned the spidery writing.

"His penmanship has not improved," I pointed out.

"Diplomats and civil service mandarins deliberately cultivate bad handwriting. It means that, should problems arise from their decisions, they can always claim that their instructions were misread by their subordinates or their reports misunderstood by their superiors."

"If I read this correctly, he is asking you to pay a visit to one of your neighbours and then report back to him."

"Indeed. I have not met the man, but I have heard talk of him in the village. His name is Sir Reginald Summersly, and he is a retired British Minister to China and the Empire of Korea, as well as Consul-General to the Empire of Japan. He now lives a reclusive existence a few miles from here, close to the sea."

"Why does Mycroft want you to intrude upon the life of a complete stranger?"

"My presumption would be that Mycroft does not wish to start any hares running. Given his position in Whitehall, his every move is scrutinised by foreign powers, as are those of his various agents. Should he take an official interest in something or someone, then that thing or that person immediately and inevitably becomes an object of fascination to others. By using me as his pawn, he disguises his plans."

"Shouldn't he have retired from his work years ago?"

Holmes snorted. "As I have observed before, brother Mycroft

is irreplaceable, both from the point of view of what he knows but also because of how he *thinks*. And besides, what would he do if he *did* retire? He can already complete the *Times* crossword in under three minutes, and believe me, that time is limited only by the speed at which he can fill in the answers. And let us not forget that Mr. Gladstone was eighty-five when he resigned as Prime Minister. Age and ability are not correlated."

We took a long lunch, provided by the estimable Mrs. Hardcastle, who visited the cottage every day to clean and cook, and then wandered outside to seek out her taciturn husband, who provided gardening and transport services for Holmes. It was Mr. Hardcastle who had picked me and my luggage up from the station a few days before. He left the plants he was caring for and, without a word, led the way to the cart that also served as a carriage, to which he had already attached two horses. The journey took us across the Sussex Downs, which undulated like a carelessly thrown green blanket. Every stone and rut was transmitted from the iron-banded wooden wheels through the body of the cart and into my increasingly old and aching back. When we passed two autocars that had run into trouble on the steeper stretches of road I found myself torn between amusement at their plight and envy of their air-filled tyres.

*

Sir Reginald's house was a good deal larger than Holmes's cottage, and provided a fine view over the Downs. I noted a grove of fruit trees behind the house as we approached, and once again wondered why my wife and I still remained in London rather than move to the countryside.

The doorway opened as we approached. Inside a footman took our coats, hats and sticks. A besuited gentleman whom I presumed to be Sir Reginald's butler approached with a silver platter. Holmes placed his visiting card on the tray, with the corner turned down to indicate that he had delivered it in person, not via a servant. The world had altered since Queen Victoria, of blessed memory, departed this life and her son Albert took his place as King; the kind of formal etiquette that Holmes and I were used to had been replaced with a more casual chumminess, but we both still felt a pull towards the old ways of doing things, and I suspected that a former ambassador to China would feel the same way. Of course, back in the last century the receiving party at home was always a woman, while gentlemen could only receive visits from men at their club, or their offices. However, in my experience this rule was more often honoured in the breach than the observance. I hoped it would be the case now.

"Mr. Sherlock Holmes and his colleague, Dr. Watson, to see Sir Reginald Summersly," Holmes murmured. The butler seemed to glide backwards with the tray and vanish into the shadows.

"I am generally a 'fan' of progress," Holmes murmured, "but it is sometimes reassuring to find that things are done now as they always were. And, I hope and trust, always will be."

Moments later a young Chinese gentleman wearing a black suit with a round, stand-up collar, of the type known as 'mandarin', emerged from what I presumed was the library, for I had glimpsed numerous books on the shelves behind him. Sir Reginald's butler followed him a few moments later.

"Gentlemen, welcome," the Chinese man said in hushed tones. "My name is Li Hsen. I am Sir Reginald's secretary. Sir Reginald is outside at the moment, relaxing and meditating in his Zen Garden, but it is nearly time for his refreshments and I know he values visitors. If you would care to accompany me, I will take you out to see him." He turned to the butler, who stood a pace behind him and off to one side. "Henderson, please ensure that refreshments sufficient for all are brought to the garden."

"A Zen Garden?" I ventured as the butler withdrew with a nod of acquiescence.

"No doubt resulting from Sir Reginald's time in Japan," Holmes noted as we followed Li Hsen down a darkened corridor towards the rear of the house. I only had time to note a number of beautiful and ethereal Asian paintings, primarily landscapes showing waves or mountains, in places where other houses would have had portraits of family members or paintings of horses.

"Hokusai," Holmes said cryptically. I was not sure if that was the name of the artist or a comment in one of the many languages in which he was fluent.

The corridor led to an orangery, and from there we exited into a well-manicured garden. The path ahead of us was straight, and led past what seemed to be a greenhouse of large dimensions, both horizontally and vertically. The glass of its construction was rendered almost opaque by condensation, and as we walked along its length I could feel heat radiating out.

"I presume," Holmes observed to Li Hsen, "that Sir Reginald brought back various horticultural samples from the various countries in which he served the Queen."

"That is the case," Mr. Hsen replied. "Most of them require high temperatures and high levels of humidity to survive. They would not prosper in the temperate climate of this country." He smiled. "Sometimes I sneak in and sit there, beneath a silver apricot tree, just to remind myself of what it was like back in Shanghai." As we approached the far end of the greenhouse he gestured to a separate brick building with a chimney, a mere few feet away. "The heat is provided by a furnace, and is carefully regulated. Some of the plants are very sensitive to changes in temperature."

After the greenhouse, as we followed a winding path through an orchard of apple and pear trees, I turned to Holmes and asked: "So what exactly *is* a Zen Garden?"

"Zen Gardens are, for all intents and purposes, miniature landscapes arranged in such a way that they reflect the essence of the natural world, so as to aid contemplation and meditation. They may contain elements of water, trees, stone, sand, moss, gravel, grass, and various simple plants. You might see them as one end of a spectrum of landscape design where the other end is the highly formalised English gardens of Lancelot Brown."

"I see."

"You will, and then it will become obvious. Bear in mind that Zen is not a religion as we would understand the term, but more of a philosophy and a way of life, and one that Sir Reginald obviously finds conducive to his well-being."

The path eventually led us out of the orchard and into a wide-open lawn, in the middle of which was a perfectly circular sea of white sand circumscribed by a low stone kerb.

The sand had apparently been raked by hand into a series of concentric circles, like frozen ripples, each set of ripples centring on a series of pure white stones that had been placed seemingly at random on the sand. Further out, towards the edge, the ripples amalgamated in such a way that the last three of them were only just smaller than the circle itself. At the centre of the pattern, on a stone plinth, sat a man. He wore a simple white suit and his head was bowed, but even at this distance I could see that he was not praying, contemplating or even sleeping. Bright red blood stained the white material, issuing from a massive depressed wound on the back of his head, a wound that was surely fatal. Nobody could survive their skull being crushed and the occipital region of their brain being traumatised in so brutal a fashion.

Apart from a few patches of blood, stark against the white sand, there was no disturbance. No footprint, no scuff marks; nothing. And no rocks or stones that might have been thrown at Sir Reginald or even dropped upon him from above. It occurred to me, as I felt Holmes stiffen beside me and Li Hsen gasp and cover his mouth with his hands, that the concentric circles of sand that formed the Zen Garden were less like ripples on a frozen sea and more like a series of target rings centred on the body.

Without thinking, I made as if to step out onto the sand. I was sure that Sir Reginald was dead, but instinctively I needed to check for any signs of life. However, Holmes grabbed at my shoulder and pulled me back.

"I fear it is too late," he said, "and it is important that any evidence be preserved." As he spoke, his gaze darted all over the sand, checking I presumed for signs of disturbance. "I see no stone or other weapon," he said, "and neither do I see any mechanism by which such an object could be projected in such a way as to reach Sir Reginald and then be removed, for example an arrow on the end of a cord. And a mechanism of that kind would leave traces in the sand, as would an attacker walking out there and back." He turned to Li Hsen, who was still choking in shock. "Mr. Hsen, when was the last time you saw Sir Reginald alive?"

"Perhaps ten minutes ago," he said, suppressing his noises of grief. "I am in the habit of regularly checking on him. He is, after all, elderly." His face appeared to crumple. "*Was* elderly."

"And were you alone?"

"No. Sir Reginald's gardener, Natsume Rintarō, was just finishing raking the sand back into the pattern you see, removing Sir Reginald's own footsteps."

"And did you leave Natsume Rintarō here?"

"No. We went back to the house together, stopping in the orchard to inspect the progress of the pears. We had been back inside the house – in the library, in fact – for only a few minutes when you arrived."

"I shall need to talk with this Natsume Rintarō," Holmes said, then turned to me. "Walk with me, please, Watson."

We walked together around the perimeter of the circle of sand, and it was one of the more macabre things I have ever experienced – a combination of ritualistic progression and afternoon perambulation. I itched all the way, wanting to rush out to Sir Reginald's side, but the more I saw of him the more I knew he was dead.

By the time we arrived back where we had started it was clear that there were no stones or other objects on the sand other than the stones at the centres of the sculpted circles, and no disturbance to those circles, which had, apparently, only just been finished when Sir Reginald was killed.

"It is said," Holmes murmured, "that the ancient Greek playwright Aeschylus was killed when an eagle dropped a tortoise on his head. Allegedly the eagle mistook his bald head for a rock and tried to use it to crack the shell of the tortoise, which it wished to eat. No eagle has ever been seen to display this type of behaviour, however, although the lammergeier, a type of European vulture, is known to drop animal bones onto rocks to crack them open and thus get to the marrow inside."

"Such an event would certainly leave traces," I pointed out, "even if the putative bird somehow managed to recover the tortoise."

"I was not suggesting it as a viable theory," Holmes countered, "merely making a historical comparison. You may, if you wish, attend to Sir Reginald now. I have seen what I need to see. Mr. Hsen, perhaps you could return to the house and send for the local constabulary."

As Li Hsen moved slowly away, looking ten years older than he had when we had first met him, I walked gingerly out into the circle of sand. I felt it crunch and shift beneath my feet, and again I was struck by the combination of the ordinary and the macabre. The last time I had walked on sand was on the beach at Cromer, with my wife. Or, as Holmes would no doubt correct me, *one* of my wives. The nature of the sculpted sand, with the circles around the white stones like ripples in water frozen at the moment the stones had been thrown in, made me feel like a clumsy intruder in a sacred space.

When I reached Sir Reginald I checked his pulse, but although his body was still warm the blood was not moving in his veins. Cautiously I examined the massive wound. Whatever had caused it had occurred within the past twenty minutes or so, given the fact that the blood had not yet fully clotted. That would be in accord with the timings Li Hsen had provided. I could see no trace of any foreign material in the wound.

Despite the fact that we had walked all around the body, albeit at a distance, looking for evidence of disruption to the sand, I now looked more closely at the area surrounding Sir Reginald. He sat – or, rather, slumped – in a circle of smooth sand about an arm's width around him. Past that, the ripples began. As I had observed earlier, apart from the splashes of blood there was nothing out of the ordinary; nothing, that is, except for the dead body of Sir Reginald Summersly himself.

I retraced my footsteps to where I had left Holmes, resisting the sudden and childish desire to walk backwards in my own footprints leaving traces that led into the Zen Garden but not out again, just to see if it could be done. Several of Holmes's cases had revolved around such a trick, but neither he nor the local constable would be amused, I judged.

*

When I reached the edge of the circle, and the treeline of the orchard, Holmes was there no longer. I glanced around in an attempt to locate him, then wandered through the orchard in the direction of Sir Reginald's house. I found Holmes crouched by an apple tree, making a careful investigation of its trunk. He straightened up as I approached.

"Have you determined anything from the body or its immediate surroundings that we did not already know?" he asked.

"Nothing. It is a puzzle."

He smiled thinly. "If by 'puzzle' you mean a situation where we only have some of the facts and have by various means to discover the rest, then yes, it is a puzzle. Our job here is to fill in those blanks as best we can."

"Then how was the murder committed?" I challenged him.

"Were we in London or any similar conurbation, I should be looking for something structural such as a crane or scaffolding, but I have examined the ground for the inevitable signs that something heavy had been installed and have found nothing. Also, if we believe the story of Mr. Hsen, then there was insufficient time to build and then deconstruct such a device."

"It occurs to me," I said, "that Mr. Hsen's story depends on the gardener, Natsume Rintarō, for corroboration, and vice versa…"

"Indeed. That thought had, of course, occurred to me, and I shall pursue this line of enquiry when I question them and the other household staff." As if he was not inclined to consider such a simple explanation, he went on, "I also considered the possibility that a web of ropes was tied between the tops of the fruit trees around the edge of the Zen Garden, allowing someone to make their way cautiously to the centre and drop a stone on Sir Reginald with a length of string tied around it so that it could be pulled up again, but we are up against the same problem – there was too little time to accomplish such a feat. And it goes without saying that Sir Reginald would undoubtedly have realised that something was amiss."

"Unless Li Hsen and Natsume Rintarō are both lying about their movements and the times at which they made them," I pointed out stubbornly.

"If those two worthy gentlemen were lying about the time and nature of their movements, then there would have been no need for such an elaborate web between the trees," Holmes reproved. "One of them could have walked out to Sir Reginald, hit him with a stone and returned while the other used a rake to cover his tracks in the sand. And besides, I have checked the trunks of numerous trees for signs they were climbed, and have found nothing." He frowned. "Actually, that is not true. I *did* find something, but that will require further thought."

"Are *we* responsible for this terrible event?" I asked. The matter had been weighing heavily upon my mind. "The sheer coincidence of Sir Reginald dying just as we were on our way to see him, at the direction of your brother, is hard to accept."

"Indeed," Holmes said, "but comfort yourself. Our visit and Sir Reginald's death are connected, but not consequentially."

"What do you mean?"

"I am making assumptions here, against my usual practice, but I believe I am justified. Consider: brother Mycroft would not suddenly decide, out of the blue, to send someone to see Sir Reginald. Something provoked him. Let us assume, for the moment, that the inciting event was the receipt by Mycroft of a letter from Sir Reginald containing some nugget of information that required further clarification. Mycroft sends us as his covert agents, so as not to arouse suspicion. However, someone else – the murderer, or someone planning the murder – intercepts either the original letter to Mycroft or the letter from him to us. They realise that Sir Reginald is on the verge of revealing something they would rather have remain secret. They immediately send an assassin to silence Sir Reginald."

I juggled for a while with the elements of the picture that Holmes had sketched out. "That would imply," I said cautiously, "that either their agent could move remarkably quickly or they already had someone in the vicinity."

"Either of those things could be true," Holmes agreed. "We need to know more. Let us repair to the house and question the staff before the police arrive. Perhaps some refreshments could be provided as well, if the cook is not too affected by the death of her master."

*

As Holmes suggested, we returned to Sir Reginald's house. The police had not arrived yet, although Li Hsen confirmed that he had sent a footman with a message. Holmes took the opportunity of asking him to send a telegram – to his brother, I presumed. While Mr. Hsen served tea and cakes from a silver tray he received from Henderson, the butler – a task I think Mr. Hsen appreciated, as it gave him something else to think about apart from the recent tragedy – Holmes sent a footman for the gardener, Natsume Rintarō, and we repaired to the dining room.

Natsume Rintarō proved to be an ancient Japanese gentleman. His voice, when he spoke, was remarkably strong and deep, and his accent slight but noticeable.

"Gentlemen, I have been instructed to tell you everything. Do you have any particular questions?"

"Just tell us about your day," Holmes prompted.

"A day that will remain with me for the rest of my life," the gardener said, with the only flash of emotion I saw from him. "I awoke early, as is my custom. I breakfasted on some rice and green tea, which I prepared myself in the kitchen, and then I went out into the gardens. For about two hours I undertook general maintenance: watering, weeding, pruning, and otherwise keeping the gardens at the level of perfection that Sir Reginald required from me. I then returned to the house, where the cook had already made me another pot of green tea. Following that, which took about half of one hour, I moved on to the orchard. An outbreak of fire blight has been reported a few miles away, and I examined all of the apple and pear trees for any signs of infection. Fortunately, there were none, but I treated the trunks with a herbal wash that I was taught to make back in my homeland from ginger root. That whole process took around one and one half hours, I would estimate. Following that—"

"You are very precise about times," Holmes interrupted, "and yet I note that you do not carry a watch. Can you explain how you can know the time with such accuracy?"

Natsume Rintarō gazed impassively at Holmes. "From the position of the sun," he replied, "and the songs sung by the birds. There are signs everywhere, if one knows where to look and when to listen."

"Very well," Holmes said. "Please continue."

"Following my labours in the orchard, I knew that it was time for Sir Reginald's regular meditation session in the Zen Garden. He meditates at the same time every day, presuming that the weather is clement enough. I went to the Zen Garden to check the sand. A fox had left footprints on it, and several leaves had drifted down from the trees. I removed the leaves and smoothed the sand, then I—"

"Do you use a special tool to smooth the sand?" Holmes enquired.

Natsume Rintarō nodded. "I have a rake, made of bamboo. I brought it with me from Japan. It was blessed by a Buddhist priest for me before I left."

"Thank you."

The gardener nodded. "I then waited for Sir Reginald to arrive. When he did, accompanied by Mr. Hsen, we talked for a while about the cherry trees he wanted to plant on the other side of the orchard. I stayed as he inspected the Zen Garden and gave me his approval. I waited until he had walked to the centre and settled himself, then I walked out with my rake and recreated the patterns that our footsteps had disturbed, walking backwards to the boundary where I stepped out and finished. Mr. Hsen and I then waited for a minute to see if Sir Reginald had any other requirements. When it was clear that he had begun his contemplations, we left together."

"This may be considered a stupid question—" I started.

"There are no stupid questions," Natsume Rintarō said softly, "merely unhelpful answers."

I heard Holmes *harrumph!* beside me, but I continued regardless. "But why did you need to recreate the pattern *behind* Sir Reginald? Surely if he was facing away from it, he would not have seen the disturbances."

"But he would have known they were there, regardless,"

Natsume Rintarō said with a slight smile that indicated I had, in fact, asked a stupid question.

"Upon returning to the house," Holmes said, "what did you do?"

"Mr. Hsen and I went to the library, where we intended to consult several books on gardening in order to ascertain which varieties of cherries go best with the varieties of apples and pears already in the orchard. We were there for a few seconds when a footman arrived to tell us that Sir Reginald had visitors. Mr. Hsen left me to continue my research. I heard him talking with you in the hall, and then I believe he led you out to see Sir Reginald."

"So if we take into account your walk from the Zen Garden to the house, your time spent in the library and the walk that my friend and I took back to the Zen Garden in the company of Mr. Hsen, how long would you say it was between your last sight of Sir Reginald and our discovery of his body?"

"Fifteen minutes," Natsume Rintarō replied. "No more."

Holmes turned towards me. "Certainly not enough time for an elaborate construction to be built to reach Sir Reginald, but perhaps enough time for someone to smooth the sand back into its previous pattern."

"I would know," Natsume Rintarō said quietly.

"I beg your pardon?"

"Any gardener experienced in the creation of Zen Gardens has their own distinct 'style'. Partly this is the way they were taught, partly it is personal, and partly it is to do with the particular tool used. When I had finished at the Zen Garden I brought my rake back with me. It currently rests against a table in the library."

"Then you would know if someone else had smoothed the sand back into place, erasing their own footsteps."

"Just as an artist would know if someone had added a brushstroke to their painting."

Holmes nodded. "Please, if you would, go to the Zen Garden before the police arrive. Examine it, and then report back to me as to whether it has been disturbed since you left it."

"Apart from my own footprints," I pointed out.

"I will account for those," the gardener said. Something about his face, expressionless as it was, suggested to me that he was unhappy at the task Holmes had set him.

"Mr. Rintarō—" I started.

"'Mr. Natsume', please," he corrected me. "That is how I was known to Sir Reginald, and to everyone else in the house."

"Mr. Natsume, I appreciate that you may feel unhappy about seeing the body of your employer, but my friend would not ask you to do this were it not important."

"'Life is uncertain; death is certain,' as the Buddha has said," he replied. "I have buried two wives and five children in my time. I will do as you ask."

"Your testimony has been a model of clarity," Holmes said. "Thank you."

Mr Natsume bowed to us, and left.

"Still it seems to me," I observed, "that the only corroboration of Mr. Hsen's story comes from Mr. Natsume, and the only corroboration of Mr. Natsume's story comes from Mr. Hsen. What if they murdered Sir Reginald together, and are covering for each other?"

"I cannot rule out that possibility yet," Holmes replied,

the world," he began, "but I was witness to some of the early signs. I saw first-hand how membership of the organisation known as the The Righteous and Harmonious Fists spread through the young and poor natives of the province of Shandong. It was the Christian missionaries who first disparagingly referred to them as 'Boxers', but that was a lazy misnomer based on the martial arts and weapons training they practised. It also ignored the high degree of supernatural belief promoted by that organisation. Its adherents truly believed that they were invulnerable to Western weapons and that an army of ghostly divine soldiers would aid them in their revolution. They swept through China, picking up new members in their thousands, and converged on Peking with the aim of supporting the Empress Dowager Cixi-Hsi and the Qing government in an attempt to throw all Westerners out of the country. It was a bloody time, by all accounts, and it took the combined military might of Great Britain, America, Russia, the Austro-Hungarian Empire, France, Germany, Italy and Japan to lift the siege. The current Chinese regime is still paying punitive reparations to all eight nations, and will continue to do so for many years to come." He waved a hand generally in the direction of the door. "And that, by the way, is another reason why it is unlikely that Mr. Natsume and Mr. Hsen would be conspiring to murder their employer. China and Japan have already fought a war over who should have the most influence over the Korean Empire, and Japan aided the West during the Boxer Rebellion. The two nations traditionally distrust one another and have opposing political ambitions in the region.

In the case of Mr. Natsume and Mr. Hsen, what appears to override the animosities between their home countries is the two men's shared loyalty to Sir Reginald. No, I cannot see them in the joint role of murderers."

"But who, then?" I asked.

"I suspect outside influence, but to establish that I need to concentrate on *why* the crime was committed, rather than by whom."

"Surely we need to establish *how* it was done," I pointed out.

"Oh, that is a simple matter," he said. "Hardly worthy of consideration. *Why* is more challenging." He abruptly slammed a hand down on the arm of the chair. "But it would be remiss of me not to investigate even the low probability that those two worthy gentlemen had formed a cabal. We should talk to the butler!"

*

In short order Henderson, the butler, was brought before us. He was pale and shaking, but it was not my friend's manner that had caused his state. It was the death of his master.

"How long have you been in Sir Reginald's service?" Holmes asked.

"Forty-eight years, man and boy," he said, the first words I had heard him utter.

"Through Sir Reginald's time as Minister to China and to the Empire of Korea, as well as Consul-General to the Empire of Japan?"

"Indeed, sir. I have travelled the globe with Sir Reginald, and during that time he has been the most charitable of men."

"And the two foreign gentlemen he picked up along the

way – Mr. Hsen and Mr. Natsume? What is the nature of your relationship with them?"

"Nothing but cordial, sir," Henderson replied. "They are both men of honour, despite their origins."

"Have you noticed any stresses or strains between them?"

"Mr. Natsume is Japanese and Mr. Hsen is Chinese. That's like putting an Englishman to work with a Frenchman and expecting them to get on – but they do, in honour of Sir Reginald." He paused, and his eyes grew moist. "Or, rather, they *did*."

"What about their relationship with Sir Reginald? Were you aware of any strains there?"

He shook his head emphatically. "Nothing, sir. The three of us were steadfast in our love for, and support of, that great gentleman."

Holmes nodded. "Two final things – first, as butler you handle all the post coming into the house, do you not?"

"Indeed I do, sir."

"Has either of those gentlemen received any letters or telegrams in the past few weeks?"

"No, sir, none." He shrugged. "In fact, I don't recall them ever receiving communication of any kind."

"Very good. And second, are you aware of any strangers – especially any foreign strangers – in the neighbourhood recently?"

"Certainly not, sir. Word travels fast around these parts. I would have heard from the butcher in the village if there were any strangers around, and from the fishmonger as well."

"Excellent. Thank you very much, Mr. Henderson."

The butler bowed slightly, and retreated.

"I can do little more until I hear from Mycroft," Holmes said, confirming my earlier supposition. "I need to search Sir Reginald's study, but I fear Mr. Hsen will not allow that without pressure from above."

"In that case," I ventured, "perhaps you would care to explain to me the exact mechanism by which Sir Reginald was dispatched."

He shrugged. "Why not? It will pass the time." Springing from his chair, he rushed out of the room. A little more slowly, due to a recurring touch of rheumatism in my left knee, I followed.

*

Holmes repeated the route we had taken earlier, ending at the edge of the orchard. Mr. Natsume was just backing away from Sir Reginald's body, which he had thoughtfully shrouded in a silken cloth. As he turned and saw us, he said:

"The garden is exactly as I left it, apart from the set of footprints in the sand leading directly to Sir Reginald's body and back again."

"Those are my footprints," I explained.

"And now also my own," he continued. "I would like to erase both sets, for symmetry and because Sir Reginald would have wanted it, but I presume you would like this place left exactly as it is?"

"Indeed, and thank you, Mr. Natsume," Holmes said. "You are an artist as well as a craftsman."

The gardener bowed, and left. I gazed out at the shrouded body. "I still cannot see how the murder was accomplished," I said, shaking my head in bewilderment.

"As the orangery leads to the greenhouse and the greenhouse to the orchard," Holmes said, "*how* leads to *who*, and *who* to *why*."

"Pray explain."

"Having ruled out cranes, pendulums and cannons, I considered what materials might be employed to project a weapon and then return it to its owner without touching the ground. It was not long before I recalled those abominable elasticated braces your latest wife has persuaded you to wear. I imagined a set – Y-shaped, like yours – but much, much longer. Initially I imagined them being rapidly secured between two trees symmetrically set on either side of the path with a heavy weight fastened in the centre. Picture, if you will, that heavy weight pulled back to the limit of the material's elasticity. The weight, when released, would be projected forwards at great velocity, stretching the elastic. At the limit of its trajectory, the weight meets Sir Reginald's skull with fatal results, but the stretched elastic pulls it back again before it can touch the ground. Its releasers catch it, detach the elastic from the trees and make their escape, leaving only Sir Reginald's corpse behind."

"Ingenious," I said, entranced – if slightly discomfited at his casual discussion of an item of gentlemen's clothing that was rarely mentioned in public, and almost always covered, as such things should properly be, by a waistcoat.

"But unsupported by the evidence. Fastening such straps would cause some damage to whatever trees were selected, and I have found no such damage."

"Then what? How?"

"Imagine the same Y-shaped braces, held by three men. One is on the path, holding the heavy weight. The other two walk quietly from the orchard towards the Zen Garden, then encircle it until they are standing on either side of Sir Reginald and slightly behind him. They will have stretched the elasticated material almost to its limit. Sir Reginald is facing forwards with his eyes closed, in meditation. Whatever sounds he hears he will put down to wildlife or his gardener. The man on the path releases the weight, with the outcome I have previously described."

"Why not just shoot him, or fire an arrow into his back?"

"Because that would leave obvious evidence, and the point was for the crime to look bizarre and inexplicable. Something supernatural."

"You used that word earlier, at the house. You were talking about the Boxers."

"I am pleased you were listening. You had an abstracted look on your face as I was speaking. But yes, I pointed out that the Boxers were inculcated with a belief in divine and supernatural powers. And that is where *how* points to *why*. Sir Reginald was a well-respected British figure. His death by apparently ghostly means would echo on the other side of the world, and perhaps act as a rallying call." He shrugged. "In fact, it is entirely possible that Sir Reginald had heard from some contact in China that another rebellion was afoot, and agents were dispatched to silence him before he could pass that message on."

"Fiendish," I breathed, shaking my head.

"And implausible," Holmes snorted. "Chinese agents

skulking around in Sussex would be as –" he waved his hand at the trees behind us "– worms in an apple, and the butler has already told us that none were seen."

"They could have hired British criminals to do their dirty work for them."

"They could have, but I think there is another explanation." He turned away, then back. "Oh, you may wish to examine the ground on either side of the garden. There are faint traces of boot prints that pay dividends if closely examined." He pulled out his magnifying glass and threw it towards me. I caught it awkwardly. "Don't bother examining the ground here, on the path. Whatever prints there might have been were unwittingly covered over by us." He turned and stalked away.

*

I did as my friend had suggested, and examined the ground at those two locations – acutely aware of Sir Reginald's shrouded body still in the centre of the circle. I found traces of the soles of boots in both places but, looking closely through Holmes's glass, I noticed black granules in the compressed soil. I picked some of the soil up and rubbed it between my fingers. The granules were harder than the soil but softer than gravel or sand would have been. Most odd, I thought.

Eventually I returned to the house and was directed by the butler to Sir Reginald's impressive study, which was panelled in a fine-grained light wood and dominated by several life-sized marble statues of rather plump, robed figures.

"Ah," Holmes said, "you are just in time."

"You have found something?"

"No, I have failed to find something. Sir Reginald had a very precise filing system. He kept not only every letter he had ever received, filed by date and subject, but also the envelopes they came in. I do the same thing. I do it for the data inherent in the postmark, the paper and the ink used; I suspect he did it because of the wide variety of foreign stamps on them."

I felt it was about time I proved that I could think as well. "I conjecture that you found a mismatch between the number of letters and the number of envelopes."

Holmes smiled. "I have trained you well, over the years. Yes, there are three letters missing, sent to Sir Reginald over the course of the past year. The letters all came from an area in the north of England. Sir Reginald also kept copies of any letters he himself sent, but I have not been able to trace any replies to those three absent letters."

I glanced at the French windows. "The letters and any responses were stolen? By an intruder?"

"Possibly, but I think not. I am informed by Mr. Hsen that Sir Reginald's son visited him two days ago. He, by the way," Holmes said with an oblique look, "will inherit the house and the grounds, but that is a secondary matter. More important is the identity of the person or people who instigated the murder. You noticed the residue in the footprints?"

"Indeed I did." I searched for the right word. "They seemed surprisingly soft. *Rubbery*, perhaps."

"You have hit upon exactly the right word, my friend."

I was about to ask for further details when the air was shattered by a sudden burst of noise and the blast of an autocar's horn from outside.

"That will be brother Mycroft, straining the suspension

of the vehicle that drove him down from London after sending the telegram that permitted me to search this study, and the rest of the house if necessary. No doubt he is eager to hear my report."

"And what will you tell him?"

He smiled. "Let us see just how far my training has percolated into your intellect." And with that he was gone.

I walked over to the window and stared out at the greenhouse, trying to piece together all the evidence in my possession, to form the picture that my friend had already seen.

"I would point out," he unexpectedly said from behind me, "that the north of England is known as its industrial heartland."

By the time I turned around, he had gone again.

Massively oversized elastic – or, in fact, rubberised – braces. Granules of rubber. The industrial heartland of England. Sir Reginald Summersly himself, and his knowledge, contacts and former senior positions. How did it all fit together?

I decided to treat the problem not like a jigsaw, but a medical diagnosis. Sometimes, when a patient came into my surgery, I would ask him to list everything that was wrong, and typically there would be a collection of symptoms that matched a disease and one or two that were unrelated and caused by other things – headaches, perhaps, or a fungal infection of the feet. The trick was to isolate the extraneous symptoms but retain and connect the important ones.

I was staring at the greenhouse, and listening without realising to the continuous chugging sound of Mycroft Holmes's car engine and the sound of voices, when a germ of an idea struck me. Granules of rubber, elasticated ropes and industry could all be connected. Sir Reginald's previous career could not. Perhaps the connection was not to him, but to the house.

Not the house – the greenhouse! A place where tropical plants could be grown in England's temperate climate! I remembered reading somewhere that all the rubber used in England – most notably in the production of tyres for autocars – was imported from the Far East by long and dangerous ship voyages. Given the increasing unrest in that region, would the manufacturers of England's rubber not wish to grow rubber trees in England? And if so, would it not be far more 'efficient' (a phrase that always made my hackles rise) to buy up an enormous greenhouse and furnace already in existence than build their own? What if they had tried to purchase Sir Reginald's house, or perhaps just his greenhouse, but had been rebuffed? What if they decided, in their heartless industrial manner, to dispense with Sir Reginald, to cause his death and blame it on a mysterious Chinese secret society, and deal directly with his more malleable scion?

From outside I heard the sound of two voices, rising above the noise of the engine. That would be Holmes and his brother arguing, but about what? Grimly I found myself wondering which side Mycroft would be on, if he had to choose. My friend, I knew, would be a firm supporter of the British countryside and British traditions. He would not wish to see the pleasant uplands of the south of England covered by factories belching smoke, despite his superficial support for progress and modernity; Mycroft, on the other hand, was a pragmatist, always looking for whatever benefit accrued to the Crown.

They were shouting now, outside.

Soon my friend would stalk back in, shaking furiously following his confrontation with his brother – a confrontation that could have only one result. I did not have to be a detective to foresee that. My job would be to soothe him, calm him, and settle him on a more stable emotional keel. That was how it had always been.

It may have said 'John Watson, M.D.' on my shingle and on my business cards, but in truth the most important thing in my life was that I was Sherlock Holmes's friend, and I always would be.

*

And here this tale must conclude. I have no doubts whatsoever that Sherlock Holmes could have discovered the murderers of Sir Reginald Summersly, but Mycroft Holmes saw to it that this did not come to pass. Perhaps the elder of the two brothers was right; sometimes larger considerations must prevail. In any case, I have decided to provide a record of these events to show that even Sherlock Holmes's pursuit of truth and justice on occasion was stymied by immovable obstacles. Such was a rare outcome indeed to one of our adventures, but I would be remiss were I not to lay out an example for the reader's contemplation. An odd aftertaste remains in my mouth upon concluding this record. I trust that I am not alone in that sensation.

THE PRIDEAUX MONOGRAPH

CARA BLACK

Holmes had left me a message to meet at dusk on a houseboat. Not a cheerful hour, and as usual he had provided me with no clue as to what the matter concerned. Weary, I made my way to the canal basin bordering Maida Vale on an October evening in the second year of the Great War.

The patter of the rain on the canal's pewter surface competed with my muted footsteps on the towpath. In the mist, swans glided, and the occasional lost seagull cried its mournful wail. Hugging the towpath were moored barge-like affairs turned into houseboats. What Holmes was doing here eluded me.

Above the tree-lined path, street lights flickered as branches whipped in the wind. Caught in the dim glow were the façades of sagging Italianate and Georgian mansions. The days of opulence were long gone. These edifices were now filled with squatters and poor families, each living in one high-ceilinged room.

My walk from Paddington left me wishing for a crackling fireplace, a warm teapot and an escape from my wet boots. A pang hit me on remembering Mrs. Hudson and our erstwhile lodgings in Baker Street. At sixty-four, I was too old for gallivanting on more investigations.

Passing by the Westbourne Terrace Road Bridge over the pool-like basin, I descended towards Delamere Terrace. I finally saw the houseboat with *Ariel* painted in turquoise on the prow. I crossed the ramp, thumping over the water-stained wood. The melodic strains of a violin came from inside.

I knocked.

"Enter, Watson."

The music continued as I opened the door. Inside the houseboat I was met by the pleasing warmth of a charcoal stove and the smell of honey. Fogged-up, round port windows, the handles in anchor shape, lent a nautical air.

"How are the bees doing these days, Holmes?"

"This time of year they hibernate, Watson, so I am enjoying the fruits of their labour, which I harvested just a few weeks ago." Holmes set down his violin in a case, closed it, and snapped the clasp. "Take some."

Holmes was wearing a simple hunter-green jacket and dark trousers and appeared prepared to venture outside.

"Ready, Watson?"

For what, I wondered, rather more inclined to rest my legs and warm up.

"Holmes, I'm not sure that I can be of help anymore. My joints have been creaking quite a bit lately."

These days I saved my energy for hospital work in a special clinic. I tended to soldiers who had received a wound to the face. The work consisted of surgery when possible, as well as the customising of masks for those men who had been so horribly disfigured that the scalpel's art could provide no relief.

"Hmmm. Face masks coming along then?"

"So-so. How did you know?"

"There is plaster stuck to the side of your shirt sleeve."

As always, he noticed details that would have passed me by.

"I see. The plaster, as a matter of fact, appears somewhat too thick for masks."

"Rubber resin should work. Much lighter."

I made a mental note to suggest this to my colleagues.

"I wasn't aware of this aquatic bolthole of yours, Holmes."

"A remnant of better days, Watson. And now a case has washed up on my gangplank, so to speak."

He gestured at some photographs – all gruesome in the extreme – caught in the glare of a torch and labelled 'Property of Scotland Yard': a man floating semi-clothed in the canal, face down, body bloated, pale feet and fingers exhibiting the unmistakable marks of nibbling fish.

Holmes pinched the bridge of his nose.

"Look closely, Watson. The canal is the one outside. These photographs were taken yesterday around midnight. Oddly, the corpse is barefoot…"

I peered at the photographs. The water gleamed like enamel and I recognised the swans. "I have just passed this bridge." I looked up. "Is Scotland Yard tempting you from retirement again?"

He shrugged. "What do you notice about the victim, Watson?"

Holmes handed me two other photos, these from the morgue, showing the man laid out face up on a dissecting table.

"His throat is slit."

My mind went to recent newspaper articles that addressed gang muggings and other violent crime in nearby Maida Vale.

"A robbery gone wrong?"

"What about the rash on his palms and the soles of his feet?"

"Ah! I should have noticed. I remember, during my internship in days of yore we had a similar case. The man's wife discovered he had been having affairs and given her syphilis. She slashed his throat with a kitchen knife."

Holmes shook his head. "Too easy, Watson. Granted, he had syphilis, but he was a swindler."

"A syphilitic swindler. And you know this how?"

Holmes held up a piece of what looked like tea-stained paper. I could barely make out a few dark smears upon it.

"A ransom note found in his back pocket. The ink has mostly washed away. But using a tincture I formulated for the Royal Navy back in the Boer War I've made most of it legible again."

I merely nodded at Holmes's feat of applied chemistry. "Does this imply he was murdered before he delivered the note?"

"That remains to be seen."

I leaned in to decipher the message:

I've what you w   Put 20,000 £ p_ _ _ _ behind
gateway post at B P Warwick Cres night for manuscri

"What do you make of this, Holmes?" My companion had
marked with pencil a number of blank spaces after the 'p'. "P
for pounds? Seems funny to spell it out."

"Indeed it does."

"What about the 'L' that's crossed out?"

He shrugged.

"And the meaning of 'B P'?"

"Too early to tell, Watson."

It had been a long day. I sat down near the charcoal stove,
drank a cup of tea and must have dozed off.

*

Holmes was shaking me. "Wake up, Watson."

He grabbed his coat from a hanger. "We are going to a séance."

"Don't tell me those are still in fashion."

"More than ever, with all the sons and husbands lost on
the front."

The missing and the dead loomed large in every family's
mind.

"I am giving my energy to the wounded these days, Holmes…"

He handed me my damp cap.

"This concerns a soldier, Watson. And we shall meet this
soldier, a generally well-informed gentleman tells me, where
the spirits are contacted."

"If it is one of our soldiers who requires assistance, I am of
course at your service."

"My car is outside. We are going to Miss Robinson's."

"Another participant?"

"Miss Robinson is the seer. The sibyl. There is always a Miss Robinson at this establishment."

"You mean they are interchangeable?"

"Not exactly. You will see, Watson."

Holmes took the wheel of his Humber equipped with a Dynamo Self-Starter, quite a modern roadster for Holmes. During our short journey, I kept my gaze on the scene outside. Sandbags ringed the gaping bomb crater on a side street left by a recent Zeppelin raid. We alighted at a public house where the signboard read 'Ale and spirits, private banquet rooms'. Inside the dark wood-panelled premises, we passed an inebriated man and ascended the stairs to the next floor. We padded over plush red carpet, past potted palms into a quiet corridor.

Here, a man with dark keen eyes and a moustache ushered us forward. "This way, *messieurs*."

"You are…?"

"*Alain, à votre service, Monsieur Holmes.*"

Alain gave a slight bow and left us at the landing.

So we were expected. Holmes paused at a double door and bade me enter.

Three people sat at a round dining table. The furnishings were heavy dark wood with red velvet curtains, while candles sputtered from nooks and crannies. The smell of candied violets came from a glass bowl on a sideboard. The young woman looked about twenty and wore a colourful headscarf and hoop earrings. A middle-aged man sitting across from her wore a drab grey suit, with an unhealthy pallor to match.

The young soldier had an expectant expression on his long face. He fidgeted in his chair. Why was he here? I sat between him and the middle-aged man.

Holmes sat across from me at the lace-covered table.

"Please join hands," said the young woman with the scarf. "We shall then ready ourselves for the guiding."

The young man closed his eyes. His large hand felt dry as it held mine in a loose grip. The woman, whom I took for Miss Robinson, inhaled and asked each of us to focus on our respective question, to keep it present in our mind. For a moment I floated back in time to a séance I had attended during Victoria's reign.

The middle-aged man squeezed my hand.

I chose the surgery question to do with facial disfigurement procedures that had been on my mind all afternoon.

"Doctor, remember your training." Her voice vibrated now with a low urgency. "Go back to your student days. The answer lies there."

My eyes opened onto the face of Miss Robinson. By Jove, now I was impressed. I wanted to ask more. Her eyes were closed in concentration. A sheen of perspiration dampened her upper lip. She breathed deeply in the flickering candlelight. I closed my eyes and thought back to what they had taught me at Netley all those years ago about the art of treating burn victims.

Her voice rang out again.

"Vyvyan, your question feels unclear. Nothing comes. I'm not hearing an answer from your brother."

The soldier next to me stirred. "Cecil's in my thoughts," he said. "He died in the trenches before we could meet here."

Here as in London? Or did he mean the séance?

Miss Robinson's voice changed, became higher in pitch, urging.

"Ask your question again."

Vyvyan whispered, "I'd like to say goodbye."

"Goodbye? He's not answering. First, you must ask a question."

Silence.

"Why am I here?"

A cold gust of wind swept the room, the candles sputtered. Two went out. A scent as of spice clove wafted through the air.

"Ah, there's your answer, Vyvyan. Your father says to look to the time when you were four years old."

"My father?" His voice wavered. "But how?"

"The way will appear, it will be clear. Be open, Vyvyan."

Again, the spicy scent filled the room, and to my surprise a green carnation had appeared on the table.

"What does this mean?"

"Your father has spoken, Vyvyan." The young man slumped and remained quiet for the rest of the session.

So far impressed with young Miss Robinson, I confess my scepticism was turning towards belief. Her straight manner and prompts seemed de rigueur for a seer. She had certainly known my question. The middle-aged man beside me was engulfed in his own private pain. Tears trailed down his cheeks and he cried out, "Marie, Marie, what should I do now?"

Miss Robinson's hands trembled on the table. A goblet behind her on the open cabinet shelf tottered. Just like that it fell with a crash. Shards splintered and scattered, glimmering in the remaining candlelight.

The young soldier beside me cried out in surprise. The middle-aged man's eyes widened. His hand clenched mine so hard it hurt.

"Marie's spirit tells me you must leave your love affair with liquor," said Miss Robinson. "Pick up the pieces. Reassemble your life. Find another port of call."

Another cold wind rushed through. Draughts whirled around my feet, the windows rattled, and we were plunged into darkness. A presence filled the room, shaking my composure.

By the time the candles were re-lit I noticed the glass shards had disappeared from the floor. The goblet – intact – was back on the shelf and now held the green carnation. But no one had come into the room. It felt as if a spirit had passed through. Uneasy, I tried to catch Holmes's gaze. The attendant in livery who had welcomed us now handed the spent medium a small glass of what looked like the common cure-all of a Guinness stout.

We rose and slowly filed out of the room, the melancholy and strangeness giving me an odd feeling. I might have attended a wake with the dead hovering, I thought, in the almost palpable miasma of grief.

On the stairs to the second landing stood Mycroft, Holmes's elder brother. The look he gave Holmes indicated that this was no chance meeting. Mycroft had aged and his waistcoat stretched even tighter than I remembered over his massive frame. His left hand rested on a cane, yet his complexion was ruddy, and he looked in good health.

"Shall we repair downstairs, Sherlock?" He inclined his head towards me. "Doctor, always a pleasure. I've engaged a private dining room. Vyvyan, please join us."

*

The bright room lit by a gleaming chandelier was a welcome change of scene after the gloom-filled séance. Flocked red and gold wallpaper, gilt chairs and linen tablecloth added another layer to my sense of well-being, not to mention the savoury smells of garlic and onion, beans and bacon. My stomach growled in anticipation.

We were served by Alain, the young moustachioed man who had directed us to the landing and had brought Miss Robinson her half-pint of stout. He now wore the long white apron characteristic of Parisian waiters, muttered in French, and tidied sauce from the edge of my plate with a linen towel, demonstrating the kind of attention to detail that I remembered from my honeymoon with Mrs. Watson in Paris.

As we dug into the cassoulet, definitely the work of a French chef, Mycroft said:

"As you might have guessed, Vyvyan, this gentleman is my dearest brother, Mr. Sherlock Holmes." He gestured towards me. "His trusty chronicler, Dr. Watson. Now tell them what you have told me."

The young soldier wiped his mouth with his napkin. He set it down, as if steeling himself.

"It's all so unexpected." He hesitated. "My wife's letter concerning my brother Cyril's death reached me last week. Cyril was shot in the trenches by a German sniper."

Mycroft touched his greying moustache. "My condolences

again. Your brother earned his battalion's respect in India and I counted him a fine captain. Worthy of the Victoria Cross."

If this gave the young soldier any solace, I do not know. He spoke with more confidence.

"We'd been separated at an early age, schooled in different countries, and after our mother died, her family kept us apart."

Holmes nodded. "Due to the past scandal of your father and his trial?"

The young soldier looked at Holmes, then down, then to me. "Dr. Watson. You need to know my full name. I am Vyvyan Holland. My father... my father was Oscar Wilde."

Wilde had, of course, twenty years ago been pilloried for homosexuality and imprisoned. People with power and influence had then repressed his works, bankrupted his estate, and all but scratched his name off his books.

Vyvyan turned to Holmes. "Yes, they never liked my father. To avoid more scandal, Mother changed our last names, refused to speak of him. The past was forbidden. If I'm honest, I feared my father was a bank robber, a con man, or that we were illegitimate."

Vyvyan took a sip of wine to fortify himself. "Only when I turned eighteen did I learn of my father's identity through his literary executor, Robert Ross, who had also been my father's friend."

Holmes set down his knife. "Had your father appointed him executor?"

Vyvyan shrugged. "I don't know." He again reached for his wine glass. "Ross pulled the estate out of bankruptcy, even solicited donations, and moved my father's body from a pauper's grave in Paris to one in Père Lachaise. A few years ago, I helped rebury him."

These words cast a pall over the table.

"Was Cyril present for this ceremony?"

Vyvyan shook his head. "Cyril had become an officer in India. We kept in touch, wrote to each other, but weren't close. Yet he was the family I had."

"When did you last see your brother? Speak with him?"

"Three years ago." Vyvyan looked close to tears again. "But we'd planned to meet here in London. It's my biggest regret. And now he's sent me a letter from the grave."

Holmes's intense look focused on the young soldier. This look, I knew, he reserved for chess problems and human beings he was keen on understanding.

"What do you mean?"

"We were a few miles apart in the trenches. I never knew. I spoke to Cyril's battery commander and the brother officer who was with him when he was killed. He gave me the bare facts, then handed me Cyril's bridle, his revolver and his field glasses. And a few days later, I got his last letter."

I watched the young man, noting his moist palms and beleaguered expression, and felt pity for him at this sad tale.

"What service can you render, Sherlock?" asked Mycroft.

My friend lowered his knife and fork. "What exactly do you wish me to do, young man?"

"Help me locate my father's supposed lost manuscript, which Cyril believed existed."

Holmes dabbed his mouth with the napkin.

"You and your brother hadn't seen each other for a time,"

he said thoughtfully. "Do you know if he trekked in the Himalayas?"

Vyvyan's head bobbed in agreement. "Why do you ask?"

Ignoring the question, Holmes continued, "Visited Tibet?"

"Yes, my brother liked adventure. He served eight years in India and he did take time to visit Tibet. I had no clue until recently that he had done so."

"Then I met your brother in 1913, at the Jokhang Temple in Lhasa."

"You, Mr. Holmes?"

"My meditation studies were with the Dalai Lama. Foreigners were scarce in Tibet. I recall your brother's dislike of *tsampa*, barley powder to make their butter tea. He carried mystery with him in a way one does who wants to eradicate the past. But never does."

"Cyril could not countenance the memory of our father. I've always thought he covered his brittle feelings by proving his manhood in the army."

Holmes nodded. "Your father I met once, at a dinner at the Langham Hotel. Watson might remember. It was around the time of *The Sign of the Four*."

"Hear, hear," I nodded. "Who could forget that case?"

"At this dinner, the editor commissioned your father to write a story that encompassed his recent ideas. The editor eventually rejected it. Your father later published it as *The Picture of Dorian Gray*. He seemed a very kind man. Extremely witty and with a turn of phrase that charmed everyone at the table. As everywhere, until the unfortunate trial."

Holmes nodded to Mycroft.

"I take it you have Captain Holland's latest military records with you?"

Mycroft reached into the inside pocket of his jacket and handed a double-folded manila envelope to Holmes.

What in blazes was going on here? Holmes's techniques, I knew, would be revealed in due time. As always, my role was to pay close attention to the events and to go along.

"You'll help, Mr. Holmes?" asked Vyvyan. "Can I count on you?"

"Yes, you can count on me. I shall need your assistance, though. Please give me the address of your father's literary executor, and the friends of your parents who visited when you were small."

Voices came in the background.

Holmes, putting a finger to his lips, shot Vyvyan a look and handed him a notebook.

Vyvyan filled the page with a number of lines.

Holmes nodded to me and stood. "Let us excuse ourselves."

I had my eye on a crème caramel, but it appeared that was not to be.

*

We remounted the stairs to the floor where the séance had been held. The potted palms and dim chandeliers looked of another age.

"Did you observe Miss Robinson, Watson?"

"I'd say she was quite accurate with her comments."

"Her rather vague reference to medicine, knowing that you are a doctor?" Holmes raised his eyebrows.

The parlour with the round table in the centre was empty. The dusty lace curtains and hollow atmosphere remained. Holmes reached for a bell pull and footsteps padded from an exterior corridor.

"Yes?"

The young Miss Robinson appeared. Her hair now hung in locks down her neck. She looked tired.

"It's late, gentlemen. Please return tomorrow evening."

"Ah, no need to trouble yourself. We are here to speak to the original Miss Robinson. Mrs. Robinson, in fact."

The woman stared.

"I have consulted her in the past and you must be—"

"Grandmother?" the woman interrupted.

"Show them in," came a quavering voice from an adjacent room.

We followed the young woman through a black curtain into a back parlour. An old woman sat with her socked feet on an ottoman. Her grey curls escaped from a mob cap, of a kind I had not seen since Queen Victoria's time.

The woman's lined face broke into a grin as Holmes produced a bottle of Madeira from his pocket. "Holmes, you shouldn't have! But now that you have, let's raise a glass. Vera!"

The young woman appeared with a tray bearing exquisite amber-coloured sherry glasses with bevelled edges.

"Did she do well, Holmes?"

"Ask Watson."

I raised my glass to the young woman. "Quite convincing, I must say."

The whiffs of Madeira brought back summer evenings on the Spanish coast, the hint of oranges, and the chirping cicadas.

"Was the young man convinced?"

"You speak through her, Mrs. Robinson. Why wouldn't he be?" said Holmes.

"Such is the tragedy of getting old; we lose our strength and must teach the coming generation."

I sipped my Madeira.

"You conducted séances in the era of the young man's parents?"

"His mother, Constance, came often, as did her set. Oscar, his father, came so often he called me the Sibyl of Mortimer Street."

She savoured the Madeira, smacked her lips.

"Hence the green carnation?" asked Holmes.

Her crow's feet crinkled as she smiled. "His trademark, always in his lapel. And his downfall. The last time I foresaw Wilde's future was here, in this room." Her eyes closed. "I remember my prophecy: 'A very brilliant life for you up to a certain point, then I see a wall. Beyond the wall I see nothing.'"

She sighed. "He heeded not the signs of danger foreseen by the spirit."

"What do you make of this request from the dead?"

Mrs. Robinson downed her Madeira, then held out her glass for another.

"It's not."

Befuddled, I lowered my glass.

"Not what, Mrs. Robinson?"

"You'll figure it out, Holmes," she said. "I'm tired."

She excused herself and we saw ourselves out.

In the car Holmes remained pensive, as was his wont. I pressed him as to Mrs. Robinson's possible meaning and was met by his reply, "Later, Watson."

*

The next morning, we arrived at a modest building in St. John's Wood, the residence of Robert Ross, Oscar Wilde's literary executor. Ross, a short, bearded Canadian in his sixties with a receding hairline, received us in his study. He wore an old-fashioned morning coat and, oddly enough, maroon carpet slippers.

"I'm so glad you've come," he said. "Frankly, I'm sceptical, but it's only right Vyvyan follows through. Poor Cyril, such a loss, alas…"

"My condolences," said Holmes. "Were you close to him?"

"Somewhat. I knew the boys well when they were small. Delightful children. Oscar asked after them constantly. Begging to visit them. Not even a letter was allowed. Shameful…" Ross paused, lost in the past, and raked his wispy black beard back from his face. "One of my favourite memories is of Oscar on the floor in the nursery playing with them for hours. Of course, that was before…" His voice trailed off.

"Do you have any thoughts regarding this lost manuscript?"

"I'm afraid not. For the past fifteen years since Oscar's death, my life's work has been to reclaim the licenses to produce his plays, but never once have I heard of such a manuscript…"

In the background, I heard someone speaking French.

"Oscar Wilde is finally acknowledged, due to my hard-won battles to keep his work in the public eye, to gather the residuals and royalties. With the scandal so much of his work was pirated. Lost."

Ross's stature gave him the appearance of a wrinkled child, a dwarf who had lived to old age. His last words, however, had carried force as if he were leading a crusade.

"Perhaps a manuscript could have been hidden in Constance's things," Ross said, regaining his equilibrium. "Secreted away by her to give to the boys when they attained maturity, and then forgotten."

He bade us sit down and offered us tea. We settled into two easy chairs, but declined the tea.

"Her family detested Wilde. Constance wanted the best for her boys and was persuaded by her elder brother to keep them 'safe' from scandal." Ross steepled his fingers. "Her brother died in Germany a month ago. Rumours float and suppositions abound. I deal in practicality, Mr. Holmes. If a manuscript ever existed, I would have known."

Yet I noticed that his brow had furrowed.

"How do you explain the letter Cyril received?" Holmes asked. "He did consider it credible enough to summon his brother from the trenches to meet."

Ross gave a mystified look. "Cyril didn't confide in me."

"Vyvyan does," said Holmes.

"In his own way, but it's more of a one-way street. I share progress on reclaiming his father's work. But why wouldn't Oscar have told me if such a manuscript existed, Mr. Holmes?"

Holmes stood and I followed, leaving Wilde's executor deep in thought and sadness. Back in the car, Holmes asked, "What did you make of him, Watson?"

"The chap garners income for the estate if the manuscript exists. Why wouldn't he be truthful?"

"That remains to be deduced."

Holmes took no notes. His mind, sharp as a blade, retentive as a steel trap, focused on details rarely apparent to me.

"No chance for us to visit Germany," he said.

"There's a war on, Holmes. Even you must acknowledge that."

*

The next morning, I returned early to the *Ariel*, where Holmes was reading the papers Mycroft had shared. I poured myself and Holmes tea from the pot on the table.

"No sugar, I am afraid," said Holmes. "Difficult to find these days."

I added some milk, then consulted my notebook. It rather felt like old times.

"How did you locate this boat, Holmes?"

Holmes's pipe had gone out. He knocked out the tobacco, put in a new pinch, lit it, and inhaled.

"The sound drew me. It was the rhythm of horses pulling barges on the towpath. More intriguing became the alteration in the sound as the horses went around the island."

Was Holmes becoming mystical with his advancing years? I need not have feared. "How sound carries, amplifies, echoes and recedes has always fascinated me," he continued. "Now, I am writing a paper on it, which the War Office commissioned for usage in battlefield strategy. I am beginning to see how it could relate to young Vyvyan's father's supposed long-lost manuscript."

"In what way, Holmes?"

"The evidence has not presented itself yet, Watson. It is all about digging out the facts."

The sound of boots came upon the deck, then a knock at the door. Holmes went to answer. Some change was passed and he tore open the telegram.

"Mycroft consulted his files, Watson."

He puffed as he read, then informed me that the Wilde boys' relatives on their maternal side had all died without issue in the bombing of their ancestral German home.

I let that message sink in and pondered its ramifications, as I watched the swans glide on the now khaki-coloured canal. "I suppose if the lost manuscript was at the relatives' house, it would now be gone."

"Possibly. But what if it had made its way to the London publishers? Or to Mr. Ross?"

It was my day off from the clinic. I proposed to Holmes that we have lunch at the Café Royal. There was rumour of veal on the menu this week. Before Holmes could reply, more knocks sounded on the door.

"Mr. Holmes?" Panting. "Dr. Watson?" Vyvyan's voice carried through the open porthole.

I whispered, "Wasn't he going to Brighton to see his wife?"

Holmes nodded and went to the door again. I sat back in the cushioned wicker chair, my leg a little stiff from the moisture on the boat.

Holmes greeted the young soldier, whose face was flushed, his lungs heaving as if he had been running. He leant over, put his hands on his knees and caught his breath.

"You have been contacted by the extortionist?" said Holmes.

Slowly, young Vyvyan raised his shoulders and face, his breath rippling in small spurts. "I was at the station, reached into my bag's pocket for my ticket, and came back with this." He waved a letter, then paused. "How did you know?"

"Pray sit. Watson, please pour this young man some tea."

The pot was cold. By the time I had brewed another, Holmes had set to work. He had donned gloves and was now carefully extracting the letter from the envelope. He proceeded to spread the letter out on a glass plate he used for photography.

Holmes then opened a concealed drawer in the boat's hull. He removed several tincture bottles I had seen previously and more with labels in Latin. The eyedropper bulbs fitting the small dark glass bottles were of indigo rubber, very expensive equipment.

"Watson, do you notice any similarity?"

I pulled my spectacles from their case, wiped the lenses, and peered closer.

"Quite similar, Holmes. I'd say it's the same colour of ink."

"Correct."

"Even the same handwriting as in the syphilitic man's note." The note read:

Didn't your brother inform you before he died? Put 20 thousand pounds behind gatepost of Beauchamp lodge 2 Warwick Avenue if you want your father's manuscript.

"That's it?" I shook my head.

"Any proof the manuscript exists?" said Holmes.

Vyvyan looked anxious. The cup of tea I had handed him was doing nothing to calm his nerves.

"Syphilis? Another note? Why didn't you inform me last night?"

Holmes nodded. "Apologies. I refrained upon the suggestion of Scotland Yard. We felt that in order to investigate the extortion threat and the individual behind these letters, it was better to keep you in the dark."

"I don't understand why." Vyvyan looked at his watch. "Now I've missed any trains going to Brighton. My wife will be disappointed."

"If you wish my assistance," said Holmes, "you must not hold back."

Vyvyan's hands quivered on the china cup.

"We found a second letter on a body floating in this very canal," Holmes continued.

"What?" Vyvyan's voice cracked with shock. "Who did you find? What's this to do with my brother?"

"It is under investigation. Now, Vyvyan, three letters. If you want my cooperation, show me the letter your brother received."

Vyvyan hugged his chest. "I never saw the letter sent to Cyril. In his letter to me, he only gave me the gist, said he'd explain when we met. He said, I'm the elder and we'll deal with this my way. Like always."

Tears brimmed in his eyes. He wiped them with his sleeve.

"Please explain to us what has happened from the very start."

"I hate reliving it yet again."

Holmes shook his head. "It will be the first time for us. It will help us catch whoever is behind this and the murder."

"All right, then. After my father's bankruptcy trial, my mother returned to our house in Chelsea. The butler had ransacked my father's office, taken things and left. She couldn't even grab our toys before the bailiffs came."

Vyvyan spoke as if from far away.

"I found out later. My mother's German family provided for us. At their behest, we changed our name, and we were forbidden any contact with my father. I was told never to speak of him. It was at my twenty-first birthday party, which Robbie Ross organised, that the stories came out. Cyril told me. We knew some valuable papers had been taken, valuable to us anyway. Sentimental value. There were hints that Father wrote a story for us. I heard the rumours and saw how hard Robbie worked to get my father's copyrighted works back."

"Did Cyril know or suspect who wrote him the letter?"

"I'm not sure."

"Who might have access to such a manuscript? Why had it not been seen before?"

"Maybe it had," said Vyvyan. "I want to ask Robbie."

Holmes nodded in such a way as to encourage Vyvyan to speak, keeping silent on the fact that we ourselves had already spoken to Ross. "When you re-buried your father in Paris in 1902, what do you remember?"

"Remember? I was young. Mostly a blur. But in 1914, when the memorial sculpture over his tomb was unveiled, I remember Ross made a point of paying my father's last hotel bill. The small Left Bank hotel was run by a good man and his family. After all these years, the hotelier remembered my father. His son was surprised that Ross was willing to settle the bill."

Vyvyan smiled. "It made me feel happy. But why would Scotland Yard ask you and mention nothing to me?"

"I consult with the Yard," said Holmes. "The homicide victim here in the canal presented a conundrum to the inspector, so he requested my assistance." Suddenly, he asked, "Do you speak French?"

Vyvyan nodded. "I attended school in Monaco. And I speak German. Does this mean you suspect me?"

Holmes registered little emotion at the best of times. His analytical mind put others ill at ease. My physician's manner helped in these situations. After all, the poor young soldier on leave faced a return to the trenches where his brother had just died.

I put my hand on Vyvyan's arm. "To solve a problem, one needs facts and details. An army goes on the attack only after the layout of the battlefield is known, eh?" I poured him another cup of steaming tea, passed him the milk.

Vyvyan sipped. I saw a faint resemblance to his father. The long full face, the fleshy mouth.

"Mr. Holmes's investigations are thorough and scientific. He needs to establish the sequence of events."

"The sequence of events? When these letters demanding money for our father's supposed manuscript came?" Vyvyan reached deep into his pack. He pulled out a soldier's diary where pay, chits, canteen bills and so on were recorded, as well as dates of service and leave. "On pay day last month I'd gone to send my wife my pay and there was the note from Cyril."

"Date, please," said Holmes.

"September the fifteenth. I marked it. Cyril said he'd received a demand for money in order to have our father's lost manuscript."

"What did your brother do?"

Vyvyan's brow beetled in pain. He seemed young for his years, and despite his exposure to the horrors of war, sheltered and naïve.

"I am waiting," said Holmes, tapping his Turkish slippers.

"I don't know any more than that Cyril arranged for us to meet here in London. He told me to request leave and we'd find out if this was authentic."

"Did you see any proof?"

Vyvyan shook his head. "Cyril was already dead when I received the letter. But it was too late to cancel my leave. I thought I'd find something here…"

"Your brother told you that you would both be attending Miss Robinson's séance?"

Vyvyan nodded.

"The séance was supposed to lead you to the right person?"

"I assumed so."

"Your brother was a spiritualist?"

Vyvyan shrugged. "I don't know. We hadn't seen each other for a long time."

Holmes paused to light his pipe. He exhaled a puff of smoke, then changed the topic of conversation: "Did your brother or the estate have funds to pay the extortionist if the manuscript proved authentic?"

"I don't know. I thought Robbie would handle it. I can't imagine that Cyril would be able to raise so much money."

The boat rocked gently in the wake lapping against the hull as a barge, pulled by draught horses, passed by on the canal. A flash of blue azure sky appeared; the greyish mists had melted. Sunlight dappled the linden tree branches.

"My leave ends in two days. I'll ask my wife to come up to London so it won't be a wasted—"

Holmes interrupted. "First, you will write a letter according to my instructions. Drop it off at Miss Robinson's and then alert me when you receive a reply at your soldier's lodgings. After that you return here. You will not go to meet the extortionist."

"Why, Holmes?"

"Vyvyan knows too much, Watson. His life is in danger. You will go in his place."

Vyvyan stood up. His body bristled with anger. "I've survived the trenches of Artois."

"Risking your life for King and country is patriotism," said Holmes, "but losing it to a greedy man who's extorting you isn't. The swindler is playing to your emotions, using your father's fame and notoriety to hook you into his scheme. You don't want him to win at this. Neither would your brother. This villain has killed once, and he will again. The final chance to make money. You're the last descendant. Besides, I haven't said that you have no role to play in what's coming."

Ten minutes later, Vyvyan made his way on the towpath to the stairs and disappeared on Delamere Terrace.

"By Jove, Holmes, the villain could have followed him here. Be waiting for him."

Holmes was going through his armoire. He tossed a set of boot inserts in my direction.

"No one kills a cash cow until he has milked it, Watson."

Maybe it was the sight of too many damaged young men, but my heart was not in this enterprise.

"Don't you realise, Watson, you'll be helping him right a wrong. This too is your battlefield. Not mending a face this time, but a heart. I cannot trust him to go himself. He would lose his nerve and commit some kind of folly. You need to go. No swindler should get away with this while our men are dying in the trenches."

Holmes was right.

*

At 11.30 p.m., I met Mycroft outside Paddington station. I took a heavy, worn travel bag from him and remounted the cab. Ten minutes later, I alighted a hundred yards from Warwick Avenue. I was wearing Vyvyan's long military coat, army cap and muffler, and also Holmes's boot inserts to make me taller. In the dark, my chances of being mistaken for Vyvyan appeared quite good. I determined to walk with a quick step and not to hunch, as age had been making me increasingly prone to do. Fuzzy old-fashioned gaslit street lamps glowed in the fog and reminded me of our investigations in the last century.

I found the address along the canal, a tall mansion that once would have been a country house outside London. The place was run down, taken over by squatters and a ghost of its former self. My heart skipped as I approached the sagging iron gate, askew on its hinges. Odours of damp foliage and canal water filled a cobbled courtyard. A fire smouldered in a rubbish bin. Sticks of furniture fuelled the flames.

Two tramps huddled over the fire, warming their hands. Neither gave me a look. I asked myself how I could leave a bag of money out here in the open, but relegated any doubts to the back of my mind. Stiffening my shoulders, I picked up my pace. Once I had reached the post, I exaggerated my movements in feeling around for a space. Then, as instructed, I placed the bag behind the post on a pile of rushes.

I looked around. Who would deliver the manuscript? The two indigents? Rustling sounds spoke of their disappearance. How did the swindler think he could make a success of this situation? Where was the promised manuscript?

Not a minute passed before I heard footsteps through the fog. My pulse increased. From the canal came the sound of rippling waves as a barge glided by.

Why had I agreed to this?

After what seemed like for ever, but must have been only a few seconds, a young boy, a chimney sweep by the look of his grimed face and sooty apron, appeared by my side as if out of nowhere.

"For you, sir." He handed me a brown paper bundle bound with string.

I shook the bundle and heard a rustling sound as of papers scraping against each other.

"Who gave you this?"

"Handed me a shilling," the boy said, shrugging, "and said you'd ask me that."

"Oh, he did?" My ire raised, I reached to grab the ragamuffin but – too quick for me – he bounded out of the gate. Thin strains of an outboard motor and the splash of water came from over the wall.

Hurriedly, I untied the string and parted the wrapping paper, while bringing the bundle to the light of the burning fire. Papers all right.

Newspapers.

I spun around. The bag I had placed on the rushes was gone. The two men I had taken for tramps were running out the gate together.

One turned and called over his shoulder, "Quick, Doctor!"

Upon reaching the towpath, it took me a moment until I could make out Holmes's *Ariel* in the fog. She sat in the canal waters and was blocking a small skiff. The stalled whine of the skiff's engine almost drowned out a man's shouts. His hands were raised above his head. Incredibly, Holmes had lassoed him by the waist and pulled him up onto the towpath. The bag of money had fallen from his hands.

"Good Lord, Holmes, where did you learn to do that?"

"Out west, Watson. Give Vyvyan a hand."

Vyvyan had appeared on *Ariel*'s deck and now jumped onto the towpath. He picked up the bag of money. It was counterfeit, as I later found out. The young soldier pointed to the man.

"Have you seen him before?" asked Holmes.

"Yes, I have! He was our waiter at Miss Robinson's place. And even there I thought I'd seen him before. He was also in the Paris hotel where my father passed away."

*

Later in the evening, we sat over a bottle of exquisite Burgundy which Holmes had produced from the hold, the small charcoal stove emitting warmth, the *Ariel* rocking as boats passed by. Vyvyan, Holmes and I drank in the lull after Scotland Yard had arrested the man, a certain Alain Prideaux.

"How did you deduce the identity of the culprit, Holmes?"

"As I have often told you, Watson, it is the process of

elimination. Everything was always tied to Paris."

"How's that?"

"You told us, Vyvyan, that you and Mr. Ross reburied your father – a costly process – and paid his debts at the hotel where he died. The father of the family who ran it, Monsieur Prideaux, had extended your father credit and figured he would likely never receive his money back. A good-hearted family, you said. The Paris Sûreté inspector I consulted agreed but said the family's fortunes had declined after Monsieur Prideaux's death. His widow, Alain's mother, married Gaston, the café owner next door on the Rue des Beaux-Arts. Gaston knew the Oscar Wilde story from Alain, his stepson – he smelled a chance of making money."

I listened, transfixed.

"Even after all this time?"

"Wilde's work would be valuable, Watson. Several years ago, Mr. Ross sponsored Alain, Prideaux's son from Paris, to find employment here and gave him odd catering jobs. We heard him at Mr. Ross's house."

Holmes leaned back, lit his pipe and puffed.

"That's where things become interesting. Gaston, his stepfather, the café owner, a womaniser, abandoned Alain's mother. Broke, Gaston came to London, demanding Alain use his connections to Oscar Wilde's estate, and extort Mr. Ross."

"That doesn't explain Cyril's letter," said Vyvyan.

"I'm sorry to say your brother's death provided the perfect opportunity. After hearing he had fallen in the trenches, Alain, with Gaston's urging, hatched a plot. Alain would write a letter, copying Cyril's style and handwriting from one of those he had found in Mr. Ross's desk. The letter spoke of a lost manuscript for twenty thousand pounds and indicated Miss Robinson's establishment as a meeting place – the villains wanted to rattle young Vyvyan to see if he suspected anything. Originally, they were going to say the manuscript had been found in the Paris hotel, which was undergoing remodelling, and call it the 'Prideaux Monograph' to give themselves a stake in the document. Gaston became greedy, unmanageable in the last stages of syphilis, and demanded a bigger cut. He had been squatting at Beauchamp Place, often half-clothed and barefoot, symptomatic of his manic condition. The other night Gaston got drunk and attacked Alain, who cut his throat. Alain then threw the body into the canal."

"Can you prove that, Mr. Holmes?"

"Sound travels over water at distinct speeds depending on the current, the depth, the location, the weather, and in this case Gaston's body weight. Beauchamp Place is just across the water; that is why it made sense with my calculations. I discovered Alain had no alibi for the time Gaston disappeared from Beauchamp Place. It would have worked. However, Alain had no idea Gaston had written another letter."

"But he hadn't delivered it yet."

"Indeed not. But he would have done so the next day. That 'p' in the letter clearly indicated a foreigner. An Englishman would have used the pound symbol, instead of writing the word. The 'l' that was crossed out stood for 'livres', French for pounds sterling, which Gaston had apparently first begun to write. I knew therefore that the body was that of a Frenchman. 'B P' was what remained of 'Beauchamp Place' on Warwick Crescent.

Oh, and as for young Miss Robinson, she was in on everything. Alain was her amour. She was arrested earlier this evening."

"What about the bag of money, Holmes? I heard nothing and yet it disappeared."

"Alain knew the grounds because he was accustomed to meet his stepfather there. The rushes on which you set the bag were a cleverly disguised basket attached to a rope. Once he felt the rope tighten, he used a handmade pulley system to lift the basket to the top of the wall. He waited, made sure the young boy kept you distracted, then made off with the money, and hopped into his skiff."

Vyvyan shook his head sadly. "Cyril didn't write me that letter and there is no lost manuscript by my father?"

"Unfortunately, there is none. However, Mr. Ross has found the fourth act of The Importance of Being Earnest. A genuine manuscript. Your father edited out the fourth act and never used it. It is a delight. If you wish, Mr. Ross said, it is yours and not for publication."

Vyvyan thought. "Future generations will see it, but not on stage – in a museum."

THE ELEMENTARY PROBLEM

PHILIP PURSER-HALLARD

For nearly a year I had received no summons from Sherlock Holmes, nor entertained with him anything but the most trivial communications. So long had it been, indeed, since we had engaged in a conversation of appreciable substance that I had come to believe that he was truly retired, in spirit as well as practice. Though he corresponded still on theoretical issues with some of the greatest cryptologists, criminologists and other scientific minds of the age, I imagined that the great detective whose exploits had thrilled the world during our comparative youth (for we both had now reached our late sixties) had finally abandoned his pursuit of adventure for the serene life of a Sussex apiarist.

For my own part, my domestic responsibilities, and the

demands, though much reduced, of partnership in the practice I still maintained, kept me agreeably occupied, though to be sure there were times when I recalled our days of perilous exploits together with a wistful melancholy.

Thus, when my old comrade invited me, not by letter or even telegram, but in a telephone call to my secretary, to visit him at his home on the South Downs in connection with "a matter of singular interest", I experienced surprised elation as well as a certain reluctance to subject my now comfortable routine to such an upheaval. Nevertheless, I made the necessary arrangements, and that same afternoon I took the Brighton line from Victoria Station, arriving in Eastbourne near dusk.

It was the early autumn of 1921, and although I had become more susceptible to the cold over the years, I found the sea breeze pleasantly warm. I took a taxi cab from the railway station to the village near Holmes's cottage, then walked the final half-mile. I found my old friend just returning from the evening ritual of tending to his bees, and in an expansively welcoming mood.

"Watson!" he cried as he removed his veil, his voice as firm and resolute as ever. "Your honest face is a steadfast sight in these changing times."

His own face was more lined than when I had last seen it, but his eyes were as keen and his smile as zestful as the day when we had first met in the laboratory at Bart's. "It's good to see you, too, Holmes," I said. "Each time we meet I feel, for a short while, less like the last relic of a bygone age."

Holmes's housekeeper had laid us out a cold supper. Holmes ate little, but I partook enthusiastically. By the time we had followed it with some of the bottled beer supplied by the local landlord (at, Holmes told me, a significant discount since an occasion when he had located the inn's lost cat and her new kittens), the twilight chill was closing in. Holmes moved a pile of books and various luminaries' letters from his second armchair, and kindled a companionable fire. We lit our pipes and took up our stations beside it.

"I'm delighted to have an opportunity to spend some time in your company, Holmes," I said with feeling, "just as in the old days at Baker Street. I confess that I'm loath to spoil our mood with talk of practicalities. But you implied that there was a particular matter on which you needed my advice, and I'm keen to know what it might be."

He smiled. "I am glad to see that age has not dampened your curiosity, old friend. Yes, a question has come to my attention in which your professional expertise would be of some assistance to me. It is a trivial local matter, but nonetheless interesting. It is not, I think, a case – or rather, if it is, then it is a medical case rather than a criminal one."

"Well then, I'm flattered as well as pleased that you called upon me. But surely there is some local doctor whom you could have consulted?"

"It is a matter of discretion as well as skill. Furthermore, our local physician, Dr. Gainsborough, has already given his opinion, and it is far from satisfactory. I need a man who is open-minded and trustworthy as much as I need a doctor."

"I see," I said, although I felt uneasy at the idea of gainsaying another doctor's diagnosis.

Holmes explained. "A neighbour of mine, a young widow

named Mrs. Brindle, has pleaded with me as a personal favour to look into the matter of her husband's death following the war. A legacy is at stake, which may amount to her livelihood and that of her young son. It is an intriguing situation, with legal as well as medical ramifications."

"It sounds so. Is foul play suspected?"

"There is nothing obvious to prompt such speculation. Richard Brindle was seriously ill, and deteriorated throughout his final months. A premature end might have been considered a mercy by some, but there has been no suggestion that his demise was anything other than the result of his condition."

"Then where is the question?"

"Nobody is quite sure what that condition was. He was invalided out of the Army very near to the end of the war, having been in rude health previously, and was only twenty-six when he died. You perhaps know the name of Nathaniel Oakenshott?"

"The coffee magnate?" I replied, a little surprised. "Of course. Didn't he die too, though, quite recently? And also after a period of ill health, as I recall."

"Indeed, and therein lies Mrs. Brindle's problem. Richard Brindle was old Oakenshott's grandson, his mother being Nathaniel's daughter. His parents died in a boating accident when he was quite young, and the old man took Richard under his wing. He was the natural heir to the family fortune, and in the ordinary course of events would have come into control of the business on his grandfather's death."

"But instead he predeceased him," I observed. "Yet you implied that Richard had a son. Wouldn't he have become the heir?"

"So one might suppose. Gerald Brindle, however, is only six years old, though there are trustworthy agents capable of running the company in his stead until he comes of age. Indeed, they are running it now, while the question of inheritance is being resolved. As you may know," he continued, "the Oakenshott family have been Quakers for many generations, and religion has a habit of complicating family affairs inordinately. The Brindles are Quakers too, though a less prominent family and somewhat less devout."

"Ah," I said, beginning to see at last where this might be heading. "You said that Richard Brindle served in the war. Despite Quaker pacifism?"

"Indeed. And Nathaniel Oakenshott was in fact a most ardent Quaker and pacifist. He detested violence in all its forms, and war most particularly. Richard Brindle, on the other hand, overcame his conscientious reservations. When the war started, he signed up to fight in France like so many other patriotic young men, although his new bride, Isobel Brindle, was already expecting their child. Nathaniel was gravely displeased by this decision. He added a clause to his will stipulating that, if Richard were to die as a result of his service in the Army, the family fortune would go, not to his issue, but to a distant cousin in America."

"That was unkind of him," I observed indignantly.

"Perhaps, Watson, but Nathaniel Oakenshott was a man of passionate morals. And perhaps by making such a stipulation he also hoped to divert his grandson from the dangerous course he had chosen. Knowing that, were he to die in combat, his wife and child would be left unprovided for might have persuaded Richard to respect his grandfather's wishes. In the event, however, it did not, and though he escaped serious injury he fell ill in France in the summer of 1918 and was forced to return to England. He died early in 1919, when the Spanish flu was at its height, though his ailment was certainly not influenza.

"For her part, Isobel Brindle was unaware of the clause disinheriting her son until the old man's will was read. Nathaniel had provided her with an allowance during the war, and she tells me that he was fond of his great-grandson. She is quite persuaded that, faced with the reality of Richard's situation, he would have amended his will to ensure that young Gerald would be provided for regardless.

"However, Oakenshott suffered a serious stroke in 1917, and was ruled legally incompetent shortly thereafter. He became incapable of making such a change, and perhaps even of understanding his grandson's condition. Isobel's allowance continued, and was sufficient, with her own savings, to support them during Richard's illness and thereafter, but it ceased on Nathaniel's death two months ago."

"And the distant cousin?"

"Is contesting Gerald's right to inherit, on the basis that the illness that caused Richard's death arose during his service in the war. The Quaker principle of charity has not penetrated so far into the remoter branches of the family, it seems. There is a pending suit over the matter that is due to be heard quite soon, hence the urgency with which I requested your services."

"I see," I said again. I understood, now, why Holmes felt the need to augment his undimmed deductive capabilities with the expertise of a medical man. "So the issue turns on whether Brindle's mysterious malady was contracted in the course of his duties, or would have occurred had he remained at home. What was wrong with him, in fact?"

"There we move from a field that is, at least, adjacent to my own, into one that is indubitably yours. Dr. Gainsborough diagnosed a combination of anaemia, gastral inflammation and nervous decay, but was unable to identify a single cause. Brindle was in constant pain. He suffered from vomiting and other digestive complaints. He experienced headaches, became dizzy and frequently fell, and did not recover readily from the injuries he thereby sustained. After a while he lost the ability to walk altogether, and began to lose his senses also. He spoke often as if he were back in the trenches, or at the abandoned factory where he was billeted late in the war. Towards the end he lost the power of speech also."

I frowned. "Such degeneration makes it sound as if he were being poisoned."

"Such was my thought also. However, no poison that I know of is capable of producing all those symptoms in combination. Besides, nobody had the opportunity to administer it with the necessary regularity. His wife was with him after his return, and Dr. Gainsborough was naturally a frequent visitor, but Brindle arrived from France already ill. He was tended there and in England by a succession of nurses."

"Perhaps some transmitted disease, then? Or an inherited ailment?"

"Again, I know of no infectious illness that matches Brindle's symptoms. The idea of a heritable disorder is of great concern to Isobel Brindle, of course. She would rather Gerald be free of his father's condition and lose his great-grandfather's fortune than that he should inherit both."

"That's very understandable," I said, imagining Mrs. Brindle's dismay should her son begin to succumb to the same fate as her husband. However, I was still mystified on one point. "But if the cause of Brindle's indisposition is altogether unknown, how can the cousin ascribe it to the war? What grounds could he have for such a contention?"

Holmes sighed. "Brindle was on the fringes of a German poison-gas attack in the trenches, in which several of his comrades perished. It was after this that he was relocated. He experienced only the milder symptoms of gas poisoning, and made what seemed a quick and full recovery. Nevertheless, it appears that his deterioration dates from shortly after this exposure. If he died as an outcome of combat, even months later, then young Gerald is ineligible to inherit."

"I've seen soldiers who were exposed to poison gas," I said. "Some of them are patients of mine. It's a foul weapon, and though the Germans bear the blame for having used it first, it will forever be a source of shame that our side retaliated in kind. However, while the lasting effects vary depending on the gas in question, none of my patients has been afflicted as you describe. I don't know of any gas used by either side that could have produced those symptoms."

Holmes nodded gravely. "My enquiries have suggested as much. But the cousin, through his lawyers, argues that, since no other explanation has been advanced, this one remains the most likely. And unfortunately Dr. Gainsborough agrees with them."

"Does he now?" I frowned. "I should like to know his reasons for that."

"It was partly to speak to him that I asked you down," said Holmes.

*

Accordingly, after a peaceful night's sleep lulled by the sound of tree leaves rustling in a breeze from the Channel, we paid several visits. The first was to Isobel Brindle, who lived in a cottage in the village. She greeted her neighbour warmly, and professed herself glad to be introduced to me. I found her an intelligent and personable young woman, though understandably careworn. While we spoke her young son ran into the house and out again, a black-and-white terrier yapping at his heels, neither of them troubled in the least by threats of destitution.

"Gerry doesn't remember much about his father," Mrs. Brindle confided. "He was only four when Richard died. They only met a few times before his illness, when Richard was home on leave, and when he finally came back from France he was so different that Gerry didn't even recognise him. Gerry is such an active child, always playing outside. We both felt it was best to spare him his father's suffering as far as we could."

"How did you find Mr. Brindle changed?" I asked, in my warmest professional manner. I used Richard Brindle's civilian title. He had enlisted as a private soldier, refusing any benefit he might have derived from his family's wealth. Regardless, I felt any mention of his rank might come as an unwelcome reminder of distressing times.

Mrs. Brindle looked upset enough as it was. "He was a shadow of himself, Dr. Watson. Richard was a fit and healthy man when I first knew him. At school he won races, and was considered a strong all-round cricketer. When he returned from France he had lost so much weight that I hardly knew him myself. He had aged so much – of course a lot of men did, during the war, but Richard had shrunk away and was beginning to go bald. He was only twenty-five."

We talked some more about her husband's illness, and she confirmed much of what Holmes had told me the previous day. "There was a short while when he seemed a little brighter, and we thought that perhaps he was beginning to recover," she said. "But then he went downhill very rapidly and we prepared ourselves for the worst." She paused, and breathed deeply. Understanding how difficult this was for her, I patted her hand. She went on. "That was when his mind began to fail him. He lost track of where he was, especially at night-time. He imagined he was back in France."

"That's not so uncommon, I'm sorry to say," I told her. "The trenches scarred some men's minds as badly as their bodies. I have had patients experience some very vivid dreams and waking hallucinations."

"So I've been told," she said, "but it wasn't just the trenches. He spoke just as much of the bottling plant where he was billeted after the gas attack, doing some kind of war work. He talked to me and Gerry sometimes as if we were his friends there. Most of them had come with him from the front when they were reassigned. He spoke most often of the one they called Sally – I never met the man, but I believe they signed up at the same time. They all had nicknames, like Blacky and Lighters and Mack. They called him Quakey, because of his religion. Sometimes…

sometimes in those last weeks, I'd call him that, to humour him. He couldn't recognise me at all towards the end."

She wiped her eyes with a handkerchief, and blew her nose, but I sensed that she had cried most of her tears for her husband long ago.

I was ready to leave her to her grief, but Holmes asked, with a gentleness that I would once have found surprising in him, "Do you know what Richard's work was while at this factory, Mrs. Brindle? I know he had been moved away from the front lines, but he had not yet fallen seriously ill. What were he and his friends doing there?"

Isobel Brindle shook her head. "He didn't talk about that. I think they drummed into him that he shouldn't, and some of those military rules stuck with him to the end. He'd get terribly upset if we showed a light in the house at night, for instance, in case the enemy saw it and used it for range-finding."

"I am sorry, Mrs. Brindle. I know that these questions must be very unsettling," said Holmes, sounding again as if he truly meant it. "One more question, if you will – do you know the location of this bottling plant?"

She shook her head again. "I couldn't tell you. He only ever called it the Château."

Young Gerry ran in again then, the terrier with him barking joyfully, and she gave a little sob and laugh and embraced them both in a struggling bundle. We left them then, at last.

*

Our visit to Dr. Gainsborough's bachelor cottage was less congenial. He was about forty, and good-looking in a sallow, peevish sort of way. Although I understood that Holmes was an occasional patient of his, he seemed disposed to take offence at our presence. I suppose that he had some right to feel this way, since after all our purpose was to call his medical judgment into question.

After outlining his diagnosis, which was as Holmes had summarised it, he concluded, "There was nothing exceptional in Richard Brindle's prior medical history, Dr. Watson. He had no allergies, no unusual childhood diseases, no family history of degenerative illness. He passed the Army medical without difficulty, and went to France a hale and hearty man. He returned a dying invalid.

"During his time there he emerged from a number of engagements largely unscathed, suffering nothing worse than cuts and bruises. His closest brush with death came during that German gas attack. It is the only thing in his medical history – in his lifetime – that can possibly account for the manner of its end."

Holmes said, "And this is what you have told the American lawyers, when they visited?"

Dr. Gainsborough bristled. "I told them the truth as I see it, Mr. Holmes. What else would you have had me do? I'm sorry, of course, about the consequences for Isobel, Mrs. Brindle – and for Gerald, naturally. Indeed, I regret them greatly, but they must lie on Nathaniel Oakenshott's conscience, not mine. It is ironic how vindictive a pacifist can be."

I asked, "There is nothing you can think of that might have produced the symptoms you saw in Brindle? I admit that I know of nothing, but Brindle was your patient. I assume that you researched his case, and perhaps consulted specialists?"

Still defiantly, he said, "I did what I could, but there was no money for specialists. In any case, who should I have gone to? His symptoms were variously nervous, gastric and haematic, and conformed to no syndrome I could identify. Besides, Dr. Watson, this was after the war, and at the height of the flu. The sick and dying were everywhere, and I was ill myself for a time. I could not expend all my energies on one invalid, however concerned I might have been for his loved ones."

I nodded sadly. He was right, of course. Even so, his manner seemed to me strangely defiant, almost furtive, and I felt that despite his denial of responsibility, he lacked the professional detachment that I would have expected.

*

"Holmes," I said, as we walked away from the physician's cottage, "I believe that Dr. Gainsborough admires Isobel Brindle. He talked of her rather than Gerald when referring to the consequences of the legal suit."

"When he spoke of Richard's loved ones," Holmes said, "I, too, did not get the sense that he had the child in mind. It may indeed be that the doctor has some tender feelings for the widow. I believe there is some gossip in the village to that effect."

Perhaps a little excitedly, I said, "You said that some might consider Brindle's death a mercy killing. Is it possible...?"

He shook his head. "I think not, Watson. When Brindle died, Dr. Gainsborough was himself laid low with the flu. A locum attended the patient in his final days. However, though it may be cynical, I cannot but wonder whether the account the doctor gave the Americans was motivated purely by a commitment to the truth. If he has hopes of marrying

Mrs. Brindle, then he would have some interest in not seeing her set up in financial independence."

"Good heavens," I said. "I do hope you're wrong there, Holmes. It would be a nasty thought to harbour of a brother physician."

"Then I shall not insist on it, my dear fellow," he said. His tone was light, but his frown remained thoughtful.

Two of the nurses who had attended Brindle in his illness still lived locally, and we called upon them also. One was out at work, however, and the other could tell us little beyond confirming the observations that Gainsborough and Mrs. Brindle had already provided.

On our return to the cottage, Holmes found two items waiting for him. One was a wine bottle, sent across (his housekeeper told us) by Isobel Brindle. A note explained that Richard had brought it back empty from France as a souvenir, and that after we left her cottage it had occurred to her that it might provide us with some clue as to the location of his mysterious winery. A label identified its long-vanished contents as 'Château Vendeux 1915'.

"Not a vintage with which I'm familiar," I observed.

"Nor I," said Holmes, "though I am sadly out of touch with such matters of late." He opened the second package, to reveal a file with Richard Brindle's name on it. "His service record," he told me. "Not especially distinguished, from what I gather, but perhaps illuminating. Brother Mycroft's name still opens some doors at the War Office."

He tore open the binding and began to read, but shortly afterwards threw the file down in disgust. "Redacted," he said. "Everything about the war work at the Château has been blacked out most efficiently, I fear beyond even my ability to reconstruct."

"But what about the gas attack?" I asked.

"Ordinary mustard gas." He passed me the file. "Vile stuff, to be sure, but in no way mysterious. Its effects are perfectly well understood."

"Then this proves that Brindle's symptoms were not produced by gas, at least."

"Perhaps, Watson," he agreed. "Whether it would satisfy a court that they were not the outcome of his war service is another matter."

Shortly thereafter, Holmes marched off to the village post office, expressing the intention of sending some telegrams and placing a call to Mycroft at the Diogenes Club. I was amused to learn that, after years of resisting the encroachment of this deplorably sociable innovation, the club had grudgingly installed a fully soundproofed phone booth for the use of its members, with a light bulb that lit up in lieu of a bell when a call was received.

Holmes returned in an ill temper, however, reporting that Mycroft had been uncharacteristically obstructive. "He admonished me that military secrets should not be pried into upon trivial pretexts, and was good enough to explain that they are kept secret for important reasons! Really, my brother can be insufferable at times."

To calm him, I suggested a walk along the coastal path to Beachy Head, and we passed a pleasant afternoon alongside the splashing waves, the seagulls above us sailing in the crisp air. After another hearty meal, we fell into reminiscence about some of Holmes's old cases and good-natured argument over some of the liberties I had taken in presenting them for literary consumption.

*

The next day, several telegrams arrived for Holmes, and another package. I did not pry into their contents, knowing that Holmes would tell me what I needed to know at the appropriate time, though I admit to some curiosity when he vanished with the parcel and the Château Vendeux bottle into his understairs cupboard, emerging a few minutes later empty-handed.

"What now?" I asked.

"Now, Watson, we take the train to Brighton," he told me cheerfully, and so we did.

As we pulled away from Eastbourne, and I watched the green Downs roll past our carriage window, Holmes explained to me some of what his telegrams had revealed.

"From Richard Brindle's service record," he told me, "and what Mrs. Brindle told us of his comrades-in-arms, I was able to identify some of those who served with him at the front before their reassignment to the Château. Blacky was one Private Samuel Blackwell, Mack was Private George MacDonald, and Lighters a corporal with the remarkable name of Hector Achilles Lightfoot. All three of them, it seems, are dead. There is limited information regarding the causes of their deaths, but like Brindle all three were invalided home and died within a few months of the end of the war."

"Good heavens!" I exclaimed. "Then perhaps there really was something in the gas."

"Perhaps, Watson, perhaps. If so, then the man we are to meet was fortunate indeed, for he received a heavier dose of it than Brindle, yet he is alive and relatively well."

I had gone on day trips to Brighton in the past, but had then been mostly walking on the Downs or taking the air on the seafront and pier, and I was not greatly familiar with the central part of the town. From the railway station Holmes hustled me confidently away from the sea, through roads I did not recognise, until we reached an unusual building sitting in an ordinary residential area: a battlemented redbrick construction with two turrets, reminding me of a prison or barracks. It proved to be a congress hall of the Salvation Army, that puritanical yet fiercely charitable sect which takes somewhat over-literally the biblical metaphor of the Church as the army of God.

"I see," I said, suddenly realising why we were here. "If Richard Brindle was Quakey because he was a Quaker, then Sally was a member of the 'Sally Army'."

"Such was my conjecture," Holmes replied. "Mrs. Brindle told us that the two of them had signed up at the same time, so it's likely that they met at a local recruiting office. I knew that the Salvationists have a thriving presence in Brighton, so I made my enquiries here."

Sally turned out to be a man in his late twenties named Fred Carpenter, a private like Brindle in the Army proper, who now wore the uniform of a lieutenant in the rank structure peculiar to his church. He was as healthy as Holmes had claimed, a slight huskiness to his voice being the only observable legacy of his brush with the Germans' chemical arsenal.

"It's put paid to my trumpet playing, too," he told us cheerfully, "and that's a blessed nuisance, but I thank the Lord I didn't suffer worse. We've brothers here who lost limbs, and others never came back at all."

Inside, the congress hall was huge, seating at least a thousand, with a large stage at the front for the brass band that typifies the sect's eccentric style of worship. Carpenter ushered us into a side room where we sat on hard chairs, and told us he was happy enough to chat about his days in France. He seemed to be one of those rare, innocent souls who had passed through the war largely unscathed in mind, despite the manifold horrors that he must have witnessed there.

I expected Holmes to ask him more about the gas attack, but he seemed to have little interest in the matter. Instead, he enquired about Brindle, and it turned out that Carpenter was under the impression that the other man had not felt any necessity to maintain contact upon their return.

"Not that I'm surprised," Carpenter said without rancour. "We'd not have had a lot in common, would we, back here in Blighty? Quakey's people have all that money from the coffee business, and here I am, doing the Lord's work with the poor. As for the others, Mack's probably an architect by now – that was his ambition – and Lighters' folk are grooms in a stables up north. Blacky's people run some business in the East End that I didn't like to ask too much about. Out there we all mucked in together – that was just how it was – but I don't blame them for not wanting to be reminded of that now. We all have our own lives, praise the Lord."

I gave Holmes a concerned look, fearful lest the truth might upset the poor fellow, but it was not to be avoided. Holmes told him, in a few sympathetic words, of his comrades' deaths, and Carpenter looked gravely shaken.

"All gone?" he muttered. "Oh, my goodness. What a thing. I knew they'd all been sick, but I never thought… Oh, my."

"We're sorry to bring such sad news," I told him, helplessly.

Holmes said, "Mr. Brindle's widow has asked us to find out some more about his time in France, Mr. Carpenter. She naturally wants to understand as much as she can about the years he spent there."

"Of course," said Carpenter. "Of course, I'll tell you anything I can." He shook his head. "Old Quakey, promoted to glory. And the others too, if it please the Lord. Well, what a thing."

There had been little of glory in the manner of Richard Brindle's demise, but it would have been churlish to say so.

Carpenter rallied quickly, and seemed pleased with the opportunity to reminisce about his late comrades and the time they spent together. "Quakey and I were pals from the start," he told us. "The others made fun of us at first, because we were both teetotal. There was a lot of drinking out there, you can imagine. When men are overworked and put upon, and spend most of the time in fear for their lives… well, the Devil thrives in places like that, and some men only get so far by singing hymns. Old Quakey didn't last long before he succumbed, I'm sorry to say. A few months and he was imbibing with the rest of them. But if he'd been a better Quaker, he never would have signed up at all, would he?"

Talk of drink led naturally to the Château, in which it seemed Holmes's primary interest now lay. "Yes, that was funny too." Carpenter smiled. "They told us it was all hush-hush, but I don't suppose there's any harm in talking about it now. See, there was I, still an abstainer after all that time at the front, praise the Lord, and there we all were, bottling wine for King and country, if you please. Not that we were allowed to touch a drop, of course – strictest orders. The wine was for the officers, I suppose, though Mack thought it might have been to sell back home, to help the war effort. Ours is not to reason why, as they say."

"So the Army reopened the bottling plant?" Holmes asked, his interest now keenly aroused.

"That's right," Carpenter agreed. "They'd found it abandoned, with all those bottles and labels left in storage, and I suppose they found the wine somewhere else, because they brought it in in barrels. Red wine it was. Horrible-looking stuff, I thought, just like blood – but then I would have, wouldn't I? The others thought it looked tasty enough. The Army gave us beer and plenty of it – stayed away I did, of course, though not the others – but we were never to be allowed even a sip of that wine. It was a queer business."

Holmes nodded in quiet satisfaction, and I could see that this confirmed his suspicions. Gently, he asked, "And did none of your friends ever defy that order, Mr. Carpenter?"

Carpenter sighed. "Well," he said. "Well, I don't like to speak ill of the dead, rest their poor souls. But I don't suppose it does them any harm to tell you now. Yes, there was one night when Blacky liberated, as he called it, a few bottles of the wine from one of the vans that took it away. He swapped them with bottles he'd filled with water and stoppered up. He said whoever ended up with them, it served them right, the greedy – well, I won't tell you gents the word he used; I'm sure you can imagine.

"I wasn't having any of it, of course, no matter how they teased me. Not just drink, but stolen drink? No, thank you. I was used to the joshing by then, so I went to my bunk and said my prayers and let them get on with it."

"And how long afterwards," Holmes asked him quietly, "did Blackwell, MacDonald, Lightfoot and Brindle fall sick?"

Carpenter was quite taken aback. "Well, gents," he said after a moment, "it wasn't long, I know that. Must have been the same week, now I think about it. They all got very poorly and got shipped off home, and soon after that I believe the whole winery business was wrapped up. Certainly I got reassigned to a quiet part of the front, and didn't see any more action before the Armistice, thank the Lord. And they all came back home and… well, they died, I suppose. Oh, my. I won't say it was the Lord's punishment, for it's not my belief that that happens in this lifetime, but it makes you think, doesn't it?"

It did indeed, though not perhaps in the way he imagined.

*

We bade goodbye to Private, or Lieutenant, Fred Carpenter and lunched at a nearby hostelry of which he and his fellow Salvationists would certainly have disapproved. As we travelled back by train to Eastbourne, Holmes spoke animatedly, pointing out landmarks on the Downs and shore, expounding upon local history, and steadfastly ignoring my attempts to draw him out on any aspect of the case.

On our return to the cottage, he vanished immediately

into the understairs cupboard, emerging some time later with a large brown envelope. "We await a telegram only," he told me, "and then the truth will be unavoidable. Our course of action less so, perhaps," he added thoughtfully.

He left to attend to his bees, and stayed with them for some time. I read and wrote some letters. No telegram arrived that afternoon, so that evening we sat again and appreciated Holmes's fire, though he seemed less at ease than the night before. After I retired, I heard him pacing downstairs, reminding me of the old days in Baker Street. I awoke at dawn to the sound of his violin.

*

The telegram came just as Holmes returned from his morning visit to the hives, and he seized it gratefully, tipping the postboy more than I imagined he would normally have seen in a month. Holmes then ripped open the missive, read it, and immediately declared to my surprise: "We start at once for London. You may pack quickly if you wish."

It had been a long time since the Army trained me to get on the move at a moment's notice, and I had not the energy of my youth. I opted to leave my things at Holmes's cottage, reasoning that I could either return or have them sent on, depending on what transpired when we reached the capital.

He left the telegram lying on the kitchen table, and before we departed my curiosity got the better of me. The communication read as follows:

VOS SPECULATIONS SONT CORRECTES. SITE FERME. RESIDU CONFIRME. QU'EST PASSE LA? MSC.

My rather rusty French took this to mean: 'Your speculations are correct. Site closed. Residue confirmed. What happened there?' Who 'MSC' might be, I had no notion.

Though he was convivial enough during our train journey, Holmes once again said nothing of import until we arrived back at Victoria, where my journey had begun. There he summoned a taxi cab and bundled me inside, instructing the driver to take us to St James's.

It had been many years since I last visited the Diogenes Club. I found it little changed, though dingier and faded, and its membership much declined in number. Those few whom we saw through the glass window of the reading room, each in his bay of silent isolation, might have been the same men who sat there on my last visit, each correspondingly older. I could have believed that they had spent the last twenty years thus ensconced, gathering dust and cobwebs, moving only when one of them died *in situ* and had to be discreetly removed by the assiduous attendants.

When Mycroft Holmes joined us, he too showed his antiquity. Always somewhat overweight, he had bloated further, and his legs had finally relinquished the task of conveying his bulk from room to room. He was brought in through the double doors of the Stranger's Room by an attendant of herculean proportions, in a specially constructed steel wheelchair.

"Well, Sherlock?" he wheezed. "I presume that you are here to continue our telephone conversation. What have you learned?"

Neither of the brothers had ever been a man for small talk, and plainly his infirmity had eroded Mycroft's capacity even further. To be frank, I found it astonishing that Holmes's elder brother was still alive, but he was extended the very best medical care by a government that could scarce afford to dispense with his services even in his seventies, and would continue working him even to his death.

Holmes shrugged, produced his brown envelope and opened it. What he brought out appeared to be a photograph of sorts – a darkened plate in which an aura glowed whitely, a blur in the rough shape of a bottle. I realised that he must have his understairs cupboard set up as a studio and dark room, although what this fuzzy image was intended to convey I could not imagine. Holmes held the plate out silently to his brother.

"Your conclusions?" Mycroft asked, without bothering to take the image. "Please don't tire me with incremental revelations, Sherlock. My patience is the only part of me that has worn thinner with age."

"Then I shall endeavour to respect its limitations," Sherlock said. "I presume that you have been apprised of the recent movements of Mademoiselle Irène Curie?"

"Naturally," sighed Mycroft.

"You will perhaps forgive my summarising them for Watson's benefit," Holmes proceeded, to his brother's visible annoyance. "Mademoiselle Curie has visited the site of the former Château Vendeux bottling plant in the Rhône Valley. She has sent word by her mother, the chemist and twofold Nobel laureate Madame Marie Skłodowska Curie, a frequent correspondent of mine, that the location is closed and remains radioactive, like that bottle."

"Radioactive?" I repeated. "Good Lord, Holmes, do you mean contaminated by radium?"

"Not quite. Radium's effects are too slow for it to be very useful as a poison. No, I fancy this residue, detectable through photography by its emission of x-rays, originates in the other novel element discovered by Madame Curie, and named after her homeland of Poland. Polonium is considerably more radioactive than radium, and there are indications that, when ingested, a minuscule dose can produce a lingering but inevitable death. So far as they have been documented, the symptoms conform to those displayed by Richard Brindle."

"So that was why those men were forbidden to drink the wine they were bottling," I said, fascinated and disgusted in equal measure. "But the intention must have been that *someone* should."

"The enemy, naturally," Holmes agreed. "I fancy it was devised as a weapon of last resort. If the Allies were forced to retreat, they would leave caches of the wine behind for the advancing Germans to happen upon. A very modern manner of salting the earth."

"Good God, Mycroft," I said, appalled. "Did you intend for German *troops* to drink this foul stuff?"

Mycroft said, "The hope was that the officers would seize it for themselves. But I admit that the plan was not a discriminating one."

Relentlessly, Sherlock continued, "You doubtless hoped that an unfamiliar poison like polonium, killing slowly after a single exposure, would take longer to detect and identify than a traditional one. When the invading German troops – or officers – began to fall ill and die from mysterious causes, the confusion and panic would have crippled their advance. It was a desperate measure, but you thought desperate times justified anything."

"Not I, Sherlock," Mycroft replied, shaking his massive head. "I was against the scheme from the start. In fact, I quite forbade it, which was why I was kept in the dark when it proceeded anyway. By the end of the war there were operations that even I was not privy to. Some actions I refused to condone, but younger, more ruthless men felt justified in perpetrating them without my knowledge."

"Nothing could justify this," I said. "It would have been an atrocity, worse even than the use of poison gas."

With, I suspected, the exception of the muscular attendant, whose face betrayed no expression, I was the only man there who had served as a soldier, and who thus understood the true enormity of what Mycroft's colleagues had authorised. "To inflict such a painful, protracted demise on men whose only crime was to serve their country – no strategic imperative could justify it. And as for our own soldiers, assigned to bottle the wine – did nobody guess that they would drink it? Have these people no understanding of human nature?"

"I think that, by the end, some of them had lost their own humanity," said Mycroft quietly. "Had I been properly informed, I should of course have ensured that Private Brindle and the others received the palliative care they needed in their final days, and that their families were provided for. Alas, I learned the specifics of the affair only once all the men were dead."

"Recriminations are of little use between us, I fear," said Holmes. "The question now is how we should proceed."

"These men must answer for this crime," I replied without

hesitation. "The British public must be told what has been done in their name."

Mycroft's sigh might have exploded from the blowhole of a whale. "In a just world, no doubt," he said. "But we live in precarious times, Dr. Watson. The nation is recovering still, not only from the war but from the epidemic. If such a scandal as this were to be revealed, public trust in the government would suffer catastrophically, as would our standing among the community of nations—"

"Deservedly so!" I interjected.

Mycroft inclined his head. "We have seen quite recently in Russia how a discontented and war-weary populace may overthrow one of the world's longest-established monarchies. It would, I believe, take a smaller spark than one might imagine to ignite similar passions upon our own shores."

"But surely this can't be concealed!" I insisted. I looked to Sherlock Holmes for his heartfelt agreement, but instead I saw that his face bore a troubled frown.

"There is another consideration, Watson," he said very deliberately. "In light of what we have discovered, it is undeniable that Richard Brindle died as a consequence of his involvement in the war. To be sure nobody ordered him to drink the tainted wine, but had he not signed up, as Nathaniel Oakenshott wished, he would never have been in a position to imbibe the poison. Given the provisions of Oakenshott's will, the effect of this revelation upon Gerald Brindle's prospects would be disastrous."

He was correct to suppose that this had not occurred to me. I had been so awash with indignation on behalf of

Richard Brindle and his comrades that I had not considered the effect of the truth upon those whom they had left behind.

Mycroft said, "The court case is pending, as you know. My colleagues will naturally ensure that no mention is made of the Château Vendeux operation, nor of the deaths of Private Brindle's associates. I can provide expert witnesses who will testify that Brindle's exposure to mustard gas could not have produced the symptoms that led to his death. Since radiation poisoning is so ill understood, we may trust that the court will rule in Gerald Brindle's favour – provided no untoward suspicions have been raised in the meantime."

Sherlock nodded sombrely, and I realised that he had reached his own conclusion some time before. I gazed out through the window into the bustle of St James's, with its speeding cars and its motorbuses loaded with tourists, and considered this world in which I now found myself. Sherlock Holmes and I were survivors: of a hundred criminal cases, of the Victorian age, of a war in which we had been too old to fight. What was it, I wondered, that we owed to the dead? Should we seek retribution or atonement on their behalf, or should we instead use our opportunities as they had, for the benefit of those who would outlive us all?

My friend has been, I believe, untroubled by the decision we reached between us that day. It was hardly the first time he had brought his own interpretation to the letter of the law, whether to save a life or, as in this case, to ensure the welfare of an innocent. And, to be sure, young Gerald Brindle – or Gerald Oakenshott, now that he has taken his great-grandfather's surname – has come into the fortune that was his by right, and before too long will take the helm of the Oakenshott mercantile empire.

In the intervening years, he and his mother have been well provided for. And yet his father's agonising and unnatural death remains a crime that will never see justice. Still, I resolved that day at the Diogenes Club that I would leave the dead alone and help the living. Since then, I have tried to learn all that I can, by reading the latest medical research and in correspondence with Mme. Curie and her colleagues, of radiation and its deadly effects.

I have been able to put my knowledge to some practical use. A few years ago, I travelled to America to testify in the case of a group of female factory workers who had become fatally ill after working for years to make luminous watch dials incorporating polonium's slower cousin radium. Though my evidence was of minor forensic value, the appearance on the witness stand of one so closely associated with the celebrated Sherlock Holmes helped to make the public aware of the case, as we were unable to do in that of Private Richard Brindle.

It is for this reason also that I set my pen to paper now. My hope is that, as the terrible violence of the Great War slowly recedes into the further recesses of our memory, my readers may be reminded of the fearful scope for ill that the use of such materials may bring. It is my fervent hope that in future those whom we entrust with power over us will recoil from such horrors, and that good sense and human decency will ensure that radiation is never again used as a weapon of war.

PERIL AT CARROWAY HOUSE

ERIC BROWN

That day, in early May of 1926, I was enjoying an afternoon brandy at my club, lost in a reverie at once painful and pleasant. I was musing upon my time with Sherlock Holmes in Baker Street, when I enjoyed the double boon of rude health and great friendship, spiced with the condiment of occasional adventure, all of which prompted an aching sense of nostalgia.

Holmes himself, of course, had always considered my accounts of his deductive feats to be little more than sensational journalism, but I was gratified to reflect upon the fact that my publisher was badgering me for another volume. The appetite of the Great British reading public for Holmes's cases appeared insatiable.

My thoughts thus full of Holmes and yesteryear, it occurred

to me that I had not seen my friend for almost eighteen months, when I had taken the train down to Eastbourne and spent a pleasant day in his company on the seafront. These days I led a quiet life, centred on our apartment in Belgravia and my club, with the occasional round of bridge and the slightly more energetic game of billiards, and rarely did I venture far from the city. My good wife had unfortunately developed a slight ailment of the lungs over recent years and occasionally went to visit her brother in Weymouth. The sea air there improved her condition, and in fact I was currently a grass widower, as she had left the metropolis three days prior.

I was drawn from my thoughts by the discreet cough of the footman, who bore a silver salver and a telegram.

YOUR IMMEDIATE PRESENCE IS URGENTLY REQUESTED. BRING AN OVERNIGHT BAG. HOLMES.

"Upon my word," I muttered. "Speak of the devil."

"Will there be a reply, sir?"

I was of a mind to ring Holmes forthwith and quiz him as to the meaning of this peremptory summons, but I well knew my friend's aversion to the telephone.

"A quick line, yes: I shall take the 2.10 from Paddington. Arrive in time for high tea. Watson."

I finished my brandy and hurried from the club, pausing at the top of the steps to contemplate the scene before me. Perhaps it was a combination of my interrupted reverie and the telegram from Holmes, but I had half expected to behold a thoroughfare chock-a-block with hansoms and two-wheelers, not a street busy with the cacophonous assault of motor cars and double-decker buses. On the way to Belgravia, I passed a newspaper vendor whose placard promised the latest on the hunger marches, and at the street corner I flipped a shilling into the upturned cap of a legless beggar. Some things never change, I thought. For all the wondrous advancements of our time, the gadgets and contraptions said to make modern life that much easier, we were in the embrace of an economic depression unknown in my lifetime.

One hour later, my bag packed, I boarded a train to the coast, and my thoughts turned from the many iniquities of the age to the possible reason for my friend's precipitous summons.

*

It was but a short walk from the station to the block of modern art-deco apartments where Holmes had lately taken up residence when life in his cottage on the Sussex Downs had become too tedious. The apartments overlooked the seafront and, to my jaundiced eye, represented not so much an architectural advancement as an unsightly blot upon the landscape. I had voiced my aesthetic grievances to Holmes on a previous visit, only to be told that his new abode had the triple advantage of affordable monthly rates, a magnificent view, and hot running water. I greeted the liveried commissionaire, said that I had come to see Mr. Holmes, and duly took the lift to the second floor.

It was some time before he answered my knock, and I was becoming impatient with the delay when the door opened and I stared down in shock and surprise.

"Why, my word, Holmes… Good God!"

"Just in time!" said he. "Now, if you would be so good as to cease your imitation of an astounded carp and come this way."

So saying, he deftly turned his wheelchair and propelled himself with alacrity along the corridor to a commodious lounge overlooking the English Channel. The room was familiar from my earlier visitations, but I could not help notice once again, and be moved by the sight of, the various accoutrements he had brought from our shared abode in Baker Street: the bearskin rug before the electric fire; the ornate ormolu clock on the mantelpiece; the rows of calf-bound reference books shelved above his workbench. Why, but for the apartment's low ceiling and modern wallpaper of a garish abstract design, I might have been pitched back in time some thirty-odd years.

Holmes pressed down on the right wheel of his carriage and spun to face me.

"But," I said, floundering, "eighteen months ago you were as fit as a fiddle and pacing the esplanade like a man half your age! What the deuce...?"

"You, as a medical man, well know the frailties of the flesh, Watson. I have succumbed to progressive scoliosis, which is quite incurable."

"You've had a second opinion?" I enquired, collapsing into a proffered armchair.

"A second, and a third. There is nothing to be done, and I have reconciled myself to my sedentary fate. It is not as if I were a young man, Watson. I count myself lucky to have reached the age of seventy-two without greater mishap."

He said as much, but quite apart from his incapacitated state, he looked drawn and haggard: his aquiline visage had never possessed a spare ounce of flesh, but now his prominent nose and cheekbones stood out in stark relief; his hair was thinning and his complexion was of an unhealthy pallor.

For a terrible second it occurred to me that the reason for his summons was to impart the dire news of some terminal illness. However, he immediately allayed these fears.

"You'll no doubt wonder, Watson, why I've—"

"I'll say!" I cried. "Are you…?"

"No, I'm not. The reason for the telegram is that, to employ the sensationalist term you put into my mouth on numerous occasions, but which if memory serves I never actually uttered –" here his grey eyes twinkled at me, "– *the game is afoot.*"

I sighed. "You know, Holmes, conventionally speaking, retirement has connotations of idleness and relaxation. I know you never stopped working, but considering this –" I gestured towards the wheelchair, "– isn't it time?"

He raised a placating hand. "I had indeed been leading a life of repose and leisure –" he indicated a side table with a stack of books upon it, "– until I received this missive. What do you make of it, Watson?"

I snatched up the letter and read it impatiently.

Dear Mr. Holmes,

I'm at my wits' end, and require your assistance in a matter most urgent. The police have proved themselves most inefficient, and it is as a last resort that I seek your professional help. You come with the highest of recommendations. If I hear nothing by return post, I will call upon you at four pm on Monday, the 3rd of May.

— Elizabeth Norton

I replaced the letter on the table and stared across at my friend.

"Well?" he said.

I gestured helplessly. "I see little herein to explain your desire to assist the petitioner."

"Note the signature, Watson."

"Elizabeth Norton," I said with a shrug. "So…?"

"The name tinkles no bells, my friend?"

"None at all. Will you please explain?" I said, exasperated.

"Cast your mind back," said Holmes, "to the March of '88, and the case you wrote up as 'A Scandal in Bohemia'."

"No, still none the wiser, Holmes. The old memory isn't quite what it used to be."

"Irene Adler, the woman… Recall: she left the country in haste, following the affair, having married one Godfrey Norton."

"'Pon my soul, Holmes. And you think this woman—"

"There is more," he said. "I spend much time, between bouts of reading and research, regarding the world from my window –" here he indicated the bow window overlooking the esplanade, "– and one afternoon three days ago I beheld a young woman of such striking mien that at first I assumed I was mistaken. The woman in question was perhaps thirty or thereabouts, and in the cast of her features and upright deportment put me in mind of no one so much as… as the woman. Moreover, she was pacing the esplanade in a state of manifest agitation, and from time to time looked up at the very window from which I observed her. After precisely twenty minutes, she departed in haste. Yesterday afternoon, on the stroke of four, I received the missive, hand-delivered."

I heard him out in silence, then nodded sagely. "And it is your opinion that this Elizabeth Norton is none other than the daughter of Irene Adler?"

"Considering all the available evidence, it is a working hypothesis," said he, "and one which might very well be further tested as the hour approaches," he went on, indicating the ormolu clock on the mantelpiece. It was one minute to four.

"Now, Watson," Holmes said, "as soon as you hear her knock, I suggest you repair to the bedroom over there. Leave the door ajar. I shall invite Miss Norton to take the seat you are now occupying, so that her back will be to you and you can overhear what passes without fear of being apprehended."

"But why the dissimulation, Holmes?"

He stroked his lean chin with a forefinger, and it was a good five seconds before he replied. "I fear there is more to Miss Norton's agitated missive than meets the eye. On observing the young lady on the esplanade the other day, I noted as she made her departure that she met a man. There was something in his demeanour – I hesitate to describe it as shiftiness – that made me wary. He too looked up at the window where I sat behind the concealing lace curtains, and he seemed to my ageing eyes to be entreating the young lady... To what end, I cannot surmise – but lo! That will be her now. Make haste, Watson!" he finished with a hiss.

As he propelled himself from the room and down the corridor, I slipped into the adjacent bedroom and eased the door almost shut behind me.

*

I heard Holmes's greeting from the hallway, and in due course the creak of the wheelchair signalled his return.

"If you would care to be seated," said he.

"That's most kind of you, Mr. Holmes," said the young woman in a light, pleasing contralto, "and so good of you to agree to see me."

Holmes murmured something in polite reply, and asked if she would care to partake of refreshment. She declined, and when I judged that the young lady had seated herself, I applied my eye to the gap between door and jamb.

Miss Norton sat with her back to me, her graceful neck and pageboy hairstyle visible above the chair's antimacassar. Her hair was the same golden hue as that of the woman whom Holmes surmised to be the young lady's mother. I observed Elizabeth Norton's right hand as it rested on the chair's arm. Her fingers were long and elegant, also reminiscent of the lady who had cast such a spell upon Holmes and me all those years ago.

I transferred my attention to Sherlock Holmes, to see what effect this vision – I might almost say this aide-memoire made flesh – had upon him.

His expression was impassive, his eyes hooded as he took in everything about his visitor's appearance. Whatever memories her presence evoked, they were not apparent from his outward demeanour.

He sat back in his carriage and stroked his chin with a long forefinger. "If I might ask," he said, "you mentioned in your letter that I had been recommended... By whom?"

"My mother spoke highly of your abilities," she said. "She mentioned you often. Of course, I was aware of your exploits, thanks to Dr. Watson's various accounts—"

Here I smiled to myself, as Holmes interrupted. "Might I venture to ask if your mother is still…?"

"She passed away peacefully two years ago," said Miss Norton, "in her sixty-sixth year."

"It pains me to hear this," said Holmes, though his expression remained determinedly neutral. "I trust she didn't suffer?"

"She had been ill for just a week, and passed away without pain. My father and I were at her bedside."

"That, at least, is of some small consolation," he said. "Still, the news saddens me, and I can only convey my belated condolences. Your mother was a most remarkable woman."

I could almost behold Miss Norton's smile as she replied, "You are not the first person to apprise me of the fact, Mr. Holmes. And she considered you a remarkable man."

This, at last, had some small effect upon my friend's vanity: his thin lips quirked in a brief smile before he swept on, "But, if you don't mind my enquiring as to the reason for your seeking my services, Miss Norton?"

My left leg aching from maintaining the same stance for some minutes, I shifted position and carefully leaned against the jamb of the door.

Miss Norton said, "As I wrote, I am quite at my wits' end, and for some time did not know who to turn to. The police have proved inefficient in the matter, as I also mentioned, and it was only on recalling my mother's high praise of your exploits that I thought of requesting your assistance. Even then, I dithered, knowing that long ago you ceased to practise as a consulting detective."

Holmes smiled and gestured with a gallantry I well recalled. "I am always willing to lend assistance to those in need," he vouchsafed. "If you would be so good as to lay before me the details of the case..."

He settled his head against the back of the chair and closed his eyes as he absorbed the details of Miss Norton's subsequent words.

Before she began, however, she crossed her legs; from this angle I could see a length of shapely calf, a finely turned ankle, and a crocodile-skin shoe of the latest design.

"One month ago, my great-aunt contacted me with a proposition," said Miss Norton. "She was due to go abroad for three months – to the spa town of Baden-Baden in the Black Forest – and was reluctant to leave her country home untenanted. She asked if I would care to stay there for the duration of her time abroad; she even offered to pay me to do so. As I was between periods of employment, and had no pressing plans of my own, the arrangement suited me to perfection."

Holmes opened his eyes. "The location of your great-aunt's residence?"

"A mile outside the village of Pursley, on the Downs, just ten miles north of here," she said.

"Pray continue."

"One month ago almost to the day, I left London and proceeded to Carroway House. I had once visited it as a small child, but never since. The house is a large, ten-bedroomed Georgian building, in considerable landscaped grounds. My aunt showed me around the place, and... and entreated me to take good care of her jewellery, in particular of a silver tiara. The piece was set with diamonds and was, I have no need to stress, of considerable value: in excess of ten thousand pounds. She kept the tiara in a safe in the library, the combination of which was known only to her."

"The library, I take it, is on the ground floor?"

"It is."

"Very good."

Miss Norton sighed, then continued, "My aunt left for Germany, and I took possession of the house. I whiled away my time with some reading and a little painting, and from time to time I invited guests from London. One week ago, I held a dinner party, and invited friends down for the evening. The dinner was a success, and my guests departed around midnight."

"And in the morning...?" Holmes said, watching her keenly.

Her head tipped forward, and I could well guess her pained expression. "In the morning, Mr. Holmes, I returned a book I had finished to the library, and was surprised to find the door unlocked. You see, I was scrupulous in ensuring that the library was locked at all times. I assumed at first that I had forgotten to lock it behind me when I left the room a few days ago. Imagine my shock when I entered now and noticed that the painting, behind which the safe was situated, was askew. On investigating, I found the safe door ajar and –" she finished in barely a whisper "– and the tiara missing."

She sniffed, fumbled with a handkerchief, then lifted it to her eyes.

Holmes murmured something inaudible, then said, "You notified the police, of course?"

"Immediately. They sent someone from Eastbourne."

"And yet their investigations proved fruitless?"

"They interviewed my six guests, I believe, but learned nothing."

"Might I ask if the tiara was insured?"

A brief silence followed the question, before Miss Norton said in barely a murmur, "My great-aunt had recently purchased the piece, and had not at that time taken out insurance."

Holmes nodded, stroking his lean jaw with a finger as he contemplated Miss Norton's sorry tale. At last he said, "I take it that you have yet to inform your great-aunt of the theft?"

The woman gave a pitiful moan. "I'm quite unable to summon the courage to do so. I live in fear of her reaction. Oh, Mr. Holmes, she would never forgive me!" She dabbed her eyes again, and went on, "It... it occurred to me that if, perhaps, you were to come to Carroway House as my guest – and if I were to ask the people who were present on the very night of the theft..."

Holmes said, "You said that they were friends?"

"Well, two were very good friends, one was an acquaintance, and the remaining three the friends of my friends – a writer, an actor and a painter. My three friends are employed in the gallery where I worked until last March."

Holmes reclined his head upon the antimacassar and closed his eyes, deep in thought. The woman sniffled from time to time. I found myself regretting my position behind the door, for judging by her comely ankle and cap of golden hair, she was a beauty I would have liked to behold.

"I was thinking," Miss Norton ventured at last, "that perhaps you could come this week..."

Holmes opened his eyes and regarded her with his penetrating gaze. "Tomorrow being the fourth. As you say, Pursley is just ten miles from Eastbourne. I could hire a car and a driver."

"Oh," the young lady said in evident relief, "if you *would* come, that would be marvellous!"

"I have one stipulation – that my good friend and confidant, Dr. Watson, should accompany me."

After the briefest hesitation, Miss Norton nodded and said, "The good Doctor would be more than welcome, Mr. Holmes."

"That is settled, then. At what time should we arrive?"

"Tomorrow afternoon, at three? I could show you the library, and whatever else you might wish to see." She smiled at my friend. "Oh, you can't imagine how grateful I am!"

Holmes smiled in return, murmuring, "It is the least I can do for the daughter of one so illustrious as…" His words trailed off, and I detected a tremor of emotion in his voice – or was I mistaken?

Miss Norton stood, and I saw that she was a tall, slim woman of elegant bearing, dressed in a lilac two-piece – the skirt being at least an inch above her knee. I stood aside, caution overcoming my curiosity.

"I shall see myself out, Mr. Holmes. Once again, thank you for your kindness—"

"There is one further thing," said my friend. "Will there be anyone else present at Carroway House tomorrow? Does your great-aunt employ servants?"

Miss Norton hesitated. "She has employed a maid for the duration of my stay," she said. "Also, a woman comes in to cook once a day, and a local man attends to the garden for two hours every morning."

"Very good," said Holmes. "Until tomorrow, Miss Norton."

I heard her footsteps on the parquet of the hall, and the eventual snap of the lock as the door closed behind her.

*

"Watson!" Holmes cried the instant she had departed. "There's no time to lose."

"What the blazes…?" I said, stepping from the bedroom.

"Follow Miss Norton," he said. "Quickly, now!"

"But… what…?" I blustered. "Why on earth should I follow the young—"

"Just do as I say, my friend, and I'll explain everything on your return."

"But what if she decides to take a train to London?"

Holmes waved impatiently. "She won't. She is lodging nearby—"

"How can you possibly—"

"Go! Time is of the essence. My hypothesis is that she is soon to meet with someone. I desire you to witness the rendezvous, then return with the details in due course. Now, for pity's sake, Watson, no more prevarication or the bird will have flown!"

Thus reprimanded, I hurried from the apartment. Miss Norton was descending in the lift, so I ran down the stairs as fast as my old legs would allow and arrived in the foyer more than a little out of breath. I was just in time to see the plate-glass entrance door to the building swing shut and Miss Norton in her lilac two-piece disappearing at a brisk clip.

By the time I emerged into the bright sunlight of the late afternoon, the young woman was perhaps twenty yards before me, making her way hurriedly through the holiday crowds along the seafront. I increased my pace, keeping her golden head in sight all the while, and wondering at Holmes's game as I did so. Miss Norton's story of the stolen tiara had seemed above board to me – but had my friend, whose ears were so much sharper than mine, noted something in her account that sat uneasily with him?

I recalled that Holmes had beheld the same woman three days earlier, and that then she had met with a man on the seafront. I wondered if it was the same person whom Holmes assumed she was meeting now.

Quite aside from the holidaymakers enjoying the summer sun, a stream of motor cars passed back and forth along the wide street, filling the air not only with the incessant din of their engines, but with noxious petrol fumes. By the time Miss Norton turned into the art-deco portals of a café-bar overlooking the sea, I was hot under the collar and in need of a refreshing drink.

The premises was one of these newfangled establishments which cannot decide whether they are a coffee house or a saloon bar retailing alcohol – and thus achieve the distinction of having the atmosphere of neither. I was attempting to decide whether I should order a shandy from the bar, or take a table and order from a waitress, when I recalled my mission and looked around for the young woman.

She was slipping into a partitioned booth at the far end of the room. Across the table from her was a pale man with a

high forehead, dressed in a sharp blue suit that bore a rather
showy carnation in its lapel. I estimated that he was closer to
forty than thirty.

I hurried across the room, passed their booth and seated
myself in the next one, ensuring that I was not observed by
Miss Norton, chary of her recognising me when I arrived at
Carroway House on the morrow.

From my seat I could glimpse the pair through a series
of chromium bars, and I had been correct in my earlier
assumption that Miss Norton was a beauty to compare with
her mother. Under the shaped curve of her golden hair, her
face was at once comely and sophisticated, with sparkling blue
eyes, a small, straight nose and a generous, smiling mouth.

The man, by contrast, could only be described as
bordering on the ugly. It was partly his deathly pallor that
suggested unwholesomeness, partly the very shape of his
face, with its bulging brow and narrow cheekbones tapering
to a weak, pointed chin.

A waitress approached them, and rather distractedly
they asked for coffee; she proceeded to my booth, and I
requested a Bass shandy.

I moved around the banquette so that I sat with my back
to the couple, who were now speaking in low, hurried tones.
I managed only to catch the odd word, a hissed "… believe
you?" from him, and from Miss Norton: "I'm uncomfortable"
and "I don't like it…"

Whatever, I asked myself, were they referring to?

If I moved slightly to my right, I could view the
reflection of the couple in an art deco-framed mirror on

the wall. Their coffees arrived and the man stretched an arm across the back of the banquette, staring at the woman in a brooding fashion, while she for her part regarded her coffee in silence. They exuded a mutual mistrust suggestive of irreconcilable differences.

My shandy arrived and I slaked my thirst.

They drank their coffee hurriedly, then fell to arguing once more, their heads close.

Of this dialogue I made out not one word, so low were their voices as they traded what I assumed could only be insults and invective. The man's face was made even uglier with a perpetual sneer, and I suddenly felt sorry for Miss Norton. Not only had she recently suffered the loss of her great-aunt's tiara, but it would seem that she was in the throes of losing a lover. Though, I opined to myself, to be without such a poor specimen of manhood would be no great loss at all.

At one point he reached across the table and snatched her delicate wrist, pulling her closer to him and snarling something in her ear. She heard him out, her face averted, then pulled herself free of his grip and rubbed her forearm.

Looking up at that point she said, loud enough for me to hear, "Why won't you just tell me, for pity's sake?"

He hissed something unintelligible in reply, whereupon she acted upon feminine impulse and, rather to my delight, slapped him in the face.

She stood quickly and hurried from the premises, while he sat in brooding silence, the mark of her slap livid on his pallid cheek. Then he pushed himself from the banquette, dropped a few coins upon the bar, and hurried out after Miss Norton.

*

I lost no time in pursuing, first leaving sixpence on the tabletop. By the time I emerged onto the street, the man had caught up with the young woman and had placed a cajoling arm around her shoulders. They proceeded along the esplanade in this fashion, with the man rocking the woman under his arm as if entreating her to reason.

In due course they stopped beside a low-slung Morgan in racing-green livery. I slowed down and watched as Miss Norton slipped into the passenger seat, folding her slim legs into the footwell with elegant economy. The man seated himself behind the wheel and gunned the engine. Miss Norton pointedly ignored him and stared across the road at the sea – his earlier sweet nothings evidently having fallen on deaf ears. The car roared off along the esplanade and within seconds was lost to sight.

Musing on what I had just observed, I made my slow way back to my friend's apartment.

"Now out with it," said Holmes as I followed him into the lounge room. "I want every detail, no matter how apparently trivial."

Taking the chair recently vacated by Miss Norton, I recounted her meeting with the unsavoury fellow in the café-bar.

"Describe him," Holmes demanded.

I did so, summoning all the detail I could recall. "And a most unprepossessing character he was," I finished.

"Evidently the very same fellow I observed from the window three days ago," Holmes said. "Did you overhear what was said between them?"

"I caught the odd word or two," I replied, "though of course caution was the watchword as I didn't want Miss Norton recognising me tomorrow."

"Quite," he said. "Now, what was said?"

"The conversation was fractious, to say the least. Recriminatory, hostile even." I recounted what I had heard pass between the pair, and went on, "Then he snatched her wrist and hissed something at her, whereupon her anger erupted and she slapped his face and walked out. He caught up with her, tried to cajole her, and they climbed into a car – a Morgan – and drove off."

Holmes sat back, silent for a space, as he contemplated everything I had told him.

"If you want my opinion, Holmes, they're lovers, and what I witnessed was an almighty tiff. Going by what was said, I rather think the fellow has been trifling with Miss Norton's affections – wouldn't be surprised if he's been paying attention to another... Miss Norton finds out and, bingo, the cat's among the pigeons."

Holmes smiled to himself. "Your vernacular, Watson, is almost as wayward as your erroneous conjecture."

I blinked. "You don't think they're lovers?"

"I would very much doubt it," said he, "though there is a possibility that it was so – not that it is in any way relevant to the matter at hand. You heard not so much a lover's tiff, as the entreaties of one person attempting to suborn the will of another."

"Your reasoning, Holmes?"

My friend reached out and took from a side-table his

ancient, and now much worn, cherrywood pipe. He proceeded to ignite it at his leisure, and soon his aquiline visage had all but disappeared behind billows of smoke.

He leaned forward, emerging from the fug, and said, "My reasoning is based on the fact that much of what Miss Norton told us, not one hour ago in this very room, was a lie."

I sat back and huffed a little at this. "A lie? But confound it, Holmes, in that case she's the most convincing liar I've ever come across! She convinced me, at any rate."

"Which is not so very surprising," he said, "as she is an actress."

"An actress? How the deuce do you know that, old man?"

"The play script in her handbag was suggestive," he said, "as was the faint blue chalk mark on the sole of her right shoe."

"A chalk mark?" I exclaimed. "But how the…?"

"Stage hands use chalk lines to mark an actor's position during rehearsals, and currently Mr. Coward's *Hay Fever* is in rehearsal at the Hippodrome. She would be perfect for the part of Sorel. Also, and this is the clincher, three days ago, as Miss Norton was pacing up and down the esplanade, she was approached by a diffident young man who proffered a programme and a fountain pen, and rather distractedly she scribbled her signature and the fellow retreated well pleased with the autograph of the pretty young starlet."

I heard him out, then said, "But what makes you assume that what she told you was a lie?"

"Oh, that?" he said with characteristic nonchalance. "Where to begin? Her hesitations; the uncertainty of expression when answering some of my questions; the way her gaze would slide off to the left when she was telling the most egregious of untruths."

"So the story about her great-aunt's tiara?"

"A flagrant taradiddle, I shouldn't wonder."

"But confound it, what on earth can she be up to?" I stopped as something further occurred to me. "And her claim to be the daughter of Irene Adler? Don't tell me…"

"That, too, is no more than a dissimulation."

"But to what end, Holmes?" I asked, exasperated.

He puffed on his pipe, emitting a series of perfect circles which floated away on the still air. He watched them go, smiling to himself. "What else can the entire charade have been in aid of, other than to lure me this week to Carroway House?"

"Good God! But… I mean to say… whatever for?"

"That, my friend, is something on which I am loath to speculate at this juncture, though I guarantee that the man of unprepossessing mien has a hand in the affair."

I sat in silence for a number of seconds, chewing my moustache and marshalling my errant thoughts. At last I looked up. "Of course, in that case we can't go to Carroway House. We'll inform the police of what we've learned and leave it in their capable hands, what?"

"On the contrary, Watson. My interest is piqued. Miss Norton – or whoever she might be – presented a pretty enough problem to begin with. What we have discovered only exacerbates my curiosity."

"But in your state, my friend…" I pleaded, gesturing forlornly at his carriage.

"*Pshaw!*" he expostulated. "*You* are as fit and able as ever, Watson."

"Well," I muttered, "I'm not as young as I once was, you know, and the old memory..."

"I am confident that, with your good self in attendance, along with the pair of Webleys which you'll find in the bottom drawer of the dresser over there, we shall acquit ourselves admirably and get to the bottom of the affair in no time."

Restraining myself from further argument, I crossed to the dresser and withdrew the handguns.

"We shall dine tonight on the potted hare that Mrs. Bains left this morning," said Holmes, "and share a brandy or two before bed. And in the morning we shall take a car and sally forth. Be so good as to pass me the *Sussex Gazetteer*, would you, Watson?"

"Speaking of brandy..." said I, handing him the booklet.

Smiling to himself, my friend gestured across the room to the decanter on the sideboard.

*

It was another hot day which saw the chauffeur of the hired car lift Holmes into the commodious back seat, arrange a travelling rug over his lap, and stow his wheelchair in the boot. I settled myself beside my friend and soon we had left Eastbourne in our wake and were climbing into the Downs to the west.

I cast my mind back to the past times I had ventured into the country with Holmes, but my memory was not up to the task. I had vague recollections of travelling to Devon on some errand involving a racehorse, and of another time when we had penetrated the wilds of Hampshire, whereupon Holmes had startled me with a meditation on the evil that dwelt in the countryside. These thoughts threatened to induce a cloying melancholia, so I cast them aside and concentrated on the verdant hills and vales flashing by on either hand.

"A penny for them, Watson," said Holmes at one point.

"Oh, I was just mulling over the past, Holmes."

"It is a terrain in which I spend an increasing amount of time these days, my friend."

"Dwelling on past glories?" I ventured.

"More the failures, old man."

A silence came between us, and at last I said, "Do you miss those times, Holmes?"

He considered the question. "I miss everything about them. Oh, to be able to return, with one's health renewed, and with the knowledge one has gained over the years, correct the errors of the past…" He fell silent, and would say no more on the subject.

Thirty minutes after setting off, we pulled into the driveway of Carroway House, a large foursquare Georgian building set into the lee of a wooded hillside.

Miss Norton – or, rather, the woman claiming that name – stood beneath a pillared portico to greet us, and once Holmes had dismissed our driver, she expressed her delight in making my acquaintance. I reversed the wheelchair and grunted as I pulled Holmes up the steps and into the house.

"I expect you'll want to refresh yourselves," she said, leading the way into the mansion, "and then perhaps you would care to examine the library, Mr. Holmes?"

My friend expressed his satisfaction at the suggestion, and she showed us a pair of comfortable rooms on the ground floor overlooking lawns to the west of the house. In due course a tap sounded at the door of my room, and Miss Norton escorted me along a corridor to a set of double doors. I could not help, as she chattered away at my side, contrasting her carefree manner of today with her distress in Holmes's apartment the day before – and not for the first time I speculated on the degree of her complicity in the affair.

She flung open the doors to reveal a sunlit room with shelves of books on three walls. Holmes had preceded me, and was stationed in his wheelchair before one of the high windows.

Miss Norton crossed to the fireplace, to the left of which it was apparent that a painting had been removed. A small safe, set into the wall, stood with its thick door ajar.

"Everything is as it was on the evening of the theft," she informed us. She hesitated, looking from me to Holmes. "No doubt you will be wanting to know more about my guests—"

"In due course, Miss Norton," Holmes interrupted. "For the time being, I wonder if I might be left alone with my friend to discuss the case?"

"Why, of course." She gave a dazzling smile, and glanced at her delicate wristwatch. "We dine at seven. It is now a little after four. I'll leave you for now, gentlemen."

I watched her as she crossed the room and pulled shut the doors behind her.

Holmes remained before the window, staring out, his gaze pensive.

"We find ourselves in an interesting situation, Watson," he said at last.

"We do?"

"We have been requested to investigate a crime that never

happened by a young woman whose involvement in the business is problematic to say the least. The notional crime of the stolen tiara is matched by a crime-to-be, you might say, just as notional as it is yet to happen."

"And that crime?"

Holmes gave a grim smile. "One that would make the theft of a tiara seem as nothing," he said. "Come here, Watson."

I crossed the room to where he sat before the window.

"Did you happen to notice the scent that greeted us as we approached the house?"

"The scent? Can't say I did, to be honest."

Holmes pointed a bony finger across the lawn. "Behold, between the trees directly in line with the sundial."

I squinted. "What am I supposed to be looking at, Holmes?"

"The gap between the beech and the fir, the pathway leading up the hillside."

I made out the start of the pathway, and a sloping timber walkway disappearing into the boscage.

"What of it, Holmes?"

"The planks have been newly cut and laid. It was the scent of freshly sawn wood which assailed us upon our arrival."

I nodded, casting a dubious glance at my friend. "And this is significant?"

"Significant?" said he. "I would aver that it is momentous." Before I could question him further, he swept on, "You have the Webley to hand, Watson, and loaded?"

I patted my flank. "As instructed."

"Excellent," said my friend. "I too am armed and ready."

"For what, exactly – if you don't mind my asking?"

His gaze returned to the sunlit lawns, and he said, "Before long, Miss Norton will request our presence. In due course she will suggest that we take a walk before dinner. She will reassure me that the terrain will be no impediment to my enjoyment of the scenery, as a walkway has been constructed by her great-aunt expressly for the purpose of allowing the elderly and infirm to avail themselves of the views famous hereabouts. You, too, will be asked to accompany us, of course, as it would seem suspicious if I were invited but not yourself." He stared at me. "But you are to make some excuse – gout or whatever – and say that you would rather rest before dinner."

I smiled at my friend. "But I'll be doing nothing of the kind, of course?"

"Five minutes after I have set out with Miss Norton, you will follow us at a discreet distance. I calculate that it will take us perhaps ten minutes to reach the viewing platform overlooking the gorge—"

"A gorge?" I echoed. "In Sussex?"

"A beauty spot, created entirely by the hand of man a century ago. I read about it in the *Gazetteer* last night," said he. "It is vital that you reach us a little before we attain the platform. I suggest you cut directly through the woods and approach us from above. I hope your eye is as sharp, and your hand as steady, as of old, my friend?"

"I'll be equal to the task," I assured him.

"Capital."

"However," I said, "why take the risk? Why not do as I suggested last night, and allow the law to intervene?"

He pierced me with a gaze. "Because, as of yet, no crime

has been committed. It would be futile to summon the law at this juncture. The criminal will reveal himself, and his foul deed, only in the act of committing his crime. Then, and only then, can we act."

A discreet tap sounded at the door, and a maid entered to ask if we should like to join Miss Norton for afternoon tea in the conservatory. I thereupon took the turned walnut handles of the wheelchair and conveyed Holmes from the library, through the house to the spacious glasshouse at the rear.

Miss Norton was seated at a wrought-iron table, smiling at us as we joined her. I admit that I was nervous as I took my seat and awaited her invitation for Holmes to join her on a pre-prandial perambulation around the grounds – if Holmes's forecast proved to be correct.

As a preamble, she asked Holmes if he had uncovered anything of significance in the library. Smiling as he sipped his tea from a china cup, he spoke at length about the safe and how easy it was to crack one of its type.

From Miss Norton's manner, as she listened politely, I could tell that she was bracing herself to ask the question: the entire success of this charade hinged, I surmised, on Holmes's agreement to her proposal. Her hand shook a little as she poured me a second cup of tea, and from time to time she nervously licked her lips.

At last, upon Holmes setting down his cup, Miss Norton smiled and leaned forward. "I was wondering, Mr. Holmes, Dr. Watson… the area surrounding the house is famed for its beauty. That is… the views are magnificent. My great-aunt had the foresight to have wooden pathways laid down, so…"

Holmes smiled, playing his part like a thespian born. "Nothing would please me more," he said, "than to take a 'walk' before dinner."

Miss Norton tried not to exhibit her relief as she smiled and turned to me. "And you, Dr. Watson; would you care to join us?"

"Do you know what?" I said. "I might sit this one out. The old gout, you know? I'll lie down in my room and read for an hour, if you don't mind."

"Why, not at all." She reached out and patted Holmes's hand. "Then perhaps when we have finished our teas…?" she suggested.

Never has Earl Grey tasted so tainted, nor a pretty young woman's company seemed so repulsive, than during the five minutes before Holmes drained his cup and pronounced himself ready for a little fresh air.

Jumping to her feet, Miss Norton took control of his carriage and wheeled him from the conservatory. I, for my part, followed them into the hallway, remembering to affect a slight limp. I assisted Holmes down the front steps, then made my way to my room.

There I hurried to the window and watched Miss Norton propel my friend along the paved path between lawn and flower bed. As they passed into the shade of the trees at the end of the garden and attained the walkway, I withdrew my Webley and checked – for perhaps the tenth time since arriving here – that it was fully loaded. Then I lost not another minute in leaving the house and crossing the lawn. Recalling Holmes's instructions to cut through the woods, I traversed a stand of shrubbery and made my way up the wooded hillside.

My course, I estimated, would soon bring me out on the crest overlooking the walkway.

The terrain was uneven, the incline steep, and I was soon out of breath and panting hard. At least, in the dappled shade of the trees, I was spared the direct heat of the sun. More than once I found myself snagged on brambles and thorns, and cursed their tenacity as I fought my way free and battled on up the hillside. Through the cover to my right, I could make out the curve of the walkway as it followed the contours of the hill. Of Miss Norton and Sherlock Holmes there was no sign.

At one point I stopped to regain my breath. Again I withdrew my pistol and checked its chambers, reassured when I beheld the bullets nestling there. I set off again, doing my best to ignore the tearing pain in my side. Very soon I would be seventy-five – hard though that was to believe! – and I felt every one of my years as I came at last to the crest of the hill and halted, hands on knees and drawing in great lungfuls of air.

I straightened up and peered down the incline; ahead I glimpsed the curve of the timber walkway, and below to my left, perhaps fifty yards distant, I made out Holmes and Miss Norton through the intervening trees.

I was about to set off again, more cautiously now, when I heard a sound behind me. I turned – but too late, and was in time only to receive a crashing blow to my brow. I pirouetted and fell face down. My instinct was to struggle to my feet and confront my assailant, but second thoughts, and wiser counsel, prevailed. As a pair of booted feet came into sight beside my head, I closed my eyes and lay very still. I felt rough fingers on my neck, checking my pulse, then heard a grunt and the sound of the boots moving off.

I gave thanks to Providence, and attempted to rise to my feet before my attacker could bring his scheme to fruition. Groaning, I slumped down again, overcome by a wave of nausea and weakness. I lay with my cheek against the noisome leaf mould, my breath coming in ragged spasms, painfully aware that every second I wasted like this, the danger to my friend increased. Spurred on by the thought that I could not fail Holmes, I managed to struggle to my hands and knees and then, by main force, push myself upright. I must have presented a frightful sight as I shambled with bloodied brow down the hillside. I bethought myself to withdraw my pistol as I surged on. I peered ahead, but of my assailant, or of Miss Norton and Holmes, there was no sign.

Then I heard a brief scream, and before I could make sense of its cause I saw, through the cluster of tree trunks between myself and the walkway, the figure of the young woman – alone now – hurrying back the way she had come with a hand pressed to her cheek in consternation.

I lurched on, veering to my left, and stumbled down the incline. As I descended, I became aware of two sounds, one of which I could not at first identify, the other horribly obvious. The first was a continuous rushing roar – which I know now to be the surging of a waterfall – while the second was the sound of two voices raised in disputation.

A wave of dizziness overcame me as I staggered forward. I feared I would pass out there and then, of little use to my friend in his hour of need. And only this thought – that, when my assistance was most needed, I would fail the commission – drove me onwards.

The surge of the rushing water grew ever louder, and with it the sound of the voices. At last, I beheld two figures facing each other on the walkway: the tall figure of the ugly man I had last seen in the café-bar, and the invalid form of my friend Sherlock Holmes in his carriage.

My vision blurred; a heat passed through my head. To prevent my imminent collapse, I leaned against the bole of an oak and, overcoming nausea, attempted to take stock of the tableau before me.

The two men confronted each other, a mere yard apart, with the headlong spuming rush of the waterfall as their backdrop. The scene was horribly familiar in a vague, nightmarish kind of way to one I had imagined many a time in the past.

"You can have no idea how much I have dreamt of this moment!" the man cried, directing a pistol at Holmes.

Holmes replied, but the sound of rushing water snatched his words away.

"The irony!" cried the man. "You, who devoted your life to apprehending those you considered villainous – and all the while you were no more than a murderer yourself!"

Holmes sneered at this, and he now also raised his voice, so I was able to hear his words. "I must remind you that it was your father who attacked *me*, lured me to Reichenbach with the express intent of having me die at the Falls, and it was poetic justice that, through happenstance, it was *he* who met his end."

Moriarty... I thought, hardly crediting my senses.

"If only it had been you who'd perished," the man averred

with bitterness, "and spared me the need for your execution! I would have had my father..." He broke down and wept, his ugly visage made even uglier in the throes of emotion. "For that – for denying me a father – you have earned your belated fate."

"How tawdry," Holmes drawled, glancing past his assailant and for the first time glimpsing me as I attempted to push myself away from the tree, "how cheap a trick to lure me to this lacklustre facsimile of Reichenbach! You should have gone the whole hog, Moriarty, and set up this pantomime in Switzerland."

I staggered forward, lifting my pistol and taking aim at the man. My vision swam, and my arm dithered, and at last I pressed the trigger... and missed!

The man saw me, turned and fired. The bullet pinged past my head – and before I could despair at my failure, a miracle occurred.

As I waved my pistol, attempting to bring it to bear upon Moriarty junior, Holmes flung aside the rug that covered his lap and leapt upright, drawing his pistol and firing. The bullet struck the man's weapon and it flew from his grasp. With a roar of rage Moriarty was upon Holmes, fighting for possession of my friend's pistol, before he could press home his advantage. They came together, clashed, young and old, good and evil, and for terrible protracted seconds that seemed to my eyes like an eternity, they fought in an appalling recapitulation of the struggle that had occurred all those years ago on the precipice above the Reichenbach Falls.

I gathered all my strength, and my wits, raised my weapon again and aimed. I fired – and this time I did not miss. Moriarty screamed, released from Holmes's embrace, and teetered on the lip of the chasm. He seemed to hang there for an age – a look of startled disbelief on his face – and then toppled slowly backwards, his dying scream diminishing as he fell.

Panting, I staggered across to my friend and, clutching each other, we peered down at the rocks far below. The progeny of the mastermind criminal was a tiny, broken figure, his lifeblood diluted and washed away in the torrential rush of the waterfall.

"I hope," said Holmes at last, still panting, "you will forgive me the dissimulation, Watson."

"The scoliosis," I said.

"On first espying young Moriarty on the seafront – and recognising in his twisted figure the semblance of his father – I devised a scheme whereby I needed to convince everyone, including yourself, Watson, of my incapacity. To that end, the invalid carriage. I borrowed it from a retired major who'd recently purchased a new chromium affair."

"You're forgiven, my friend."

"At first, I could hardly bring myself to credit his scheme," Holmes went on, dashing a streak of blood from his cheek, "but then I saw him with the girl, whom he selected because of her striking resemblance to *the* woman, and when I received her letter, I *knew*."

"And her part in this scheme?"

"A dupe, no more," said Holmes, "cajoled into luring us hither by a man tortured by grief and hatred. Her part in the affair need not come to light…"

He fell silent, staring down into the ravine for long minutes.

"Holmes?" I said at last.

"I am contemplating the past, Watson, the 'happy highways where we went, and cannot come again...' 'The Scandal in Bohemia', as you entitled the affair, and *the* woman. And later, the dreadful tussle above the Reichenbach Falls... It was contemplation of this, not a week ago, that clinched it, Watson: it occurred to me that the anniversary of that fateful day was fast approaching."

"Good God!"

"Thirty-five years ago to the very day, the fourth of May, 1891, Moriarty and I came together above the Falls." He fell silent as we stared down at the man's shattered corpse.

"Holmes."

"Yes, my friend."

"I was thinking... we really shouldn't leave it another eighteen months before we meet again."

Holmes smiled. "On that point, I concur," said he. "And now, Watson, to the house, where you shall phone the local constabulary and apprise them of all that has occurred."

We left the raging torrent and, our arms about each other, two old men, bloodied perhaps but not broken, we made our slow way back along the timber walkway to Carroway House.

ABOUT THE EDITOR

Martin Rosenstock studied modern literature at the University of California, Santa Barbara. After job hopping around the colder latitudes of the US, he decided to return to warmer climes and took a teaching position in Kuwait. He has contributed stories to *Sherlock Holmes Mystery Magazine*, *Mystery Weekly* and *The MX Book of New Sherlock Holmes Stories*. For Titan, he has edited *Sherlock Holmes: The Sign of Seven*. When not brooding over plot twists, he spends too much time travelling.

ABOUT THE CONTRIBUTORS

Derrick Belanger is an author, publisher and educator most noted for his books and lectures on Sherlock Holmes and Sir Arthur Conan Doyle. A number of his books have been #1 bestsellers in their categories on Amazon.com. Derrick is co-owner of the publishing company Belanger Books, which published the first ebook editions of the original Solar Pons books by August Derleth. Derrick is a board member of Dr. Watson's Neglected Patients, the Denver-based Scion Society, and in 2019 was inducted into the Praed Street Irregulars. He currently resides in Broomfield, Colorado. Find him at www.belangerbooks.com.

Cara Black lives in San Francisco with her bookseller husband, Jun, and their dog. She is a *New York Times* and *USA TODAY* bestselling author, a San Francisco Library Laureate, as well as a Macavity and three-time Anthony Award nominee for her Paris-set series, Aimée Leduc Investigations. Cara has also received the Médaille de la Ville de Paris – the Paris City Medal, which is awarded in recognition of contributions to international culture – and invitations to be the Guest of Honour at such noteworthy conferences as the Paris Polar Crime Festival and Left Coast Crime. Her latest Aimée Leduc novel is *Murder at the Porte de Versailles*.

Eric Brown was born in Haworth, West Yorkshire, and has lived all over the world, in Australia, India and Greece. He has won the British Science Fiction Award twice for his short stories, and his novel *Helix Wars* was shortlisted for the 2012 Philip K. Dick Award. He has published over seventy books and his latest novel is *Murder Most Vile*, the ninth volume in the Langham and Dupré mystery series set in the 1950s. Forthcoming is the SF novel *Wormhole*, written with Keith Brooke. He lives near Dunbar in Scotland, and his website is at: ericbrown.co.uk.

David Stuart Davies is the author of nine Sherlock Holmes novels and of *Starring Sherlock Holmes*, which details the detective's film career. David's two successful one-man plays, *Sherlock Holmes: The Last Act* and *Sherlock Holmes: The Life & Death*, have been recorded on audio CD by Big Finish. His latest play, *Sherlock Holmes: The Final Reckoning*, premiered in Edinburgh in February 2018. David is the author of other works of crime fiction. His latest novels are *Blood Rites*, *Oliver Twist & The Mystery of Throate Manor* and *The Darkness Rising*. He is a Baker Street Irregular, a member of The Detection Club and edits *Red Herrings*, the monthly magazine of the Crime Writers' Association, for twenty years.

Stuart Douglas is an author, editor and publisher, who has written four Sherlock Holmes novels for Titan Books, and contributed stories to the anthologies *Encounters of Sherlock Holmes*, *Further Associates of Sherlock Holmes* and *The MX Book of New Sherlock Holmes Stories*. He runs Obverse Books and lives in Edinburgh.

Andrew Lane is the author of, amongst many other things, the eight *Young Sherlock Holmes* novels, which ask the question: what was Sherlock Holmes like as a teenager? What had to happen to him to turn him into the complex character we know and love? He has contributed short stories to the Titan anthologies *The Further Encounters of Sherlock Holmes*, *The Associates of Sherlock Holmes* and *The Further Associates of Sherlock Holmes*, and Titan has published his adult SF novel *Netherspace* (written with Nigel Foster).

James Lovegrove is the author of over sixty books, including *The Hope*, *Days*, *Untied Kingdom*, *Provender Gleed*, and the *New York Times* bestselling *Pantheon* series, and his work has been translated into fifteen languages. He has written eight Sherlock Holmes novels, a collection of Holmes short stories, and a Conan Doyle/Lovecraft mashup trilogy, *The Cthulhu Casebooks*. He has also written four tie-in novels for the TV show *Firefly*, one of which, *The Ghost Machine*, won the 2020 Dragon Award for Best Media Tie-in Novel. He contributes two regular fiction-review columns to the *Financial Times* and lives with his wife, two sons and tiny dog in Eastbourne, not far from the site of the "small farm upon the South Downs" to which Sherlock Holmes retired.

David Marcum first discovered Sherlock Holmes in 1975 at the age of ten, and since that time, he has collected, read and catalogued literally thousands of traditional Holmes pastiches. He is the author of over ninety-five Sherlockian pastiches. His books include *The Papers of Sherlock Holmes*, *Sherlock Holmes and A Quantity of Debt*, *Sherlock Holmes – Tangled Skeins*, *Sherlock Holmes and The Eye of Heka* and *The Complete Papers of Sherlock Holmes* (containing seventy-seven of his stories in five massive volumes). He has edited over sixty books, such as the ongoing series *The MX Book of New Sherlock Holmes Stories*. He is a licensed civil engineer, living in Tennessee with his wife and son.

Philip Purser-Hallard is a writer and editor of science fiction, fantasy, crime and criticism. He has written three Sherlock Holmes novels for Titan: *The Vanishing Man*, *The Spider's Web* and *Masters of Lies*, with a fourth to follow. *Publishers Weekly* believes his work 'ranks among the top novel-length Sherlock Holmes pastiches' and shows 'remarkable facility at conjuring the spirit of Conan Doyle's originals'. He edits and has written for the Black Archive series of critical books about individual *Doctor Who* stories. His trilogy of urban fantasy political thrillers, *The Pendragon Protocol*, *The Locksley Exploit* and *Trojans*, is available from Snowbooks.

Cavan Scott is a *New York Times* bestselling author whose work includes novels, television, comic books and award-winning audio dramas. He has written for a large number of high-profile series including *Star Wars*, *Doctor Who*, *Assassin's Creed*, *Pacific Rim*, *Transformers*, *Back to the Future*, *Star Trek*, *Vikings*, *Adventure Time* and many others. His latest creator-owned comic book series, the supernatural urban fantasy *Shadow Service*, launched in 2020 from Vault Comics. He has written two Sherlock Holmes novels for Titan Books, *Sherlock Holmes: The Patchwork Devil* and *Sherlock Holmes: Cry of the Innocents*. Cavan lives in the west of England with his wife and two daughters. His passions include learning the concertina, folklore, the music of David Bowie, and scary movies.

Peter Swanson is the *Sunday Times* and *New York Times* bestselling author of eight novels, including *The Kind Worth Killing*, winner of the New England Society Book Award and finalist for the CWA Ian Fleming Steel Dagger; *Her Every Fear*, an NPR book of the year; and *Eight Perfect Murders*, a *Kirkus Reviews* Book of the Year. His books have been translated into over 30 languages. He lives on the North Shore of Massachusetts, where he is re-reading the tales of Sherlock Holmes while working on his next novel.

Amy Thomas is the author of *The Detective and The Woman* novel series featuring Sherlock Holmes and Irene Adler. She lives and works in South Florida, where she hones her understanding of true crime by working in the legal system, proofreading case transcripts, and listening to too many podcasts. In addition to attending Sherlock Holmes

ENCOUNTERS OF SHERLOCK HOLMES
EDITED BY GEORGE MANN

The spirit of Sherlock Holmes lives on in this collection of
fourteen brand-new adventures. Marvel as the master of
deduction aids a dying Sir Richard Francis Burton; matches
wits with gentleman thief A.J. Raffles; crosses paths with H.G.
Wells in the most curious circumstances; unravels a macabre
mystery on the *Necropolis Express*; unpicks a murder in a
locked railway carriage; explains the origins of his famous
Persian slipper and more!

FEATURING ORIGINAL STORIES FROM

**MARK HODDER • MAGS L. HALLIDAY
CAVAN SCOTT • NICK KYME • PAUL MAGRS
GEORGE MANN • STUART DOUGLAS
ERIC BROWN • RICHARD DINNICK
KELLY HALE • STEVE LOCKLEY
MARK WRIGHT • DAVID BARNETT
JAMES LOVEGROVE**

ASSOCIATES OF SHERLOCK HOLMES
EDITED BY GEORGE MANN

For the very first time, famous associates of the Great
Detective – clients, colleagues, and of course, villains – tell
their own stories in this collection of brand-new adventures.
Follow Inspector Lestrade as he and Sherlock Holmes pursue a
killer to rival Jack the Ripper; sit with Mycroft Holmes as
he solves a case from the comfort of the Diogenes Club;
take a drink with Irene Adler and Dr Watson in a Parisian
café; and join Colonel Sebastian Moran on the hunt for a
supposedly mythical creature…

FEATURING ORIGINAL STORIES FROM

**JONATHAN BARNES • KARA DENNISON
LYNDSAY FAYE • SIMON BUCHER-JONES
NICK KYME • ANDY LANE • TIM PRATT
JAMES LOVEGROVE • WILLIAM MEIKLE
CAVAN SCOTT • JEFFREY THOMAS
IAN EDGINTON • JAINE FENN**

FURTHER ASSOCIATES OF SHERLOCK HOLMES
EDITED BY GEORGE MANN

Once again, famous associates of the Great Detective –
clients, colleagues and, of course, villains – tell their own
stories in this collection of brand-new adventures. Meet Lucy
Hebron years after Holmes's only ever failed deduction; follow
your nose down the streets of London with Toby the Dog;
join Mrs Hudson on her first ever case; greet an ambassador
from Mars alongside Lord Holdhurst; and confess your sins
to your cellmate, Professor James Moriarty…

FEATURING ORIGINAL STORIES FROM

STUART DOUGLAS • JONATHAN GREEN • STEPHEN HENRY
ANDREW LANE • MARK A. LATHAM • JAMES LOVEGROVE
DAVID MARCUM • IAIN MCLAUGHLIN
PHILIP PURSER-HALLARD • MICHELLE RUDA • SAM STONE
NIK VINCENT • DAN WATTERS • MARCIA WILSON

For more fantastic fiction, author events, exclusive
excerpts, competitions, limited editions and more

VISIT OUR WEBSITE
titanbooks.com

LIKE US ON FACEBOOK
facebook.com/titanbooks

FOLLOW US ON TWITTER
@TitanBooks

EMAIL US
readerfeedback@titanemail.com